Inside Her

A SAPPHIC LOVE STORY

LISA J. EVANS

With thanks

Special gratitude goes to the love of my life, Alex Brown, whose un-wavering support made this book a reality. I also extend my heartfelt thanks to the incredible people who contributed their expertise and encouragement: Trev Gilham, the mastermind behind the cover de-sign; Jennifer Kay Davies, my wonderful editor; and a circle of trea-sured friends, mentors and advisors including Kerrie Hughes, Holly June Smith, Matt Bielby, Rachel Moses-Lloyd, Hannah Evans, Sara Morgan, Jo Frei Hill, Caitlin Stanley, Alice Scott, Stacey and Nathan Cotter, Laura McArthur, Sarah Moolla, Lydia Tewkesbury, Harriet Noble, Emma Savage, Chloe Michelle Howarth, Emma Teagle and Siân David. Your guidance and generosity have been invaluable.

Content warning

Note to reader: Trigger warnings include, but are not limited to, sexually explicit material, domestic abuse, sexual assault, harassment, stalking, BDSM, self-harm and suicidal intent.

Mum, Dad, if you're reading this, stop now. For the love of God, please stop now.

Prologue

I think the world is full of monsters.

My therapist told me to start this diary. Weird that I have a therapist. No other kids my age do. She said it might help me 'feel better' or 'let things out' or whatever. I don't know if I believe her, but I don't want to talk anymore. So now I'm writing.

Everything changed when it happened. Nobody talks about it, but I know they're all thinking about it. Like it's stamped on my forehead. The thing that makes me dirty, ruined. Mum's smile is different now. And Dad... he never used to cry. But now he does. They don't stop hugging me. I hate seeing them sad. It's my fault.

When I have to leave my house, I try to be invisible. I try not to speak or take up too much space because the more I'm here, the more I'm seen. The more I remember. The more I remember him.

I hate him.

How can I move on when every time I close my eyes, he's there? He's in the dark. In every man that passes me on the street. I feel like I'll never be safe again. Not from the monsters. Not from the memories.

I guess it's not just men I'm afraid of. It's people. All of them (apart from my family. And Li). They walk around like they're normal, like they're safe. But they're not. Even the kind-looking ones can hurt me.

Sometimes it's like I'm just pretending to be a real human and everyone knows and is secretly judging me for it. My therapist says I wear a mask – not a real one, it's just imaginary – to act the way people want me to.

Maybe writing will help. Maybe it won't. But I'll keep trying because if I don't, I feel like the monsters will win.

And I can't let them.

PS I have a boyfriend now. I don't want one. But it's safer this way.

Chapter 1

'I left him,' Li said after a long pause, her soft voice barely rising above the quiet hum of the pub. She watched for my reaction, her expression shifting from mild anxiety to barely suppressed laughter as my jaw dropped wide open. 'If you're surprised now, you'll have to prepare yourself for the rest.' She took a deep breath. 'I left him... for a woman.'

An elderly man at a nearby table flinched at the sound of my gasp, tipping the frothy head of his pint onto his woolly sleeve mid-sip.

I raised a hand in apology, which he returned with a chuckle, before I leaned closer to Li and whispered, 'You can't be serious.'

She nodded, and I noticed she was shaking slightly as she lifted her glass of lemonade to her lips. 'I met her – Bex – at work a few weeks ago.' She took a hurried sip, her dark hair catching the amber glow of the hanging lights as she shifted. 'She's a new starter at the firm.'

I'd sensed something was up – there had been a secret buried in her voice for weeks – but this?

Her cheeks flushed and she smiled as if she couldn't believe it herself. 'I know. Nine years with Nathan, and I finally figure out I like women.'

I bit my tongue. It was the perfect moment to share the doubts I'd been having about my own sexuality, doubts that had been eating away at me, doubts I had intended on sharing with Li that very evening. But I didn't want to steal the focus, especially as Li had opened up to me of her own accord – which she rarely did without encouragement.

'You're not freaked out, are you, Jess?' She was trying to act casual, but I could tell she was nervous from the way she chewed the inside of her cheek – a habit she'd had since we were kids.

'Of course not. I'm just surprised, that's all.'

Her cherubic face was edged with worry. 'You're the first person I've told. I'm going to introduce her to my mum and dad soon. After that, I'll have told everyone I care about.'

It meant everything to know she trusted me with this before anyone else. Moments earlier, I had been about to do the same with her.

'I haven't made you uncomfortable?'

I smiled. She was always putting others' feelings before her own. I felt a rush of affection for her, my wonderful Li. 'Not at all.' I rotated my engagement ring, the lie on my finger, and itched to tell her I thought I was the same as her. 'I'm honestly over the moon for you.'

The tension seemed to melt from her shoulders. I reached across the table and squeezed her hand.

'I actually think I'm in love,' she whispered, her voice catching in her throat.

My heart swelled with pride. 'Li Jing-Mei!' I squealed, and she laughed at the use of her full name. I sprang up from my seat and wrapped her in a tight hug, her head tucking neatly under my chin.

She was the only person I knew who was shorter than me; every time we hugged, I felt like I was her big sister.

The four middle-aged blokes at the bar looked over at us, their conversation halting as if one of them had quietly pointed us out. Their eyes drank us in before they turned back, smirking at each other.

'I knew you'd understand, Jessica Louise Davies,' Li said brightly, oblivious to the stares, her voice muffled against my shoulder. 'You've always been on my wavelength.'

'Now more than ever by the looks of things,' I said before I could stop myself.

She pulled back and looked up at me. 'What do you mean?'

My heart began to gallop. I sat down, adjusting my top to hide my cleavage in case the men looked again. I noticed my phone had lit up – my boss, the news editor of *The City Post* was calling. I turned the phone face down. Surely it could wait.

'Jess?' Li said, waiting for my answer.

My hands instinctively found my long red hair, and I tossed it back over my shoulders, as if that would lighten the weight of the moment. Then, before I could lose my nerve, I said it. My words hung there in the silence.

Li's expression shifted between confusion and surprise, her eyes widening as she processed what I'd just admitted. She beamed a smile. 'Wait.' She let out slow exhale. 'You're saying... we both... all this time?'

I nodded, a soft laugh of relief escaping as a tear rolled down my cheek. 'What are the chances?'

Chapter 2

Twenty-four, twenty-five, twenty-six. I counted Joe's thrusts, enduring them, knowing it had to be over soon; they normally ended in the thirties. I scrunched up my face and stroked through the sweat on his back – sweat that always seemed to burst from him when he made the very first thrust into me. I couldn't take my hands away; he'd asked for them there. He liked me to slip them up and down through the wetness, over his coarse skin, while he whispered, 'You see what you do to me?' in my ear.

It made me queasy, but it was better than the alternatives, like when he demanded I remain motionless and pretend I was a sex doll: 'Stay limp,' he'd say, and I wasn't to move or react.

I glanced at my phone on the bedside table, the sight of it stirring up the worry I'd felt since missing my boss's call the night before. As one of the on-call Sunday reporters, I should have answered or at least returned Glyn's call. But the evening had been so emotional with Li, both of us crying and spilling our feelings – her joy, my fear – that there just wasn't an opening. I did text him when I got home from the pub, guilt gnawing at me. I never missed work calls; my ambition demanded it. Or maybe it wasn't my ambition so much as wanting to be seen as reliable and dependable. Liked. Glyn had texted back, telling me the other on-call reporter – Whatshisname – had it covered. I hated feeling like I had failed. But there was only one missed call; it couldn't have been that important.

My neck ached from the effort of keeping my face turned away from Joe. His hot morning breath and body odour combined into a nauseating mix of rotting food and the mustiness of an old book. Every couple of thrusts, he'd flick his tongue into my mouth and I would taste the salt of its rough surface.

I could always endure it so long as I thought about women. Women such as the waitress at the restaurant where Joe had proposed the year before. In my mind, she would secretively grab my hand as I headed towards the toilets, the spark in her eyes and the smirk on her lips making my pulse jump. She'd silently pull me into the pantry, pressing me hard against the spice shelves, the scents of cinnamon and pepper mingling with the heat radiating between us. Our mouths would crash together, her kiss fierce and unapologetically hungry, her tongue sliding against mine, as if she couldn't get close enough, couldn't taste enough. Her touch would roam all over me, urgent and searching, fingers catching on the fabric of my dress, pulling, claiming. I'd glance at the door, nerves prickling at the thought of someone walking in at any second, catching us. Then she'd drop to her knees in one swift, fluid motion, her hands gripping my hips to keep me steady as her mouth found its way up my thighs, each kiss hot and demanding. I'd clutch at the shelves behind me, feeling the world blur as she pulled my underwear to the side and held me there, her tongue tracing patterns that were as wild and insistent as she was. My legs would tremble, my breath coming in short gasps as her rhythm intensified. As I felt myself teetering on the edge, she'd sense it too, and her fingers would slip inside me, rhythmically pushing into me, each movement precise and relentless. Her mouth and hands would work together in perfect, frenzied sync, driving me forward, pushing me past the last shred of control.

Thirty-nine, forty. He was done, his mess oozing on my thighs. I had never enjoyed sex with men. But you can't stay in a relationship unless you have sex, so I'd always just... kept having it. At the very least, it was a break from Joe's rants; he always seemed to be angry unless he was inside me.

Regardless, I was engaged to a man, and we had sex. It was what it was. It had to be. I needed to be in a relationship after what happened. And a man, especially a six-five one with seventeen stone of muscle like Joe, could keep me safe from the world and its threats.

My mind, however, was elsewhere. My thoughts about women were all-consuming. I saw them naked when they walked past me in the street, I pictured what it would be like to touch their bodies, and my head created stories about them throwing me up against walls and having their moans kiss at my ears. What I wanted I couldn't have, and what I had I couldn't want.

When it came to my urges, one minute I'd feel complete shame, and the next, dreamy optimism, as if my thoughts rode a rickety rollercoaster along a splintering wooden track held together by loosening nuts and bolts. There were steep inclines, vertiginous drops and sudden changes of speed and direction. Constant unstable fluctuations and undulations.

I had never pursued my fantasies. I had spent too many years with Joe to back out; it would have been too much effort to start again. My plan was to be married by the time I was twenty-five and then try for a baby, so I was already slightly behind schedule. If I left him and started dating again – something I'd have to do immediately, for my own safety – I would have to wait much longer to start a family. Joe would do. And besides, I feared what he'd do to me if I left him.

Chapter 3

The moment I stepped into the newsroom, I knew something big had happened. All the phones were either ringing or occupied, and reporters were dashing between desks, the urgency buzzing in the air like static electricity. Normally nine a.m. on a Monday was a slow ease-in, with the newsdesk swapping weekend stories or engaging in dull chatter about sports results.

Then I saw it. The morning edition, still warm from the presses. The headline blared up at me: Masked Gunmen Raid Cardiff Jewellery Store – Shop Owner Fighting for Life. My stomach plummeted. This wasn't just another story; this was huge – a career-making front page that would leap from our city paper to national networks within hours. And I'd missed it.

My eyes scanned the story. Whatshisname had secured an exclusive: an interview with the terrified cleaner who had been inside the store when the van crashed through the glass frontage and was the sole eyewitness to the owner's shooting.

My boss beckoned me over.

'So,' Glyn said, smirking over his shoulder at me as he closed the door, sealing us both inside the meeting room. 'What lesson did we learn last night?' His gut led the way across the room, the rest of him just trying to keep up.

'Never miss a call,' I muttered, his motto bitter in my mouth as I chose a chair adjacent to his at the head of the table.

'Never miss a call!' he repeated heartily, pointing a stubby finger that almost touched my nose, a self-satisfied grin plastered across his face as he soaked in my frustration. 'Spot on, Jess.'

'Sorry, Glyn,' I said, disappointment bubbling beneath my forced composure.

His fingers tapped at what should have been his chin, the point where his face sloped into his neck – a continuous curve of soft flesh, pebble-dashed with large, dark moles. 'Not like you to miss a call.'

I opened my mouth to explain, but he cut me off. 'You know,' he said, his voice dropping into that patronising-meets-sleazy tone that always made me want to scream, 'it's not just about answering the phone. It's about being vigilant. Always having your ear to the ground. That's what good reporters do.' His eyes narrowed slightly as they traced the line of my shirt.

I couldn't understand why he thought there was time for this when he should have been in the newsroom to help with the biggest story we'd had in months. Then again, it wasn't entirely surprising – he had a habit of pulling the female reporters aside for impromptu chats throughout the day.

He leaned back in his chair, crossing his arms over his stomach, slimeball-smiling. 'Whatshisname has already done an early-morning interview with the chief constable, and now he's working on an updated version of the story for the afternoon edition. A journalist award is practically in the bag for him.' He paused, his fat pink tongue peeking out between his lips as he blatantly eyed my chest. 'You're smart, Jess. You could go far here, you know? You've got the brains, the looks.'

'Thanks,' I said flatly, forcing a smile while my skin crawled.

'Just don't let another one of these slip through your fingers, yeah? We're all on the same team here.' He winked at me, like we shared some secret bond, then waved a dismissive hand.

I nodded stiffly and stood, feeling him give me the usual full-length once-over. 'It won't happen again.'

The humiliation clung to me as I walked back to my desk. Missing the story was bad, but dealing with Glyn was worse.

Carys, the photographer, swivelled in her chair to talk to me as I sat down. 'Mental, isn't it?' she said, holding a copy of the paper and staring at the photo on the front page – the jewellery store's glass front shattered, debris scattered on the pavement, police tape cordoning off the scene. She shook her head. 'I didn't know people even owned guns in Wales.'

I offered a distracted 'mmm', still processing my disappointment.

'A sawn-off shotgun of all things. Sounds like something from a mafia movie.'

'It does. Great picture, though, Carys. Well done.'

'It's a good job Carys answers her phone, isn't it, Jess?' Glyn chimed in condescendingly as he waddled past.

Chapter 4

I turned off the TV in a huff and threw the remote on my sofa. The robbery was still the top story, as it had been for the whole week. The store owner had died from his injuries, the gunmen were still on the run, and Whatshisname's byline had made its way into all the national papers. Glyn's smirk flashed in my mind, and I groaned.

I needed a break from thinking about work. A night out would do it. Li had invited me to join her and her new girlfriend at Freedom, a gay club in the city. Just the thought sent a spark through me. I smoothed my hands over my tight patchwork dress, wondering if I looked the part. It was just a club, right? Just a club. The first gay club I would ever set foot in. No big deal.

Staring at my reflection in the living room mirror, I felt relieved that Joe wasn't home to critique it. I checked my makeup – the black stitches drawn across my face and neck in eyeliner, the wispy false lashes, the smoky eyeshadow – before uncapping a lipstick and painting my lips as vibrantly red as my waist-length hair. Sally from *The*

Nightmare Before Christmas was looking back at me. Even if it was just a Halloween costume, it felt good to be someone else for a while.

I had briefly considered dressing as Jessica Rabbit, but the thought of it gave me flashbacks to school, when the boys would call me that name, make hourglass-figure motions with their hands, and hump the air. I'd always wondered what it would be like to have Li's lean frame – the way her hipbones jutted out when she wore low-rise jeans, and how her small chest allowed her to run without pain – but I had developed curves before I even hit my teens, feeling like a foreign object with my sudden breasts and hips and waist. It wasn't my body that inspired my nickname, though; it was my hair – a long, flowing curtain of dark red, not ginger, but an unnaturally bright scarlet. Even when I was a toddler, people would ask my parents if my hair had been dyed that colour.

I waited downstairs, in the communal foyer of my block of flats, hoping none of my neighbours would come in or out and see me dressed as I was.

The knot of nervous excitement in my stomach had been tightening all day; I'd always wanted to go to a queer club. Added to that knot was a fierce protectiveness of Li. I was about to meet her new partner – her first girlfriend, the woman who had made Li realise she was gay and ultimately led her to leave an almost decade-long relationship. More than anything, I wanted to be sure that Bex was good for her.

'Well don't you look just wonderful, bach,' said a frail voice behind me. It was Gwen, one of the residents on my floor, making her slow way down the stairs, clutching a rubbish bag, on her way to the recycling bin outside.

I tottered up the stairs in my stilettos to meet her. 'Let me take that for you, Gwen,' I said loudly, knowing she wouldn't hear me otherwise.

She gave me a soft, toothy grin as I took the bag from her. 'You're a good girl, you are, Jess.' Her Welsh accent was much stronger than mine, lilting and sing-song. She took another step down.

'Don't worry about coming down, Gwen; I'll take this out for you.'

She chuckled and nodded, clearly missing what I'd said, and linked her arm through mine as she continued to shuffle down carefully. 'Who are you dressed as, my love?' she asked, turning to admire my outfit.

I smiled, positioning my hand over the bare skin on my chest, which didn't seem appropriate for her to see, the bin bag bumping against my stomach as I did so. 'I'm Sally from *The Nightmare Before Christmas.*'

She blinked at me blankly, her enthusiastic smile never fading.

'She's a ragdoll from a Halloween film,' I added.

She laughed delightedly. 'Oh, isn't that absolutely wonderful. Is your lovely Mr. Griffiths joining you tonight?'

I stifled the urge to laugh at the use of the word 'lovely' to describe Joe. I'd told him I was going to a work event – a Halloween-themed team-bonding night for all the editorial staff at *The City Post*. He didn't like me going out to clubs; I knew he wouldn't let me go if he knew the real plan. Lying, even to him, made me feel uneasy, but it was the only way I could go out without causing a scene.

'He's working tonight,' I said, offering her a disappointed smile.

'Oh, there's a shame,' she said, squeezing my hand.

I saw car lights outside. 'I think my ride is here, Gwen,' I said as loudly as I could without breaking into a shout. 'Do you want me to help you back up before I go?'

'You are an angel,' she said, her eyes crinkling into tiny crescents as she grinned. She reached out with her arthritis-knobbled fingers and patted my cheek. 'Don't worry about me, cariad. Taking the rubbish out is my daily workout; it keeps me young, it does.'

I waved back at her and dumped the bin bag before heading over to the car, Bex's car. Li was already standing on the pavement, dressed as the most adorable witch I'd ever seen – despite her clear attempt to look scary with green face paint. She practically bounced towards me and wrapped me in a hug.

'Elphaba?' I asked, smiling, already knowing the answer. We had seen *Wicked* in the theatre at least five times; Li was obsessed with it.

'Of course,' she said, smiling proudly. And you are... Sally?'

I nodded. We loved surprising each other with our Halloween outfits. On regular days or nights out, we'd call to find out what the other was wearing. Halloween was our only exception.

'You look awesome,' she said before lowering her voice to a whisper and discreetly pointing towards Bex, who was waiting in the car. 'I'm praying you'll like her.'

Li tilted the passenger seat forward so I could feed myself through the gap, onto the backseat.

'You're going to get a bit squished back there, sorry,' Bex said from the driver's seat, flashing me a wide smile. 'Small car problems.' She was dressed as a circus strongman, in a red and white striped vest top and matching shorts, with a lopsided handlebar moustache hanging off her top lip.

I smiled. 'Don't worry, I've only got little legs.'

She laughed enthusiastically, a double chin forming as she did so, and reached out her hand for me to take. It was meaty, large like a baseball mitt. She placed her other hand on top, enclosing mine in a surprisingly gentle handshake. 'Great to finally meet you, Jess.' Her voice was kind. 'I've heard so much about you – mostly how you're a complete badass.' Her moustache fell off as she said the last word.

Li giggled from the passenger seat and picked it up.

'Oh, that's just Li's very biased opinion of me,' I said, digging in my handbag. 'I doubt I've ever done a single badass thing in my life.'

'Well, there's always tonight,' Bex said with a warm chuckle.

I handed her my tube of lash glue. 'This will keep it in place,' I said, gesturing to the moustache.

'Tidy!' She said, flashing me a grin. I remembered Li mentioning that Bex had started picking up Welshisms since moving to Cardiff, even though she was the only one out of the three of us who hadn't grown up in Wales.

As Li helped her affix the facial hair back in place, I studied Bex, trying to gauge whether she was the kind of person who would treat my best friend well, or if she might end up breaking her heart. It wasn't personal; I would have approached anyone with the same caution. 'I've heard a lot about you too – mostly good things,' I said, making sure there was light-heartedness in my voice.

Bex flashed a silly, disarming grin. 'Good things, eh? Does that mean I pass the Jess approval test?'

'Still to be determined,' I said semi-seriously, just then noticing that Gwen was still standing at the doorway waving goodbye. I waved back through the tiny window.

'I'll be on my best behaviour,' Bex said, sitting up soldier-tall, her head reaching the roof of the car, giving a three-finger salute. 'Scout's honour.'

Li leaned towards Bex, grinning. 'Jess is just protective, but I can already tell she likes you.'

I raised an eyebrow. 'Hmm. We'll see. I'm sure you know the drill, Bex – hurt her, I kill you.'

Bex boomed a robust laugh again. 'And you said you weren't a badass. I'm just glad you're here to keep me in check, Jess.'

I found myself softening. She had the kind of easy warmth that made strangers feel like old friends.

'I'll think of a way to win you over,' she said, flipping on her indicator. 'I'm pretty good with jokes – maybe a few laughs will do the trick.'

'Try me,' I said, waving once more to Gwen as the car pulled away from the curb.

'What do you call a man with no shins?'

'What?'

'Tony.'

Li giggled.

I pursed my lips together, struggling to keep a straight face, not wanting to smile too soon. 'You'll have to do better than that,' I teased.

'Right,' Bex said eagerly, taking the challenge seriously. 'Why did the baker have brown hands?'

'Why?'

'Because he kneaded a poo.'

Bex glanced at me in her rearview as I grinned. 'Yes! That one broke a smile at least. OK, OK, let me think,' she continued, almost to herself. 'Li told me you're a reporter, so I need a writer joke.' She paused for a moment, and I saw her eyes light up again in the mirror. 'I bought the world's worst thesaurus the other day – not only is it terrible, it's terrible.'

I laughed, not just for Bex's benefit. Li did too. And Bex joined in, raising her fist in the air, shaking it in vigorous celebration.

I hadn't known what to expect of Bex. Yes, Li had described her looks – mixed race, short hair, broad, tall (though everyone seemed tall compared to me and Li) – and her character – a goofball, with a heart of gold. But it was another thing to meet her and form my own opinions. Li had picked a good one if first impressions were anything to go by. Also, Bex's jesting had eased my nerves about going to the gay club.

'I just need to pick up my friend Georgia, and we'll be on our way,' Bex said. 'It'll be like a double date.'

'She's joking,' Li said quickly, before I could feel uneasy.

As Bex drove on, I watched as Li's dainty hand gently stroked the back of Bex's head, where the hair was shaved close, her fingertips skimming the tight bottle-blonde curls at the crown. Her painted nails inched down onto the nape of Bex's neck and onto her fleshy shoulders. Li's hand looked tiny against the expanse of Bex's bare skin, which was framed only by thin vest straps. Their golden skin tones – Li's much lighter and Bex's much deeper – looked as if they were painted from the same palette. I could *feel* the love between them. I hadn't seen Li touch Nathan like that in all the years they were together. She wasn't normally the PDA type.

'That's her house there,' Bex said. She parked in front of a row of terraced houses and excitedly unclipped her seatbelt. 'Back in a jiff.'

'It's not *actually* going to seem like we're on a double date, is it?' I asked Li after Bex closed the car door behind her.

'Not at all,' Li said soothingly as she turned in her seat to face me, tucking a strand of her silky black hair behind her ear. 'It's just a casual night out. It's me and my friend, and Bex and her friend. Nothing more, nothing less.'

I let out an exaggerated breath. 'How are you feeling about going to a gay bar for the first time? Nervous?'

'A bit, but once we settle in it'll be fine. I'm sure of it.' She looked out the car window and pointed. 'There she is. That's Georgia.'

I turned and looked. Something wild and warming burgeoned in my heart as she walked towards the car, lit by the glow of the porch light. It was as if she were moving in slow motion. I watched her make her way down the driveway. Her cropped brunette hair caught the light and shimmered with hints of burgundy as the wind played with it, her sweeping fringe blowing back to reveal her stunning bone structure and peachy skin. My eyes trailed down her body, which was somehow both feminine and masculine, hard but with soft curves. As she neared, I tore my gaze away and fumbled for my mirror, pulling it out of my handbag. I quickly checked my makeup, smoothing out any smudges, then ran my hands through the lengths of my hair, adjusting it so it wasn't covering my cleavage. I snapped the mirror closed as she climbed into the back seat next to me.

'Hi,' I said brightly.

'Oh. Hey,' she replied, seemingly confused that I was in the car. She turned her attention to Bex. 'Did you bring the eyepatch and pirate bandana for me to borrow?'

'Yep. It's in the boot with my foam barbell,' Bex replied.

Apart from that, we didn't acknowledge each other throughout the drive to Freedom. I busied myself with Li, making stilted conversation, stumbling over my words, and struggling to concentrate on what I was saying while trying to listen in on Georgia's conversation with Bex. Now and then, I laughed a bit too loudly at Bex's jokes, even though I wasn't really hearing them, perhaps hoping to draw Georgia's attention without having to speak directly to her. I was careful not to let my knees brush against hers, though the space between us felt impossibly small in the back of Bex's Audi TT, and I kept my gaze away from her – not intentionally, but as if I were trying to look at the sun, my eyes instinctively knowing better. Georgia's presence – her tempting scent, calm voice, and her steady energy – seemed to fill the space, making Li and Bex fade into a distant background hum. I nodded, smiled and shook my head at guessed intervals as Li spoke to me with her soundless voice. I only heard Georgia, heard her even when she wasn't speaking. A heat started to tingle between my legs.

Chapter 5

Freedom's sparkly sign was flanked by two flags – one rainbow and the other a Welsh dragon. The entire front wall was mirrored like a disco ball, and on the far left, the open double doors let music and neon spill out.

A wave of intimidation hit me. I imagined everyone inside being completely at ease with themselves, confident in their identities and sexualities. They would be right at home, comfortable in their own skins, while I would be the outsider, the intruder. I didn't want to make eye contact with the bouncer, worried she might think I was in the wrong place. As the four of us were given the nod to approach, I could feel her looking at me – as if she knew I was engaged to a man. She asked me and Li for our IDs, which we hadn't thought to bring, considering we were in our mid-twenties, but Bex and Georgia – who were regulars – vouched for us.

As I stepped through the door, the air was what hit me first – alive, swirling, charged with energy, thickened by body heat and layered with perfume and alcohol. Then, as I rounded the corner, I saw the sea of women. I couldn't tell you how many there were; it could have been as few as ten or as many as fifty. It was like seeing a new world open up before me. Women. Uninhibited, fearless, dancing close to each other, their bodies – painted multicolour under the strobe lights – moving to the rhythm of the bassy music, the beat thumping through me. Some were wrapped up in each other, completely lost in the moment, while others twirled and bounced with playful energy, flashes of their laughter rising above the noise. There were probably gay men there too, but I don't remember any. A warm flush spread through me when I spotted women kissing passionately, right where they stood, openly and without any attempt to hide, their desire bold and unashamed. I stole a glance at Georgia and felt the urge to pull her close and share that same sense of freedom.

Li and I looked at each other, speechless, before following a seemingly unfazed Bex and Georgia across the space. I felt women turning their heads to look at me as I passed. I imagined their thoughts. How bright my hair was, how well my dress hugged my body, how big my boobs were. I imagined it really hard so that the other thoughts didn't creep in, like how I didn't look gay enough to be there and how I wasn't welcome.

'Shall we go to the dancefloor?' Bex asked.

'I'm going to have to grab some shots first if we're doing that,' said Georgia.

'I'll come with you,' I said quickly, seeing my chance to talk to her with no one listening in.

'I'll pass on the shots,' Li said, her hands lifting in a gentle, almost protective gesture. She'd never been much of a drinker. 'I'm driving Bex's car back later.'

Georgia and I made our way across the room, with her briskly striding ahead while I followed. As we stood side by side at the bar, she kept her head turned away from me, her attention fixed on the bearded bartender theatrically shaking up a cocktail to the beat of the music.

'Does it take a while to get served here?' I asked her, just to say anything.

She turned her head, but not her eyes, towards me. 'It's usually pretty quick.'

I stared at her side profile. I thought she must be the most beautiful woman I'd ever seen – high cheekbones, a sleek jawline, full lips, lightly freckled skin and the cutest bump on the bridge of her nose. 'So you're thinking shots?' I asked, my eyes drifting to her toned forearms, exposed by the rolled-up sleeves of her shirt.

'Yeah,' she replied in a matter-of-fact tone, adjusting her bandana, not yet wearing the eye patch.

'What's your go-to shot?' I asked the side of her face, not waiting for an answer before I continued, 'I can't stand sambuca, but I like tequila. I've heard it doesn't give you a hangover. Do you like tequila?'

'Could I get four Jäger shots, please?' she asked the bartender, not acknowledging my question.

Despite the loud music, the silence between us was painful as the shots were poured. I looked around the room and saw two girls kissing – one dressed as a cat and the other as a devil – their tongues moving slowly, and the cat-girl's face paint smudged onto the devil-girl's face, creating a grey five o'clock shadow. 'I haven't had a Jäger shot before,' I said, still watching them, confident that Georgia wouldn't clock my line of sight anyway. 'Are they strong?'

'Well, yeah, shots are always strong,' she said bluntly, handing a ten-pound note to the bartender. As he returned with the change, Georgia's eyes flicked to the small heap of silver coins in her palm; after barely a glance, she handed him back two ten pence pieces. 'This is too much,' she said, her voice steady and clear. 'The change should only be one pound twenty.'

'How much do I owe you?' I asked, trying to keep things direct after my previous attempts to chat had been met with such indifference.

'Nothing. I only bought two each for me and Bex, as that's what we normally get. Sorry, I thought you were getting tequila. Do you want me to—'

'No, it's fine. I've got it.'

She nodded once, without making eye contact, and walked away, leaving me standing there.

While I waited, I looked around the room again and realised I was the only one in heels. I was always the odd one out, no matter the reason. Everyone else seemed to know what to wear, how to act, what to say. They spoke in riddles I couldn't quite understand, as if the world had a secret language I was never taught. For as long as I could remember, I'd been mimicking the way people interacted just to pass as normal. If I were a bird, I'd be the one who pretended I loved to fly.

Queer people had always been the *most* elusive. Before Li came out to me, I had never met a real-life lesbian. To me, gay people were all part of a secret society I couldn't access. I wanted so much to be a part of it, but I didn't feel worthy. I was a fraud.

'Georgia's not a fan of me,' I said, leaning close to Li's ear over the blasting music while we swayed on the dancefloor.

'She is,' Li replied emphatically. 'Who wouldn't be? You're wonderful. She's probably just shy.'

I scanned the club for Georgia but didn't spot her at first. My attention was drawn by Bex, on the other side of the room, chatting with a girl who was dressed as a mermaid. Bex twirled her moustache before lifting her foam barbell above her head – her armpit hair on full display – grimacing and staggering as though it were a real challenge, making the girl throw her head back in laughter.

I turned my gaze to Li, who had her phone pressed to one ear and her finger in the other, focusing intently on whatever was being said on the call. I caught her eye and nudged my head towards Bex, giving Li a questioning look that asked, *Are you cool with that?* knowing how upset she used to get when Nathan flirted with other girls. Her calm expression replied, *It's just Bex being Bex; she never crosses any lines.* She seemed more relaxed, more carefree with Bex than she ever had with him.

I finally spotted Georgia standing alone, elbows resting on a tall table. I got the impression we were both outsiders in our own ways.

'Not much of a talker, is she?' I said in Li's ear when she'd hung up the phone, subtly pointing at Georgia.

'Bex says she warms up,' Li said, putting her phone away in her bag. 'I've only met her fleetingly when I went to watch Bex play football once, but she seems nice.'

'Who was on the phone, anyway?' I asked.

'It was a voicemail from my manager.' Li rolled her eyes in an attempt to convey annoyance, but her round, angelic face coated in pea-green paint made it hard to take her seriously. 'On a Saturday night of all times. She's as bad as your boss!'

***

I hadn't expected Georgia to want to continue the night at Bex's; she had seemed so distant at the club. Bex and Li dashed off to the kitchen, leaving me and Georgia alone together in the living room. I was incredibly aware that it was just the two of us. The space seemed to become bigger, our silence bouncing off the walls. If I stayed quiet, surely she'd come out with something? I tried it.

'So how long have you known Li?' she asked after a few agonising moments, brushing imaginary crumbs off her knees and watching for where they landed on the floor.

'Oh, she's my oldest friend; we met in nursery when we were two years old. What about you and Bex?'

'Only earlier this year, through playing football together. But we actually connected more over statistics, weirdly. We both keep track of the team's performance. I like to work out the probabilities of different strategies we could use during matches.'

I raised an eyebrow, intrigued. 'So you're the analytical type,' I said, remembering how quickly she had noticed noticed the bartender had given her the wrong change earlier that night.

'Have to be. I'm a maths teacher at Bayside Comprehensive School.'

'That's impressive,' I said, and I meant it.

'What do you do?'

'I'm a senior reporter at *The City Post*.'

'That must involve a lot of critical thinking, too.'

'Maybe that's why Bex thought we'd make a good match,' I said playfully.

'What do you mean?' she asked, and I thought I saw a hint of disdain on her face.

'Bex joked it was a double date, that's all.' I laughed, trying to keep it light, though I was offended by the minutiae of her expression.

'She didn't tell me that. I had no idea it was a set-up.'

'She was only messing around,' I said, the ego injury apparent in my tone. 'No need to be annoyed.'

'No,' she said, actually looking at me properly for the first time, and I noticed how blue her eyes were. 'If Bex had told me you were coming, I could have prepared myself to see such a beautiful girl tonight. Do you realise how off I've been since getting into Bex's car and seeing you? I didn't know they were bringing anyone, let alone someone as stunning as you.'

I breathed out a surprised laugh, feeling relieved – and flattered – that her night-long standoffishness had been because she was attracted to me.

'Anyway,' she continued, 'when I asked Bex about you earlier tonight, she said you had a boyfriend.'

I smothered a smile, secretly pleased to hear that Georgia had been asking about me. 'I do have a boyfriend, a fiancé, actually, but I didn't want to feel like a misfit tonight at a *gay* club.'

'So you were just playing dress-up tonight? And I don't mean all of that,' she said, gesturing to my makeup and costume.

'No, I—'

'Spaces like Freedom exist for a reason. They're not for people who want to pretend they belong.'

That really hit a fucking nerve.

'Woah, what's going on in here?' Bex said in the doorway, holding a tray of pink drinks complete with paper umbrellas.

I grabbed my bag and manoeuvred around Bex, careful not to bump into her or the tray as I made my way to the door.

I heard a kerfuffle of hasty whispers behind me.

'Hold on,' Georgia said, softly jogging towards me in the hallway. 'That was really rude of me. I shouldn't have said that. Any chance we can start again?'

I paused, rubbing the back of my neck. 'Well... I feel uncomfortable now.'

'What about if we have those crap-looking Barbie drinks they've made for us and then I'll make sure you get home safe.'

Just looking into her eyes made me forgive her. 'One drink.'

'Are you OK?' Li asked in a hushed, concerned tone, giving my hand a reassuring squeeze when I walked back into the room.

'Yeah, just a misunderstanding.' I offered her a grateful smile.

Georgia took a sip of her drink and winced. 'Bloody hell. What's in this, Bex?'

'Duw duw,' Bex said in mock affront, making us all laugh. 'It's a raspberry gin cocktail. Don't you like it? It's my favourite.'

Given Bex's large, solid frame with its hint of masculine attitude, it was endearingly at odds that her favourite drink was something so delicate and pink.

'Yeah, lovely,' Georgia said sarcastically. That was the first glimpse of humour she'd shown all night, and it was the first I'd seen of the smile-activated dimples in her cheeks.

When Bex brought out Trivial Pursuit, Georgia came to sit next to me, and there were gentle hand touches and a few fleeting glances that made my tummy flip. Georgia answered every question with such ease that we all started joking she must have been cheating. Her mind seemed to work on some advanced level, effortlessly pulling facts and details from every corner of knowledge.

After the game, Georgia and I caught a taxi together, and during the drive she asked for my number, which I gave to her, as a friend. She made sure I was dropped off first even though we passed her house on the way to mine – so she ended up having to backtrack for twenty minutes – and she didn't let me pay.

'Least I can do,' she said, leaning towards my side of the taxi as I stood gripping the open car door to steady my half-cut body. 'Let's have another "friend date" at some point; it turned out to be pretty fun.'

Chapter 6

'A work night, yeah?' Joe said in a low voice from the dark of the bedroom, startling me as I crept in. 'Do work nights often finish at two in the morning?'

'Sorry,' I whispered, being as careful as I could not to slur. 'Time got away from me. I didn't know it would run on that late.' I recited the lines I'd rehearsed while walking upstairs to the flat, realising these premeditated lies almost made me as bad as him – nowhere near as bad, actually, but I still wasn't proud of it. 'I wanted to stay until the end to make up for having missed that big story last weekend.' His silence made me ramble on. 'If I want to get back in their good books, I have to attend all these things. I need to keep myself on the radar of the decision-makers if I want to become news editor one day.' That last part wasn't a lie.

He turned the bedside lamp on. 'I bet you made a fucking stellar impression,' he said through snarled lips. 'Assuming you even went to a work event tonight. Look at the state of you.'

I slid my heels off and climbed into bed without replying, my hands trembling slightly.

He yanked the covers away and flung a pillow at me. 'Do you really think you're sleeping in here?'

Without hesitation, I made my way down the hall to the living room, clutching my pillow. I knew in that instant that I shouldn't have walked away from him. He wanted an argument; he wanted me to defend myself so that he could prove me wrong – and this was one of those rare occasions he had every right to be angry, not that I'd admitted that to him.

I heard him scrambling down the hallway after me. 'You fucking bitch,' he said under his breath. 'Don't walk away from me when I'm speaking to you.'

I instinctively ran from him, but he grabbed me and bundled me over to the wall – not just any wall, it was always the same one, the one in the kitchen, on the left side of the room, because that was an outside wall, not connected to the neighbouring flats. It was solid brick and barely made a noise when he flat-handed it or punched it while towering over me. The interior walls of the flat must have been plasterboard; they sounded hollow, so he didn't use those; besides, they would have probably dented or cracked under a fist. He'd drag me over to that kitchen wall regardless of what room I'd aggravated him in.

He pushed my back against it and squeezed my face in his hand while bending himself down to my eye level. 'Are you lying to me about where you were tonight?'

'No.'

'So if I call your office in the morning, they'll confirm that?'

'Yes.'

He thumped The Wall millimetres from my face before returning his stare, standing over me, his face contorted in an ugly display of rage, his arms blocking my escape. His strength meant he could easily keep me in one spot, not that I dared to squirm away.

'Your outfit is fucking trashy. If it *was* a work event, you've fucked your chances of being taken seriously by wearing that.' He grabbed the flesh on the back of my arm and shook it. 'How many times do I have to tell you to wear outfits that cover this? Nobody wants to see your flabby arms, Jess.'

He yanked me forward and pulled at the back of my dress, searching for the label and reading it. 'A medium. When I met you, you were a size small.' He shook his head. 'You need to start taking care of yourself. I'm not going to marry a fat slob. Imagine how good you could look in your wedding dress if you lost weight.' A hint of a smile played at his lips. 'Say it,' he whispered. I knew he wanted me to repeat his words back to him. He grabbed my face. 'Say. It!'

I closed my eyes, detaching myself from emotion. 'I could look good in my wedding dress if I lost weight.'

'Look at me and continue.'

'I need to start taking care of myself.'

'And?'

'I need to get back to a size small.'

His smile grew. 'Pathetic.' He turned and began walking back to the bedroom. 'Get some sleep; you're a fucking mess.'

His behaviour had become near to normalised in my brain. Just as a doctor becomes desensitised to blood, I had grown numb to Joe's cruelty; it was like I was under anaesthetic, paralysed but conscious, aware of the pain yet powerless to stop it.

When I heard the bedroom door shut behind him, I took my phone out of my pocket. There was a text from Georgia:

'Hope you're not feeling too rough after Bex's Barbie drinks.'

A warm sensation flowed into me, mixing with the fear Joe had just stirred up. *Don't get attached*, I thought. *She's just a new friend*. Up popped up another text:

'Fancy going to the cinema next weekend?'

Chapter 7

The thought of seeing Georgia again had catapulted me through the week. Days always seemed to zip by in a high-energy blur regardless – news never stops, especially at the city's biggest paper – but all the more so when the prize of seeing Georgia waited at the finish line.

A thrill shot through me every time I pictured her. We'd texted and called all week, and I learned so much about her: she captained the local football team; had a past relationship with a girl named Ruth, who also played on the team, which bothered me a little; she loved Fat Max burgers; adored her Boston Terrier, Pickle; and still lived with her dad, Mike, and younger sister, Gemma, despite being twenty-seven – two years older than me.

Her mum never came up in conversation; she'd always change the topic. I wanted to know everything there was to know. Despite our weirdly rocky start, I felt something real forming. A friendship. Only a friendship. I had a fiancé. When the weekend landed, my stomach felt like it was being tased from the inside. I was about to see her face again, her smile, those incredible eyes.

We sat side by side in the deep cinema seats, looking straight ahead at the screen while both trying to put our drinks in the same cup holder. The accidental touch of our fingers sent a charge through me; I felt it zap straight through my arm, leaving goosebumps in its wake. We answered each other's awkward smiles and she swapped her drink to the other side.

I stayed as calm as possible, pretending not to notice that there was more feeling in our pinkies brushing than in the whole act of sex with Joe, or with anyone for that matter. Still staring straight ahead, she crossed her legs towards me. As she leant away to take a sip through her straw, the side of her shoe travelled ever so slightly up my shin and back down as she returned to an upright position. She kept her foot resting softly against me. I felt the heat of it through my jeans like it was being tattooed there. Was she meaning to do it? Could she feel what I felt? There was a high-pitched ringing in my ears, and my heart was pounding so hard I was sure it was visibly rocking me in my seat. How could something as subtle as her foot touching me feel like the aftershock of a bomb? When the lights went down, I wanted so much to kiss her, though I knew I wouldn't.

Scenes of a bustling 1950s Manhattan department store in the pre-Christmas rush unfolded before us, a virginal shopgirl serving an elegantly dressed older woman. I held myself still in my seat, trying to focus on the film rather than Georgia's closeness, or the way the stolen glances between the women on screen felt far too much like how we looked at each other. The movie followed their tentative first conversations before the pull between them became undeniable. I gripped the armrest, struggling to concentrate, my mind drifting to what it meant that Georgia had brought me to see a story about forbidden love.

Somewhere around the one-hour mark, the women kissed. My face burned, and I felt like I had forgotten how to breathe normally. When I finally dared to glance at Georgia, she was focused on the screen, her eyes glassy as the older woman faced losing custody of her child because of her relationship with another woman. She leaned slightly closer, her breath warm against my ear. 'I'm so glad we don't live in those times.'

***

The next afternoon, Georgia and I joined Li and Bex for a picnic at Lake Calon Park, one of the serene pockets of nature nestled in the city.

I hadn't said anything about my feelings for Georgia, but Li knew. Her eyes seemed to be twinkling with knowing as she glanced at me.

'Quick stroll?' I asked Li, eager to speak with her alone.

'Absolutely.' She hopped up from the picnic blanket. 'Lead the way.'

I nodded my head towards the lake, which sparkled like a field of diamonds under the crisp November sunlight. Despite the season, the day was mild – a continuation of the unusually gentle autumn we'd been having.

'You better not eat all the Welsh cakes, Bex,' Li said over her shoulder as we walked away. She turned her attention to me, her smile unguarded – the kind that belonged on a child on Christmas morning.

'So...' I began, my own grin breaking through. 'Last night went well?' I had called her the previous evening to ask how introducing

Bex to her parents went – we'd spent two hours on the phone – but I wanted to replay it, in person.

'Amazing.' Her voice brimmed with excitement. 'I wasn't worried; you know how they are.'

I wrapped my arm around her shoulders as we walked. 'I'm so unbelievably happy for you.' I knew Jim and Anne would be supportive – there was never a doubt. They'd always been Li's biggest fans. Twenty-five years ago, they'd flown all the way to China to adopt her. Not out of some grand humanitarian gesture, but simply because they wanted to be parents. They didn't know anything about her background; the adoption report said Li was found on the orphanage doorstep, her umbilical cord still attached, and described her as 'a healthy baby with shining hair and smart eyes'. Anne had told me the story countless times during sleepovers, when she'd tuck us in and sit at the foot of the bed, saying how grateful she and Jim were to Li's birth parents.

'They were so excited to meet Bex,' Li continued, throwing crusts from her sandwich to the ducks and swans. 'It was like they'd known her forever. They wouldn't stop squeezing her hand across the table.' I could picture it easily. 'Bex cried when we got in the car after. She was so chuffed. I'm so lucky to have the three of them. Everything just feels... right.'

Listening to Li, I found myself daydreaming about coming out to my own parents, telling them I'd called off the wedding to Joe and was seeing a woman. But then I remembered why I never would. After what had happened when I was eleven and seeing their faces when I broke the news, I couldn't bear the thought of giving them another life-altering surprise. It wasn't that I thought they'd be sad or angry, I just I loved them too much to risk delivering any shocking news ever again. Their expressions from that day were still etched in my mind.

'Anyway,' Li said, giggling as a gaggle of geese waddled over for the last of Li's crusts, 'enough about me. Tell me more about the cinema.'

'I told you all there is to tell.' I tried my best to hide a shy smile.

'You and Georgia seem to be getting on well.'

'We are.'

She looked up at me, that knowing glint in her eyes again.

'We're just friends,' I said, trying to convince myself as much as her.

She nudged me softly. 'I know. But you *would* make such a lush couple—'

'Li,' I said semi-seriously, barely suppressing a grin. 'Don't.'

'I can see it in your eyes. You—'

'Stop!' I fixed my hand over her mouth, laughing as she tried to talk underneath it.

'Alright,' she said with a chuckle after I let go. 'You're just friends.'

'Thank you,' I said with a sigh, relieved she was dropping it.

'As long as she doesn't replace me.'

'Never.'

'Besties for the resties,' she said, holding out her pinkie.

I linked it with mine, feigning annoyance. 'I hate when you say that.'

She laughed. 'I know you do. But it's always been our thing.'

'It was cute when we were, like, five, but now it's just cringey.'

Li grinned and wrapped an arm around my waist. 'Besties for the resties!' she declared, a little louder, her voice full of affection.

I tutted through a smile as warmth spread through my chest.

***

'Where did you two get to?' Bex called when she saw us approaching.

'Just a little stroll around the lake with my *bestie*,' Li said, grinning up at me before glancing back at the glittering water. 'It's amazing here. Thanks for suggesting it, Georgia. I haven't been here for ages.'

'It's beautiful, isn't it?' Georgia said, turning her gaze towards me as she responded to Li, a smile playing on her lips as she locked her eyes with mine. 'I could stare at this view for hours.'

I felt my cheeks burn as I smiled back at her, settling onto the picnic blanket beside her. She spoke animatedly to Li and Bex, reeling off facts about the lake – how it was half a mile from end to end and fourteen feet deep. I watched the way her words slipped through her lips. She was paralysingly beautiful. It wasn't just the way she looked that attracted me to her, it was the workings of her mind, her intelligence. I realised Li was probably staring at me while I stared at Georgia, but I didn't care; Georgia had me constantly intrigued and captivated in a way I wasn't used to. I was turned on by her intellect, dizzy with a desire to kiss her.

'It's not a picnic until somebody pulls out their sausage,' Bex said, breaking me out of my trance. She hooted at her own joke while pointing at Li, who had a mouthful of sausage roll.

I started belly laughing, mainly because Li was turning pink and couldn't get a word out after taking such a huge bite of the pastry. Her eyes began to water as she silently laughed, her hand covering her full mouth, with the occasional flaky crumb shooting out.

'If you love sausage so much, why did you leave your man for me, Li?' Bex teased, poking Li's cheek.

I held my ribs as I laughed.

Li gently batted Bex's hands away.

'Come on, hurry up and deep-throat that sausage; we've got to go soon.'

'Be-ex!' Li finally managed after swallowing. 'Stop it!'

'Right, as much as I'd like to do this all day, me and my little sausage gobbler have to go,' Bex said, patting Li on the back. 'Are you two going to stick around for a bit longer, or...?'

Georgia glanced at me. I thought for a second I might drown in those eyes. 'If there's cake to finish, I'm staying,' she said, pointing to the leftovers on the picnic blanket.

'Me too,' I said, smiling.

'Bex, I'm going to get you back for that, you know,' Li said with a mischievous grin, standing.

'Oh yeah? You'll have to catch me first.' Bex ran off, shouting her goodbyes to me and Georgia over her shoulder as Li chased her.

I couldn't help but laugh at their childish flirting. Li in her mid-twenties, and Bex, pushing thirty, seemed to become kids when they were around each other. It was good to see Li so happy and carefree. She'd always had a childlike, playful spirit – a trait I doubted she'd ever grow out of; even if she lived on into a wrinkled, hunched, hobbling old age, she'd probably still want to play games and chase butterflies. That side of her had always been slightly dulled whenever I saw her around Nathan, despite her once worshipping the ground he walked on. With Bex, though, the real Li was shining through.

It was strange to imagine them both in their professional roles at Cymru Protect, the insurance firm where they worked – Li as an underwriter and Bex as a risk analyst – being all serious in their stiff corporate outfits, determining policies, typing up reports, and handling important phone calls. It seemed so at odds with how they were in the real world.

As they disappeared from view and Georgia and I had finished laughing at their silliness, a silence fell, not uncomfortable, but a flutter of nervousness trilled through me nonetheless. In the moment of quiet, an off-lead pug came trotting up to us.

'Oh, hello, handsome,' I cooed in a high-pitched voice, lowering it when I noticed how ridiculous it sounded. 'Where did you come from, sweet boy?'

I stroked his little head, and Georgia joined in with the pats, her shoulder brushing against mine. Despite my love for dogs, all I could think about were Georgia's lips, mere inches from mine.

The pug sniffed at the bara brith on the picnic blanket.

'Oh, you can't have that,' Georgia said in a baby voice, similar to the one I'd used. 'Raisins are bad for your belly.'

I felt a smile spreading across my face. 'I'm so glad you do that, too,' I said, feeling both amused and touched by how her usual calm demeanour gave way to this tender, adoring side.

She laughed. 'I can't help it; they're so cute, they bring it out of me.'

'They really are the best. I'd love to have one, but my landlord doesn't allow pets. Adopting a pug is at the top of my bucket list, though. One day.'

'If Pickle, my baby, didn't have a bad leg, I'd have brought him today. You would have fallen in love.'

'I'm sure I would have,' I said, flustered at the mention of love – a feeling that was a little too close to home at that moment.

The pug climbed onto my lap and lay down, belly to the sky, licking my arm.

Georgia laughed. 'He must be able to sense how amazing you are.'

I felt my cheeks redden. I couldn't remember the last time I'd been complimented on anything other than my appearance – except by Li or my family. The word 'amazing' suddenly pulled me back to secondary school. I could almost hear the girls in my class talking about me – *She thinks she's amazing; so stuck up; full of herself* – the taunts and sneers coming easily to them. Li always had my back, whether they were gossiping about me, making up mocking songs, or trying to cut off my long red ponytail during assembly. Li stood up for me so often that she was bullied by association, with kids pulling their eyes into slits and calling her 'Ching Chong'.

'Sorry about him,' the pug's owner called, jogging over to us. He laughed at the sight of the dog on my lap. 'He's daft as a brush.'

'We can't get enough of him,' I said, grinning, and Georgia agreed.

He chuckled. 'Come on, Dave, that's enough flirting.' The dog's tongue lolled out of his smiling mouth as he ignored his dad. 'Dave. David. Come on. Biscuit?' The dog popped up at the last word, making us all laugh. 'Come on,' his owner said again playfully, beginning to walk away. 'I'll make sure he gets extra biscuits for being such a charmer today, girls.'

'Be good, Dave,' Georgia called.

We packed up the rest of the picnic and set out on a walk around the lake. The water was framed by a blaze of fiery oranges and rich browns which the gentle breeze set aquiver, coaxing leaves to break free and spiral downwards to carpet our path in a tapestry of rustling hues. My hand brushed against hers as we walked. My heart skipped. When I rubbed my arm nervously, she glanced at me.

'Are you cold?' she asked, already starting to offer me her jumper.

I accepted it, smiling gratefully before pulling it over my head, smelling her sweet, woody perfume on it, feeling a warmth that had nothing to do with the fabric.

Chapter 8

Georgia, Li, Bex and I began to spend most of our free time together. I squeezed in lunchtimes with them on workdays, and in the evenings, when Joe left the flat to go to the pub or hangout at his friends' houses, I would meet the girls. We usually went to Bex's place since she lived alone, but sometimes we'd go to Li's shared house – though her housemates didn't like us using the living room or making any noise. Once, we went to Georgia's when her dad was out. I didn't invite them to mine because I hated the thought of Joe coming back and finding us all there. He didn't like anyone in his space – even though it was *my* flat.

In the early stages of mine and Joe's relationship, I'd been led to believe we'd be one of those cute couples who cooked three-course meals for our couple-friends; we'd sit around our beautifully decorated dining table, laughing all evening and getting sophisticatedly tipsy before calling it a night and kissing our guests goodbye on the cheeks at the door. But no, we were the couple that didn't invite people over, and we weren't invited anywhere in return.

Instead, he prioritised other pursuits, like his frequent 'business' trips to London with Matty, the co-founder of his tech start-up, JoMatTech. They often took their entire team – five employees, all women – on all-expenses-paid trips, staying at The Ritz or The Savoy and celebrating 'jobs well done' at exclusive clubs over magnums of champagne. I only knew this because I'd seen the receipts once. I nearly choked at the amount he'd spent. It was particularly infuriating because he never contributed a penny towards my rent or bills, despite practically living in my flat. He'd always insist he 'hadn't officially moved in' and that he'd 'just brought some of his things from his mum's house'.

I didn't allow myself to wonder about what really went on while he was away with his mainly female team; I knew what went on, but I was fine with sweeping it all under the rug. That's what people did in relationships, I thought. And anyway, I was pleased to have that extra time with Georgia and the girls. His work kept him busy, so I didn't pry.

Joe claimed JoMatTech was fast becoming a recognised name in the tech world. Although I never fully understood the intricacies, it revolved around cyber security. He was proud of being what he called an 'ethical hacker'. He'd even landed a contract with one of the UK's leading entertainment companies by hacking their computer network and then convincing them to hire JoMatTech as their digital bouncer to protect their system from 'real criminals'. He would brag about infiltrating the systems of big-name brands, banks and private hospitals. It all sounded sketchy to me, but he always insisted he was on the verge of making it big. 'Just wait,' he'd say, 'the money's tied up right now because we're making investments, but soon you and I will have a huge house and a big garden for our kids and pugs to play in.' The promise of a stable, secure life was always on the cusp of reality.

That was how I'd initially fallen for his charms; he had a knack for spinning exciting yarns about our imminent future.

Chapter 9

G eorgia stared at me with her azure-blue eyes, a half-smile on her face.

I beamed back at her over my white wine spritzer. 'Wha-aht?' I asked, my voice soft with shyness.

'Nothing,' she said, holding my gaze. 'I just thought what you did earlier was really cool.'

I fought the urge to bite my lip. 'Really?'

'Yeah, the way you took charge and sprang into action.'

'Real springing into action would have been running inside the building and putting the fire out myself,' I said. 'All I did was call *The City Post* and tell my boss about the fire.'

Earlier that evening, while driving to the pub, we had spotted smoke pouring from the upper windows of an office building, thick and black against the twilight sky. I instinctively pulled over and called it in to the paper, just as I always did whenever I saw something newsworthy. I'd felt a familiar twinge of guilt that my first instinct had been to notify the office, not call 999 – an unwritten rule of being a reporter – and it gnawed at me, even though, as I spoke with Glyn, I could hear the distant sirens of the fire engines approaching.

Georgia smiled at me again from across the table. It was our second night alone together, our first since the cinema. Not a date. Just friends having a drink together.

There was this feeling as if we were the only people in the room, in our own little scintillating bubble. Our eye contact lingered, and there was an active holding back of hands that wanted to reach out and touch, and sometimes they did, just fleetingly, like when she passed me a coaster and our fingers brushed, or when she laughed at something I said and pressed a hand lightly on my forearm, raising my goosebumps and leaving a blotch of heat where her hand had been, causing me to imagine what it would be like if her contact lasted longer. But still, we were just friends.

It's hard to explain, but it felt like we communicated more through our bodies than we did through talking. Every time we touched, it was like I'd been plugged in. There was electricity between us – charges, sparks and flickers. It was as if she knew my soul's true language, and I didn't have to waste my energy decoding it for her. She made me feel so safe, so heard, so seen after a life spent hiding in plain sight. I could let go of my ego in her presence, and I inched my mask off as I felt her encouraging me to be entirely myself.

She described her perfect woman to me – curvy, shorter than her and ambitious. And I described mine – brunette, athletic, taller than me and smart. We knew we were talking about each other, but neither of us admitted it.

While we sat there, it was as if I were watching us in a sappy movie; I could 'see' us. The subtext of our body language was loud, the way we were so interested in each other. I wanted to whisper my feelings to her. I knew I loved her. Not just as a friend, who was I kidding?

'I feel as if I could tell you anything,' she said. 'Is that strange considering we haven't known each other for very long?'

'God no, I feel the same. It's like we were meant to meet.'

'Jess, I've never really opened up about this before, but I want to tell you something.'

'Anything,' I replied quickly.

'You know when you've asked about my mum and I've always changed the subject?'

'Yes...'

A visible heat crept up her neck. 'Well, that was because my... my mum passed away when I was younger.'

Compassion spread like ink through me. Whenever I'd asked about her family before, she'd tell me about living with her dad and sister but would always deflect the conversation back to me, eager to hear about my parents, who I'd duly describe with quiet pride – Dad, a garden centre manager, who always whistled when he washed the dishes, who would catch spiders in glasses and release them into the garden, and who woke at five a.m. every day so the dog would always get a morning walk; and Mum, a bookseller, who knitted me a new jumper every Christmas, who went to Zumba every Thursday, and who loved nothing more than reading a book while snuggled under a wool blanket on the sofa.

'Oh, Georgia, I'm so sorry.' I reached out and held her hand in both of mine, stroking it.

'It was a brain tumour,' she said, her voice wavering. 'It was awful to see her go through such hell. It felt like my whole world was crashing down. And I couldn't... I couldn't do anything to stop it.'

'I can't even imagine what that must have been like for you.' I squeezed tighter, wanting to dart around to her side of the table and hug her. I felt such a great need to comfort her and ease her pain.

'Sometimes I still feel like that scared little girl, you know?'

'It's OK to feel that way. Losing someone you loved so much... the pain must never leave you. You're so strong for carrying that with you, but it's OK to not be strong too.'

She sniffed and nodded. 'I haven't really talked about it with anyone.'

'Thank you so much for sharing it with me,' I said, stroking my thumbs over her hand while she used the other to wipe her eyes. 'I feel privileged that you told me, and I'm here for you. You don't have to carry this alone.' I reached up to her face to wipe her falling tears. She placed her hand over mine while it cupped her cheek.

I heard muffled sniggers coming from across the room. I clocked a group of tattooed blokes – all clones of each other – watching us. Georgia followed my line of sight and leant back in her chair when she noticed them. I eased my hand out of hers and she quickly dried her face. There was an instant distance between us as the boys' laughter cut through our tender moment like a blade.

I focused my attention on my drink, swirling it in the glass, and then studied the back of my shoe, pulling it into place on my heel even though it was already in the perfect spot.

'Lezzers!' they took turns shouting, under coughs and through laughs.

I was so used to the male gaze, but not like that. I'd been looked at in many ways – in lust, in desire, in superiority – but never in derision; I'd always been too agreeable to elicit derision. I was experienced at being what men wanted me to be, and in doing so I kept myself safe and in control, knowing all too well that sometimes compliance buys safety. For boyfriends, I was the 'cool girl' who liked whatever they liked, acted in ways that pleased them, and never nagged. I'd let them do what they wanted to me in bed; I was their object, someone to brag about. For strangers, I'd stay seated when they sat next to me on an otherwise empty train; I'd apologise when they 'needed' to steer me out of their way with their hands on my lower back; I'd be gracious to my bum-gropers so they wouldn't become aggressive; and I would smile in the street when strangers asked me to. When it came to male bosses and higher-ups, I would ask them for their intellectual input when I didn't need it, amassing a network of blokes on whose guidance I appeared to depend for my every move. Men might label that as manipulative, but women are aware of the complexities at play. Glyn was completely oblivious to the fact that all the females in the office were repulsed by him, probably because we'd all force smiles – knowing how he'd reacted to 'rude girls' in the past, all of whom hadn't made it past their probationary periods – fortifying his delusion that we actually enjoyed his behaviour. I told myself I shouldn't get angry at him, that I should be grateful to him because he was the reason I had a job in the first place – not to mention the fact that I wanted his job one day. So, no matter how he acted or what he said, I forced myself to showcase a facade of appreciation for him, like a display of fine china in a glass-fronted cabinet, hiding all the broken plates in the back where he couldn't see them.

Men don't like troublesome women. They don't like criticism from women. They don't like ambitious women. Often, they just don't like women. To get around this, I had to abuse my feminine wiles and adopt chameleonic personas – acting fragile and obedient, or empathetic and nurturing, or seductive and magnetic – trying to gauge what each man needed me to be – or sometimes, what *I* needed to be, for my own safety. I would make myself not only palatable, easy-to-swallow and digestible, but the best meal they'd ever had. Their death-row dinner.

'Don't worry about them,' Georgia said in a hushed voice, tilting her head towards the group of boys who were still mocking us. 'They just don't know how to act when they see lesbians.'

'I'm not a lesbian,' I said with quiet force as if in defence of myself. I wasn't sure if she'd heard me; I hoped she didn't.

I wanted to scream at them for ruining my otherwise perfect evening with Georgia. But that just wasn't something I would ever risk doing. It was always as if, around men, especially groups of them, the ability to express myself in the moment was stifled. I'd think of the perfect thing to say after the fact, but when I was face to face, anxiety took over.

I barely looked at them, but the one time I did, the guy I happened to lock eyes with ran his tongue between the V of his index and middle fingers – to his friends' amusement – and in the next second, he came right for us. I shrank in my seat as he stood next to us, studying us individually, with big hungry eyes. I felt like a thing to be gobbled up, picked clean to the bone.

Then he asked with a building smirk, 'So, who's the man?'

'Get a grip,' Georgia replied while I flashed him a biddable smile to keep the peace.

'Nah, come on, don't be like that,' he said, placing the heels of his hands on our table and glancing over his shoulder at his clones, who were wheeze-laughing. 'We were just wondering if you strap it on, that's all.' He waited for our response, leaning over us. When he didn't get one, he continued. 'Anyway, why do lesbians use strap-ons? If you like cock, why not just have sex with men?'

'Ask them if they squirt, Shagga!' came one of the pantomime voices behind him, raising another roar of laughter.

Georgia made unwavering eye contact with *Shagga*. 'Piss. Off.'

'We're only messing with you; calm down, yeah?' he said, kissing the air at her.

Georgia stood abruptly.

'Whoa!' came the rapturous chorus of male voices.

'The lesbians are fucking nuts, boys!' *Shagga* said gleefully, as if pleased he'd roused a reaction, before jogging off, laughing.

'We should go,' I said to Georgia, fumbling for my bag.

'No, we shouldn't have to leave. I'll talk to someone and have them thrown out.' She pushed back in her chair.

'No, don't,' I said, hushed and insistently.

'They need to realise that they can't act like that,' she whispered over the table before walking off towards the bar.

I sat there alone, not daring to glance their way again, wondering why *Shagga* thought it had been acceptable to probe so lubriciously. If I had been a straight girl with a boy, he wouldn't have even thought about approaching us. Thankfully, Georgia returned within seconds, followed closely behind by a large balding man.

'What seems to be the problem, ladies?' he asked, wiping his hands on a grubby-looking tea towel before flinging it onto his shoulder in a huff.

'That group of boys,' Georgia said, pointing them out, 'they're making us uncomfortable.'

He exhaled hard through his nose and regarded us for just a moment longer than was needed, as if he thought we were being problematic, and then trudged over to their table. We couldn't hear what was said during the exchange, but when he returned, he said, with his shoulders shrugged, 'They're just on a night out having a laugh, ladies. Nothing to get upset about. Just ignore it if you want to stay. If not, the door's there.'

As soon as the manager was out of sight, one boy threw a handful of peanuts, which landed on our table and in my lap. We made to leave, but I knocked my glass over, causing the boys to jeer. I felt hotness fluster behind my cheeks as I held back self-conscious tears.

Georgia thrust her middle finger up at them and one of them stood. I took her hand and ran. It felt right to run. Every woman I know has had to run, or at least thought of running, from men.

We climbed into my old, rattling Renault Clio and I sped off, even though they hadn't followed us.

'That was horrible,' I said, breaking the silence.

She sighed. 'Sadly I can't say that was the first time I've seen boys act like that.' After a pause, she continued. 'When men saw me and Ruth together, they would sometimes react in that sleazeball way. And if we didn't acknowledge them or play to it, sometimes they'd get abusive.'

My heart jumped. 'Abusive?'

'Never physically; just insults.'

'Like?'

'The only thing that springs to mind is them calling us bitches for ignoring them. Or they'd act as if we were damaged goods, and they'd say it was a "waste" for a woman to be with a woman. It always feels so aggressive even though they make out as if they're joking; I used to worry that it would escalate, and we'd, you know, get attacked.'

Deep down, I knew that being with a man would mean avoiding all of that; I could have an easy life. I'd gain no pleasure out of that life, but I could be safe and treated as a 'normal' person. I could do what I did best, what I had a lifetime of practice in – I could blend. And, most importantly of all, a man could protect me from other men, which, after what happened when I was little, was vital. The world wasn't mine to live in unless I had a man to defend me in it. A woman couldn't protect me; a target couldn't protect another target – paired together, we'd offer double the surface area and be that much easier to hit.

But was I just exaggerating? Was the world really so dangerous? Maybe I was just scaring myself, terrorising myself with my own thoughts.

Was it all the news stories I'd read (and occasionally written) about women being violently attacked and killed at the hands of men, and often blamed for it themselves?

Was it the fact that nowhere was deemed safe? Forget the dark alleys and quiet corners. Work, home, the gym, shops, schools and even hospitals were potential places for harm.

Was it that my septuagenarian driving instructor liked to put my seatbelt on for me, brushing over my breasts as he did so?

Was it that all the girls were given rape alarms in our welcome packs on the first day of university by a bright, cheery student ambassador who clearly thought nothing of it?

Was it that the girls at my graduation party were upskirted, and male students took turns guessing 'whose ass is this?' over social media?

Was it the fact that new inventions, like pocketknives hidden in lipsticks, and strange contraptions to make sure my hotel room door remained locked, and pepper spray that would turn my assailant's face blue were constantly being introduced to the market?

Was it the useless facts that raced around in my head, such as the odds of being attacked by a shark are one in four million, while a woman's odds of being raped are one in just six?

Or was it the teenager that dragged me into the bushes when I was eleven years old and he... I can't even repeat it.

Those reasons were as much a part of my world as the knowledge that I would be putting myself at risk if I went out in shoes I couldn't run away in; as much a part of my world as the fear of a taxi's automatic door locking system; as much a part of my world as always avoiding the shortcut; as much a part of my world as never wearing earphones at full volume while outside alone; as much a part of my world as the keys I held spiked through my knuckles as I walked home; as much a part of my world as knowing I needed to scratch my attacker so their DNA would be under my nails.

I blinked and I was back in the car, still driving Georgia home.

'Jess, can I ask you something?' she said.

'Of course.'

'On the topic of men who don't respect women. Why are you staying with Joe when you deserve a million times better?'

I hadn't told her much about him, but she knew enough.

Chapter 10

How could I even answer Georgia's question? The answer was: I was staying with Joe because I was terrified to leave. Equally terrified of what he'd do if I left and terrified of the world without a man to protect me in it.

Joe was my bouncer, my bodyguard, but he was also a person I needed protecting *from* most of the time. Why would I stay with someone so wrong for me? Because leaving him could mean an even worse fate. It's not that I thought he would kill me, but I knew he could make my life a living hell – worse than it already was.

'There's something hard about walking away after devoting years to someone,' I said.

'I get that, but you have to want to stay. Do you *want* to be with him?'

I stayed quiet, watching the road.

'The way you talk about him, I don't think you do, Jess. It's not wrong to want to find happiness, you know.'

I'd given so much effort to hone the person Joe needed me to be that part of me didn't want to throw all that effort away – I almost felt like I owed it to myself to stay, otherwise it would have all been for nothing, all the tears and sadness.

I knew I wasn't in love with Joe, but until meeting Georgia, I hadn't realised I was capable of falling in love with anyone. I'd considered it *my* problem, a shortcoming I had, and why would I have bothered to find someone new, again, if I was incapable of love anyway? I'd already tried four times, with four men.

The four had come one after the other, and I'd spent years with each. Whenever I felt my partner's interest in me wane, I'd line up my next relationship, ready to jump into it when the existing one ended. Every time I entered a new one, I became completely stuck inside it. It started to feel as if I'd been trapped inside their skin, like I had no control at all. It must be, I thought, how the weaker one of a pair of conjoined twins feels – the one without the control of the arms or the legs or the speech.

Truly, I wanted to walk away from him. I did. I wanted Georgia. But I also wanted a safe life. But I also wanted freedom. But I also wanted choice. But I didn't want to choose. I wanted everything all at once.

I was scared of being tied down once again after promising myself that if I ever managed to be free of needing a man, I would have the courage to honour that freedom; I would live it and experience it – be single and date women, lots of women, in secret. I'd finally embrace my fantasies, and the world would never have to know because it would all go on behind closed doors. But I didn't want to be without Georgia. If I chose Georgia though, I'd be outed. I was terrified of what revealing my true self, my queerness, would do to my life and to how men perceived me. If I came out as a lesbian, I saw two things happening. Either I'd alienate men completely, sending the message that I wasn't interested in them – even though I never had been. It would be like holding up a placard that read, *Men, you're not good enough for me*, and inviting their anger and violence. Or I'd become even more sexualised, fetishised, and turned into a pornographic idea in their minds. Or both. Either way, I'd be in danger, and either way, I'd lose the siren song I'd spent a lifetime refining.

***

'It's late,' Joe said harshly as I walked into my living room. I hadn't expected him to be home; he'd normally stay out with the boys until the bitter end of the night, sitting in one of their houses smoking weed and playing video games. 'Where have you been?'

'Just out with Li,' I lied, worried I'd get myself into trouble otherwise.

'Only it wasn't Li, was it?'

I didn't know how to reply. If I'd been spotted at the pub by someone he knew and they'd reported back to him, then chaos would ensue if I confirmed my lie. But maybe he was just trying to catch me out.

'I was out with Li, and one of her friends joined us, but then Li had to go, so I was left with the friend.' I was aware how convoluted my story sounded.

'I highly suspect that is bullshit. Will you just—'

'I—'

'Jess!' He paused, lowering his voice to a whisper before starting again. 'Jess. Don't fucking interrupt me. I was going to say, just kindly tell me the fucking truth about where you've been.'

He didn't like to be loud in my flat. He needed to keep his squeaky-clean image with the neighbours, who had no clue that his exceptional charm was superficial, or that he was a monster behind closed doors. I couldn't blame them for not realising; I was sucked in at first too.

'That *is* the truth.' I looked at the floor, feeling his stare bore through me.

'It better fucking be.' He stepped closer. 'Look at me. Fucking look at me,' he repeated, grabbing my face. 'You tell me where you are at all times, and with who. If Li leaves and someone new joins, that's something you tell me in the future. Yes?'

'Yes.'

'What if you got hurt and I didn't know where you were? What if someone took you? There are human traffickers out there just waiting to pounce. There are acid attackers. There are men out there who want to rape girls like you, especially girls who wear things like that.' He tugged at my skirt while squeezing my face in his other hand. 'I just want to know you're safe.'

'Let me go. That hurts, Joe.'

'I'm not hurting you. You're acting like a fucking victim, Jess, when you're the one, yet again, who is sauntering home late at night without a valid reason.'

'You're hurting me.'

'For fuck's sake, you're not even focusing on the problem at hand, you're just diverting to get out of having this conversation.' His thumb and fingers were gripping my face so hard my teeth ached.

'Get off me, Joe.'

He jerked my face out of his hand. 'I can't win. All I ever do is try to protect you and you won't even have a fucking conversation with me. You're always making me out to be the bad guy.'

He stormed out of the flat, gently closing the front door behind him for the neighbours' benefit. But a minute or two later I heard an almighty smash. His hot-headedness had won, and he'd put his fist through the window of the stairwell door.

In the A&E waiting room, a cascade of his usual apologies gushed from his mouth. He lowered himself in his chair and smeared a sheepish, scared look across his face – how a puppy looks after it's chewed your slipper – as he glanced between me and the glass in his knuckles. He was a fine artist when it came to his expressions; he thought the right one could manipulate its way to solving any problem.

His primary concern upon returning to the flat in the early hours of the morning was how to explain his actions to the neighbours; he was panicked that his outburst had exposed his true nature. Sleeplessly, he waited for the clock hands to strike an acceptable hour before making his rounds, knocking on every door, with his bandaged hand front and centre, ready to tell his version of the story. Through the thin walls of my flat, I heard him in the hall explaining to each neighbour how he'd heard a noise late at night, got up to investigate, and in his half-asleep state, accidentally stumbled into the glass partition, causing it to shatter. At Gareth's door, he praised his daughter's progress in the coding classes Joe had been giving her for free. I could hear her giggling – she had a crush on Joe and, as a result, despised me. At the recently moved-in couple's door, he complimented a recipe they'd shared with him, lying that he had tried it and found it delicious, eliciting pleased responses. Finally, at Gwen's door, he offered to fix her leaking tap, and I heard the faint sounds of his work and her heartfelt gratitude drifting through the walls.

People were always so charmed by him. He could turn his charisma on in a flash. Girls were jealous of me for getting to spend my life with him, old ladies pinched his cheeks, and men admired his work ethic, never suspecting the darker truth hidden beneath the smiles.

He'd drawn me in all those years ago, just as he did with everyone else he encountered. In a world of rat-race routineness, I was enticed by his surface-level exceptionality. Somewhere along the line, I'd questioned what the hell I was doing with him, but clarity only came with hindsight.

More people, I've realised, seem concerned with why women stay in abusive relationships than why men abuse women. There are so many reasons we stay; some are simple, some are complex. Once Joe had hooked me in, he stripped me of agency, devalued me, ground me down, and all but brainwashed me into believing that this was how a relationship should be. He convinced me that my expectations were too high or that I was being too emotional, and tricked me into thinking I would never find anyone else.

I think it might have been a kind of Stockholm syndrome too, or a trauma bonding, whereby I became dependent on the hormonal rollercoaster his abuse sent me on. In the beginning, it started with an offhand comment here or a mild insult there, but he'd apologise, and I'd write them off, thinking he was perfect for me in every other way. He was a genius at pretending to be everything I'd been looking for in a partner, so much so that he would create bizarre lies and draw them out for months. Like how, when we were first dating back in university, he'd said he owned a Ferrari – which he kept at his mum's house in case people thought he was a show-off. He held onto that lie for six months, and when he finally took me to meet his mum, I asked him, in front of her, if he would take me for a spin in his Ferrari, and she cackled and called him out hard. And when I was mad at him – for the lie, not specifically because the Ferrari didn't exist – he accused me of being a gold digger.

There were so many lies that I hadn't known were lies early on; I thought I'd found a one-in-a-million bloke. He love-bombed me with so much affection that I thought *that* was the real him, and I assumed that the minor slip-ups he was having were my fault. I found myself wanting to please him and wanting to keep him happy so that the slip-ups wouldn't happen again. But they did happen again, and they became more frequent and more vicious – which I reacted to by becoming even more accommodating and subservient to counteract the situation and win back his affection.

It happened so gradually, so slowly, that I didn't really notice it building up. It was like gazing out of a car window and seeing the details pass by one by one – houses, gardens, a post office, a park, shops, a school, a pub – taking them in as separate components without realising they were amounting to an entire village.

I became too tangled in it to back out – caught in his well-made web of gaslighting, control and intermittent handing out of 'love' for the times I 'behaved'. After an argument, he'd always have such conviction in his own story that my account of it would fall apart.

His abuse was insidious and slow, like an IV drip laced with trace amounts of poison. He'd never hit me though. For me to admit that I *wanted* him to, just once, well, it would sound nonsensical. But I always held that as a point of no return, a justification for leaving him, a reason to call the police on him, to have some solid proof of his cruelty, and hopefully even get him punished for it.

But he was too clever for that. He knew to stay in the grey area. My word against his. And with charm like his, of course everyone would believe I was the irrational one. Anything that didn't leave a mark on my body went unnoticed.

Chapter 11

When Christmas arrived, two months after I'd first met Georgia, I didn't see Joe; we spent the day with our own families. My day was filled with well-meaning but relentless questions from my aunties and uncles: When would I finally book the wedding venue? Was I planning to try for a baby on the honeymoon? That particular question made my parents visibly uncomfortable, and my dad quickly put an end to the conversation.

Joe and I had exchanged presents on Christmas Eve. He gave me a non-value-specific voucher for our local shopping centre, and I gave him the top-of-the-line webcam he'd specifically requested – only for him to point out that it wasn't the latest model and ask if I still had the receipt.

I met Georgia that same night, after Joe had gone out with the boys. We were sitting in her car, parked near what had become 'our spot', Lake Calon, and at the same time, we both pulled out gifts, neither of us expecting it. I'd bought her some fuzzy socks since she was always complaining of cold feet, and she gave me a giant bag of my favourite sweets. They were token gifts, but thoughtful.

'These taste different,' I said, chewing a mouthful of the Skittles. 'I must have had these a thousand times, but they've never been *this* good.' I wondered if they tasted better simply because she had bought them for me, and my feelings for her made them even sweeter. That was until she spoke.

'Really?' she asked, a playful smirk crossing her lips, the little dimple in her cheek becoming visible.

I squinted at her suspiciously, still chewing. 'Why do they taste better? What have you done?'

She laughed through her nose.

Turning on the passenger light, I peered into the bag. They were all purple.

'I know they're your favourite flavour,' she said, 'so I bought ten packs and put all the blackcurrant ones in there.' She pointed to the bag in my hand.

I felt a rush of emotion. 'But the pack was sealed, how did you—' I held the bag up and noticed the underside had been sealed with tape. I shook my head, smiling. 'That must have taken you ages.'

I spent New Year's Eve with Georgia too, as well as Li and Bex, at Freedom Club. Joe had organised a three-night celebration in London for him and his friends, complete with a boat party on the Thames at midnight – happily leaving me behind.

I'd wanted to kiss Georgia at midnight. I didn't, of course.

On New Year's Day, I invited her to my flat for the first time, knowing Joe would be away for two more nights in London.

'Hi,' I said, beaming when I opened the door to her. It would have felt so natural to have welcomed her with a kiss, but I wrapped my arms around her instead. 'Come in.'

'Lush place,' she said, looking into each of the rooms as she walked along the corridor to the living room. She was just being polite; it was a basic space, with bare walls – the landlord wouldn't allow artwork – laminate kitchen worktops and brown-beige storage heaters on the walls instead of radiators.

I gathered the snacks and wine and we settled next to each other on the sofa in front of the TV to watch *The Notebook*. Our shoulders were touching only ever so slightly, but enough to send static through me, spreading a buzzing sensation through the top of my arm.

'I liked the lead-up to that kiss more than the kiss itself,' I said, giving a directional nod towards the screen where Rachel and Ryan had their tongues down each other's throats.

'Why's that?' She flicked her gaze from my eyes to my mouth and back again.

'I always love the tension before a first kiss, when neither person knows for sure if the other feels the same way.'

'I know exactly what you mean,' she said, tucking in her bottom lip and wetting it with the underside of her tongue.

I swallowed hard. 'It's the anticipation that makes it so electric. Like, you can feel the air between them crackling.'

'And,' she said, pausing, her face lit by the colours of the TV, 'the build-up can't be considered cheating, because you're not even touching.'

'That's right.' I felt my heartbeat creep up to my throat, making me gulp.

'How would it start – the lead-up, I mean – if we were in a movie right now?' She turned her body towards mine, shifting her weight so she was sitting sideways on the sofa.

My heart hammered and my breathing grew heavy. 'I guess by looking into each other's eyes.'

She locked her eyes with mine.

'And then we'd probably admire each other's faces?' I said as calmly as I could manage, glancing down at her mouth and back up to those captivating eyes, the colour of the sky on a perfectly clear day.

She started exploring my skin with her eyes, and I hoped she wouldn't spot the hurried beat of the vein in my neck. 'And then maybe they'd start edging a bit closer?' she asked tentatively.

I nodded and she leant her body a fraction towards me.

'And maybe I'd put my hand here,' I said, trying hard not to let my voice shake, and I placed my hand on her knee. 'Like this, just for the cinematic tension?'

'That feels right – for the viewers' sake, I mean,' she said, her eyes penetrating mine with a visible longing.

'What next?' I asked, breathing out the words.

'I suppose we'd get to about here, and just... stop?' she whispered, her lips a few inches from mine.

'Because we'd have to be careful not to ruin it all by letting our lips touch,' I whispered back, hearing my own heartbeat louder than I could my words.

'We would. But maybe a little closer would be better...' She sounded so sure, so confident, but I could hear the almost inaudible tremor in her voice.

We were so close, our lips just a whisper away from touching. Tears pricked at my eyes; I wanted to cry out with the craving raging beneath the surface. I moved my hand up her leg slightly, pressing into her thigh with the pads of my fingertips. The sensations were volcanic and ached to burst through in any way possible.

Her breath was shallow. 'And then maybe...' She tentatively reached out her hand, ghosting it over my cheek, touching my face for the first time ever. 'I could put my hand here.'

It was hot against my skin. She stayed silent, a few centimetres from me. Then she held my face in both hands, hands that I wouldn't have realised were faintly trembling were I not so in tune with her at that moment, like she'd spent as long wanting this as I had.

The tips of our noses touched and I closed my eyes. My longing had me by the throat. I could smell her perfume – a woody, honey-laced, narcotic sweetness – and it was all I could do not to bite straight into her neck.

Somehow, without me even noticing, we ended up on our knees on the sofa, my chest pressed to hers. I could feel her heartbeat against my own, the heat of her chest beneath the fabric of her T-shirt. We moulded to each other; I wanted us to fuse like that, I wanted to be soldered to her, I wanted our bodies to merge.

We moved frantically but barely at all, our foreheads pressing together, then our noses, and back to our foreheads, then we pecked at each other's cheeks and nuzzled each other's necks. We moved as if choreographed, pressing ourselves into each other. Her fingers gripped the back of my head and tugged slightly at the roots of my hair. Our bodies were alight, as if we'd touched two lit candles together and they had merged into a single flame, high and dancing, popping and crackling, their intense energy burning, creating scorching heat and velvet smoke.

Our grips changed on each other, constantly finding new ways to hold on tightly. I wanted to beg her to kiss me; the only words I could think to say were 'please' and 'I love you', but I could only manage whimpers – I heard them escape; they sounded like sobs.

The humidity of our breaths settled on the peachy hairs on my face; it felt as if there was an aura around us that would have surely been glowing in the dimly lit room if I had been able to open my eyes and look. I felt as if I'd been transported to a space I didn't know existed –

between reality and make-believe, as if I were under hypnosis, or lucid dreaming, or having an out-of-body experience. We were floating, weightless, rising vertically.

And then my lips were on hers. They were meant to be there. Hot tears streamed down my cheeks as an emotional bomb softly exploded inside me and rippled through my limbs. I was barely able to kiss her as my lips were quivering and holding back cries. It was as if every secret glance, every fleeting touch and every internal butterfly had led us up to that moment.

I couldn't pull her close enough, hold her tight enough, kiss her deep enough. I descended into the drunkenness of it. Nothing had ever felt so right – like it was the thing I had been waiting for my whole life. She could have done anything to me in that moment and I'd have been hers.

Chapter 12

Drowsy rumblings of rain pitter-pattered on my living room window and I felt myself float to the surface of sleep and bob into wakefulness.

I opened my eyes, realising I was lying on my tiny two-seater sofa, with Georgia's head nestled into my chest. I felt delirious, as if in a post-drunken stupor, but it was a glowing, warmed-through sensation. It was the first time we'd slept side by side.

I lay there smiling, my heart fluttering as I looked down at her. I'd kissed plenty of people before, but they'd all been men. Kissing men had always been transactional, obligatory – a societal norm rather than a personal desire. I'd never truly lost myself in a kiss. But with Georgia, everything changed. With her, it was as instinctive as breathing, and I never wanted it to stop.

As she began to stir, our eyes met, and we exchanged meek smiles that quickly morphed into laughter.

I rested my arm on my forehead and stared up at the ceiling. 'I have never experienced anything like what happened last night,' I said, the memory a sweet rush. 'How the hell can a kiss, *just* a kiss, be better than any sexual experience I've ever had?' I could hardly contain the joy still bubbling inside me. The undeniable happiness.

'Tell me about it,' she said, her voice soft and warm, still resting her head on me, but then worry crept into her tone as she said, 'Do you feel guilty?'

The weight of reality crashed down on me. I had a fiancé. I had kissed someone else. I had cheated on him – not that there was a doubt in my mind he hadn't been doing the same to me in London on his three-day bender.

'I do,' I said, 'but if last night wasn't a sign that I need to end things with Joe, nothing is.'

She looked up at me and a smile pulled gently at the corners of her mouth. I wanted to kiss her again; I even felt myself leaning in instinctively. But I had to do the right thing. I had to end things with Joe first. I pulled myself back, as hard as it was. 'Anyway, enough about him,' I said, unfurling myself from around her before standing and stretching, clicking out the bones that had curled during sleep. 'Breakfast?'

She checked her watch and laughed. 'Breakfast or lunch? It's nearly midday.'

'Oh!' I couldn't remember the last time I'd slept in that late. I walked to my open-plan kitchen, collecting our empty snack wrappers and wineglasses from the coffee table as I went. 'Shall we go out for brunch somewhere in that case?' I asked, placing the glasses in the sink. 'Hopefully the rain will die off soon.'

'I like that idea,' she said, stretching out on my sofa, looking so at home, and I couldn't help but wish I could wake up to her every day.

'Oh god, I look like shit!' I said, laughing as I caught my bed-head reflection in the mirror.

'Trust me, you look anything but shit, Jess. You're always beautiful.'

I beamed at her, shaking my head shyly and tucking my hair behind my ears. Then I heard something down the hall, the front door opening.

'I'm home.' It was Joe's voice. My heart leapt in my chest. What was he doing back so early? He was supposed to be gone until the following morning. My eyes darted around the room to check for evidence that Georgia had slept over. There was none – we were still fully clothed, and there were no blankets or pillows around because we hadn't planned to go to sleep.

'You've only just arrived, OK?' I whispered to her, wide-eyed as I listened to him lumbering down the hall. She nodded quickly and started smoothing down her hair, sitting bolt upright on the sofa.

'Hello?' he called again.

'Just in here,' I said, talking to the doorway, hearing him approach. 'I thought you were going to be away until tomorrow?' I kept my voice indifferent. 'What happened?'

'Jeez, on my case already? You sound like my mum; you want to put a tracker on me or something?' he said, appearing. 'I—' He clocked Georgia. 'Oh, hi,' he said, his bright, charming manner appearing like the sun coming out from behind a cloud.

'Hi, I'm Georgia,' she said, standing. 'I just came over so that Jess and I could walk to brunch together. But I can go – let you two catch up...'

He blinked a twinkle into his eye. 'Nice to meet you, I'm Joe.' His voice had gained a chocolatey-smooth quality. 'You stay, honestly. I fancy a nap – long night – so you stay and enjoy; it's a lovely day for it, apart from the storm.' He released a strategic laugh.

As he talked, I noticed the wineglasses in the sink – out of his line of sight, around the corner of the L-shaped floor plan. They were a giveaway that she'd stayed the night.

'That's alright,' I said to him, smoothly making my way into the kitchen. 'Georgia and I can catch up another time.'

I silently opened the cupboard above my head and then gently gripped the stem of one of the glasses, being careful not to make a *tink* noise as I picked it up out of the metal sink. 'I'm happy you're home,' I said loudly, placing the unwashed glass in the cupboard cautiously and closing the door as softly as I'd opened it. 'We don't mind rearranging.'

'No, that's fine,' he said from right behind me, making me jump. Had he seen me put the glass in the cupboard, or had he appeared around the corner just after? 'You two go and enjoy.' He smiled at me, his side profile intentionally on show to Georgia, so that she could see his benevolent expression.

I knew I had to end things with him, and that morning was as good a time as any. I darted my eyes to Georgia, who understood the look I gave her.

'Thank you anyway, but I've just had a text from my sister saying she needs me, so rain check, Jess?' she said while slowly walking away.

'Yes, no worries, hope everything's OK with Gemma.'

'Nice to meet you,' Joe said cheerily, pausing before turning to face me and setting his glare over me, his jaw ticking with impatience as he waited to hear the front door shut. When he heard the latch click, he let all the muscles in his face drop, even the ones in his eyelids, leaving his pupils peering through hooded slits.

'Why didn't you tell me you'd be having a guest over? You know I don't like it when I don't know who's in my flat.'

It's my fucking flat.

'And who is she, anyway?'

'She's one of Bex's friends,' I said, faltering, realising I hadn't told him who Bex was either. 'Bex is Li's—' I stopped myself saying 'girl-friend' in the nick of time. 'Friend.'

'And why is a friend of a friend of a friend in my flat?' he asked, his nostrils flared and whitening.

Your flat?

'Because she lives close by, and it was just easier to meet here and walk over to the café. And we were going to meet Li and Bex there too,' I lied, swallowing down the nervousness churning inside me. 'But I'll just text them and say I'm not going now.'

He stared at me. 'I told you, Jess, I don't like people in—' He glanced at the kitchen countertop, the snack wrappers and the empty wine bottle catching his eye. 'You been having a party or something?'

'I got a bit carried away last night and finished the bottle while watching a film by myself.' I discreetly covered my throat with my hand so that he wouldn't see me gulping.

'And you ate all that yourself too?' His face contorted to disgust as he picked up a handful of the wrappers and let them rain back down onto the surface. He poked my stomach. 'I can tell. Anyway, I'll help you outside,' he said, anger rumbling under the surface of his words. 'Come on, you've made a big brunch plan without telling me, so go see it through, eh?'

He grabbed my arm and started pulling me out of the kitchen and down the hallway. 'Come on,' he said faux playfully as I struggled to free myself while calmly saying his name over and over.

'Out you go,' he said, practically throwing me out of the flat and shutting the door on me.

It wasn't a door that could be opened without a key from the outside – it locked immediately – not that I wanted to go back in.

Thankfully, my phone, my lifeline, was in my pocket. I walked down the first few steps, dialling Georgia.

Fast footsteps came from behind me. 'Get back in the flat, you cheeky bitch,' Joe whispered from the top of the stairs. I did as he said.

As I turned back, my heart pounding, I heard the creak of another door down the hallway. Gwen appeared, a small rubbish bag clutched in her hands, her face lighting up with her usual elated smile when she saw us.

'Happy New Year, both,' she said, waving.

In unison, we wished her the same, then Joe started his customary charm offensive. He strode towards her holding his arms out.

'You're looking young as ever, Gwen,' he said, kissing her on both cheeks. 'Honestly, you put the rest of us to shame. What's your secr—' But before he could finish, Gwen interrupted, probably because she hadn't heard him.

'Everything all right, cariad?' she asked me, concern in her eyes as she gave me a soft pat on the arm. 'You're looking a bit flushed.'

I swallowed hard, forcing myself to tell her I was fine, making sure to nod so the message would come across visually too.

'Well, have a little lay down just in case. And give me a knock if you need anything, bach. You know me – I've always got something to help.'

With one last reassuring smile, she shuffled off slowly towards the stairs, humming softly to herself as she went.

The second the door clicked shut behind us, Joe's expression darkened. 'What the fuck are you playing at? You were actually going to walk away then, weren't you? You weren't even going to attempt to come back in and make amends.' He waited for my answer. 'Don't just stand there, you cunt, speak!'

I stared through him, silently picking up the courage to end it. If something as minor as having a friend over could push him into such a rage, I knew that breaking up with him could spell disaster. But suddenly, I didn't care. I wasn't afraid. My mind was made up.

'God, you look like shit today,' he said. 'Were you honestly about to go out looking like that? Have you even brushed your hair? Look how wrinkled your clothes are. You're going downhill in the looks department rapidly, Jess. You'll be one of those worthless women who go to the shops in their dressing gowns and slippers soon. Do you have no shame?'

I stared, emotionless, unreactive to his slurry of invective. I knew he didn't like that. He liked to see me cry, be offended, act hurt. The simplest way to endure life with him was always to fall into character, to pretend his provocation was working. For every criticism he threw my way, I'd assess what reaction he was looking for – sadness, anger, suspicion, affront – and I'd play that part, for an easy life. And after I'd put on my show, he would then tell me I was an idiot for feeling any of those emotions he'd deliberately sought to stir in me, and he'd recline and nestle in them, prop them up like goose down pillows behind his back, lounging in his victory.

Not today.

'You disrespectful cow,' he said through gritted teeth. 'Why are you ignoring me?' He pushed me down the hallway, backwards, into the left side of the kitchen, so that he could pin me against The Wall by my throat.

'All I fucking want – and this is me being polite, Jessica – is that you simply *ask* me before you have people over,' he said, centimetres from my face.

I could smell his oily skin and his booze-soured dank cave of a mouth. I just glared at him, swallowing calmly against the pressure of his hand, as if it wasn't bothering me.

'Fuuuck.' He silent-screamed the word. I knew he wanted to yell it but he was thinking about the neighbours. He opened his mouth as wide as he would have if he were yelling and bared his teeth, letting out a hard, long whisper version of the howl again. He glared at me, taking solid breaths. 'I guess you want to do this the hard way?' He adjusted his grip, from my neck to my shoulders. He didn't like to hold on to any of my body parts for too long, in case his hands caused marks that people would see.

Now or never. 'I don't want to be with you,' I said, projecting as much courage as I could. 'I'm not willing to live like this any longer, with a man who thinks it's fine to treat me so badly.'

'What?' He backed up, keeping me pinned, but at arm's length. 'Who treats *you* so badly?' He laughed without smiling. 'I'm the one coming home to my boundaries being crossed. I've told you a million times that I don't want anyone here unless I know about it. It's a simple thing and yet you don't even respect me that much. How is this now my fault?'

'It's never your fault, is it? It's always mine. Even though you manhandle me and abuse me, it's all my fault.'

'Abuse? Never use that word.' He lowered his voice further. 'I've never fucking hit you.'

'Abuse doesn't always have to mean hitting. Look what you're doing to me right now, Joe.'

'You're delusional, Jess.' He took his hands off me. 'Always so dramatic. Always playing the victim. You've been doing it since you were a child. I wouldn't be surprised if that poor guy who's in prison because of you never even touched you.'

'Don't say that!'

He put on a whiny voice and said, 'Mummy, a boy took me into the bushes and put his peepee in my weewee.'

'Joe, stop!'

'He pinned me down. Boohoo. I'm a little eleven-year-old bullshitter making shit up for attention. Ruining men's lives.'

'I want you out, Joe. I'm done.' I kept my tone and volume controlled as I twisted the engagement ring off my finger and held it out for him in my trembling hand. 'I should never have said yes to you.'

For a moment, he just stared at me, the air between us heavy with unspoken threats. Then he stepped back. I could see the tension in his jaw, the way his fists clenched at his sides. 'You think you can just walk away from this?' His voice was hushed and dangerous. 'You think you can just toss me aside like I'm nothing?'

I took a deep breath, summoning every ounce of mettle I had. 'Yes, Joe. That's exactly what I'm doing.'

His face twisted into a sneer. 'No one will ever love you the way I do. You're nothing without me.'

I stood my ground, even though my legs felt like they might give out. 'I'd rather be nothing than be with you.'

His eyes darkened further, and for a terrifying moment, I thought he might lash out. But instead, he took the ring from my hand and examined it, turning it over between his fingers. 'You'll regret this,' he said quietly, his voice trembling with barely contained rage. 'Trust me.'

I shook my head, tears welling up but refusing to fall. 'No, Joe. I'm done being scared of you.'

He gave a cold, humourless laugh. 'We'll see about that.' He slipped the ring into his pocket and leaned in close, his breath hot against my ear. 'Remember this, darling, you'll never be happy without me. Never.'

He walked to the sofa and sat down, spreading his arms along the back of it. 'You think you can just kick me out? This is my home too.'

'This is my flat, Joe. I pay the rent. I'll give you a day, but you have to go.'

He stretched out, making himself comfortable. 'I'm not going anywhere.'

The realisation dawned that this was far from over. I walked out of the room and locked myself in the bathroom, starting the shower, feeling the need to wash the fear and the feeling of his hands off me.

I checked my phone. Multiple missed calls and texts from Georgia:

'Are you OK?'

'Text when you get this.'

'Worried about you.'

'Shall I come back over?'

I typed quickly:

'I'm OK.'

She replied:

'You're welcome to come to mine whenever you want. My dad's on a date with his girlfriend, and my sister is out, so it would just be us.'

Joe rapped at the door. 'What the fuck, Jess? You're going to shower in the middle of trying to dump me?'

I didn't answer; I knew he wasn't about to break the door down – that would have been too loud and the neighbours would have heard. I finished up, came out of the bathroom in a towel and headed to the bedroom for a change of clothes.

'What are you doing?' he said, following me. 'Stop ignoring me, Jess! Fuck. Jess.' He raked his fingers aggressively through his thinning hair in a gesture of exasperation, pulling at its roots and growling. 'It's like you expect me to be a perfect man all the time! No one can be perfect.' He purposely softened his voice. 'I'll admit, I've made some mistakes in the way I've acted towards you, but I'm working on myself, for you. Sometimes I go too far, and I'm sorry, but flawless people don't exist. You know that, right? All I do is try to make you happy.' His face shone with grease under the harsh bedroom light.

I gathered my hair into a ponytail. 'I need to get out and clear my head, Joe.'

'You're overreacting. Why are you being so crazy?'

I stayed silent.

'Answer me!' He leapt towards me, ripping the towel from me and throwing it to the floor before hurling my naked body onto the bed and pinning me to it.

He gathered my struggling wrists into one of his hands, keeping them immobilised with ease, and with the other, he grabbed at my bare breasts. 'If we have sex, it'll help,' he said insistently, keeping me restrained by sitting on top of me. He started unbuckling his belt with his free hand. 'It will calm you down. Make you see sense. You need to remember how much you love me.' He yanked the waistband of his boxers down and his erection sprung free.

'If you don't let me go, I'll scream this whole fucking place down,' I said, my voice timorous but assertive.

He stared at me silently, as if in disbelief that I would stand up to him. I watched as he weighed up whether to progress or back down – violence and defeat battling for victory. In that moment, rape seemed inevitable and impossible at the same time. I was terrified that this was the sole remaining card in his ever-dwindling deck of choices.

A moment later, he pressed his free hand over my mouth, but just as quickly as he'd placed it there, he removed it – before I could even thrust my waiting scream into my throat. And, miraculously, he climbed off me. I shakily threw on a zip-up hoodie, leggings and a pair

of trainers as fast as I could and rushed out of the front door and down
the stairs before he changed his mind.

Chapter 13

Before my knuckles even made contact with the door, it swung open to reveal Georgia draped in a plush dressing gown, seeming taller than usual. I stepped in, shaken by what had just happened with Joe but eager to tell her my news. After grabbing her hands, I held them out in front of her with mine on top. I smiled and gestured for her to look at my left hand, still quivering, my palm facing down. Her pupils expanded as she registered my bare ring finger, an indent there made by the engagement band after fifteen months of sitting in the same place.

'You ended it?' she asked, her neck mottling with crimson.

'I ended it.'

Her eyes were glossed with tears as she looked up at me. 'Does that mean I can kiss you?'

I seized her face and pressed my lips to hers, closing my eyes and feeling the brightness, colour and dizziness set in, while Pickle barked at my ankle. It was rare that I ignored a dog, but this was without a doubt one of those times.

I edged Georgia backwards to the foot of the stairs and she took a step up, managing to keep her lips locked with mine. She took my hand and pulled me up. We started running.

We burst into her bedroom in a frenzy of passion, stopping for just a moment to usher a jumping, barking Pickle out. Once the door was closed, Georgia grabbed my hoodie and pulled me to her. Her lips collided with mine and she let out a groan that hit the back of my throat. I felt myself crumple. I pushed her dressing gown off her shoulders and wrapped my arms tightly around her, wanting to cry, sinking into her body's enveloping warmth as my heart hammered.

Holding me closely, Georgia said, her voice almost inaudible, 'Are you sure you want this?'

'I've never been more sure of anything,' I replied quickly.

'Nothing has to happen, OK?'

'I know,' I whispered, swept by the tenderness and safety of her words. 'I want it to happen. I hope I can show you how much.'

We all but floated down onto the bed. I settled myself onto her, my body between her legs as her hands travelled inside my top, over my sides and up my braless back. I had never felt her skin on so much of my skin before. We held on to each other, sighing and moaning between slow, deep kisses.

'Shall I switch the light off?' she whispered, her voice low and husky with desire.

'No, I want to see all of you.'

'God, Jess. I do too. You're beyond beautiful.'

There was nothing I wanted more than her in that moment; desire for her eclipsed everything else. With inexperienced hands, I touched over her pyjama top; there was nothing else underneath. I could feel the suppleness of her breasts cupped by the material; they were full and warm under the thin cotton. I was desperate to touch her and to feel her touch. I wanted to rip her clothes off, but I also felt the need to discover her body slowly, inch by inch. My trembling hand began a timid exploration down her torso, lifting her top just enough to kiss the satin skin around her belly button. I inched the material up, planting kisses as I went, pushing it higher, feeling her stomach contracting as my lips roamed over her. I pushed the material higher still, until it came to the undersides of her breasts. I continued, millimetre by millimetre, kissing and licking her forgiving flesh, longing to expose her nipples, but enjoying – and hearing her enjoy – the sweet torture of the wait.

'I want you so much,' she whispered needfully. 'Oh god, Jess.'

I felt for her nipples, hard and pining through the stitching; I needed them in my mouth. As I moved, the beating inside me grew heavier. I eased her top up a little further, feeling her shiver in anticipation, and saw the pink crescent shapes appear, and then there they were, as flushed as her cheeks and requesting to be sucked. Her moans were music as I took each tight nipple in my mouth and flicked my tongue over them, squeezing at her incredible breasts as I did so, feeling them overspill in my hands.

Pressing my thighs together in an attempt to assuage the throbbing between them, I ran my hands over her strong feminine shape in gentle wonder, exploring her – the firm contours, the beautiful curves, the delicate hollows, the exquisite softness, the slender, athletic, sculptural lines of her – needing to kiss her body, caress it, taste it, suppressing the urge to bite into it. Gasps rippled through Georgia's light, rapid breathing as I slipped my hand under her waistband, feeling her thrust herself onto my palm. A carnal tide surged through me as I cupped her warmth in my hand. I sighed painfully when I found the abundant evidence of her desire, my middle finger sliding between silky contours, gathering her wetness.

I reached my other hand down to pull off her pyjama bottoms; she helped tug them free and I pulled them off one of her legs before opening her and seeing her in full. I stared, unblinking, in open-mouthed awe, powerless to stop the burning need blazing inside me as my eyes feasted on what had for so long been forbidden. She spread her legs wider for me. I was transfixed at the sight, at the pink flesh gleaming with slick moisture. Even the hair there was sexy – neat and dark. For a long moment, I couldn't move, couldn't do anything but gaze in amazement. She was exposed entirely for me. I felt my own body shiver with a powerful rush, starving for her.

'You're unbelievably beautiful,' I said, and she produced a faint, desperate sound – part sigh, part plea – in response.

I moved to kiss over her hip and along her taut stomach with light, tasting strokes of my tongue, bringing my mouth down to where I wanted it most, not wanting to waste another second, my mouth watering. She exhaled completely, forcefully, as my tongue spread her apart. I groaned at the contact, dizzy with lust, aching with how much I wanted her. She tasted so sweet and felt as smooth as silk against my tongue.

The quiet room seemed to magnify every sound – the hitch in her breath, the gentle rustle of sheets, the wetness of my mouth against her skin.

Her fingers tangled in my hair as I kissed her there, open-mouthed and gentle. I struggled to believe what I was doing. As I ran my tongue over her swollen clit, I eased one finger into her, sinking inside, feeling all but sucked in, and hearing her gasp. She felt like liquid velvet, smooth and hot.

My every movement was guided by how her body responded – her hips lifting slightly, her breathing quickening, the way her thighs trembled under my touch. I was acutely aware of how well I knew my own body, how I could anticipate the sensations she must be feeling. I added a second finger, crooking them, hitting a spot that raised her moans an octave, the pleasure of her pleasure blooming inside me. She rocked her pelvis rhythmically under my face, clasping the sheets at her sides as I lapped at her insatiably and pressed and twirled my fingers into her, feeling the walls of flesh clasping and beating, her warm thighs soft against my shoulders.

My body, awash with desire, was alive with a fierce animal hunger that was almost frightening to me. I glanced up at her and met her eyes, which were blazing with raw craving as she stared back at me.

My clit throbbed as her moans increased; I maintained my pace, attuned to the strength of her responses. She grabbed at my hair, pulling me into her until I could barely move my tongue, her hips continuing their rocking undulations and her soft whimpers lending courage to my every move. She tightened and fluttered against my fingers' strokes, her soft sequence of moans like kisses to my ears. Then, through her mouth, she propelled out the strength of what was building and her body grew taut. A lifetime of unexplored passion surged through me, and mini orgasm took over me just from knowing I was making the beautiful woman beneath me climax. As I moaned out my own ecstasy – momentarily overwhelmed not just by its brief intensity but by the fact that it had happened without physical touch – I felt Georgia's body coil and strain. It lasted a few glorious moments before a strangled cry escaped her throat.

I revelled in the waves of euphoria that rolled through me, feeling her spasming around my fingers, almost unable to believe they were my own. My tongue and fingers continued their ministrations, and I watched as she began to shake with pleasure, her thighs quaking against my cheeks, until she slowly dissolved.

I gradually slipped my fingers from her, still gently lapping my tongue over her, desperate to savour the taste of her climax as her incredible body writhed weakly underneath me.

I crawled up the bed and pressed my body against hers, resting my head on her chest, nestling it into her, kissing her throat and feeling her pulse tick gently under my lips while I listened to the jagged ends of her pleasure. I wanted to whisper 'I love you' in her ear, but I stopped myself and burrowed into the feelings of gentleness and belonging instead.

Then came her hands. They undressed me and left trails of fire on my bare skin. 'You're incredible,' she whispered roughly, and I felt it to my toes.

My body was electric with pleasure; I gasped as Georgia's hand made its way between my legs, heat pulsating from the point where her fingers met me. She slid herself into me effortlessly, her tongue caressing mine with deep strokes synchronised to the kneading of her fingers. I desperately grabbed her wrist with a trembling hand and urged her even deeper, the first teasing ripples of orgasm trilling through me.

I felt her thrusts all the way up to my throat, and I clutched onto her as she plunged into me. She showered kisses down my body like warm rain, raising goosebumps to the surface of my skin, pressing her lush curves against me as she went. After kissing over the tops of my thighs while still pushing into me, her breath was between my legs. She eased her fingers out of me and used them to spread me. We both groaned at the first stroke of her tongue, its liquid heat setting me alight with paralysing pleasure, and I half growled and half screamed when she pushed it inside me.

She swapped her tongue for her fingers, then drew my clit into her mouth, sucking on it. Holding suction, she ran her tongue over it in a steady rhythm. I couldn't stop my hips from rising to meet her mouth, hearing the slippery sounds of my wetness and her tongue combined. Her mouth was amorphous against me; I couldn't tell the difference between her lips and tongue and fingers, I just felt a hot, wet, frictionless, delectable mess against me.

My whole body was ablaze, my senses engulfed and stunned by the intensity of the feelings. Tingles surged over my skin. I was light-headed, my vision was blurred and I was aware of every inch of my skin – so sensitive that I could even feel the thread count of the smooth bedsheet beneath my body. The delicious, molten mingling of sensations rocked through me, stealing the breath from my lungs.

Then an instant weightlessness came over my body as if I were hovering. I couldn't focus on anything except this rising, inexplicable wave, growing high to a tsunami-like height in my body, sucking my breath into its swell, and reaching its peak before crashing down over my skin and rushing through my veins, bringing with it an oblivion of shimmers, flashes and colours that shattered behind my tightly closed eyes. My limbs crackled and fizzed and my body jerked from the intensity of pure ecstasy. I wanted to scream savagely from the most primitive depths of myself.

I lay there bewildered and emotional as the ecstasy crested and mellowed – my body languorous and contented, my heart slamming itself against my chest. As she settled light kisses on my still-convulsing thighs, the endorphins still racing through me top to toe, I realised that *this* was the type of sex people had been talking about. *This* was what I'd been missing out on. Not just the pleasure of it, but the emotion of it, the connection of it, the pure safety of it. I stroked the palm of my hand down my throat, hoping to dislodge the painful lump that had taken up residence there. There was nothing I could do to stop the tears. I understood then that I'd never had a genuine sexual experience before. I had always forced myself to believe the only sex that counted was sex with a penis in me. I realised how out-of-body it had been with men, how unnatural it was, and how I'd always felt unsafe and used, like I was just a vessel to them. I had never properly identified that before. This was my moment of realisation; *this* was how it should feel. And when I was finally able to have that comparison, it was heartbreaking; I felt like I had betrayed myself so extensively, over and over again, for so many years. The grief of the lost time hit me right between the eyes.

I sought the tightness of Georgia's arms, our bodies yielding against each other, fitting together, and when I glanced up at her, I saw that she was crying too.

Georgia. Oh god, Georgia. Why couldn't I have met you sooner?

Chapter 14

I opened my eyes to see I was in Georgia's room; it was dark, but I instinctively knew it wasn't night anymore. There was a different hue to it – more of a violet-grey than a midnight blackness. I'd slept over. Joe would be apoplectic. How would I explain this? And then I realised, I didn't have to. I wasn't with him. I'd given back my ring. I had taken back control.

But Joe didn't like to lose; he was obsessed with power. He was always so focused on how wily, shrewd and intelligent he was, or how well he could play a situation. I couldn't imagine how he'd feel at being outmanoeuvred by his own fiancée. *Ex*-fiancée.

Georgia turned towards me, smiling, her eyes flickering open, and all felt well in the world again. My face melted into a reciprocal expression as she held onto my hand underneath the warm covers. Pleasure shockwaves traced a line from my brain to my clit when thoughts of the night before flashed up.

Our heads were positioned on the edges of our pillows, the tips of our noses almost touching. She slowly lifted my hand to her mouth, kissing the pads of my fingers one by one. Feeling suddenly starved of her, I leant in and kissed her; she kissed me back without hesitation, letting out a feathered moan through her nose. Need radiated through me as everything outside of her became non-existent.

I stroked her arm under the covers, bringing my hand slowly over her incredible breasts, her nipples tightening beneath my palms. How did I get so lucky? She shuffled closer to me in bed, pressing her naked chest onto mine, the warmth of her body glowing through me, and placed her hand on my hip. She traced her hand over the front of my thigh until it was between my legs, her fingertips dipping inside. My head tilted itself back, and my leg instinctively draped over her to give her better access. She poured a gentle 'Shhh' into my ear; I could tell she was smiling by the shape of the sound. I'd obviously started making noises I wasn't aware of.

'My dad is back,' she whispered. 'He's in the next room with his girlfriend.'

I reached between her legs as she sank into me, her hips jerking at the contact. I pushed into her slick heat and touched her in sync, our bodies in rhythm with each other, our strokes deep, slow and thorough.

I heard voices on the landing outside her unlocked door. It excited me a little, knowing we could be caught at any second. I tensed up in pleasure, burying my face into her neck to muffle my cries as she thrust solidly in and out of me, her fingers as deep as they could be, taking me hard and fast, heat consuming and enveloping us.

I clenched to hold on to the sensation until my body finally gave in and the best feeling hit. I felt her internal muscles start to convulse around my fingers as I continued to beckon them as best I could while my own body shuddered with release, the prolonged sensations flowing through the whole of me, leaving behind a diffusion of gratification opening and expanding as she continued to fuck me.

I revelled in the tight resistance that met my thrusts, biting my lip as I watched her face scrunch and felt her body stiffen; it was like seeing a pot of water boiling over – a slow build rising to an intense, unstoppable overflow. Her mouth opened as if she was about to scream; I covered it with my free hand, while she covered my mouth in return, our muffled moans filled with desperate need.

We slowly inched in and out of each other, our wet fingers continuing to caress sensitive flesh, savouring the sensation of one another's aftershocks. Every muscle was soft and melting; it was pure pleasure and peace. Her body pressed against mine felt like home.

Minutes later, I felt her slow kisses on my neck, chest and stomach. I closed my eyes at the sensation of her balmy, travelling mouth, and she spread my legs. Suddenly self-conscious, I told her I hadn't showered yet – as if she didn't already know that, seeing as we'd just woken up together – but she said she preferred it like that.

'I want to taste *you*,' she said.

Between my trembling thighs, she dipped her head and began tickling my clit with the tip of her tongue and teasing her fingertips back inside me. She waited for me to settle into the sensations before sinking into me up to her knuckles, filling me. Her name emerged from my mouth in a whimper as she closed her lips around my clit and jackhammered her tongue directly onto it. I clamped my hands over my mouth to stop myself from screaming. She glanced up at me with pure lust in her eyes, and I promised myself I'd never forget how good it felt to be desired like this.

Then came the onslaught of quakes and tingles before the mind-blowing release of endorphins burst through, again. She lapped at me until the rapture softened – until I felt myself drifting back down to earth, every cell in my body languorously repeating 'Yes, yes, yes!' with as much post-climax enthusiasm as they could muster. A heaviness closed over my wearied eyes as her mouth trailed up my body before claiming my lips.

Her house was awake; the smell of coffee and bacon slid itself under the bedroom door like a note from a stranger. I wanted to be able to leave for work without Georgia's dad or his girlfriend seeing me. Not because it mattered that I was there – Georgia said they'd be fine with that, and they'd have seen my car parked on the double driveway anyway – but because I felt shy about having spent the night; they would surely know what it meant. We were too old to be having sleepovers. And besides, I wanted to at least look presentable – and be wearing a bra – when I first met her family.

Georgia glanced back at me with a reassuring smile as she led the way down the stairs. As we reached the bottom, I took a deep breath, smoothing my hair down, before following her into the kitchen, my heart fluttering.

'Gem, can you grab the plates from the cupboard?' Georgia's dad, Mike, said, his voice rich and deep.

'On it,' Georgia's sister replied.

'Stace, do we have any of that fancy syrup left?' he asked his girlfriend.

I stepped into the room behind Georgia, and all three heads turned towards us. Gemma, still in her pyjamas and leaning against the counter, wore a playful grin on her face; Mike greeted us with a warm smile; and Stace stood beside him, her welcoming expression radiating kindness.

'This is Jess,' Georgia said, staying close to my side, and not offering any further details.

'Good morning, Jess!' Mike boomed, his eyes sparkling with friendliness. 'I hope you're hungry. We've got plenty.'

'Morning!' I said, perhaps a bit too enthusiastically.

'Tea or coffee, babe?' Stace asked me.

'Tea please.'

'Sit, sit,' Gemma said, rubbing her eyes sleepily, and I felt overwhelming relief at not having to stand awkwardly anymore. Georgia, Gemma and I settled at the kitchen table while their dad whistled a merry tune, piling pancakes on a big plate as Stace prepared our drinks. No questions were asked – although I could tell Gemma saw right through us – and I was grateful for that.

The laughter, the love, the warmth – they were all pieces of a puzzle I hadn't realised I needed. Joe's parents had never liked me.

As we all chatted about our plans for the day, everything felt natural and easy. They didn't pry into how we knew each other or why I was there; the elephant in the room felt more like a tiny mouse. I didn't know it yet, but I would come to love them. All I knew in that moment was that I felt like I fitted in without trying.

Chapter 15

'Where have you been?' Joe asked in a whispered shout when I made it through the door of my flat.

'I went to stay with a friend; things were too heated between us last night and I needed some time,' I said, pushing down the desire to scream, *Because you almost fucking raped me.*

His jaw hardened. 'You can't just leave when we're in the middle of something like that, Jess.'

'I need you to move out,' I said matter-of-factly while my heart thudded with the dread of what might happen next. 'We're not together. You can't stay here.'

'We're engaged, Jessica. That's not something you can just end at the snap of your fingers. We need time to talk it through, to work it out, to go to couples therapy – I don't know.'

I knew he wouldn't just up and leave at my command. He would only leave if it were his choice. I thought about how I could get him to go. I could have called my dad and asked him to chuck Joe out – Joe would have never put a foot wrong around my dad; he wouldn't have wanted to ruin the squeaky-clean fiancé image he'd cultivated so well.

'Look, I know last night went too far, but what was I supposed to do?' He took a few steps towards me. 'I was pushed to my limit, and I reacted badly. I hold my hands up.' He stepped closer and swept my hair from my face. 'Do you forgive me, baby? I promise that will never happen again. Can we just start over?'

'I'm sorry, but... no.'

'Don't be like that, baby.' He stroked my cheek with the back of his index finger. 'I promise you; I've learnt the error of my ways, and everything's going to change from now on. I know how close I came to losing you last night; I'll never let my anger take over me like that again.' He cupped my face in both hands. 'I'll never let you go.'

'I need to get ready for work,' I said.

He reached into his pocket and pulled out my engagement ring before getting down on one knee.

I shook my head frantically. 'Joe, don't.'

'My love,' he said, trying to reach my hand as I took a step back. 'This is my promise to you that I have changed.' He paused to wipe tears from eyes – tears that I was certain he could summon on command. 'I love you more than anything.' He sniffed dramatically, holding the ring in the fingertips of both hands. 'I learned such a huge lesson last night. It kills me that I almost lost you.'

I looked down at him and realised how often this type of speech had worked in the past. He'd always get me to believe that his last slip-up would be his final slip-up, even though I had been proven wrong countless times. And normally, *I'd* end up saying sorry, and for some reason, it always actually felt right to do so.

He watched me with put-on obliviousness as I continued to inch further away. 'Baby girl, come here.' He held out his hand.

'No, Joe. I'm sorry. It's over. I need you to go. I'm sorry.'

'Jess, listen,' he said, standing, and I could tell he was fighting to keep his tone reasonable. 'Can't you see I'm doing everything in my power to make this right? Don't throw this back in my face.' He closed the gap between us.

'I meant what I said last night, Joe. I can't do this anymore; I don't want to do it anymore.'

He grabbed my hand, trying to force the ring on my finger, still acting calm. 'I love you, Jess.'

I pulled back but he didn't let go. 'Stop,' I said loudly.

'Don't shout. The neighbours will think something's wrong.'

'Stop or I'll fucking scream.'

He let go. 'What are you talking about? I'm literally trying to re-propose to you. You'll find any excuse to make yourself a victim, won't you? I'm expressing my undying love, and you're threatening to scream for help. Make it make sense.'

***

As expected, he didn't leave that day, or that night; he just got into bed and turned over. I slept happily on the two-seater sofa where Georgia and I had shared our first kiss.

Days later, he was still living at my flat – and I was still on the couch, with backache. He was acting as if nothing had happened, still calling me 'baby'. All he had at mine was a suitcase-worth of clothes, so it would have been simple for him to go. I told him to go back and live with his (horrible) mum, who still referred to me as 'that girl'. He said he would fight to get me back and wasn't going anywhere, and that, if he left, it would feel like he was giving up. He cooked a 'romantic' dinner, as he referred to it, and served it by candlelight, he washed the dishes, he did the laundry, and he fixed the wardrobe doorknob – which had been hanging off for the past six months – as if any of it would help.

I told him I'd have to call the police if he didn't leave. He cried, pleaded, apologised and utilised every emotional tactic he had. He said he would change. He pleaded. He said he'd go to therapy, that he'd stop going out with the boys so much, that he would start paying for rent. Then, when all of that didn't work, he told me I wouldn't dare leave him, that he could ruin me. He threatened my job and my home – he said he would anonymously call my boss and my landlord and complain about me to both. He said he loved me, he had me against The Wall several more times, he turned on music and tried to dance with me, and he attempted to seduce me. And when that didn't work, he grabbed a knife.

He held the blade to the side of his neck and spat that he would 'do it' if I didn't take him back. *Be my guest*, I thought. I had become so accustomed to his drama that it no longer caused alarm. I knew this meant he'd run out of options for gaining back control. He'd tried everything, until only the threat of suicide remained.

'Please put the knife down, Joe,' I said, knowing he wanted me to play to the drama. 'Don't do anything stupid. Come on, now.'

'Say you still love me.'

I never loved you.

'Look, this has gotten out of hand. I need you to put the knife down, Joe.'

He kept it to his neck, his hand shaking with how tightly he was holding it. I wanted to roll my eyes at him. I knew this would stop if I took it off him – he would put up a fake struggle and then he'd simply let it go. If I didn't take it from him, I knew it could go on all morning, and I had to get to work.

I stepped forward, faux-tentatively, touched his arm and then lightly grabbed his wrist. 'Give it to me,' I said, prising his fingers off the handle. 'It's over, Joe. Stop fighting for us; it's done.'

He grabbed the knife back off me, pushed me against The Wall and held the blade to my throat. 'If you're ending this because you've met another man, I'll kill him.' A few flecks of his white spittle landed on my face as he spoke. His jaw muscles were so tense that everything from his collarbones up quivered, the cords of his neck protruding and the vein in his forehead as thick as an earthworm. 'You hear me? I'll fucking kill him.' He spat in my eyes and released me, throwing the knife to the floor as he walked away.

***

When I came home from work, he was gone. That was, until the day after, when I found that he'd let himself back in to scatter love notes about the place.

You're making a mistake.

I can be better.

I love you so much it makes my heart ache, baby.

I kept thinking I had found them all, and then I opened the fridge and there was another one, and I picked up the toothpaste and there was one taped around the tube, and I pulled back my bedcovers and there was one in the middle of the mattress.

There was nothing romantic about someone who had a key to my flat and no respect for my boundaries. I called him to tell him firmly and in no uncertain terms that this was the end, and that I would call the police if he let himself into my flat again.

The next morning, I arranged to have the locks changed, but the locksmith I'd been recommended couldn't come until five p.m., so that was another full working day out of my flat knowing Joe had a key.

At work, I realised I'd left my phone in the flat. It was a good excuse to pop home and check that the place hadn't been burnt to the ground.

No love notes, no fire, nothing missing, nothing trashed, my phone on the bedside table where I'd left it. Relief. Everything was as it should have been. I locked up.

For the rest of the day, my mind raced with thoughts of Joe letting himself into my place while I was still at work. When I finally arrived home, I parked outside the flat and noticed the locksmith already at the front door, toolbox in hand.

I jogged over in my heels. 'Sorry I'm a few minutes late,' I said to him, smiling, letting him into the building.

'No worries,' he said merrily. He had a bulbous, pock-marked nose, a friendly face and was exceedingly chatty.

'Lost your keys or something have you?' he asked as we ascended the stairs. 'That's one of the top reasons people call little ol' me.'

'No. There's just someone who has a key, and I don't want them getting in.'

'You've got yourself a stalker have you, love?' he asked through a light chuckle.

'Something like that.'

'Nothing worse.'

I laughed politely, showing him through my door – making sure to keep it open, as I always did when a contractor came in, such was my fear of men, no matter how seemingly friendly.

'Any chance I could use your bathroom quickly, love?' he said.

'Sure. Just through there.'

He closed the door behind him and then opened it again immediately. 'Uh, love, have you seen what's in here?'

My stomach flipped as I hurried to the bathroom, where a pile of my clothes lay on the floor, soaked. At first, I thought it was just water – until I noticed the yellow splashes around the edges and realised what it really was. In the blind rage I felt at seeing the contents of my entire wardrobe marinating in Joe's piss, I dialled 999.

Chapter 16

Georgia's dad had breakfast waiting for us. He whistled while placing the toast and crumpets on the table along with a jug of orange juice and a pot of tea.

'M'lady,' he said in his gravelly voice as he pulled a chair out for me.

'Thanks, Mike,' I said, amused.

He was a handsome guy, with a great bone structure, and tanned in an outdoorsy way. He had a buzz cut, which he shaved himself to save money, Georgia said. She told me he'd been conscious of money ever since his wife – Georgia and Gemma's mum – passed away when Georgia was eleven and Gemma was nine, and he became the sole provider for his two girls.

'Anything else I can get for the three queens?' he asked me, Georgia and Gemma as we sat there in our pyjamas like kids.

'Dad, ease up,' Georgia said with a smirk, 'you'll scare Jess off.'

'No, no,' I said, my grin widening. 'I could get used to this.' I turned my attention to Georgia and Gemma. 'Is breakfast time always like this?'

'Pretty much,' Gemma said before lowering her volume. 'But he's hamming it up for you. He loves visitors.'

I caught the corners of Mike's mouth pulling up before he turned away to fetch some spoons from the drawer, pretending not to hear her.

There was a knock at the front door. Pickle barked, his paws slipping on the floor as he tried to take off, skidding in place like a cartoon character before managing to scamper down the hall. Stace let herself in through the unlocked front door, following Pickle, who excitedly led the way. His paws tapped the kitchen floor in a frenzied rhythm. I bent down in my chair and beckoned him over, giving him a scratch behind the ears. He responded by circling my feet like he'd known me forever.

Mike pecked Stace on the cheek in greeting.

'Morning, loves,' she said brightly, her gaze sweeping over each of us in turn. When her eyes landed on me, her smile grew sympathetic. 'How are you holding up, Jess? Mike told me about what happened yesterday. Joe sounds like a right bastard.'

'I'm fine, thank you.' I nodded appreciatively, covering my mouth with my hand as I'd just taken a bite of a jammy crumpet. 'I mean, it would have probably been safe enough to stay at my flat last night – I had the locks changed and reported Joe to the police – but I was still a bit on edge. I was so glad for the invitation to stay here, just to be on the safe side.' I felt a pang of guilt for not taking my parents up on their offer for me to stay, but they lived too far out of the city. 'And I'm being treated like royalty,' I added, flashing a grateful grin at Mike.

She rested her head on Mike's shoulder, giving his chest a gentle pat. 'He's a good egg, this one.'

'I try,' Mike said with a modest shrug. 'Do you have time for a cuppa, love?' he asked, wrapping an arm around Stace's back.

'Just a fleeting hello this morning, sadly; I've got an early meeting. I just wanted to check on Jess.'

Hearing that made me feel even more part of the family than I already did.

'Oh, thanks,' Mike chimed in with mock offence.

'And you, Mike.' She rolled her eyes and we all chuckled. 'And you, girls.'

I could easily imagine my parents laughing along with Mike and Stace; they shared a similar sense of humour and brightness. I smiled at the thought of our two families meeting, but that couldn't happen. Mike and Stace didn't ask questions; I was just Georgia's new friend as far as they were concerned – or at least they didn't let on if they thought otherwise – a friend who needed a place to stay. If I introduced Georgia to my parents, now or anytime in the future, they wouldn't be as unconcerned with the details as Mike and Stace. They were always curious, full of questions – especially Mum – and I could already picture the dozens they'd ask if I brought Georgia for a visit. Not in a prying way, but with genuine interest. They'd want to know everything: how and where we met, who she was, why now. I wasn't ready for that. I wasn't ready to risk slipping up or for them to notice something in the way I looked at her. After all, I had only recently broken the news to them that I didn't want to marry Joe. I couldn't bring myself to give them anything else to digest on top of that. Saying that, after I'd told them the news about me and Joe – over the phone, so I wouldn't have to see their worried, concerned expressions – Dad actually said, 'Well, love, we never thought he was right for you, anyway.' Mum agreed, adding something about Joe always being 'too slick for his own good.' I had to smile. I'd been dreading their reaction, afraid I'd worry them, only to find they'd been quietly hoping for this moment all along.

Stace's laugh brought me back to the room. Looking around at everyone's smiling faces felt bittersweet – as if by deciding in my head not to let my family meet Georgia, I was leaving my parents out, depriving them of this kind of around-the-table warmth and closeness. Depriving myself, too.

I stayed at Georgia's another night at Mike's insistence. 'Just to be cautious,' he said. 'Stay as long as you like. Any friend of Georgia's is a welcome guest.'

In those two nights, I had a taste of what it would be like to live with Georgia – morning snuggles in bed; brushing our teeth side by side; strolls at our favourite spot, Lake Calon; coming home after work and drinking wine on the sofa; eating dinner together. There wasn't any room for negative thoughts when I was with her.

Waking up to her felt as if I'd come back to the world after being dead – as if all the things I'd taken for granted in my previous life, things that I'd thought of as dull or monotonous or grating, seemed wondrous when I was gifted the opportunity to experience them again after dying. Oh, how grateful I was to hear the alarm clock blaring at me – I could hear again! And I'd enthusiastically welcome a new pimple to my face – I couldn't get spots when I was dead, but my skin was alive again! And what a sensation it was when the shower ran out of hot water and suddenly left me shivering – I could feel again!

***

As the weeks went on, I realised that the lifelong fear I'd had about not having a man to protect me was just that: a fear. Nothing happened. This newfound sense of security, or maybe rather the absence of terror, further fuelled my feelings for Georgia. I craved more and more of her. The longing to kiss her or to hold her hand in public was over-powering, but I held back, worried about what people would think. Sometimes, I wouldn't realise I was acting on my impulses until I was in the middle of them, like when I kissed her shoulder while we were waiting in line at the post office; a panic crawled over me, wondering who had seen, and my body froze up. From behind us, a lady with a cloud of purple hair and little round glasses tapped my shoulder and said, 'You shouldn't kiss friends, people will think you're dykes.'

When Georgia would unconsciously knit her fingers between mine in public, she'd pull her hand away quickly, remembering that I wasn't ready for the world to see, not yet. But I'd feel myself dissolve at her touch, like candy floss in water. Why was I trying to deny myself of such a feeling? I craved it; I constantly felt the hypnotic, irresistible pull of her, the inexplicable urge to physically connect. The secrecy around us was turning from exciting to excruciating. Why was I hiding her, hiding our relationship, when I wanted to shout about it from the rooftops? Why was I prioritising the feelings of closed-minded bigots? There was always a niggling feeling that someone might laugh at us, feel sickened by us, fetishise us, criticise us, or confront us. Being a lesbian in public meant being on constant alert.

I hated that I always needed a closed door to be part of the equation when it came to us. A bedroom door. A changing room door. A toilet stall door. I longed not to care about doors anymore. The unspoken rules said if we weren't behind a door, we could only touch each other secretly under a table or in the dark when we were out in public. But there were a few exceptions, like when we visited her mum's grave and held hands and hugged without worrying about anyone watching, or the time she took me to Lake Calon, pulled out strawberries and a bottle of champagne from a cooler, and I kissed her without thinking. For a moment, I'd wondered if she might be about to propose, but since she knew I wasn't ready to 'come out' or admit we were in a relationship, I was sure she wouldn't do that. She never wanted to rush me. She was so patient; I appreciated that more than she knew. It must have been hurting her on some level.

The only time I felt comfortable with full PDA was in the gay bars – more than comfortable, actually; I loved the feeling of being watched by queer people and showing that I was a member of their club, part of something real. And, of course, I was always happy to touch and kiss Georgia around Li and Bex, as long as we were in one of our homes. We were together almost every day of the week; whenever I wasn't alone with Georgia, the four of us were joined at the hips. Work was pretty much the only time I was without them.

God, I loved Georgia. I never wanted to stop touching her. It felt like a movie type of love, a fairy tale love, too good to be true. It was as if nothing else existed until I saw her each day. And the moment I'd lay eyes on her, desire – even just to hold her – would bombard me.

And the sex, my god, the sex. We may as well have spent every moment together naked – although that would have been challenging to do at her dad's house. When we were alone, behind one of the closed doors, the only times our mouths came off each other was to tear off our clothes. And, sometimes, we were so eager that we didn't even have time to undress.

Chapter 17

'I can't believe how different sex is with a woman,' I said, lying on my side with my head nestled on her chest, the golden sunrise peeping through the gaps in her curtains. We'd had another mind-blowing experience the night before. Thankfully, only her sister had been home, and her room was on the other side of the house, so we hadn't been too concerned about noise levels. It would have been simpler if Georgia had just come over to my flat every time we'd wanted to be alone together, but I'd grown to adore her family, and I loved being in her space too, seeing her in her world. 'How have I been missing this my whole life?' I asked, looking up at Georgia, sweeping her choppy, mulberry-tinted hair away from her eyes. 'It had never entered my mind that sex could just be for me sometimes; the fact you can get your kicks from just pleasuring me is insane.'

'If I was told I had to choose between only giving you pleasure or only receiving pleasure, I would choose "give" without a moment's hesitation,' she said, cuddling me. 'It's the sexiest thing on this planet to me – to make you feel like that – there's nothing like it.'

'Before you, I felt like my pleasure was a burden,' I said, hearing my receiver complex and remembering how Joe would yawn while his fingers were inside me. He would always act as if he was doing me a favour when it came to foreplay. 'I feel worshipped by you.'

'I hope so.'

I smiled. 'There's so much I want to learn about your body.' I propped myself up on my elbow as I spoke. 'I want to give you more pleasure than you've ever felt, I want to know exactly what you want, I want to know all the tricks. I want to find out your kinks that you don't even know you have.'

'You already do know my body,' she said, laughing, tucking my hair behind my ear. 'You blow my mind.'

'But I want to know more.'

She chuckled again. 'I swear to you, everything you do is what I want. I couldn't ask for more.'

'Would you show me how you would do it if you were alone?' I asked.

Her eyes widened. '...As long as you showed me.'

I nodded, grinning.

'Oh my god,' she said, squeezing her fists. 'We'll need to do it at your place, so we're undisturbed.'

'This is turning me on so much already. It's going to be hot as hell, but I want to treat it like a class; I want to know exactly what you do to yourself. I want a class itinerary!'

'Hang on...' She hopped out of bed wearing just her tight box-er-short underwear and a white vest top that hugged her body just right. I could see the shape of perfectly round breasts, the material of her top just thin enough that I could make out the outline of her nipples. I wanted to pinch myself that I got to see her like that; her beautiful body, all mine.

She padded across the room softly in the socks I'd bought her for Christmas and then rummaged through the back of her wardrobe and produced a roll of A3 paper. 'I brought it home from an art class I taught last month,' she said. She taught maths at the comprehensive school she went to as a kid. I was always so impressed by her intelligence – she could do any sum in her head – but she didn't flaunt her cleverness; she was extremely modest with it.

Now and then, the school would ask her to substitute-teach for a different class. She liked taking the art students; she said it was treat seeing them get creative. I had always loved art in school – it was the only subject where I felt no pressure, where the focus wasn't on getting the right answer or being perfect. It became my escape. I could lose myself in a sketch or painting and let the world slip away for a while.

She tore off a sheet of paper and popped the cap off a pen. I scooted to the end of the bed, loosely covering my naked body with the duvet, to watch what she was doing.

'Right,' Georgia said, scrawling the word 'Itinerary' at the top of the A3 page, sounding it out and smirking as she wrote. 'What about if we do Round One: show each other how we touch ourselves, and the rule is the other person can't get involved, they can only watch.'

'It'll be *so* hard not to touch you, but yes,' I said, my heart fluttering as she started writing it down. 'And the other rule should be that we have to do it as we would if we were alone, no exaggeration allowed.'

'Yes.' She wrote it down. 'Round Two can be: using what we've just watched, we try that on each other. So, I touch you the way you've just touched yourself – same speed, same technique etcetera – and you do it to me too?' she asked, pen poised.

'Definitely,' I said, my quick breaths a rhythm of anticipation. 'Then, for Round Three, I want you to demonstrate what you'd like me to do to you, by doing it to me first.'

'Like a show-and-tell round?'

'Yes! So, Round Three: fucking each other the way we want to be fucked, but keeping it education-centred, you know?' I winked at her.

'Je-ess,' she said, screwing up her face, not appreciating my crude language.

I laughed. 'Sorry. "Make love" to each other the way we want to be made love to?'

She cringed, wrinkling her nose. 'I like that wording even less,' she said with a smile, rolling her eyes and continuing to write. She clicked the cap back on the pen and stared at me with glitter in her eyes.

'No, wait. Let's add more,' I said, the saliva in my mouth changing taste with excitement. 'It's our game, we make the rules. What about if we add a Round Four? We could try some wild, experimental stuff. But the rule is we can't lie about liking it if we don't; this experience is one I want to learn from, so we have to be honest. Maybe we can even discover a few things about ourselves – our hidden kinks and fetishes.'

'The wild card round,' she said, writing it down, her bottom lip disappearing between her teeth. 'This is going to be fun.'

'Yes, but we have to control ourselves, "as per the rules"!' I said, air-quoting and grinning. 'When should we do it?' I added, wide-eyed.

'I mean, if I had my way it would be right now,' she said, standing up, leaning over me and kissing just under my ear, sending frisson through me.

'But Gemma's here,' she said, letting out a gentle laugh, 'and my dad will be back soon. We'd have to be so quiet. We should do it at your place, set out a whole day for it.'

'But it's Sunday today,' I said, faking a childish pout. 'That'll be an entire week of waiting until we have another full day together. I don't know if I can wait that long.'

She was resting her hands on the mattress while standing in front of me; I kissed her and got out of bed. 'I'm going to jump in the shower,' I said, standing there naked, stretching, purposely enticing her. 'Want to join me?'

We kissed fervently under the hot cascade of water in her en-suite shower, pressing ourselves together tightly. I traced the contours of her body, cupping the smooth outer curve of each breast; they were perfect – full, perky, and so good to play with. She ran her palms over my hips and thighs delectably slowly, her touch sending shivers through me while her tongue stroked mine with a slow and deliberate rhythm.

'Let's do it today,' she whispered through smiling kisses.

I breathed in a rush of air and jerked my face skyward. 'Yes!' I breathed.

We used our fingers to stroke and wash the sensitive flesh between each other's legs, fingertips dipping inside, trying to resist the temptation to go any further, electric with anticipation of what was to come.

Patting each other dry, we lay side by side on her bed, naked, our eyes dancing over each other, taking in every inch as the lemony haze of the morning light filtered through the room. We traced over curves, angles, grooves and freckle constellations, our skin fresh-from-shower plumped.

'Ready for Round One?' she asked.

Chapter 18

I glanced at the A3 sheet on the floor:

Itinerary

Round One:

Show each other how we touch ourselves.

Round Two:

Pleasure each other in the way we've just watched.

Round Three:

F*ck each other the way we want to be f*cked.

Round Four:

The wild card.

'I want you so badly,' she said in the most sensual of voices, her eyes burning over every naked curve of my body. She kissed down my side until she reached the outside of one of my thighs, running her tongue over the top of it while opening my legs and lying on her stomach in front of me. With her warm arms wrapped around my thighs, she pulled me towards her mouth, planting a juicy open-mouthed kiss on my clit.

I threw my head back and gasped. 'George,' I said with a mixture of pleasure and feigned scolding. 'That isn't how Round One is supposed to go.'

'But look at you, how am I supposed to control myself?' she moaned lustfully, not taking her eyes from between my legs. 'OK, I'll play by the rules. Round One,' she said before softening her voice to a whisper. 'Touch yourself for me.'

Her words lit a fire in me. She backed up and knelt on the bed, her pinpoint gaze unfaltering. I wanted her to see every part of me – every detail, up close. Opening my legs wider, I spread myself with my fingers. She sighed painfully, arching her eyebrows upward and sucking on her lower lip as if pining for what she was being shown. I offered my fingers to her mouth; she sucked on them before I used them to circle my clit, my mouth falling open and a rough moan slipping past my lips as I did so. Exposing myself to her admiring eyes, I relaxed into the feelings and honoured the simplicity of what I would do if I were alone, sans vibrator.

'I want to see you too,' I said huskily, still circling, my pulse beating hard in my head. 'I want to do it together.'

She swallowed hard before picking the scatter cushions up off the floor, propping them behind her at the end of the bed and leaning against them. I traced my eyes over her bare body, over her post-shower skin which had sprung into its fullest conformations. My eyes lingered over her breasts and tight nipples before trailing down her taut belly and sculpted legs. Her inner thighs looked so soft; I wanted to bite into them as if they were ripe peaches and let the sweet juice trickle down my chin. Her fingers wandered over her body in a teasing exploration, drifting over her chest and skimming her nipples before lowering between those thighs. She was glistening wet as she slid her fingertips over herself in an up-and-down motion, and the middle finger of her other hand pressed inside her. She shifted her thighs further apart to allow me to see everything. I looked on hungrily, helplessly, as she continued to touch herself.

'I'm already close,' I whispered, my breaths becoming increasingly ragged. Just the fact that she was watching me and I was watching her was enough of a turn-on to get me to feel the ascent towards climax in moments.

'Let me watch what happens as you orgasm,' she said quickly, knowing from my pause in breath that it was about to happen.

I kept circling at a fast pace, trying to keep my hand out of the 'way' as much as I could for her viewing pleasure. A rush of intensity sparked in my clit and spread, somehow slowly and all at once, through my legs, torso and arms, firing tingles through my toes and fingertips. I subdued my moans as much as possible, but knowing her family might hear me heightened the thrill. As my body juddered and the ribbons of pleasure curled through me, I held myself apart so she could examine my ecstasy and aftershocks, her moans amplifying my pleasure.

When I opened my eyes, she was on the peak, stuck on the inhale with her mouth open and her eyebrows furrowed, and I knew she was about to release. I saw how wet she'd become, saw how the muscles in her upper thighs trembled, saw how the colour had risen in her cheeks. I watched wide-eyed as she continued to touch herself. She used her fingers so differently from how I used mine – she didn't circle, she almost skated her fingertips over her clit one at a time, in an upward motion, in a fast, rhythmic pattern, while two fingers of her other hand worked internally.

Then came her powerful exhale; her abdomen tensed and the tremors of intensity began. I watched her fingers work slowly while she rode the surf to the end, letting the last waves wash over her before she all but collapsed back. I was enthralled.

We lay there opposite each other, breathing out soft sighs and groans for the long moments it took to recover.

I glided my hands over her calves, and her eyes flickered open as her breathing relaxed and her limbs loosened. With her legs still wide open, I pressed gentle, slow kisses up them until I reached her centre, eliciting a drawn-out moan, and with the lightest of pressure, I gently started Round Two – using what I'd just learnt to pleasure her.

From what I'd watched, I realised she preferred upward motions on her clit, so I ran my tongue slowly from the bottom to the top of her wetness, feeling her body spasm involuntarily as I did so. I savoured her honey-sweetness and revelled in the softness of her thighs against my cheeks. With a firm grip on her hips, my tongue traced over her lightly, opening her, teasing a path through to her clit. I breathed heat onto her and felt the hotness of her against my mouth in return, the wet-on-wet combination of textures of her against my tongue and lips so luscious. She tasted so fucking good.

My upward laps were delivered at a glacial pace, and her body moved in time with them. I smiled against her flesh and used my whole tongue, relaxing it onto her, planting its warmth against her, feeling it mould to her lust-swollen shape, manoeuvring it deliciously slowly, knowing how sensitive she'd still be after her orgasm. I reached my fingers underneath my chin and sank them into her. Her hands slipped through my hair with synchronicity. Deep inside, I swirled unhurriedly, deliberately, as if we had all the time in the world, my tongue in matching cadence – my movements making her gasp and sigh. I maintained my pace, enjoying listening to the delicate whimpers escaping her mouth, and to the subtle slick, wet sounds of my fingers inside her as they manipulated her G-spot.

My speed was measured; my goal wasn't to get her to peak again – not straight away – instead, I wanted her to bask in the sensations, to feel desired. I found myself in disbelief that I was getting to experience this; it was even better than how I'd dreamt it could be.

She was holding her breath, her eyes were closed, and she'd gone completely silent. I knew what that meant. The muscles in her thighs started to twitch against my face, and inside she clasped around my fingers.

'Faster,' she said through high-pitched sighs.

As I turned my long, languid flattened licks into rapid flicks, bouncing her clit around on my tongue, her breath returned, but it was irregular and ragged. Her body tensed as her tender cries increased, and I felt her melt in my mouth while I was buried in her clutching warmth. Thank god for multiple orgasms.

I could have slept after that. With my eyes closed and a smile etched on my face, the lure of just a quick nap tugged at me, but her kisses brought me back. She invaded my mouth as if it belonged to her. Her lips trailed down to one of my nipples, which she sucked on until it hardened in her mouth, and then she released it with a light pop before offering attention to the other one. It seemed it was my turn for Round Two.

She kissed and licked every inch of my body, leaving my clit for last, until I was twisting with desire, my longing raging out of control. She brought her lips to the hollow of my groin and drifted a whisper of kisses across me until they landed on my clit, gradually increasing the weight of them so that I could adjust as I squirmed under her. Then came the all-encompassing heat, wetness and softness of her mouth. She spread her tongue out, laying it over me, circling with varying degrees of pressure, dispersing thrills through me. Around and around she swirled the flat of her tongue, and her fingers – three, I think – slid into me, one by one, as deeply as they could, so deep, jerking slowly yet rhythmically, filling me, stretching me, pushing inwards and upward, massaging and thrusting.

My heart pounded as the pace intensified; she drove into me deep and hard, the fullness almost too much, my desire turbulent. She locked her mouth onto me, sucking, her groans vibrating on my clit as I gyrated against her, enveloped by a haze of swirling, dizzying lust. I whined as she fucked and ate me, getting her face wet, nose to chin, and using the pressure and contours of her face to grind into me.

After I came, she stayed inside, keeping her fingers still as I pulsed against them, and ran endless gossamer kisses over me before gently pulling out and settling onto her back, her chest still thumping in exertion.

***

We acted as normal as ever in front of her dad and Gemma while we made sandwiches in her kitchen, chatting and laughing away as if we hadn't been blowing each other's minds all morning. I hadn't known Mike and Gemma all that long, but they already felt like my extended family. Gemma knew that Georgia and I were dating, but her dad still never asked questions. He must have known we were more than friends, but, being such a polite man, I don't think he considered it his place to ask. He had a genuine heart, which he'd passed on to Georgia.

'Right, we're just going to go chill upstairs now,' Georgia said while taking our plates over to the dishwasher and loading them in.

Her dad gave a thumbs up and Gemma threw me a knowing smile, to which I shook my head and poked my tongue out cheekily.

***

'Close your eyes,' Georgia said, exhaling the words close to my ear after undressing me and having me lie on the bed.

My eyes widened momentarily at the unexpectedness of the instruction and then obediently slid shut.

'Are you ready for Round Three?' she breathed against my neck.

I nodded eagerly, replaying the description for the round in my head: fuck each other the way we want to be fucked. I loved that she'd censored it with asterisks when writing it down; it was endearing. I heard her rummaging in a drawer before feeling her arrange something satiny across my eyelids.

'Is this OK?' she asked, her voice dripping with desire as she blindfolded me.

I breathed a yes in luxurious acceptance.

'What about this?' her silken voice whispered as she slowly and gently tied my wrists together with something strong and leathery.

'Yes,' I whisper-moaned, not yet knowing how intense my penchant for bondage would become in the near future.

'Stay still.'

A hundred warm kisses covered my body; I felt them air-dry and cool as she descended, leaving my skin tingling and tightening one section at a time. She slowly found new ways to make me squirm and twist without even touching any of the obvious areas. Even the way she ran her tongue over the inside of my ankle, or the way she stroked over my waist and down onto my hips, made my toes curl and my skin quiver.

She pulled me to the edge of the bed and knelt on the floor in front of me before kissing, licking and gently nibbling at my sensitive inner thighs. She parted me with her fingers. 'God, you're so beautiful,' she said, the temperature of her words rippling over my exposure as I became breathless. As she held me open, I knew she was studying me, taking in every detail. I heard her breaths and sighs escalate, the occasional 'Oh my god' or 'Wow' barely detectable as my thighs trembled. It turned me on in indescribable amounts, and all she was doing was looking between my legs.

I writhed under her gaze and felt her gently blowing on my clit, the airflow steamy and hot as her mouth was mere millimetres from me. I felt my whole body grow pink, shivering at the pleasure it brought me, my arousal savage and pounding, my legs open, my body on full display while I lay blindfolded and bound. To allow her face so close to my most intimate parts, to let her get an up-close look at my excitement in the full light of day, I had to give up control – surrender. I felt both goddess-like and powerless opening up for her inspection.

I wanted to watch what she was doing, see how her face looked as she anchored her attention between my legs, but seeing only the dark insides of my eyelids made the sensations even more acute. I bit my lip in delight at the sensuous torture. Then I felt the tip of her tongue, teasing in circular motions, and when my moans increased, she slowly pushed her whole wet, slippery tongue into me, burying it. She didn't move it in and out, she kept it deep inside, and I could feel her rolling and winding it before she began thrusting. When she brought her tongue out, I felt my wetness trailing with it and landing back on me.

She started back on the gentle flicking of her tongue over my entrance, her fingers still holding me open. She moved to light, slow upward licks with just the tip of her tongue, not yet touching my clit. I heard myself beg unexpectedly. I was so wet and red hot; my arousal was painful. She was taking her time; it wasn't a rush job to get me to finish; she was taking me on a pleasure journey. I was so used to let's-do-this-as-fast-as-possible, goal-orientated sex with men that I still wasn't used to this kind of play.

The area directly below my clit felt just as sensitive as if it were a second clit; she concentrated there, seemingly knowing that. Then, when I was practically shaking with need, she widened and softened her tongue and planted the whole thing against me in one soft, slow, wet lick; there it was, the magic touch I'd been waiting for, and it was heaven. My bound wrists pressed together above my head, and although the ties weren't attached to anything, I left them in place, imagining they were. The rhythmic all-consuming laps continued, their effect soporific, hypnotic.

'Oh fuck, keep doing that,' I begged, my mouth barely moving.

'If I keep doing that, you'll finish, and it's not time yet,' she said against my clit.

My frustration mingled with the furnace-like heat of her words alone might have been enough to send me into oblivion. She opened me again and blew warmly on me before fluttering her tongue, as fast and soft as a butterfly wing, over my clit, barely touching it. With wet lips, she kissed it. Her lips surrounded it, sucked lightly, and slid off it with a kiss, and again, and again, and again, the same metrical motion: surround, suck, kiss; surround, suck, kiss.

'You,' kiss, 'taste,' kiss, 'so,' kiss, 'good,' she said, and on the final word she speared her fingers into me. 'There we go. Stay still, keep your arms above your head, legs open; that's it.'

Her words made me tingle as much as her fingers did. She'd never talked dirty to me, not like that anyway. I think I loved it. I squeezed my eyes tighter under the blindfold knowing she was watching her fingers sliding in and out of me, deep and slow. She turned her fingers while they were still inside me, sweeping them downwards.

She kept delivering words that sent shocks through me.

'I love seeing myself inside you.'

'If only you could see what I can see.'

'You feel so good.'

'Keep those legs wide open for me.'

It was driving me insane. I began to shake in her hold. Never had words had such a visceral effect on me; it had unleashed a new kind of desire. This was what she wanted from me, too – Round Three was 'fuck me as you want to be fucked', after all.

And then came her mouth again, her whole mouth, devouring me. Her fingers plundered faster and faster, striking an internal electric button every time she thrust them in. Both feelings melted together and lusciously blurred, thrumming pleasure through me all the way to my ears, muffling my moans and rising higher until I felt that drop in my stomach as if on a rollercoaster. The tension imploded inside me, gushing through my limbs like a waterfall with a current running through it, leaving thousands of tiny effervescent bubbles slowly sailing across my skin until I turned to liquid.

I lay there trembling, unable to form a sentence, as the heat of our bodies hung in the air. She stroked my face as I tumbled into a semi-dream state, my mind grappling with my internal detonations. After a few minutes, my haze lifted, and I moved to taste myself on her tongue; I sucked at it and bit at her lips. How could I still be so ravenous for her after three orgasms?

When she asked if I was ready for Round Four, I laughed with what little energy I had, my eyes barely able to open, and told her I needed to recharge. 'I can't remember what Round Four was supposed to be anyway,' I said, my jaw and tongue moving slower than the words.

'It was your idea,' she said, laughing, kissing me again. 'Round Four is the wild card, trying new, experimental things on each other.'

'You basically just did Round Four on me, then,' I said slowly through the numbness of my mouth, softly holding her hand in mine and kissing my way up to her fingertips, tasting myself on them. 'That was incredible. I want to be tied up all the time, and I loved how you spoke to me like I belonged to you.'

'You do belong to me,' she said, smiling, kissing my shoulder, pressing me into her. 'You're mine.'

The words made my breath catch. I wanted her to possess me, to own me; I wanted to be only hers, and for her to be only mine.

'Before we even discuss Round Four,' I said lethargically, kissing at her neck and ear, 'I do believe it's your turn for Round Three, Miss Morgan.'

With the realisation that I loved being tied up and praised – and with the new awareness that she must have wanted that too – it was obvious that I should repeat what had just been done to me, perhaps even adding a touch more intensity.

On the bed, there was a black satin sleep mask, which was what she'd used to blindfold me. And there was a black leather belt lying next to it, which she'd used to secure my wrists. I dressed her in both, but I looped the belt around a slat in the headboard, restraining her properly. I had such a desire to tie her feet apart and attach them to the corners of the bed, but I had no way of doing it. My mind raced with thoughts of future kinky possibilities.

I stared down at her in awe, marvelling at her naked beauty. My desperate hands roamed everywhere, beginning a fervent and thorough exploration of her body. As my blunt nails ran over her firm stomach, she arched her back, and I saw her smooth skin contract and stretch over the ridges of her ribcage. I slid my hand lower down her body, spreading her thighs before splitting two fingers between her legs, parting her, revealing her glistening pink centre as her breath turned into a pant. I flashed my eyes over the length of her body while I held her open. She lay there blindfolded and tied up, her naked body on full display for me as she writhed deliciously on the sheets in anticipation of what I was about to do next. It was a sight which drove me to the brink of madness.

I felt a pounding between my legs, a pleasure so intense it bordered on painful, a constant potent throbbing. Incapable of leaving her untouched for any longer, I let my fingers play, gently, slowly, knowing her body must have felt as sensitive as mine. She writhed even more eagerly beneath me, her hips rising slightly as if seeking a firmer touch. I used a little more pressure to stroke over her clit with a wet fingertip, hearing her soft, high-pitched whimpers emerge. I slid my fingers deep into her, then pulled them out slowly, staring, transfixed at how they glistened, at how dripping wet she was. I had to taste her.

My mouth descended, the scent and taste of sex, sweetness, salt and sweat sent me into a state of dazed ecstasy.

'I can't believe you're mine,' I whispered, my lips lightly brushing over her clit as I spoke. 'I couldn't want anyone more. I can't get enough of you.'

I slapped the outside of her thigh to see her reaction. She moaned, whispering 'yes' almost to herself. I licked with more pressure, more speed, stopping when I saw that she was close – her body stiffening and arching. Reaching up to untie her wrists so that I could get her in a better position, I said quietly but firmly, 'I want you on your knees.' She crawled into place and waited for me to secure her with the belt. I spanked her again – harder, but not so hard that it would be too loud. It would be years before I knew how violent a true spanking could be.

While she was on her knees, I pushed into her with two fingers, reaching over her hip with my other hand to stroke her clit. 'That's it,' I said. 'Tell me what you want.'

'I want you to keep surprising me,' she said breathlessly.

I used my thigh to push my fingers in deeper, thrusting hard and fast, and when I felt she was almost on the brink again, I stopped and untied her. 'Lie on your back.'

She did as I said, and I interlaced my legs with hers, moving into a scissor position. I shifted myself until I found that sweet spot where we connected, my hips circling slowly as I moved over her, both of us so wet, the slick heat of our centres slipping and gliding together. The silky friction sent waves of raw pleasure through me. I felt her textures and details slide over me as she whirled against me, the pressure perfect, the temperature delicious. I could feel her warmth spreading through me, inviting, intense. Our bodies found a rhythm, a slow, intoxicating dance as we moved against each other. The wetness between us made every shift seamless, effortless, our pleasure melding into one. I could feel the softness of her vulva, the subtle ridges and contours of her pressing onto me with each roll of our hips. Our breathing grew heavy, in sync, each exhale mingling in the space between us as we pressed harder, wet and grinding, our bodies locked in a rhythm that felt both primal and tender. I closed my eyes, losing myself in the slick warmth, in the sound of our bodies meeting, a quiet symphony of gasps and sighs. Our motions became bolder, more desperate. I tightened my grip on her, urging us both to the edge, the pressure building until every nerve was on fire. After a few more moments, her breath hitched and she sighed out a choked cry of release, her body shuddering before collapsing languidly in the aftermath of spent pleasure.

She grasped my hand and gently drew me down beside her, holding me close, her fingers threading through my sweat-dampened hair. A sudden wave of sleepy contentment washed over me again; I had one foot in an enveloping dream and one in reality, straddling the two realms. Georgia placed her palm on my forearm. The heat of her hand radiated up through my arm, all the way to my shoulder in seconds, lighting a glow through my skin and muscles. It crept up to the side of my face and smouldered red, relaxing me. My head, just on that one side, had its own heartbeat and my neck veins pulsed just on that side too, the side she was touching, my vessels expanding. The feeling continued to slide down my side, emanating over my ribcage and down to the dip above my hip.

She gently lifted her hand off my skin, maybe as she thought I'd fallen asleep, and it was as if she had unplugged from me – she the charger and I the device – and I went black, my power deactivated. I reached for her hand and knotted my fingers with hers, feeling the glow return as soon as her skin touched mine.

'Are we admitting defeat?' I asked, my eyes still closed. 'Will our "wild card" round have to wait?'

She laughed. 'No, we're going all the way. But, saying that, I'm so hungry. Should we get dinner?'

Chapter 19

The rumble of her car was almost too much for my post-orgasm sensitivity. We were heading to Fat Max, the nearest drive-thru. She would never order her favourite burger when we went there – even though I always encouraged her to – because she knew I was trying to become a fully-fledged vegetarian. I wasn't the type of vegetarian to feel sick at the sight of meat; it was the opposite problem for me – I wanted it, badly. Her favourite burger order used to be my favourite burger order back in my meat-eating days, so she wouldn't buy it in case it tempted me to give in.

She always showed me small acts of affection and thoughtfulness like that. Some were so small they could have gone unnoticed by someone else, but to me, the little things weren't little – 'This reminded me of you', 'I appreciate you', 'Of course I remember', 'I'm proud of you' – they all meant the world to me. There was, for example, the small gesture of how many kisses we'd put at the end of a text. At the start of our relationship, it was one kiss, and then it increased in increments, with both of us always matching the amount each time, and, by that point, it had grown to eleven kisses. We'd never acknowledged the text-kisses in person; it was an unspoken promise that we would always match them, meaning that, without doubt, we counted the kisses every time a text came through, just in case an extra one was added.

There were the big gestures too: the romantic, candlelit three-course meals she would make, for which she bought a vegetarian cookbook especially; or the surprise weekend away to a boutique country hotel with a deep roll-top bathtub; or the time she booked us tickets to the red panda experience at the safari park a few hours from us because she knew they were my second favourite animal, after pugs.

Not that I needed the big gestures; although I wholly appreciated them, it didn't matter to me how we spent our time. As long as we were together, I didn't care where we were or what we were doing. I wanted to be wherever she was, next to her, even if she was asleep. I had no idea a relationship could be that way; she treated me like the most important person alive.

I loved all of our getting-to-know-you moments too, like finding out her favourite writer was Sylvia Plath, and seeing her dry her hair for the first time and watching the face she pulled when the blow-dryer was on. When I asked her why she made that face, which featured a wrinkled nose and a pulled-up top lip exposing her teeth, she said it was because she was rushing to finish. 'I always rush through the boring bits of life so I have more time for the good stuff,' she'd said, and I thought that was beautiful. And I loved how organised she was in all aspects of her life, even down to the clothes she wanted to wear – she'd choose them the night before so she wouldn't have to think about putting an outfit together the next morning. She was such a reliable, methodical, dependable person; her ducks were always in a row.

And there were the serendipitous moments we shared, like when we both surprised each other with potted blue orchids on the same day. We found out that day, by chance, that we both loved blue flowers – for me, it was because they were rare, and extra effort had to go into finding them. For her, it was simply because blue was her favourite colour. That was the first time either of us had been given flowers, and we'd bought each other the same ones.

And of course there was the sex – the passionate, all-consuming, hot-blooded, incredible sex.

We arrived back at her house recharged after our meal, eager for what was next.

On to Round Four: the wild card. This was the experimental play round, where we would explore and see if we could uncover any hidden kinks neither of us knew we had.

'Latex, pantyhose, feet... balloons.' Georgia read aloud from a list of sexual fetishes on a random website she'd found, while we made faces and giggled like school kids. 'God, they just get weirder as the list goes on: humiliation, asphyxiation – or "breath play", that's a lovely way of putting it – and electro-stimulation, which uses "power sources to stimulate the genitals".' She stared at me aghast, shifting her sitting position on the edge of the bed as if the kink descriptions were getting between her legs.

'Keep going,' I said, chuckling at her reaction.

'There's bondage, but we already know we're fans of that after today.' She winked at me cheekily. 'And there's water sports, but I think you've had enough of pee for a lifetime after what Joe did to your clothes...'

I shuddered at the memory of picking up my piss-sodden dresses with my marigold-gloved hands and throwing them onto the shower floor one by one.

'Tell me about the sex you and Ruth used to have,' I said, smirking naughtily.

'Jess.' Georgia's expression shifted as she met my gaze, a hint of seriousness in her eyes while she smiled. 'I really can't talk about that. I need to respect her privacy.'

'Oh, I didn't mean to pry. I'm sorry.'

'It's alright,' she replied gently, still smiling. 'I just never talk about sex outside of a relationship.'

I nodded, grateful to know she'd never talk about me to anyone else either.

After a brief pause, I encouraged her to continue, and she seamlessly picked up the conversation again, as if I hadn't just interrupted the moment.

She continued. 'There's, bloody hell, I can't even pronounce this one. Knism—'

I knelt behind her, hugged my arms around her waist and peered over her shoulder at the phone.

She sounded it out: 'Knis-molag-nia – "pleasure from tickling or being tickled". I don't think we're going to find anything on this list for us.'

I smiled. 'I'm not even a hundred per cent certain I could orgasm again tonight anyway.'

'We'll see about that,' she said, bringing the back of my hand to her lips and kissing it, causing a sharp shock of arousal to flash through my body. She scrolled some more. 'Role play? That's more of a your-place activity.'

'Nurse and patient?' I kissed her neck, raising goosebumps on her skin. She tilted her head to one side, inviting more kisses. 'Masseuse and client?' I kissed her again. 'Flight attendant and passenger?'

Her eyes were closed as she breathed, 'Anything. Everything.'

I could have devoured her. I pressed my lips against her heated flesh, feeling love beyond anything I thought I could experience. I knew that even an eternity with her wouldn't be enough. I missed her even when she was in my arms. She turned her head and kissed me, holding my face. Nothing else mattered when she kissed me.

Before I realised it, I was on top of her, straddling her lap, and the passion resumed – no craziness, no tricks, no plan, no experiments, no kinks, no over-the-top sex moves, no act, no performance, no 'wild card'; just simplicity and desire and effortlessness, our bodies moving together as one, blazing under each other's touches, abandoning ourselves to sensation. And it was perfect.

We fell against each other in a jumble of clammy skin, with our arms and legs interlaced.

'My girl,' she whispered as I drifted to sleep with a smile decorating my face. 'I could never have enough of you.'

Maybe keeping it simple was what we were best at. All the fancy stuff was unnecessary; we'd never even used toys. We weren't in it to be 'dirty' or experimental; our bodies knew what they wanted to do when they were together – I never had to think when I was around her.

Chapter 20

'Wait a sec,' Georgia said, adjusting the ball in front of me. 'OK, now move just a little more to the left,' she instructed, her voice calm and encouraging. 'You want to aim just slightly off-centre.'

I shifted my weight, glancing anxiously at the few people dotted around the field. Two teen girls sniggered as they walked by, and I felt my cheeks flush, convinced they were mocking me – wearing a short skirt, a full face of makeup, and my bright red hair whipping into my eyes – as I struggled to figure out how to 'bend' a football. The sense of being watched made it impossible to focus, even though, for all I knew, their laughter could have been about something entirely unrelated.

Georgia must have seen my discomfort and stepped closer. 'Take your time,' she said. 'Imagine the ball is a paintbrush, and you're curving a line into the goal. Stand at a forty-five-degree angle,' she continued, positioning me. She stood behind me, her hands on my waist, and we held there for a moment, my frame inside hers, and I wanted to turn and kiss her.

'Now,' she said, 'take a mental photo of your target, and when you kick, make contact with the base of your big toe. Think technique, not power.'

I nodded, trying to take in all the advice, although it made no sense to me. I lined up my shot and kicked with a careful motion. It missed the goal by miles.

'Nice try,' she said reassuringly, and I laughed. 'No, seriously, soon you'll be bending them right into the net. You almost had it, it just takes practice.'

She'd taken me to the field in Lake Calon Park to help me let off steam after an awful day at work. My boss had pulled me into the meeting room early on to comment on my outfit, telling me he liked the colour while his eyes roamed all over me. Later, just when I thought I had a solid lead ready for the afternoon edition of the paper, Glyn called me in again.

'Jess,' he said, leaning back in his chair. 'This piece you've written? It needs a major overhaul. We need a different angle.' I clenched my jaw. I'd written it exactly as he'd instructed, despite suggesting a different approach. Yet there he was, circling back to my original idea, as if it had never been mentioned. As if that wasn't enough, I was saddled with six downpage filler pieces and a vox pop, all due by the end of the day.

I was grateful to Georgia for trying to help me decompress in the way that she liked to, by having a kick about. I was open to trying it, even though it didn't exactly come naturally to me, and I appreciated that she wanted to help.

'Is it time to go for food yet?' I asked casually, not wanting to make her feel as if I was bored of learning football skills.

She checked her watch. 'It is actually. Bex and Li might even be there before us for once.'

'I doubt it, you know what they're like. Never on time.'

As we walked, the sun hung low in the sky, coating everything in honey. We wandered down a beautiful tree-lined street, passing imposing detached houses that overlooked the picture-perfect lake. But within minutes, the scenery shifted. The impressive buildings and manicured lawns gave way to convenience stores with faded signs, kebab shops wafting the smell of hot oil, and the hum of traffic growing louder. That was how it was all over the city – a quick change in backdrop, almost without warning. One moment, you'd find yourself in a neighbourhood of tightly packed terrace houses where everyone knew each other's secrets, where curtain-twitchers peeked out of windows – out of curiosity or vigilance – and the next, you'd see an imposing old private school or a street adorned with luxury cars and grand homes and behind tall gates. Then the colours would shift again as you walked by a busker with a guitar, his voice drowned out by the cries of seagulls eyeing the rubbish toppling out of public bins, while fly-tipped sofas leaned against alley walls. The city had multiple faces, constantly shifting. No matter how beautiful or grim a place, though, I always saw the danger. The potential muggers, the weirdos, the perverts... the rapists. Sure, in the rougher areas, it seemed more obvious – the figures in hoodies smoking outside corner shops, the ones loitering at bus stops. But the suited men giving polite nods, the ones in the clean streets, had the potential to be just as dangerous. You never really knew. They walked among us, blending into the fabric of everyday life. But if I looked past the people, there was something undeniably magical about the city I called home. It felt like a place with stories in every corner. The fantasy-like castles with their fairy-tale spires and towers, the historic landmarks, the stadium where rugby matches and concerts brought the city to life, the bustling market which smelled of cockles and laverbread and the sea, the museums, the universities, the lively pubs and shops bringing their own flavour to the mix. But no matter where I was, the people always scared me.

'*There* you are,' Georgia said, grinning as she spotted Bex and Li making their way across the pub to us.

'Better late than never, boyo,' Bex replied, a huge smile on her face.

Li sat down next to me and hugged me, squeezing me tight. 'It feels like it's been ages.'

I laughed. 'We only saw each other a few days ago.'

'In friendship years, that's practically a lifetime,' Bex said. 'What's new with you two?' She waggled her eyebrows, a teasing glint in her eyes as she glanced between Georgia and me.

'Just been practising our footy skills,' Georgia said before nudging me with her elbow. 'Jess is a natural.'

'Right, I'm the queen of the pitch,' I said rolling my eyes, my cheeks warming slightly.

'I'll have to see that,' Bex said, rubbing her big hands together. 'Li and I will be your cheerleaders.'

I smiled weakly and wagged a finger. 'Not a chance.'

'Sorry Glyn was such a git to you today,' Li said, noticing my expression. She was aware of what had happened earlier, thanks to my multiple texts.

'He's awful.' I shook my head. 'What happened with *your* awful colleague today?'

'Oh, Richy? He actually changed his tune after we had a chat today,' Li said. 'He's sweet deep down.'

'And how was *your* day, Georgia?' Bex asked in a tone mimicking a concerned counsellor, clasping her hands together, playfully mocking mine and Li's conversation.

'Oh, you know.' Georgia sighed dramatically. 'Just another day trying to make arithmetic sound fun. One kid asked if we could skip fractions because "life's too short for halves".'

Bex burst into laughter, setting off a chain reaction that had us all giggling uncontrollably. It was moments like those I was happiest. I'd never had a group of friends to call my own before, and I cherished our bond. I looked at Georgia, her smile lighting up her beautiful face; at Bex, whose infectious laughter filled the air; and at Li, my biggest supporter. I felt incredibly lucky, like nothing could ever break the four of us apart. If only I had known then what I know now.

Chapter 21

From the back window of Mike's car, I'd spotted a gorgeous woman and had pictured the way she and I would rip each other's clothes off. I squeezed my eyes closed and shook the thought away. Those kinds of fantasies had crept in daily for as long as I could remember. They were no reflection on Georgia; I knew that. They played in the background, constantly, as if on a dusty old record player I could hear through the attic floorboards of my brain. Nothing had changed about the thoughts, except they had started to make me feel guilty. I'd never tried to stop them when I was in relationships with boys, but with Georgia, it felt like cheating. I had fallen in love for the first time, with a woman – my dreams had already come true, so why wouldn't my mind catch up?

The fantasies weren't needed anymore; I had the real deal, a girl-friend (not that we called each other that) – someone exceptional, and perfect for me in every way. I wanted to be able to control my brain – to tell it to stop allowing other women in – but it had a mind of its own and was detached from, and unresponsive to, my conscious thoughts.

I could judge and criticise my longings, but I couldn't seem to modify them. Years of secret thoughts were difficult to cut ties with. They had become a habit, and I needed help to quit.

Everywhere I went, I developed crushes: mums on the morning school run, my hairdresser, the salad lady I sometimes visited for my work lunch, police officers, delivery drivers, women doing any sort of 'traditionally male' job – the gamut.

I didn't like how the thoughts made me feel – like a lecherous, perverted nymphomaniac. If I was going to have them, they should have at least been more wholesome, more respectable good-feminist ones. I felt depraved sexualising women; men had sexualised me all my life, and I didn't want to be like them.

I wondered for a moment if I should have been listening to my inner desires. Were they trying to tell me something? If I were a cavewoman living in the Stone Age, I would have certainly acted on my yearnings. Modern society and my own morals told me not to, but hundreds of thousands of years of evolution were urging me to go for it. Cavewoman-me wouldn't have hesitated – just the same as a lion wouldn't hesitate to mate with multiple lionesses. Maybe it would have made more sense if I were a man craving all those women, because I could blame it on the biological drive to mate and reproduce. If I were a man, my yearnings would be put down to me being human – nothing more than that.

But it was OK, because I knew what was important to me, and it certainly wasn't hooking up with other girls. My important was Georgia. If the fantasies kept playing out, my plan was just to let them. There was no point in worrying about something I had no control over. Soon enough, they'd die out. Wouldn't they?

'Just give me a call when you're ready to come home,' Mike said from the driver's seat as we all clambered out of his car.

'We will, love,' Stace replied, her voice as giddy as a schoolgirl's, before leaning in to peck him on the lips through the open window.

Still beaming, Stace tottered up the steps behind me, Georgia and Gemma. 'I feel young again,' she said, practically bouncing with excitement. 'Thanks for inviting me, girlies.'

We were meeting Li and Bex at a new bar in the city, and judging by the sea of people inside, it seemed like half the city had shown up.

After weaving between tables and getting bumped into by a few tipsy patrons, we spotted a booth opening up near the back. We darted over, staking our claim just before another group could swoop in.

By the time Bex and Li strolled in – fashionably late as usual – we'd already gone through a couple of rounds, and the buzz was starting to hit. Bex threw her arms up in apology as she walked towards us, her customary bright grin plastered across her face. 'Sorry, sorry. Traffic was a nightmare.'

'Yeah, sure, traffic,' I teased. 'More like you couldn't tear yourself away from each other.'

Li snorted, giving a playful shrug. 'Just cuddles – PG stuff!'

'I don't want to picture that, even if it is PG,' Georgia said, covering her eyes. 'I'm going to get the next round in. Bex, Li, come give me a hand?'

Once they'd gone to the bar, Stace leaned closer to me. 'So, what's going on between you and Georgia then, babe?' she asked, her voice full of curiosity.

I felt my stomach flip. It was the first time either Stace or Mike had asked the question head-on. Gemma grimaced at me from across the table, her expression saying, *Busted*.

Stace sipped her drink through her straw and rubbed my arm, the speed of her blinks slowed by alcohol. 'I can see you two are getting closer,' she said understandingly. 'And I just want you to know, you don't have to pretend – if it is something more, I mean. I know Mike would be fine with it. Right, Gem?'

'Dad would be fine.' Gemma nodded. 'He'd just roll with it. He didn't ask any questions when Georgia and Ruth were together, but he must have known what was going on.'

I hesitated, heat rushing to my cheeks. 'I – I want it to be something, but I'm scared,' I said, surprised by how vulnerable I sounded.

Stace tilted her head. 'Scared of what, babe?' Her tone was gentle, her concern genuine.

'So many things,' I said, my throat tightening. I was desperate not to ramble, but the words started pouring out. 'I'm not "out" yet. What if everything changes? What if people look at me differently? It's terrifying – the unknown.' I made myself stop, and I smiled sheepishly. 'Sorry, that was too much. It must be the wine talking.'

'No, don't be silly, I *want* to know.' Stace rubbed my arm again, her voice soft. 'Georgia doesn't really like to talk about these things. I obviously won't tell Mike – or anyone else. Change is scary, babe, but you shouldn't let fear decide your fate. That's what my friend Caz always says. Life's too short to worry about what others think. You need to focus on your happiness.'

I glanced towards the bar, catching sight of Georgia, still waiting to be served. She looked effortlessly stunning, wearing rust-coloured jeans rolled up at the ankles, an oversized white T-shirt overlaid with dainty gold chains at the neck, and white trainers. She was the kind of woman who didn't even have to try to be the most attractive person in the room. I ran my eyes down her body, and my mind flashed back to the weekend before, to the memory of her standing in my bedroom in that tight police officer's uniform we'd ordered online – a dark blue shirt with silver buttons, a badge over her heart, and fitted trousers that hugged her curves, with a leather belt holding faux handcuffs and a large truncheon at her side. I was dressed in a black-and-white-striped prisoner's top and a tight matching mini skirt that barely covered a thing. I thought of how she'd pressed me against the wall, arms behind my back, snapping the handcuffs into place with more expertise than I'd expected, her breath hot against my ear as she whispered 'Spread your legs' in a low voice that sent a shockwave straight through me. And to make things even spicier, we filmed the whole thing on my phone. Watching it back later was another kind of thrill altogether. It was so out of the box for us – something we'd never done before – but that didn't mean we couldn't experiment. And God, it was so fucking hot. I blinked away the memory. Not the kind of thing to be thinking about in front of Stace and Gemma.

'You're right, Stace,' I said, exhaling slowly. 'I shouldn't let fear decide my fate. Thank you.' I stood up, feeling a sudden surge of resolve. 'I'm going to go talk to her. Right now.'

Stace's face lit up as she pulled me into a tight hug. 'Go for it,' she whispered. 'She's lucky to have you, and you're lucky to have her.'

Gemma joined the hug, and I couldn't help but laugh; it felt so good to feel part of Georgia's family. To feel liked.

I weaved through the crowd, making my way to Georgia, who was still yet to be served. She stretched out a welcoming arm when she saw me approaching.

I bit my lip nervously. 'Can we go back to mine?' I asked, leaning into her, feeling her arm curl around me, her fingers nestling into the dip along my spine.

'Now?'

I nodded quickly, feeling hundreds of eyes landing on us as we touched, though it was just as likely no one saw.

'Shouldn't we wait for Bex and Li?' she asked, glancing around. 'They went to the toilet together a few minutes ago.'

I wanted to pull her by the hand through the mass of people and take her to my flat, but I held back, knowing the right thing to do was to save their place at the bar.

'Still not served?' Bex's voice cut through the noise behind us, Li next to her.

'Nope. It's like I'm invisible,' Georgia said, rolling her eyes.

'I need to steal Georgia – sorry, girls,' I said quickly, giving them an apologetic smile. 'There's something I need to talk to her about.'

I saw Li's eyes scrunch with tenderness; she instinctively knew what I wanted to talk to Georgia about.

'But the night is young,' Bex said disappointedly.

Li smiled, nudging her playfully. 'Go on, lovebirds. We'll make sure Stace and Gemma get their drinks.'

'Spoil sports,' Bex said, jutting out her bottom lip. 'Fine, be off with you. I'm ordering a white chocolate cherry cocktail to cheer myself up.'

'That sounds disgusting, Bex,' Georgia said.

Li squeezed my hand, giving me an excited nod, silently wishing me luck.

I pulled Georgia towards the door, glancing back at Li and Bex. They were both smiling at us, Bex wrapping her arms around Li's waist from behind, stooping comically low to accommodate the height difference.

Just as we stepped onto the pavement, a deep voice stopped me cold. 'Jess.'

My heart dropped. I'd recognise that voice anywhere.

Chapter 22

'Joe.' I froze, fright seeping into me even though I knew he'd never do or say anything in public to expose the man he really was.

'Hi,' he said, too casually, as if he had planned for the encounter. Suspicion curled in my gut. He flashed his signature smile. 'And Georgia, lovely to see you again.'

Georgia stiffened beside me, her body language matching mine, but we both managed to force polite smiles.

'You look great, Jess,' he said, his eyes easing down my legs. 'How have you been?'

'Fine, thanks.' I kept my voice short, my nerves biting just under my skin.

'That's so great to hear,' he continued, the familiar charm masking something darker. He tilted his head slightly, as if studying me. 'I always knew you'd be fine. You were always stronger than you gave yourself credit for.'

I could feel the subtle dig in his words – the way he twisted things to remind me of the control he once had. That feeling of self-doubt crept in, despite knowing better.

'Not everyone can handle things the way you do,' he added with the faintest of smirks. 'It's impressive how you can get on with life so quickly.'

Georgia cleared her throat beside me, breaking the uncomfortable silence.

'Well, I won't keep you,' Joe said, flashing that grin again. He stepped a little closer, leaning in just enough to make me feel trapped. 'It was really wonderful to see you. I hope to bump into you again soon.'

I forced a smile that felt more like a grimace. 'Take care, Joe.'

'Always do,' he said, the words almost a whisper, before walking into the bar, leaving the weight of his presence lingering in the air.

***

As soon as Georgia and I were inside my flat, I closed the door behind me, resting my back against it and taking a deep, juddering breath, holding back tears even though nothing terrible had really happened.

Georgia reached out and gently touched my arm.

'I'm sorry,' I said. Just looking into her eyes made me feel safe. 'Seeing him again... it just stirred up so much.'

'You don't have to apologise. Come here.' She pulled me into a comforting hug, and it made me remember the urgency with which I had brought her here, wanting to tell her everything I had longed to say. I held her tight, letting the moment be enough until I was ready for more. I kissed her neck, almost crying, my breath hitching as I fought back tears. But the tears had nothing to do with Joe anymore; they were filled with love, safety, understanding.

She tilted her face towards mine, kissing one cheek and then the other. 'Don't let seeing him upset you,' she said, kissing my lips quickly before continuing, 'he can't hurt you now.'

I drew her face back to mine, light kisses deepening into something more passionate, feeling love ache inside my bones. I needed to tell her how I felt; showing her wasn't enough.

'I —' I couldn't say it, I couldn't say that I was ready to come out, or that I wanted to call her my girlfriend, officially, or that I fucking loved her with my whole heart. Why couldn't I say any of it? 'I want you,' I managed shakily, and in a second, I had her up against the wall and was frantically undoing her jeans while she kicked off her shoes. I slipped my hand into the waistband of her boxer shorts, wanting her so badly I could have burst. It was always a surprise to me how our passion seemed to increase every time we got our hands on each other; I'd think it couldn't get any more intense than the last time, but it always did. It was a fall-in-love-all-over-again type of connection.

With my fingers dipped inside her warmth, my words felt stuck in my throat. 'I think I'm—' My heart slammed against my chest. 'Falling in love with you.'

A heartbeat passed. 'I've already fallen,' she whispered before grabbing my face again and kissing me wildly.

We kissed frenziedly, hugging and squeezing our bodies against each other as I continued to plunge my fingers in and out of her, while on the verge of tears. Like lionesses, we rubbed our faces, heads and necks against each other, the animal sides of us in tune and our animal urges just as strong. Tongues tangled, we fell into a raw, primal, savage world of sheet-clawing sex, hungrily tasting each other's flesh, our cravings wild, voracious, fierce and feral. She lunged at me, pinned me down, bit my thighs, lapped at me, tore into me and ravaged me. We growled, screeched, scratched, sucked, cried and fucked without restraint, our bodies unravelling as we repeated our untamed 'I love you's.

***

In a half-awake state, I felt her arm reach around my waist and hug me into her body as the morning blazed through my flimsy bedroom blinds.

'Please, please tell me you remember what you said last night when you were drunk,' she said.

I turned to face her in the bed, moving my hands over her warmed-from-sleep nakedness, and through slow, smiling kisses on her neck and lightly freckled shoulders, I said, 'What's that? That... I love you?' I let the words toddle off the tip of my tongue and patter into her ear.

She exhaled, almost growled, in relief, and grabbed my face, caressing me with her expression for a moment before kissing me, the matching smiles impressed into our faces making us bump teeth. I felt groggy with love; only absorbing into her skin could have felt better. I was overflowing.

'Tell me I'm yours again,' I said.

'You're mine.' The gravity of her words settled over me like a reassuring weighted blanket.

I breathed her words in, feeling them infuse into my body. I lay there holding her, feeling my contentment. It shocked me how comfortable and natural I was with her, in every moment – even just-woken, 'ugly' moments.

With Joe, I would have only slept on my back to stop the makeup that I'd deliberately left on overnight from smudging, so that in the morning I would look presentable. I thought my looks were every-thing, my currency. I thought my worth and value were controlled by attractiveness.

When Joe and I were at university together, I vividly remember the first night we slept together in his room in halls. Afterward, Joe went into the communal kitchen next to his room to get us some post-sex drinks. The walls must have been paper-thin because I could hear everything he was saying to the boys from his floor, who were all congregated in the kitchen after their night out. I peered through the peephole at them all sitting around the kitchen table, with Joe directly in my eyeline. They were all patting him on the back at his 'conquest', and in what he must have thought was a voice low enough not to be heard by me, he started detailing what we had just done in bed – most of which was exaggerated beyond belief. The last thing he said before he made his way back to the bedroom was, 'Let's see if she goes from a ten to a two in the morning like most girls do, lads.' They all laughed and one of them said, 'That's why I always take them swimming on the first date, mate.'

That should have been a red flag, and it was, but I thought all men had red flags, and if I didn't accept one type of red flag I'd have to put up with another anyway. So that night, I slept perfectly still, got up before dawn to touch up my makeup using what few products I had with me in my handbag, brush my hair, and freshen up in case he wanted morning sex. Then I returned to stillness until he stirred, and when he turned over and saw me – my hair without a single knot, my cheeks rosy and my lips glossy – I knew he was impressed. He didn't compliment me, but I was confident that he would at least tell his friends that I woke up a ten. *She's not like other girls*, I imagined him saying. *She's wife material.*

I had to keep up that facade throughout our years together, never wanting him to find out I was anything less than perfect. I'd keep a mirror next to the bed and sleep with chewing gum in my mouth every night – which would often fall out and land in my hair while I slept. Being immaculately groomed became my whole personality; anything that stopped me from looking my best was off the agenda – any outdoor or hair-wetting exploit was a no; any activity that I couldn't feasibly wear flattering clothes to was a no; anything that involved messy food was a no. Everything fun was written off. I didn't care if I came across as boring, because at least I was beautiful.

I felt a tear roll down my cheek. I was free now. From the very first morning with Georgia, things had been different. I hadn't felt that creeping anxiety, the dread that I needed to be perfect before she opened her eyes. I didn't wake up early to fix my hair or paint my face. I didn't feel the need to impress her. Somehow, I just knew she wouldn't measure me by the smoothness of my skin or the way my hair fell perfectly into place. She'd always look at me like I was enough, like I was flawless even when I didn't try to be.

The first night we slept together, I woke up before her. My first instinct was to reach for my makeup, to start my usual routine. But then I stopped. I glanced over at her, still asleep, her face soft and relaxed, and I felt a wave of calm wash over me. For the first time in years, I let myself just be. I felt vulnerable, but also... safe. She didn't compare me to other women or hold me to impossible standards. She didn't make me feel like I had to compete. It was like she saw me – the real me, the woman underneath the mask – and that was who she wanted.

Chapter 23

I remember the very moment it all started unravelling.

The music was so loud I could feel it reverberating in my chest. That particular gay club we were at, Freedom, was my favourite, but it wasn't a place in which you could easily chat. Georgia, Li, Bex and I – the 'Fab Four' as we had begun calling ourselves – sat at a table, people-watching and sipping our drinks. My sour margarita shot thousands of miniature pins into the roof of my mouth as I danced in my seat. I was excited and alive. I had a fresh, new, vigorous appetite for life and a sense of real belonging.

Georgia's mouth approached my ear, and she asked me if I wanted to leave, go back to hers and snuggle. She said nights out weren't doing it for her anymore – she was over them. Her cheek pressed against mine as she explained how she couldn't care less if she never saw a dancefloor again, and I felt a frown carve itself between my eyebrows. I was just getting started on this new life of mine; our nights out in the gay clubs were collectively forming into the best good-old-days memory in my reminiscence bank, ready to be dusted off when I turned old and grey.

Senior me would wipe them over with her woollen sleeve, bring them closer and then further away from her face so as to let her eyes adjust to them, and then she'd clutch them to her chest, smiling. She'd feel the memories come flooding back, transporting her to those clubs where the air nettled with excitement and where her young heart drummed with energy.

What Georgia was bored with, I was riveted by. It was the law of the lever; when one side of the seesaw went up, the other had to come down. That was fine though; relationships were all about balance, give and take, compromise and negotiation, working around the small eddies beneath the surface. I knew we could find our way around all challenges – trivial or significant – as they presented themselves.

Someone walked up to our table and stopped at me. My eyes widened seeing that it was Carys, *The City Post*'s photographer. Her mouth opened wide in a silent burst of enthusiasm, and she started speaking. I pointed to my ears, shaking my head to convey that I couldn't hear her over the music.

She leaned closer. 'What are you doing here?' she yelled animatedly.

'Just with friends,' I mouthed silently, pointing at the girls, trying to seem indifferent to her presence.

'What?' she shouted.

'Just with friends,' I yelled back.

'I didn't realise you came to gay bars; you're not gay, are you?'

'No way!' I shouted back immediately, laughing nervously. 'Just having a night out with friends.'

'Oh cool. I'm with my cousin.' Carys rolled her eyes playfully. 'She's like, *super* gay. You know, rainbows on everything, watches *The L Word* on repeat, the whole deal. See you on the dancefloor later?'

I gave her a thumbs up while nodding heartily and then turned back to the table. I felt Georgia bristling next to me and turned to meet her eyes, which were pooling with hurt.

I tried to explain how I didn't want people to gossip about my sexuality at work, but she turned away from me.

'Come to the toilets with me,' I said quickly, worrying.

She stood without looking at me and started walking towards the back of the room where the toilets were.

'I'm so sorry,' I said, closing the door to the cubicle that we'd previously had sex in twice – the memory of the most recent time flashing into my mind, giving me a surge below. A week or so before, she had pushed me against that very wall, crouched down in front of me, reached under my skirt and slowly pulled down my thong while looking up at me. I stepped out of it and she put it in her back pocket for safekeeping before inching my skirt up and then sliding her tongue onto me. She'd had her hands on my ass, with her forearms pressing on the outsides of my thighs, ensuring my legs stayed together so that she could part me with her tongue only; she'd never gone down on me in that position before – most of the other times I'd felt her tongue on me, I had been lying down with my legs apart. It had been so surprising a sensation; I think gravity had some part to play – maybe the erogenous blood rushed down there faster than it would have if I were horizontal, or maybe it was just the new angle she was hitting with her mouth and fingers. After a few minutes, she pushed my legs apart and hooked one over her shoulder, so that she had better access to me. I'd held the back of her neck, closed my eyes and allowed myself to get lost in her fucking me to the beat of the music that was thumping through the speaker in the bathroom.

'Carys caught me off-guard,' I said pleadingly now, 'and I just said the first thing that came to mind, to protect myself. I'm not ready for everyone at work to know yet.'

'It's like you're embarrassed of me,' she said, her voice steady and calm but tinged with sadness. 'The way you shouted "No way!" when she asked if you were gay – like that would be the worst thing in the world.'

'In all fairness, we haven't had that conversation, not properly. You've always been so patient with me when it comes to me not being ready to come out. I didn't think the pressure was on all that much.'

'You told me you loved me, Jess. I assumed that meant you wanted to be together and that you were ready.'

'I do love you, but I'm not ready to out myself. They are two separate things.' She looked away from me, but I continued. 'I'm not ready to let the world know yet. Why complicate things right now? They are so perfect. I don't have to explain myself to anyone but you. I'm living the life I've always dreamed of, but I want to do that privately for now.' I just wanted to continue as we were – secretly being with her, in our own bubble. What was so wrong with wanting to keep quiet – so that I wouldn't have to worry my parents; or be judged by my colleagues; or confuse Gwen or my other neighbours; or offend strangers? I just wanted to fit in with society and not be stared at or treated differently. I wanted to be safe around the lunatics out there who thought gay people either didn't deserve to be happy or were mentally unhinged. And I wanted, maybe needed, to retain the impact I had on men – an impact which afforded me safety – that would surely fizzle and die if they knew I'd chosen a woman over them.

I knew we couldn't stay a secret forever – that would mean not being able to share important life events with family and friends, never marrying her, never having a family with her. It would mean not being able to fully share life together, and that would certainly be a time-limited relationship. But I just needed a little *more* time.

'Being gay isn't a criminal offence; we don't have to hide,' she said, her voice still calm, contained.

'No, we don't have to, but my life will change, and everyone will see me differently,' I said, my voice brimming with vulnerability and panic.

'Doesn't love outweigh anxiety? Are you really willing to lose what we have over the chance of feeling uncomfortable around the people who care about you – people who will continue to love you and learn to accept this new part of you when they see how happy it makes you?'

I looked at her and knew, with absolute certainty, as certainly as I knew I would die one day, that I loved her more than my own life. 'It's not that simple,' I said, staring at the floor. 'Or perhaps it is. But it's the unknown, and I'm not ready. Plus, this is my first go at a relationship with a girl; how am I supposed to know it's worth coming out for?'

The silence gaped as dread engulfed me. Why the fuck did I say that? I hadn't meant it; the wrong words just slipped out of my mouth. There was no taking them back.

'No, wait!' I blocked the door as she went to unlock it. 'That came out so wrong. I'm so sorry. I meant, what if one day you left me after I exposed everything?'

She stayed silent, tonguing her cheek, not looking at me. My face started to burn and my stomach stirred with a fear that she was just going to walk away from me, and that would be it.

'I'm so sorry. I didn't mean that at all – I promise.' I hugged her tight and continued to speak over her shoulder, horrified, scolding myself silently. 'I meant, what if I upheave my entire life and then once we're "official" it doesn't actually work because the secrecy and fun is gone and you want to leave me?' What if the glue that bonded us was just our shared excitement over this undercover life we were living? What if once we were out, we couldn't hack the attention? What if we were followed and attacked? I was scared by it all. Staying as we were would avoid all of that. 'Please say something.'

'If you think that, then that answers the question, Jess.'

'No! It doesn't. What you're asking is to choose you or life as I know it. I could never go back to normality if I came out. You've been so patient with me, please don't just spring this on me. I've hidden my feelings about women my entire life, so I can't come out of hiding at the drop of a hat.'

'Well, why should *I* hide?' she asked.

I couldn't answer that. 'George, I want everything you want. But what if holding your hand and kissing you in public leads to terrible things? We can't control other people's reactions, and you said yourself that when you were with Ruth, men would approach you and say abusive things; you said you were worried that someone might even attack you for it.'

'I should never have said that. That was stupid. I don't actually think anyone would hurt me for being a lesbian.'

'It's not stupid. It happens all the time.'

She closed her eyes.

I lifted her chin and locked my eyes with hers. 'Please, please know that even if our relationship isn't seen by other people, it is still just as important. It's the best thing that's ever happened to me. I don't want you to feel like our love is somehow lessened if we can't show it off. We can have this incredible connection without anyone else witnessing it. I promise it won't be this way forever, but it doesn't mean that what I feel right now isn't legitimate. I want so much to be free to show off what we have, parade it, but I'm just not quite there yet.'

She put her palms to her temples. 'I don't want to be waiting around for years if that's how long you think it will take.'

'It won't be years. I'll just have to tell you when I know, when I feel it. It's a process; it's not black and white. George, this isn't about you; it pre-existed you. I've been in the closet my whole life.'

She still wouldn't look at me. 'I think, if I said right now that I was going to walk away unless you were ready to be with me, you'd let me.' She sounded so defeated, so close to giving up, and I felt a bright flare of panic; I couldn't lose her. But I was also angry at her words, the nature of them, the way they cornered me and towered over me.

'Don't say that.'

'Ruth was never ready either, and look how that turned out.' She looked at me and I could see the anguish underneath her mask of calm.

'I just want time,' I said. 'Time to think, talk and take baby steps towards this. It should be a good, exciting feeling to come out, and I want to wait for that, and I know it's around the corner somewhere. Please know that I love you incredible, unspeakable amounts.'

'There's a queue out here,' shouted a voice from outside the cubicle, followed by a few bangs to the door. 'Seriously, come on, we need to piss.'

Chapter 24

Li and I huddled at the edge of the field under an umbrella – a typical summer's night in Wales – watching Bex, Georgia, and the rest of the football players fight for control of the ball under the harsh glare of the floodlights. Around us, small groups were scattered, their cheers faint in the cool night air. It wasn't a big crowd, but enough to give the match a pulse.

The players dashed through the mist, boots trampling and occasionally slipping on the slick grass. Breathless shouts emerged as they jostled shoulder-to-shoulder, vying for possession, rain trickling down their faces and mud flecking their legs. Georgia's passion was alive, sexy, her focus unwavering as she kept her eyes locked on the ball. It came flying towards a teammate beside her, who met it with a solid pass to Georgia. Without hesitation, she stretched out her leg and, with a powerful strike, sent it soaring into the net, past the goalkeeper's desperate dive. Her team erupted into cheers, and her ex, Ruth, was by her side in an instant, clapping her on the back. If Ruth's hand lingered a bit longer than necessary, nobody noticed except me.

When the final whistle blew, Bex jogged over to Li and grabbed her face with muddy hands, smearing dirt on her cheeks as she kissed her, which Li took in stride, grinning back at her. Georgia didn't stop to join us. She only shot a brief, tight smile our way before heading towards the car park, where her VW was parked about twenty metres away. It had been days since we'd talked at the club – the longest we'd gone without seeing each other. I watched her walk, shoulders tense, as she opened the boot of her car and pulled out a towel. I wanted to go over, to say something, to apologise, but before I could move, Ruth passed me, quickening her pace to catch up with Georgia. A bitter knot of jealousy twisted in my gut as I watched them talk. Georgia's expression stayed neutral, barely acknowledging Ruth, which soothed me a little. But the way Ruth leaned in, her eagerness to be close to Georgia, made my chest tighten.

***

'I think Ruth is still in love with you,' I said while Georgia was driving me back to my flat.

'What?' Georgia screwed up her face while turning a corner, using just one hand – the flat of her palm – to turn the steering wheel; even her driving skills were erotic. 'There's no way. She dumped me for a guy, remember? A six-foot, muscly man fifteen years older than me – the opposite of me in every way. And then she married him.'

'Are you still close?' I asked, starting my tentative line of questioning, aware that I was entering volatile territory as she was still upset from our recent argument.

'No, not at all,' she said reassuringly. 'We don't see each other outside of footy, and even then, it's not a one-on-one thing; all the girls just chat together.'

I believed her. It was a strange feeling, knowing unequivocally that my partner was telling the truth. I hadn't experienced that with anyone before; I'd always assumed they were cheating on me – and later had my suspicions confirmed on a few occasions – it was just something that I accepted happened in most relationships.

'What was she talking to you about when she sprinted over to you earlier?' I asked.

'She congratulated me on my goal and talked about how the game went,' she said. 'I kept trying to end the conversation. I can tell her to back off if it makes you uncomfortable – she is my ex, after all.'

'I am a bit uncomfortable as she seemed really into you, but I'm not going to ask you to stop talking to her. That would be super awkward for you.'

'No it wouldn't.' She shrugged and shook her head. 'I would just tell her straight; it doesn't bother me. I don't owe her anything. You matter more.'

She always had this way of putting me first, which seemed to come so naturally to her. I glanced down at her mud-stained hand on the gear stick – such a sexy hand; gentle but strong, with skilled fingers that had been inside me so many times. I felt a spasm between my legs.

She always rested it on the gear stick while driving. I would nervously drive with my hands at ten and two, but she was so relaxed, and she never went over the speed limit – she was fantastically safe like that, such a rock in every way.

'Why are you being so nice to me after what happened the other night?' I asked. 'I feel like such a dick for what I said.'

'You don't have to feel that way,' she said. 'I was in the wrong for springing all that on you; I just felt out of my mind for a second. I'm impatient because I love you, and I want all of you, and I want everyone to know you're mine.'

My mouth formed itself to say *I want that too*, and I meant it, more than anything, but I stopped myself in case it was a confusing message. I put my hand on top of hers instead.

'Sorry, that wasn't me trying to put pressure on you again,' she said. 'I promise.'

Shit. *She* was apologising to *me*? I suddenly felt like Joe – when he'd do something wrong and would manipulate me into apologising for it. Was I a Joe? Did she feel compelled to say sorry even though she'd done nothing wrong? I leant in to kiss her at the traffic lights as there was no one around. I seized her face in both hands and she clutched onto my thigh.

Suddenly, a car behind us beeped.

'Fuck, the light's green,' I muttered, startled, realising we needed to move quickly. Georgia fumbled for the gear stick, but the aggravated driver – a large man in his forties, with orange, reflective wrap-around shades on – pulled around us and slammed on his brakes when he was parallel to her car.

'Fucking lesbians,' he shouted through his open window. 'The world would be a much better place if you lot disappeared.' Then, I was sure he added quietly, 'Just fucking die already.'

Chapter 25

I watched her spirit slowly erode with each day I kept her holding on for an answer as to when I was going to be 'ready'. I wanted to come out from hiding with her, I did, but something was stopping me. I was scared of what coming out would mean for me, but the new pressure on me had made me dive deeper into my reveries about other women. I had tried so hard to push them down, but my fantasies were so close I could almost touch them.

When I had been with men and had my regular fantasies about women, they felt dream-like, fantastical and so far away. But I finally knew what it was like to touch a woman and to have one touch me. And I wanted more. I wanted to fly off in all directions, like the flares of a firework. But I also wanted to float back down to earth after my colours had filled the sky and be with Georgia forever.

I knew I couldn't stay in limbo for long and I had to make a decision. It was a constant ticking clock. Being granted time didn't feel like a luxury. It was sands through the hourglass, and every day, time was closer to running out while I remained in decision paralysis.

Even though, since that night in Freedom's toilet stall, Georgia hadn't brought it up again, it had become an unspoken yell in my ear every morning I woke up; I *felt* her waiting. Each day brought with it this giant, dark looming presence; it was in every room I walked into; it lurked in the corners or followed me outside. It was a beast of a thing; slowly advancing, nibbling away at my edges. I thought of myself in Georgia's shoes and how she must have felt: small, neglected, unimportant and unchosen; a dirty, shameful secret. If I had been the one ready to come out and she wasn't, I'd feel worthless, and I'd wonder why she didn't love me enough to take a risk for me.

'So, what's your lesson plan for today?' I asked as we sat down for breakfast at my dining table.

Georgia looked up from her coffee, her eye contact evasive. 'Combinatorial game theory.'

'What's that?'

'We'll look at simple games, like noughts and crosses, and how they relate to mathematical strategy.'

'That sounds fun,' I said, trying to keep my tone upbeat. Every conversation we'd been having felt more and more forced, uneasy or insincere because there was only one thing we knew we should have been talking about, and we were avoiding it.

'Yeah, it's a good way to show how maths can be applied in a real-world context.'

'Do the kids enjoy it?'

'Usually, especially when they see the patterns emerging.'

'That's great,' I said, nodding. The atmosphere ached with a longing for me to shout, *Oh fuck it! I'm ready!* I yearned to say it and I knew she burned to hear it. But the finality of those words petrified me; there was no going back from them – that would mean the start of the unknown, the start of a new forever. I couldn't go back and forth on my word; I had to be sure. So I stayed quiet, like the coward I was – the coward that was being offered everything she'd ever dreamed of on a silver platter, but wouldn't take it. 'It's amazing how you make maths so accessible.'

She smiled. 'Thanks. I hope I do.'

There was a heavy silence after that, punctuated only by the clinking of cutlery. Georgia's gaze wandered, and I could feel the weight of the unspoken conversation hanging between us. My heart was breaking, and it was my doing.

I kept mulling over what coming out would mean. 'The lesbian' – that would be how people would see me. It would be my identifier. But I liked to be a shapeshifter, morphing into what each person needed or wanted me to be, and I wouldn't be able to do that if I was 'the lesbian'. I wouldn't be able to continue pulling on any chosen mask or don any personality depending on who I was with at any given time. I didn't want my sweet old neighbour Gwen to see me as anything other than the lovely girl who always popped in to see how she was doing. I didn't want the girls who sat next to me at work to worry that 'the lesbian' would look at their bums when they left their seats. I didn't want the guy flirting with me at a media networking event to think I hated men.

My shape-shifter nature was why I liked to keep my friends separate too. I didn't have groups of friends – apart from the Fab Four – instead I had one friend here, one friend there. They were acquaintances more than friends, really. If they had ever all been in a room together, I wouldn't have known how to act; they all knew such different versions of me.

I was a chameleon. Whatever someone wanted me to be, I became a facsimile of that for them. Like when Li felt too shy to order at restaurants or bars, I'd take charge and take care of it. It was like my anxiety had a loophole, that if somebody else was more uncomfortable than I was, I developed the sudden ability to take control. I couldn't ask for a drink refill for myself, but if Li wanted one, I was out of my seat in a second.

And past versions of me – made for friends I'd since lost or left behind – included the hyper one; the sombre one; the motherly one; the insecure one; the body-positive one; and the fiery one who didn't take any shit. Whether my acquaintances were looking for a carbon copy of themselves to expound their interests to; or if they were power-hungry and wanted someone to push around; or if they were timid and needed someone to take the reins, I was that person for them. It made them like me and feel good about themselves.

It wasn't like I missed being 'myself' with any of them, because I didn't know who I was anyway. I didn't know which version of myself I aligned with most, or what my hobbies were, or what music I liked, or what interested me. I was still searching for all the answers to those questions that came so naturally to everybody else. Not knowing myself had its perks, though. I could pass it off as an air of mystery.

Acquaintances seemed drawn to my unknowability; it intrigued them. I was an enigma. And while I pretended to them, I could pretend to myself too. I had become reliant on self-deception. Before finding the queer scene, I didn't have a place in society, nowhere that I neatly fitted in, so when I acted a part, it meant I morphed into someone people would respect. I learnt to mirror, mask and mimic so well that I could befriend almost anyone, but I rarely felt a genuine connection with any of them. And the friendships never lasted very long; I didn't feel good enough for them and would push people away before they could do it to me. Joe had slowly reinforced the belief that I was a good-for-nothing, sorry excuse for a human, and years of being told just that – not to mention the arguments it would create if

I pushed back – had me immobilised with self-doubt. He had drip-fed the comments, by degrees, and like a frog being gradually boiled alive, before I knew it, I was soup.

Li was the only true friend I'd ever managed to hold on to; she was my special one. The Fab Four was all I had at that point. Li had bought us all cringe-worthy matching Besties for the Resties bumper stickers for our cars; we felt like a proper team. I was relaxed around them and felt more myself around Georgia than I did around anyone. I was getting to know myself as much as I was getting to know her.

Maybe that was the reason I longed to explore my feelings and fantasies about other women, because the real me was desperate to be found, and finding yourself comes from experience. Some people long to travel, and they find themselves through adventure; their feet learn how to form their own paths and their hearts begin to beat to different rhythms. My longing for adventure had always been in the form of women and the freedom to get into bed with as many as I wanted to. I want to bite into life, tear at it, rip it to shreds.

I pined to experience what I'd always dreamt of, but giving myself wholly and fully to Georgia would mean the closure of those opportunities. I had reached a point where this was my one and only chance to explore. I'd never had a spontaneous hook-up, not with any gender; my record was spotless in that regard. Georgia was proof of how amazing sex with a woman could be, and part of me craved more experiences like that with others while I was still young. But I also just wanted her, desperately and forever.

If only I could have split into two and lived both lives; I was torn and tortured by the choice – the near-misses, the what-ifs, the regrets, the relief, the wonder, the excitement, the awe of each. I'd never know the reality of the choice I'd left behind.

***

'Don't be nervous; she's going to love you,' I said to Li over the phone. She was getting ready for her trip up north to meet Bex's auntie for the first time. After Bex came out as gay, her parents had severed ties, kicking her out of the family home when she was just eighteen. That painful rift still lingered, but her auntie had always been supportive.

'I really hope so,' Li said. 'I've got a big box of chocolates and a bunch of flowers for her. Should I take anything else?'

'I think that's perfect.' I heard my voice waver. 'When do you leave?'

'Bex is coming to pick me up in about ten minutes.'

'What are you wearing to meet her?'

'One sec.'

My phone chimed – she'd sent me a picture of her wearing a respectable blouse and tailored trousers.

'Beautiful on the surface and all the way through,' I said, my voice catching again.

'Thank you.' Her voice adjusted with concern. 'Jess, you don't sound yourself. Is something wrong?'

I sighed hard. 'Can I ask you something really personal?' As I spoke, I picked up a pen and started mindlessly doodling on a pad of paper, swirls and shapes forming on the page without any real thought behind them.

'Always.'

'Do you ever feel, because Bex is the first girl you've been with, like you're missing out on new experiences... with others?'

'In all honesty, no. I love Bex. She's all I want.' After a pause, she continued. 'Talk to me, Jess.'

'I love Georgia. I love her so much it hurts.' I meant that. 'But I keep having these thoughts that won't go away. I locked myself down with boys for so many years, and now I'm confining myself to one woman, closing myself off again.' All future opportunities were dangling before me and, as I watched them, they were all shrivelling, rotting and dropping to the floor like Sylvia Plath's metaphorical figs. I traced a thick line through the doodle, feeling some of my frustration transfer into the pen.

Li's response was gentle, almost as if her words were wrapping me in a warm hug. 'I think it's normal to have curiosities. They don't make you a bad person, Jess. You shouldn't feel pressured to fit into a box or live up to any expectation; your feelings are your own, and it's OK to have them.'

'Silly question probably, but how do you know you're lesbian, Li?'

'Well, because I'm in love with a woman, I guess.'

'But that's like saying you were straight when you were in love with Nathan. People can't suddenly "turn" lesbian, surely? Sexuality is about who you're attracted to, not who you've slept with, after all. Or maybe you're bi, or pansexual, or some other form of queer...'

'I hadn't thought about it like that,' Li said, as if wondering to herself. 'I guess it's the label I most align with, if I had to have one.'

'I think I'm having an identity crisis.' I laughed, but I meant it. It felt like my mind was consumed by wanderlust for the queer world and the desire to find my perfect place within it. 'I've even been reading up about polyamorous people in case that's what's going on with me. I've been trying to think of all possibilities as to why I feel this way. I've even wondered if I'm just making things up; like, am I just looking for drama? Trying to give myself an edge? Am I pretending? Or maybe that awful thing that happened when I was a kid made me so scared of men that my brain tricked me into thinking I wanted women.' I forced another laugh. 'Sorry, Bex is picking you up in a few minutes; this is a big day for you and I'm wittering on.'

'I'll always have time for you. No matter what. Have you told Georgia any of this?'

'God, no. I don't want to upset her, and besides, I don't even know what I'm feeling right now; my head's a mess.' I stared at the page, my drawing now a tangled, messy maze of lines and swirls. 'There's no point in worrying her for nothing.'

'You don't have to have all the answers,' Li said, and I knew she'd be squeezing my hand or rubbing my back if she had been next to me then. 'Let's take our time and figure this out together.'

'I'm going to let you go now, otherwise I'll make you late, Li.'

'It's no problem, I—'

'Li. Have the best day. She will love you.'

'Call me if you need me, OK, Jess?'

'I will. Good luck. You've got this.'

After hanging up, I padded across the hall to Gwen's flat in my slippers and made us both a cup of tea. I always told myself these little visits were for her – so she'd have some company – but the truth was, they were just as much for me.

That night, I dreamt of Georgia. We had landed on an unknown planet. She was standing in front of me, smiling, and as I looked beyond her, the landscape unfolded in a breathtaking panorama. Lush blue, purple and pink undulating mountain terrains dominated the horizon; vast unexplored plains sprawled out, an invitation into the unknown; ethereal swirling rivers of iridescent colour painted the atmosphere in a mesmerising spectacle; and distant coos and shrieks of never-before-discovered life echoed behind her.

She remained the focal point in my vision. She stood on terracotta rocky land, ochre dust blowing in loose swirls at her feet, her frame absorbing the radiant light, and she was reaching out to hold my hand, ready to escort me into a little house made just for us.

She didn't attempt to explain what was going on, but I somehow knew that if we entered the house, the door would deadbolt and we'd be inside forever; the two of us would exist in an eternal sanctuary, cut off from the wonders outside. I'd only be able to peer out of the windows, never experiencing the new world in person. If I were at the right angle and looked out of the window at the right time, I'd be able to spot the two suns filling the sky with their luminous palettes that I didn't know existed, their rays intersecting to create a technicolour sunset. From behind the windows, I'd also be able to glimpse the many moons pinned overhead, and the ballet of shooting stars; and I could watch the way the enormous flowers of all colours bloomed spectacularly by day, and sealed themselves by night. Behind the glass, I'd marvel at how high the geysers would shoot their luminous jets into the air, and how their shimmering mists would eddy around in the atmosphere; and maybe, if I was lucky, I'd spot one of the sapient species passing on wing, foot or belly – traversing in manners beyond my understanding. But I could never leave the house.

Confined within those walls, I'd remain a spectator, forever separated from the allure of the unexplored. *But perhaps it would be safer inside,* thought my cowardly side. *The creatures on this planet may want to hurt us. It would be a sheltered life, but a secure one.*

I owed this new world to her, but everything in it beckoned me to discover it – like a faint, sweet song drifting in the air that I needed to follow. But if I chose to explore, it would mean I'd be cast out of the house; I'd be homeless, alone in this new world.

In the dream, I let go of her hand and started to run into the unknown. But then my steps became slower and slower until I wasn't even walking anymore and I was back outside the door of the little house. My sprint had taken me in a full circle. I was standing and staring at the house, stuck to the spot, willing myself to move forward towards it. I didn't know what to choose – even my subconscious didn't have an answer.

A heightening mess of thoughts piled up in my mind like a mountain of unread letters on the hallway mat of a yet-undiscovered dead homeowner. If only I'd had the chance to be single, even for a brief while before meeting her, I would have been exactly where I needed to be – with everything out of my system. But having such a hole in me, an unfulfilled, eager, excited, cavernous space brimming with possibilities, just couldn't be ignored, even though I tried every day. The frustrating truth was emerging: I could no longer ignore the greedy demands or the persistent nagging of my own imagination.

Chapter 26

S ince the age of twelve, I had been locked inside secret hiding
places. There were four in total. Each hideaway was constructed
from the skin of the boy or the man who chose to offer me refuge.
I suppose this might sound strange, but it's how I understood my
relationships when I was younger. Each new relationship felt like
slipping into a bunker, a den, a protective shell that shielded me from
the world. Like I was inside their skin. At that tender age, and given
the trauma I'd experienced, I saw things differently – everything was
shaped by my need for safety and protection.

As soon as one hideaway deteriorated, which always took an un-
predictable number of years, I immediately entered the next; I never
left one without having another lined up ready to jump into.

After that boy forced himself on me when I was eleven, I knew I
needed protectors to keep me safe from predators like him. Coupling
up was all I'd known since then. It made me realise that this was
everyone else's world, and I was just living in it. Everyone knew I wasn't
supposed to be in this world, but I didn't know how to leave. I never

belonged. I was an outsider, and the all-knowing eyes of the rest of the world judged me as an alien. They exchanged glances and whispered about me. Somehow, everyone else seemed to know what to do and how to act, as if everyone had the rulebook except me.

When I found a boy or man who wanted me, or even accepted me, I eagerly clambered into the skin prison they so readily offered me. I huddled down, hugged my knees and welcomed the pressure of the hermetic sealing process. I savoured my final deep inhalations of fresh oxygen before the structure became airtight and impenetrable, pressing down on the back of my neck as I bowed my head and submitted.

I was secure when inside, I didn't have to brave the world alone. I blended in. Hidden as part of a two. Veiled in flesh.

She must be one of us, people would think when they did, on occasion, spot me. *One of our own has accepted her.* And I could be carefully carried around inside my suffocating, claustrophobic disguise forever – undisturbed, within the cover of another's microbiome.

Of course, beneath the security and protection of these enclosures, there was no light, no control, no joy, no love, no freedom. But I chose incarceration. It was the lesser of two evils, staying inside a skin container. It was the safest I could be. Even so, there always lingered the knowledge that even just existing and breathing in that one spot was me taking up too much room in the world.

Then, in a whirlwind, I found myself climbing inside Georgia's skin. It was soft and warm inside her; it made me feel nourished, as if in utero. I'd been floating serenely, immersed in the bath-warm amniotic tranquillity of not only being safe but, for the first time, also being truly loved. And I truly loved her in return. But I was no longer invisible. Attention was being drawn. And attention was dangerous. People stared harder at me than they did before, their discrimination suddenly two-fold because, not only was I an outsider who didn't belong in the world, but I was a queer one – more alien and more 'other' than before. And I was about to be outed.

Inside her, inside Georgia's skin, was where I was meant to be. But despite my happiness, the longer I stayed, the more people were turning to look – and the more curious, critical and condemnatory they were becoming. They were edging closer and closer, reminding me of zombies who slowly cricked their necks towards any slight noise or movement made by the living. They were all listening for me, searching for me, trying to spot me in the crowd. It was as if the walls of my once-secure skin sanctuary were slowly turning transparent. People gawped at us, laughed at us, shouted at us through car windows, threw peanuts at us, and tossed death threats at us. As far as they were concerned, a woman wasn't supposed to be with a woman, and I was far too conspicuous when I was with her. I lived in constant fear of being discovered. And Georgia *wanted* it to be that way, she was ready to take that on; she wanted to show me off to the world. But I still wanted to hide.

The longer I stayed in there, in her skin, the more chance I had of being outed, and I wasn't ready. Onlookers inched closer, gathering in numbers. I needed to find my way out, and fast.

I patted frantically around the inside of the living structure searching for a weak spot in the vessel-rich walls. I took out my pocketknife – which I kept on my keyring at all times for protection – and it glinted as I flipped it open. I made my first cut into the ceiling of my beloved skin sanctuary, the only place that had felt right in my life.

'I think I need to have some time to myself,' I told Georgia, the words sharp and sudden. 'A pause to figure out what to do.'

'What does that mean?' she asked, her eyes widening; I felt her stomach drop just by looking into them. She wilted on the bench, our bench, at Lake Calon, her mouth vulnerable.

'I just feel like there's so much pressure for me to come out and—'

Her lips opened. 'Wait!' she interrupted, almost vomiting out the word. 'I haven't put any pressure on you since that night at Freedom. I've been waiting patiently and haven't spoken a word about what I've been feeling.' Her words shook their fists with insistence, and she was absolutely right.

'Exactly. And I could *feel* that. I could feel you holding back,' I said, continuing my stabs and incisions from the inside of the relationship. 'The thing is, we've barely had anything else to say to each other because there's been nothing else on our minds apart from this one topic.' For weeks, it was as if a fire had been raging in the middle of the room and we had just been pretending it wasn't there, even though the flames were making us sweat and the smoke was thick and up to our chins, and we were having to raise up out of it on our tiptoes just to breathe. 'It's all on me,' I continued, as sensitively as possible to the crown of her lovely head as she hung it, watching a fine mist of drizzle start to cling to her hair. 'You're ready for this. I'm not. So I'm the one the focus is on. You've barely kissed me since that night at Freedom,' I added, bracing as I drove the knife in deeper, feeling the sinews catch on the blade, trying my best to avoid any more of the tiny blue vessels, several of which were already spurting and spraying like burst pipes and threatening to flood my skin sanctuary. 'It's like I'm being punished. I don't feel free to choose to come out or not; I feel like I've been pushed into a corner. If I have an alternative opinion, it will upset you; there's only one answer you're looking for, and I'm just disappointing you.'

'So, in other words, you feel trapped?' she asked, the choked-out words limping their way across the bench to me.

'Not trapped, I just... need a breather from it all.'

A pale knowing washed over her face. 'Does a "breather" mean you'd be single?' Her voice wavered, and she swiped at her teary eyes aggressively, like she didn't have time for crying.

I hesitated, not knowing what to say. The answer was yes, I would be temporarily single, but I racked my brain for some conciliatory phrasing, searching for wording that would hurt less. While my mouth was on pause, I continued to chop and hack at the skin container's fibrous structure from the inside, readying myself for escape, even though escape wasn't what I wanted. Not really.

'I'm not for a second saying I want to be with anyone else, nor do I have any plans to be,' I said, focusing on the floor, hoping she wouldn't see the lie in my eyes. 'I just want to feel completely free for a moment.'

She was spluttering and shaking all over – it wasn't a constant shake, just every few seconds – her body was convulsing with it; it was taking over her jaw when she tried to speak, her mouth and tongue seemingly rigid and unable to form words properly, like when you're terribly cold. Or maybe she *was* just cold, as the wind had picked up and we were wearing T-shirts, caught off guard by how the warm day had turned suddenly brisk.

Tears poured from her, dispensing directly onto the gravel and dirt because of the angle that her head hung, her chin resting on her chest as she sobbed. It pained me to see her distress, but I still kept hacking away.

'You feel no sympathy, do you?' she said, pushing rich sobs out of her lungs, scanning my dry eyes as I felt myself slowly turn to stone, frozen, too aware of the heads turning to look at us, our heated argument disrupting the peace of the surroundings.

'Of course I do,' I said with sincerity and some anger in my voice, the blood from the relationship's injuries making my hair and clothes heavy. 'I care about you more than I care about anyone. It fucking terrifies me how much I care. And I'm so sorry. I just don't know what else to do.'

Neither of us spoke for a few excruciating, fragile beats, the chill in the air between us becoming increasingly apparent.

'I just don't know what to do,' I repeated, feeling numbness seep through my body, just wanting the conversation to be over so as to pause her pain. Or was it to get away quickly with my act of subterfuge? 'I'm at a standstill.'

'You just want a break so you can have sex with other women and get it out of your system before coming back to me and settling down, don't you?'

'That's not true,' I said emphatically, secretly frustrated by how well she saw through me.

'I won't be here for you at the end of it if you do that.'

'But see, that's you putting barriers up, and I need complete freedom otherwise this isn't going to work.' I could hear the manipulation in my voice; it was like something out of Joe's playbook, and I hated myself for it. I wanted to take it all back immediately and stop being such a monster to the woman who loved me, and who I loved in return. But the words wouldn't retreat. Why couldn't I just be honest with her? Why couldn't I just tell her I needed to explore my queerness, outside of a relationship? Honesty would break her heart, that was why, but her heart was shattering regardless – I was all but sawing it in two as we spoke.

'So you're happy to lose me?' she asked, and I could see the hope in her bloodshot eyes that I would take everything back.

'I love you so much, but I think I'll have to take that risk for a short while, because I can't stay where I am at the moment; it's driving me insane. But please, please, please can we still be friends and see each other during the break?'

Her jaw dropped. 'Friends?' she said loudly. 'Just be honest with me and tell me you want to play the field. You want to keep me on the sidelines until you're ready to come back to me. You just expect me to be patient while you go mess around and then accept you back with open arms on your terms.'

She wanted the unvarnished version, the raw, horrendous truth. I wished she would just accept my circumlocution. I didn't want to tell her that I couldn't stop thinking about change and excitement and freedom, and I didn't want her to know that I was wondering what it would feel like to have other women's hands on me. I wanted the freedom to touch any woman I liked, to snake my way through crowds of them, rubbing past their legs and tasting them with a forked tongue as I went. I wanted to move stealthily, avoid being seen by anyone except the women I selected, and then move on to my next conquest, and then the next, and then the next – never staying long enough to be spotted by outside eyes, and never feeling pressured to slither into their skin containers to be held captive. No, I was going to be in control this time; if there were any prisoners, I'd be the one taking them. I would be the one in charge. I was sick of my every move being for others.

'You want the truth?' I said, knowing I still wasn't going to fully give it to her, for fear of losing her completely.

She nodded then squeezed her eyes shut and bared her teeth as if bracing for impact.

'I'm at a point where I want to immerse myself in our relationship,' I said, carefully preparing each word and feeding them into her ear. 'I want to say yes to it all, I want to dive so deeply into this together that we drown in it, I want to shut out the noise around us and have it just be me and you – fuck what anyone says, fuck the judgement, fuck the worry. I want a life with you. I want to experience every high and every low with you by my side. You're all I want and all I care about. You're my person, who I'm willing to risk it all for, because what's the "all" without you anyway?'

That was all true. I meant every word.

'That's everything I could ever want to hear,' she said, her words bumping the sides on the way out.

'But,' I said, angling my head down and closing my eyes, 'as much as I mean all of that, I haven't lived a day as a single woman. I love you so much but I've never been on my own, independent, because the thought of being alone has always terrified me. I've always wanted to escape the confines of the life I'd created for myself, and I promised myself that if I ever had the courage to leave Joe, I would stay single. But then I met you. Actually, meeting you was the *reason* I left him. So what the hell am I meant to do?'

'Why wouldn't you want to be with someone you've fallen in love with?' she asked shakily, the marble sky darkening dramatically behind her like a stage backdrop. 'That's what I don't understand. We've found something rare; not many people find something so special, not even if they spend their whole lives searching. So many people just have to settle for as good as they can find. Why are you willing to take such a big risk of never finding love again, but you won't take the risk of accepting the love you have for me? You want me – you just said that – so why can't you treat this as a chapter of your life where you just simply get to be happy?'

I glanced around at the damage I'd already done to the skin container – to our relationship – its sawn-through nerve endings hanging limply overhead like stalactites, twitching, the skin contracting and tightening disturbingly.

Georgia was crying like an injured animal. Raincoated dog-walkers slowed their pace, rubbernecking and exchanging concerned glances, their whispered speculations hanging in the air. Eyes everywhere, with us at the centre of an unintended performance, our emotions laid bare for all to see.

'Why do you want to take this risk to find out if you might be happier?' she asked, her words catapulting out between convulsive catches of her breath. 'You could end up without me entirely, unhappy and single. This have-your-cake-and-eat-it cliché is not like you, and it's not fair. I'm not going to just wait for you while you hurt me.'

I stayed silent. I saw through her words and temerity; they looked like glass. I peered through their transparency. The fact was, I *knew* she would wait for me. And I was going to take advantage of that so I could straddle both the lives I craved: one with her, and one as a single woman.

I made my final cuts through the membranes, sensing I was nearing the outermost layer of skin. There it was: the light, the freedom – it beckoned. It was just a temporary freedom, of course – I only wanted a taster, and then I would come back to her.

Angry clouds brewed overhead, arching their necks downwards for a better perspective, readying themselves to rain down in torrents when I emerged – even nature was against me.

I hoisted myself out of the skin container, sitting on its ledge, staring down at my feet, which were dangling into the blood-soaked, freshly cut escape hole I'd made. I wanted so much to slide back in. There I was, perched on the precipice between love and adventure, terrified of finally having something worth losing.

I briefly considered jumping into any nearby male skin container to hide myself away; it would have been easy. I was an experienced performer and I could have persuaded a man to let me in – with flirtation or an invitation of sex. I then considered running to a place where no one knew me, and starting anew, freshly unboxed, alone. Then I considered repairing the wounds I'd inflicted on the love of my life and begging her to forgive me before braving the world with her by my side.

While her head remained drooped, I quietly climbed my way down the outside of the skin container and crept away from her, unnoticed. How could I be so callous? I had become what I despised. The voice of regret was burning inside me before I'd even taken the first step away from her. *Go back to her!* it shouted. *Stop what you're doing and go live your dream life.* Why wouldn't my body turn back? I felt stuck to the spot unless I moved away from her, like a character in a video game – blocked on three sides, only able to walk straight on, even though, somehow, I knew it was going to lead me into the enemy's arms.

Chapter 27

I cried for two days after walking away from her. I couldn't understand my decision; it felt so wrong. Why did I choose to leave when being with Georgia was the only thing that had ever felt right? Nothing made sense.

I needed something, anything, to help untangle the mess inside me. I pulled out an old sketchbook from the bottom of my wardrobe. It had been years since I'd properly touched it, and the spine creaked as I opened it, revealing half-finished drawings and forgotten doodles. I flipped to a blank page, grabbed a pencil, and let my hand move. The lines came out disordered and chaotic, mirroring the whirlwind of emotions I couldn't put into words. It wasn't pretty, but I felt myself begin to breathe a little easier. By the time I finished, the weight in my chest felt lighter, if only slightly.

I'd told Li everything that had happened with Georgia and, knowing me better than I know myself, Li had booked the two of us in for a spa day that weekend – just me and her, like old times. When she came into my flat that Saturday morning, I was in the middle of texting

Georgia a long apology. I was taking back everything I'd said two days ago and pleading for her to forget the entire ordeal.

'Don't send it,' Li said. 'Today is about talking everything through; I don't want you to make an impulsive decision that you regret down the line. Let's just take today, and then you can send that text when we're home in a few hours if you still feel the same way after having a nice long relax, OK?'

I looked at her, and then at the text. She held out her hand. I locked my phone without sending the message and handed it to her. She carried a chair from the dining area to the kitchen and climbed up onto it before placing my phone on top of the high cupboards, which she could barely reach.

'It's going up here for safekeeping, and you can have it back when I bring you home. Out of sight, out of mind.'

This was what I needed: someone to take control, a day to clear my head.

***

My masseuse was bird-like and pretty; her hands were gentle and a little weak, and they shook when applying pressure to my body. As I lay face-down, I watched her bare feet pad around beneath me – pearlescent pink toenails and skin like caramel chocolate. Her hands slid over me sensually and I wondered whether she was trying to make her strokes feel sexual on purpose. When she asked me to turn over, she held my towel in front of her face to give me privacy, but I saw her peer over the top of it, and I allowed her to see my breasts before she arranged the towel back over me.

She rubbed at my shoulders, bringing her fingers down onto my chest and ever so slightly under the lip of the towel. My breathing wanted to get heavier, but I subdued it, which made it tremble a little. When she started to rub my feet and legs, I caught sight down her top as she leant forward. She moved up my legs in slow strokes, and when she reached my thighs, I felt her fingers brush over my underwear.

When Li and I finally emerged from our massages, our limbs jelly-like, we sank into the inviting warmth of the hot tub.

'What's their story?' Li asked, smiling at me expectantly, nodding towards the woman with the younger, muscular man beside her in the pool.

'Definitely having an affair,' I whispered. We'd played this game since we were kids – inventing lives for strangers. She was trying to cheer me up.

'Yes, and her husband is at home with the kids, worked to the bone.' Li laughed. 'And here she is, living her best life.'

'And look at that guy alone over there.' I pointed to a man in the shallow end, letting the water ripple around his waist as he stood against the side. 'He's the PI the husband has hired.'

Li squinted, feigning seriousness. 'He's got a waterproof camera tucked into his shorts, waiting for the moment they kiss to snap the incriminating shot.'

'He's probably telling himself it's just a job, but really, he's hoping for some drama. Maybe he'll even join in.'

Li shook her head, laughing. 'It'll be the best day of his life.'

I forced a smile, but it felt heavy on my lips. I couldn't keep playing, and Li could see right through me.

'Shall we talk about it?' she asked cautiously.

'I want to, yes.'

'Do you want to vent, or do you want advice?'

'Both.'

'OK. So what's the latest? When did you last speak to Georgia?'

I took a deep inhale. 'I've texted her asking how she is, but she's blanking me; I don't think she wants anything to do with me right now.'

'Do you think she knows you want to – you know – be with other girls?'

'I think so. I haven't admitted that I want that, though.'

Li tilted her head thoughtfully. 'You both must be feeling so overwhelmed right now; it must be really tough.' She took my hand under the water. 'But having said that, you have to put yourself first right now. You have never been single, not since we were in school. You should listen to what your gut is telling you.'

I rubbed my free hand over my face, dragging it down over my mouth. 'I can't stop thinking about being with her – like, properly being with her. But I also can't stop thinking about what's out there that I'll never get to experience.'

'On a moral level, all you have to do is be honest with her. You could maybe tell her you *do* want to be single and that you want to get some life experience, and tell her that if she still wants you at the end of it, you'll be there with open arms. It would need to be a proper breakup, though, so she knows where she stands; and then, if she's willing to give you a second chance when everything's out of your system, you'll know it's meant to be.

'What you shouldn't do,' she continued gently, 'is pretend you don't want anyone else, because if you do get with someone, she'll feel betrayed, and then you could ruin your chances with her.' She stroked the back of my hand, clearly noticing I was about to cry.

'Knowing how big this world is, knowing how many women are out there, if I limit myself to just one person, I wonder if I'm always going to wonder,' I said. 'I love Georgia. But if I stay with her, we'll be at a stage where I *have* to come out soon, to show that I'm serious about her, but if I take a break and get with other girls, there's no pressure on me to do anything.'

'But would you be willing to risk your whole relationship with Georgia for some strangers?' There was so much concern in her eyes as she waited for a response I didn't give. 'If so,' she continued, 'you should think about properly breaking up with her; don't let go of your morals.'

I shook my head profusely. 'I can't *properly* end everything we have. We're just having a break.' I thought for a second about losing her, and the rush of dread it instilled made me backtrack. 'Or maybe I don't even want the break. I want her. I couldn't imagine life without her. Oh god, Li, what am I doing?'

'It's OK,' she said soothingly, hugging me. 'You haven't done anything wrong. Not yet. As long as you choose what to do, one way or the other, it'll be alright. But I don't think there's a middle ground you can take; I personally don't believe there is such a thing as a break.'

'You don't?'

'I wish I could tell you otherwise, but I don't think it would be fair on her. I'm sorry to say, I think you have to choose. Honesty is the best policy.'

I sucked at my bottom lip, frustrated by her tough-love approach – well, tough for Li, at least – and the fact I knew she was right.

'Put yourself first for once, Jess. You deserve to live your life – don't feel guilty about wanting to do that. Whether that means staying with her or leaving her is up to you. Just as long as you do the moral thing and be honest with her, it'll all be OK.'

***

Back at my flat, the first thing Li did was climb up onto the chair in the kitchen and retrieve my phone for me. She handed it over with a sympathetic smile. 'You've got this, my darling girl. Do what feels right for you.'

After I'd shown Li out, I opened the text draft of the apology I'd been writing to Georgia earlier that day, lingering on it and hovering over the send button before locking my phone and walking to the kitchen. After cracking open a bottle of sparkling wine from the fridge – the crisp glug of the pour so satisfying – I settled on the sofa and took a refreshing sip. I stared at the text again before finally clicking off it and downloading a dating app, Li's voice echoing in my mind, repeating, *morals, morals, morals.*

I selected *Just Friends* under the *Looking For* section, skipped the sexual preference question – I wasn't about to out myself, even on a queer app – toggled the location settings to only show people who lived in or near Cardiff, and added three selfies. The rest of the profile could be filled in later.

A notification appeared on my screen. I'd been 'liked', by someone called Daeva Valentine – it sounded like a porn star name – and then a message popped through from her:

'My mum's called Jess. If I date you, you're going to have to change your name.'

I replied:

'Just looking for friends over here!'

'You'd know that if you'd bothered to view my profile,' I muttered into my glass, the sound reflecting back at me. I preferred people who did their research, and it's not as if it would have been laborious research either, just a glance at my bare-bones profile was all she would have needed to do. She was clearly a careless veteran of the app.

She countered:

'On a lesbian app looking for friends? I can be your friend.'

I chose to ignore her; she seemed toxic. Attractive, yes, but there was something about her eyes; even though they were the lightest-coloured eyes I'd ever seen, there was a darkness in them. Her pictures seemed to leech venom; I wanted to wash my hands after scrolling through them. She had piercings all over her face and tattoos covering ninety per cent of the skin she had on show. In most of the shots, she wore a black bandana over her raven hair – which was styled somewhere midway between a '70s shag and an '80s mullet – and her pose of choice was to brandish a peace sign with her fingers and to raise one side of her top lip.

I locked my phone and set it down while I went to make some toast. When I returned, eight new messages were waiting for me. It felt good to be wanted. I opened the first one, from some girl I now don't remember the name of:

'Looking for friends? Hmm. You know there are specific apps for friendless people to use, right? You don't have to come on here and waste people's time – it's obvious what everyone wants on a dating app. Delete your account.'

I snapped back by sending a screenshot of the app's description: *LGBTQ+ dating and community app, to find soulmates or just mates.* And I messaged her saying:

'This is a friend *and* dating app. I'm just trying to find like-minded people in the queer community; since when was that a crime?'

Why had I even bothered to send that? I opened the next message from another girl:

'Fuck's sake, just another bi-curious person wanting to use us as an experiment.'

Ugh! Next:

'I don't understand people who won't announce their sexuality on an app like this. How hard is it to be honest?'

I threw my phone down onto the sofa and crunched into my toast angrily. Picking the phone up again, I tapped back onto Daeva Valentine's profile and squinted at her pictures, which were glowing at me with bright, artificial light. I rubbed my tired eyes, wondering if I should just turn off the phone and go to bed, but then I typed out a message:

'Fancy a friendly drink, then?'

I hesitated, scrunched up my nose, and thumped send. My phone chimed with a reply instantly:

'Next Saturday?'

I sipped my wine slowly, glaring at the word over the rim of the glass before bashing out:

'Does The Leek and Daff pub at 8 p.m. sound good to you?'

'See you there, friend.'

This felt like trouble.

Chapter 28

I headed into The Leek and Daff and grabbed a table; I was deliberately early so that I didn't have to be watched by Daeva while walking in. Guilt swirled in my stomach. I knew I shouldn't be doing this – especially not after the conversation with Li, who'd made me realise there was no such thing as a break. Either I was in or I was out. Yet, here I was, choosing the non-existent middle ground.

Daeva walked in, her bandana pulled snugly over her hair. There was a toughness to her; she was short, about my height, but she looked solid, with broad, strong shoulders and hands clenched into fists as she walked. It didn't come across as if she was particularly proud of her sturdiness, though; if anything, it seemed as if she was trying to cover it up with the oversized clothes she was wearing.

'Matey,' Daeva said loudly, followed by a metal-studded smile stretched strangely wide. She reached out her hand and I gave her an awkward half-high-five, half-handshake, not knowing exactly what she wanted. She laughed. I obviously did it wrong.

My two courage-builder Long Islands that I'd ordered came to the table. I was hoping to finish one before she arrived and then I would have just had the one in front of me, but instead, I looked like an alcoholic. I handed her one, as if I'd meant for her to have it.

Every other word from her mouth was 'fuck', but she smiled non-stop while speaking, as if she were cursed to appear happy regardless of what she was saying, her voice mellifluous and unnerving. In the brief moments that she wasn't smiling, I could see how creased her lips were – not chapped, just stretched so much by her Cheshire-cat grins that they looked like flaccid accordions when they relaxed. Her freakishly light-blue eyes were almost white at a glance, with pinprick pupils that punctured through frosted centres. Her glare was probing and severe, reminding me of a time from my childhood when I visited a zoo and the tiger behind the glass wouldn't take his eyes off me; I was a chubby bundle of meat, and his predatory instincts were activated. I couldn't tell if Daeva's stare was confident, violent or seductive, but it instilled the same panic in me as the tiger's. She wore, ironically, a bulky silver tiger's head ring on her middle finger and kept tapping it against her glass; the noise was setting the nerves of my teeth on edge, like how a clock's ticking becomes unbearable right after you've noticed it.

She didn't hold back when it came to conversation, choosing to strike up only the most controversial of topics. The mask that seemed most fitting to don around her was one of composure, one that portrayed I was unfazed by her boorish language and inappropriate questions. After asking me about my body count, my favourite sex position and whether or not I was a lesbian, she got on to the topic of comp-het – the only semi-interesting subject of the night.

'Have you heard of it before?' she asked.

I hadn't.

'It means compulsory heterosexuality. I reckon fucking loads of women are sufferers of it.'

'What do mean, sorry?' I asked, arranging my listening face.

'Being straight is expected. No one "expects" a baby is going to be fucking gay when they grow up. Kids accept their sexuality because they're told who they should like. It's fucking always, "This is a girl. This is a boy. They kiss".'

I nodded.

'By the time you're old enough to realise that you might want something different, you've already been brainwashed, and you have to fucking struggle to find the truth.'

I nodded again.

'The struggle for me was never that I was gay; it's the way society treats us that's the issue. It was hard enough being a teenager when I barely knew what "gay" even meant; I was made to feel like it was something strange or wrong. Comp-het makes people confused about what they're actually feeling versus what they're told they should feel.'

I raised my eyebrows and tried to seem engrossed in what she was saying; I kind of was, but I needed to focus so that my facial expressions would show I was actively listening.

'So,' she continued, her smile wider than it had been all evening, 'reckon you're having a sapphic awakening after a lifetime of comp-het?'

I laughed along with her as boisterously as I could, careful not to admit to anything.

When someone tried to pass by our table, she lifted the spare chair off the floor with one hand and shifted it out of the way. I watched as her bicep flexed through the baggy sleeve of her checked shirt. And it wasn't a flimsy chair, it was one of those weighty wrought-iron ones with a fancy, sturdy back. This girl was strong.

'Do you fancy coming back to mine for a nightcap?' she asked, grinning. 'No funny business, friend. My flatmates will be there, so you don't have to worry about going back to a quiet house with a stranger.'

I thought about it; I didn't like the idea, but it never occurred to me to say no.

'Cool, it's just a few minutes' walk that-a-way,' she said heartily, pointing with both index fingers after pushing her chair under the table.

A few minutes' walk turned into thirty. I was desperately out of my comfort zone; my legs were walking, but they wanted to stop. Was this going to be my first one-night stand? I didn't want it. All I could think about was Georgia. We'd agreed to stay friends during our break – she had finally texted me back to say she would try – so I knew I could just text her right then and there, hop in a cab and go see her. I could arrive at her house and tell her how this was all a big misunderstanding, and that I didn't need a break after all because I was positive that I was meant to be with her.

Daeva closed her front door behind us. 'Hello?' she shouted upstairs, waiting for a reply that never came. 'They must be out.'

Did anyone else even live in the house? I followed her through the hallway, my shoes squeaking on the mosaic brown, orange and blue Victorian tiled floor – the same as my late grandma had had at her house. The hallway was filled with an overbearing sprawl of framed posters that covered the walls from floor to ceiling – mostly band photographs and album covers – and a thick blanket of cloying radiator heat made me instantly groggy. Why was the heating on in the middle of summer?

'Drink?' she asked while leading me through to the kitchen as I fanned myself. 'I make a mean cocktail.'

'Uh, go on then, surprise me,' I said, perching on a breakfast bar stool and watching her every move to check she wasn't drugging my drink.

She brought over two negronis and stood on the other side of the kitchen island to me, leaning her elbows on it. 'I didn't think you were going to suggest meeting up, I'll be honest,' she said after swallowing a huge glug of her drink, almost knocking it back in one. 'You weren't putting out that vibe. I can't work out if this has been a date or not. You're still only looking for friends, yeah?' Beneath her eyebrow piercings, the darkness in her eyes glittered – I wasn't sure whether I was seeing evil or pain in them – they were indefinably peculiar. She smiled as a serpent would if it were in human form, and the smile never felt real – a faker can spot a faker. It was as if she knew when she was supposed to smile, so she did. I wanted to reach over, grip her face and remove its human facade to see what was underneath – something grotesque, snarling and twisted no doubt, frowning, with wild, wide eyes.

'Um, I'm not too sure right now,' I said, taking off a layer of clothing, feeling faint from the heat. Maybe that was why she kept the radiators cranked up – to make sure any woman she invited over would end up having to strip. 'To be honest, I'm new to this so I didn't want to say outright "single and looking to fuck around" on the app. That would have drawn the wrong kind of attention, and it's not something I'm entirely sure I want anyway. I mean, if sex naturally happened, then that's different to having it as a goal, you know?'

From the way she was eyeing me, I worried she was going to make a move, so I quickly threw in a 'And I wouldn't want that to happen straight away anyway, that's not the type of girl I am; I like to get to know a person first.'

I watched her blink away her lustful thoughts and her face returned to a grin. 'Oh, so you're looking to date, then?'

'I don't want to date,' I said quickly, wrapping my hands around the icy glass for respite from the sickly warmth hanging in the room. 'But if I say "no" to wanting to date and "no" to wanting to fuck, well, I guess that only leaves friends again – so that's probably a good thing to stick to right now. I just want to meet people like me and experience the gay scene as a single person.'

'You're shit out of luck if you want me to show you the queer scene,' she said, laughing from the pit of her stomach. 'I'm past that – I'm almost forty – I don't do clubs anymore, only house parties. Oh, I do love a good house party – they're stocked full of free booze. This house is in a student area, so there's always a party close by. I just let myself into the loudest houses and no one ever says anything or even realises I haven't been invited. It's hilarious.'

'Are you serious?'

'Yeah. Why the fuck not?'

She reached into the pocket of her black skinny jeans and pulled out her wallet. 'Mind if I just have a little bump?' she asked, flopping a bag of white powder onto the counter. Her question was clearly rhetorical; she was already digging her key into the stuff.

'Oh,' I said, immediately uncomfortable. 'You do you, it's your house.'

'Fancy a little hit?'

'No thanks. I've never done it before so chances are I'd react badly.'

She laughed hard again. 'Honestly, nothing will happen; it's just a little coke. All it does is make you feel more awake. You're not going to pass out or fucking shit yourself.'

I smiled respectfully. 'I'm not brave enough. Where do you think your housemates are, by the way?'

'Just out. Honestly now, if you try a bit, I'll be here to protect you and make sure nothing happens. It'll just be silly and fun. Do you trust me?' Her intense eye contact sent a shiver through me.

'I'm a chicken when it comes to anything like that,' I said, discreetly wiping beads of sweat from my forehead. 'I can't even handle my alcohol that well, let alone class As.'

'You'll be fine, I swear, I do it every day, even at work.' She chuckled, holding the heaped key inches from my nose. 'Everyone in the office does it – we wouldn't be able to stay in sales otherwise.'

I held my hands in front of my face and waved them, trying my best to hide my discomfort with a smile. 'I'm OK for now, thank you though.'

She sniffed it herself, and every few minutes from then she took another hit.

'I think I'm going to head off soon,' I said through a faked yawn.

'What? Why?' she said, her pinprick pupils having turned to saucers after the drugs had stretched them out. 'The night is young. Bit of a lightweight, aren't you?'

'Yeah, I totally am; I'm ready to get tucked up into bed.'

'There's one upstairs I can tuck you into if you want?'

I feigned a giggle and put my phone to my ear, having dialled a taxi. I hung up, realising I'd have to give my address, which I didn't want her to hear. 'What am I doing? It's the modern day.' I laughed. 'I'll use my app to grab a cab.'

'Woah,' she said, putting her hand over my phone and gently trying to take it from me over the countertop. 'Stay for a minute. Chill out; you're a bit uptight.'

I held on tight to my phone and tugged it gradually out of her grip, careful not to snatch it away. 'Oh, I have to wake up early tomorrow,'

I lied through a smile, continuing to book the taxi while talking. 'Sundays are always really busy for me.'

'I thought this was going to be a really good night,' she said with a disappointed, slightly aggressive edge. 'Never mind, then.'

'It *has* been a good night; sorry I have to end it so soon,' I said, even though it was nearly eleven p.m., which to me was an entirely late night, especially with a stranger. 'The app says the taxi is already outside; that was quick. Thanks for tonight, it was great.' I turned around to grab my coat from the bar stool.

'Wait,' she said in a low voice, suddenly standing next to me, making me gasp. 'Will I see you again?'

'Yes, sure,' I said as calmly as I could while heading for the front door. 'Got to run now though – these bloody taxis only wait a few minutes.'

I stepped lithely down the hallway and turned the handle on the front door, looking forward to some fresh air. It was locked. I scanned its length searching for a latch or a bolt – there wasn't one. She must have locked it with a key when we came in. I looked behind me and she dangled a ring of keys in front of her. I breathed out a bogus laugh and backed up so she could get to the lock.

'I can never remember which one it is,' she said in a pondering voice, studying the keys in her palm while leisurely stepping towards the door. 'Maybe this one?' She tried it. It didn't work. She tried another. Same thing. And a third. My stomach dropped a level each time. 'Hmm, well, maybe none of them work?' she said, turning her head to me. She took a step closer while my back was against the wall. I heard a car drive off and knew it was the taxi.

Chapter 29

'I feel a bit sick is the thing,' I said to Daeva, turning my face away from her and bringing my hand up to my mouth. 'I really do need to go now; sorry to ruin things.'

My phone lit up with a notification:

'Driver could not find you. Press here to rebook.'

I pressed it.

The stained glass of the door shadowed from the outside, and the doorbell rang. *The taxi driver,* I thought. Daeva shoved the correct key in the door and opened it a crack. 'What the fuck are you doing here?' she said to whoever was on the other side.

'Are you going to let me in or what?' said a slurring female voice from the doorstep.

'No. I'm going to bed; I'll call you in the morning.'

'What, I'm not invited into your bed anymore, am I?'

Daeva rolled her head back and jerked the door open, dragging the girl in by her forearm and shutting the door again, locking it, pocketing the keys.

'Don't touch me like that!' the girl said, rubbing her arm. 'Who the fuck is this?' She glared at me.

'This is Jess; we went on a date, OK?' said Daeva coolly. 'So fucking shoot me.'

'A date,' said the girl; it wasn't even a question.

I started shaking my head.

'A fucking date,' she repeated. 'Well, how fucking wonderful for you.' She started clapping slowly.

'Not a date,' I said firmly, frowning at Daeva. 'I told you I'm not dating right now. It was just a friendly meet-up.'

The girl just stared at me, her arms folded and her tongue in her cheek. Her long blue-black hair was messy, and something was gluing the ends of it together on one side – maybe a spilled drink that had dried in.

Daeva frowned and smiled at the same time as she turned to me. 'Yeah? A friendly meet-up? That's why you said you wanted to fuck me?'

I held my hands up in defence, mainly for the girl's benefit. 'At what point did I say that?'

'You said you're looking to fuck around, and you came back to my house after a date, so... the pieces all fit.'

'Look, I'm going to go,' I said curtly. 'Can you unlock the door, please? My taxi is going to be outside any minute. I can't miss it again.'

'You promised me you wouldn't bring any more girls back,' said the girl, practically growling the words into Daeva's face.

'You don't make the fucking rules!' Daeva shouted at the top of her voice, getting closer to the girl's face.

I thought about the neighbours on either side of the terraced house – how they'd be able to hear everything, and it was so late at night.

'You going to fucking hit me again?' the girl said with wide eyes. 'Do it. Fucking do it and see what happens.'

Daeva laughed as if in disbelief. 'I've never hit you.' She reminded me of Joe then.

'Here we go with the lies now that you have an audience. Where did my black eye come from last month then?'

'I told you. I was taking off my top, and I accidentally elbowed you in the face,' Daeva said, spacing her words out carefully, like you do when someone doesn't speak your language.

'Bullshit.'

'I was taking off my fucking t—'

'Can you open the door please?' I interrupted, looking down at the taxi notification on my phone.

They both acted as if I hadn't spoken a word.

'You hit me on purpose. Why can't you just admit that?' asked the girl through gritted teeth.

'Do you *want* me to fucking hit you? Maybe I should, just so you know the difference.' Daeva balled up her tattooed fist and raised it. 'You'd know it if I meant to hit you. Trust me. You wouldn't be conscious.'

'Right,' I said loudly, shoving my trembling arm between them. 'Why don't we just step outside for a moment and calm down.' I pulled Daeva by the waist, aiming to guide her to the door, but I couldn't budge her; there wasn't so much as a hint of movement in her body as I tugged at her – it was like she was a stone statue fused to the floor, sturdy as a brick wall.

'I suppose it's the same as how you "didn't" rape Sara, yeah?' said the girl, inches from Daeva face.

'Don't you fucking dare bring that up, you little cunt!' Daeva shrieked, spitting the words out, grabbing the girl by the throat and throwing her to the ground in one sweeping, effortless movement.

I screeched, crouching to the floor to help her up.

'I didn't rape anyone!' yelled Daeva.

'Well, why were you taken to court for it then?' said the girl, making her way back up to a standing position.

'I hadn't realised she was asleep! You know that. She was making noises, so I thought she was awake. It was pitch-black in the room.'

'You hit me, and you raped Sara.'

Daeva pushed the girl hard against the front door, so hard that the wooden frame shook. She cried out and held her lower back.

'Let us out of here right now,' I barked.

My phone chimed:

'Driver could not find you.'

Daeva unlocked the door and manhandled the girl through it. 'Get the fuck out!' she shouted, inflamed.

The girl ran down the street, crying out loudly. Daeva grabbed me firmly by the wrist as I tried to leave. She smiled faintly and said in a hushed, mellow voice, 'Jess, look, don't listen to anything she just said, she's fucking obsessed with me and she does this kind of thing all the time. She lives off the drama. I'm not like that, she just knows how to push my buttons. I'd never lay a finger on her, or any woman.'

I nodded and tried to step away, but she still had my wrist in a vice-like grip.

'I need your word that you won't believe anything she just said, Jess.'

'Of course,' I said in a neutral voice. 'She was so drunk; she didn't know what she was talking about.'

'So, I can see you again, right?'

'Yes. I'll message you on the app.'

Relief rushed through me when she let my arm go, and I welcomed the tingling blast of cold night air as I power-walked down the street. When I made it around the corner, I called for a cab with hands that were shaking so much that the phone practically dialled itself, and straight after, I held my finger down on the dating app, deleting the thing.

After studying the taxi driver's eyes in the rearview and making a mental note of what he was wearing – as I always did when catching a cab alone, in case I was attacked and had to identify him at a later stage – I texted Georgia from the back seat:

'Would you be up for hangover out tomorrow?'

Predictive text had changed *hanging out* to *hangover*.

I sent a correction:

'Hanging out*'

We hadn't seen or spoken to each other properly since we started our break. I needed to get on my knees and beg for forgiveness.

I texted Li too:

'Went out with a girl from a dating app. Regretted it immediately.'

Li wasn't best pleased that I hadn't been honest with Georgia about what I really wanted, but as ever, she had my back.

As the taxi neared my street, we had to stop short – a flashing ambulance was blocking the road.

'Here's fine,' I said, already mentally preparing myself to ring the on-call reporter at *The City Post*. It was probably another car crash; the street had a tight corner, and accidents weren't uncommon. I hoped no one was seriously hurt as I dialled.

I turned the corner towards my building, holding my phone to my ear, ready to reel off information. But there was no crash – just a group of my neighbours, huddled together outside. A heaviness settled in my stomach. That was when they wheeled the stretcher out of my block, the body bag unmistakable.

'Hi, Jess, what have you got for me?' asked the voice on the other end of the phone. I hung up.

One of the women from the floor below me approached, her face pale. 'It's Gwen,' she said, her voice sombre. 'She had a heart attack on the stairs, love.'

Chapter 30

I practised the conversation out loud to myself in my car before I pulled up to Georgia's house. First, I would ask her if we could go for a walk around Lake Calon, then I'd explain how stupid I'd been and that I'd made the biggest mistake in the world by thinking I needed a break from our relationship. After that, I'd ask if we could start fresh and pretend the whole thing had never happened. Mid-walk, I'd ask her to be my girlfriend, and when she said yes, I would grab her and kiss her in public, preferably when there were lots of people around to see, and we'd walk hand in hand back to her house, not giving a care to anyone who looked our way.

That was the plan, at least.

But even as I rehearsed those words, my mind kept flickering back to Gwen. I couldn't shake the weight of her death. She'd been like a surrogate grandma to me. The idea of her dying alone on the stairs haunted me. It felt wrong to be focusing on Georgia when I hadn't even properly mourned Gwen yet.

'Hey,' Georgia said apathetically as she opened her front door, barely looking at me. It felt so strange not to kiss her when I saw her. She walked away as I slid my shoes off – she never normally left me to it; she would always offer a hand or an arm to balance me while I was taking them off.

'You OK?' I asked as I followed behind her.

'Yep,' she said with mock enthusiasm. She was so off with me. I deserved it, I knew that, but it seemed so strange.

'I was thinking we could go for a wander up at the lake, get some fresh air?'

She glanced out of the window. 'It's probably going to rain. I'd rather stay in, watch a film or something.' She handed me the TV remote without looking at me. 'You choose something and I'll get drinks.'

We usually chose the film together. I felt my bottom lip tremble. I stood there with the remote in my hand, watching as she left the room. 'Maybe we should just have a *quick* walk?' I called into the kitchen after her, hearing footsteps on the landing above me. 'Hopefully the rain will hold off. It would be good to be alone, just us, for a little while.'

'You've changed your tune after last night,' she said.

'What do you mean?'

'The text you sent me.'

I thought back to what I wrote. It wouldn't pop into my head, so I checked it while she poured the drinks:

'Would you be up for hangover out tomorrow?'

Then the correction:

'Hanging out*'

She was right; that was a pretty unfeeling text, and I didn't put our usual eleven kisses at the end. And I had just said how much I'd wanted to be alone with her – the two didn't match up. Emotion never really comes through via text, but I could have tried harder.

She handed me a fizzy drink and walked past me to the living room. I noticed that the light behind her eyes had gone out. I had to reignite it before it was too late.

'Georgia, I—'

'Hey, Jess.' Gemma came downstairs. She plonked down on the sofa. 'What are we watching?'

Goodbye, privacy.

I sat through some sappy made-for-TV rom-com – Gemma's choice; I had given her the remote – and I waited patiently for it to end so that Georgia and I could go out before it got too dark.

I scooted to the edge of the sofa when the end credits rolled; I stretched and casually asked Georgia if she fancied that walk. She didn't.

'Well, it was lush to see you both, I better be off,' I said, hoping Georgia and I would at least have a chance to chat alone by the front door.

'See you soon, Jess,' Gemma said cheerfully.

'Yeah, bye,' mumbled Georgia.

I put my shoes on slowly in the hallway, waiting for Georgia to come and show me out like she always did. She didn't appear.

I stepped back into the living room doorway; she was still sitting there on the sofa, scrolling through her phone. 'I'm off now,' I said, hopeful.

She said bye again.

I'd seen her break open, and now I was watching her close back up.

'Well, that was the worst feeling in the world,' I said to myself when I was back in my car. 'What the fuck did you expect?' I replied, putting my seatbelt on. 'She fucking hates you now. You've fucked it. You've ruined everything.'

My plan had been to make everything right, to ask her to be my girlfriend, but she wouldn't give me a chance. I could tell by her eyes that she didn't want me; she didn't want anything to do with me.

My knuckles leached of colour as I gripped the wheel and floored the gas. Hot tears start to pour, burning down my cheeks. I could barely see the road; everything was blurred and doubled, my surroundings becoming a haze, the road a watery smear of distorted colours and shapes. I desperately fought to blink my sight back into focus as I sped along.

Suddenly, I felt a harsh jolt and the car lurched. I had no idea what I'd hit. I instinctively swerved away from whatever it was and the car fishtailed. My vision swam with red spots and my heart pounded in my ears as I fought to regain control. What had I hit?

Just as my sight cleared, a cyclist materialised in front of me, barely a few feet away. I desperately swerved, barely avoiding them, their scream piercing through my panic.

I skidded to a stop at the side of the road, my whole body trembling as I discharged a long scream, pounding the steering wheel over and over with my fists.

'You idiot!' the cyclist yelled. 'You nearly killed me!'

I mouthed frantic apologies through the windscreen, tears streaming down my face as I cried hysterically.

'I watched you hit the kerb, and then you nearly took me out. What the fuck were you doing?'

The kerb. Relief flooded through me – thank god, the thing I hit, it was just the kerb.

The cyclist's curses faded into the distance, but the terror remained, gripping my chest in an iron vice. I almost killed someone, and I could have killed myself.

I closed my eyes, curling my trembling fingers around the steering wheel, drawing in a shaky breath, willing the fear to dissipate. The metallic tang of fright lingered, but I forced myself to focus on the steady rise and fall of my chest.

Slowly, deliberately, I released my grip and sank back into the seat, letting out a tremulous exhale. With hands that still shook, I reached for my phone and texted Li:

'She doesn't want me anymore.'

Li called me immediately and tried to calm me, but it was no use. I could barely get any words out, but she knew I needed her.

'Where are you?' she asked with urgency. 'I'm coming to you, just tell me where you are.'

I pinged her my location.

'Stay there, I'm on my way.'

She parked up behind me. In my rearview, I spotted the Besties for the Resties bumper sticker, and it made me feel better. It was so silly that she'd stuck it to the front of her car; who does that? We'd all teased her for it. Everyone knows bumper stickers go on the back, where the other three of us had put them. I watched as she launched herself out and ran to me. She opened my passenger door and sat inside, immediately hugging me into her. I sobbed on her shoulder, feeling my whole body shake and my heart hurt.

It was over between me and Georgia. I could feel that it was over.

Chapter 31

The sharp hiss of the coffee machine made me jump again. I was at a café trying to get some work done on my laptop because the office had been driving me mad that morning. Too much noise, too many distractions. The sales team, taking up one side of our big open-plan office, had just hit their quarterly targets, and that side was in full party mode. Laughter, cheering, high-fives, and even speeches filled the space. It was like that every quarter. The reporters had to compete with the excited chatter for hours. The advertising director had even brought in party hats and games. Chaos. At least at the café I could focus with no interruptions.

'Hey, Jess,' said a voice. I looked up to be met with the smiling face of my colleague Carys. 'I haven't seen you since that night at Freedom. You still owe me a boogie.'

I realised Carys didn't have a clue what had happened between me and Georgia that night. And Carys also didn't know that she was the detonator of the great fucking fuck-off life-changing bomb that had gone off in my relationship. I couldn't be mad; it wasn't her fault.

I laughed politely. I didn't tend to see Carys in the office all that much because she was constantly out on shoots. She popped in now and then, but nothing much. 'I do still owe you a dance, you're right.'

'It's a cool place, Freedom, isn't it?' she said, sipping her takeaway latte. 'My cousin's dragging me to Scissor tomorrow. You know it?'

'I've heard of it,' I said, anxiously wringing my hands, desperate to get back to my write-ups.

'Any time you want to come out with me and my cousin, just let me know, yeah?'

'Thanks, that would be great,' I said noncommittally.

'Tomorrow, then? Or is that too short notice for you?'

'Sounds good,' I said, just trying to shake her off so I could get back to work.

She tugged her phone from her back pocket and hit a few buttons. 'Sorted, just bagged you a ticket to Scissor; there were only a couple left. So it's a ten p.m. start tomorrow. See you there, yeah?'

Panic settled over me. I wasn't actually planning to go. And it clashed with the takeaway-and-movie night I was meant to be having with the girls. Li had arranged it especially for me to have a chance to be with Georgia in a neutral environment. I couldn't – and didn't want to – cancel that. I mentally made a plan: I could go to Bex's place at about 6.30 p.m., stay until about ten, and then drive to Scissor – on the other side of the city – aiming for fashionably late. I couldn't let Carys down after she'd spent money on a ticket for me.

***

Georgia and Li were already at Bex's when I arrived; I was late leaving the office because one of the junior reporters, Aled, was in tears after Glyn had torn into him earlier that day – Glyn didn't like boys.

I sat with Aled after everyone had left and we worked through his article. He had a lead on the council trying to cover up a massive overspend, but he couldn't find the proof and no one believed him. So, we pored over my list of contacts until we struck gold. An opposition councillor I knew answered my call with a warm 'Jess, great to hear from you', and after a few minutes of small talk, he dropped his voice and said, 'It didn't come from me, but...' and I knew we were in. He leaked details about a £10.5 million overspend and he emailed the documents straight to us. By the time we were done updating the piece, it was a solid story. We printed it out and left it on Glyn's desk, so it would be the first thing he'd see in the morning.

Georgia was as distant with me as the last time I saw her, if not more so; she was becoming a shell of herself, withdrawn and detached. It took me back to when we first met and she was as aloof as a cat, and actually quite rude. I reminded myself that she admitted she was so unapproachable that night because she fancied me and didn't know how to act around me. Maybe she just didn't know how to act again; sometimes people's need for connection can look a lot like rejection, after all.

At least Bex wasn't treating me any differently. I had assumed that either Li or Georgia had filled her in on our troubles, but she remained friendly, as if nothing had changed between us.

I kept encouraging Li to start the film, anxious that I had a time-frame to stick to, but she kept dithering about in the kitchen, attempting to make popcorn, and burning it, twice.

'It doesn't matter, we don't need snacks, the takeaway will be delivered soon anyway,' I said, hurrying Li back into the living area.

'Oh, the takeaway,' she said. 'Has anyone ordered yet?'

I frowned – she had said she was on top of it. I took out my phone and ordered. The food arrived gone nine p.m. and I had to pretend I was too tired to see the film out to the end. I was aware I was acting out of line, but I didn't want to let Carys down. I wanted to keep everyone happy.

Chapter 32

I told the bouncer at the door that there should be a ticket behind for me, for Jess Davies. She gave me the nod, unhooked the burgundy rope from the gold pole it was attached to and stepped aside to let me in without a hint of eye contact for the entire exchange. Within seconds, a thickset tomboy approached me and asked if I fancied a drink. Flattered by the attention, I made for the bar with her – where I was heading anyway – and she ordered for us. The bartender handed over my small white wine spritzer and her large beer. The girl raised her pint, thanked me and walked away. I hid the embarrassment from my face as I paid for both drinks.

'That's just Bobby,' Carys said behind me, laughing, having witnessed the tail end of what had happened. 'She preys on newbies and gets them to buy her drinks. Don't worry, it happens to the best of us.'

I pretended to see the funny side and pushed out a relaxed laugh. 'How much do I owe you for the ticket?'

'Nothing, they're free,' Carys said. 'It's just a place you have to book before coming, that's all – so they know how many people to expect, I guess.'

So I wouldn't have been letting Carys down if I hadn't turned up. I thought about leaving and heading back to Bex's, but Carys started introducing me to her cousin and her friends, and it would have been impolite to walk away. They all seemed nice enough, but I had no desire to be social with strangers; what was the point of wasting my energy? I smiled and babbled along all the same.

'So are you on the prowl tonight, Jess?'

I tried to figure out which one of them had spoken. I hated speaking to a crowd; I preferred to make eye contact with just one person, but the whole group stayed quiet and awaited my response, staring at me, judging me in 360. Bringing my glass to my lips, I took a sip to buy myself a moment, then I smiled and shook my head, hoping the questioner would move on.

They then started talking about butches – something to do with how we 'need more butch-on-butch romance in the world' and 'of course butches can fancy each other', but I was distracted from the conversation by a girl on the dancefloor who had gorgeously wild leonine hair – butter-toffee-coloured ringlets. I couldn't stop staring.

'See something you like?' Carys asked me. 'Why don't you go say hello?'

It was like something my mum would say to me when I was a kid on holiday with no one to play with. She'd point to a kid doing handstands in the pool and she'd nudge me and tell me to 'go say hi'.

I would have felt stupid going over to the girl then, as if it were Carys's idea that I was just following like a little sheep. She'd taken away my control of the situation. Minutes later, someone else in the group asked if anyone fancied dancing; I saw my chance to get close to the lion-haired girl.

After inching my way towards her on the dancefloor, I found myself right next to her; she smelt so good, like freshly bitten pears. The warm, low light bounced off her smooth, bronzed shoulders as she danced – her moves playful, comical, even.

'Can you teach me how to dance like that?' I asked her loudly over the music, smiling when we locked eyes – hers shimmering under the club lights.

'It's all about not giving a fuck,' she shouted, grabbing my hand to twirl me. I was conscious that Carys was probably watching, and I was definitely giving a fuck. I danced her further into the crowd for cover.

'Your hair is incredible,' she said, twirling a stand of it around her finger. 'It's the colour of cherries; looks good enough to eat.'

'Thanks.' I laughed. 'Yours is amazing too. Like twirled caramel.'

She put her hands on my waist. Her lips were near mine; she was super tactile. Laughing, we threw one purposefully wacky dance move after the other, our limbs flailing wildly as the music throbbed around us.

'Wait, we have to get a picture of this!' she said, already pulling my phone out of my hand. She held it up, snapping a shot of us mid-laugh, our cherry and caramel hair contrasting in a delicious display of colour.

She turned her back to me, pressing herself against me as she bent over, her hands resting on her thighs. I tentatively grabbed her hips and moved with her. Suddenly it wasn't funny anymore. My teeth grazed my lower lip. All I would have needed to do was lift her skirt and I'd have been touching her. I stroked over its soft, hugging material; her hips felt equal parts firm and supple underneath it. I ran my hands over her sides to feel her shape, and then down her thighs. She'd stopped laughing too. Her side profile, looking back over her shoulder, was sultry, and she was still grinding into me.

She turned to me, still dancing, and put her hands on me, running them along my back, hips and sides as we moved to the music. Our faces were close; she was eyeing my lips.

'I know it's early, but do you want to get out of here?' she asked, her hair lit from behind like a halo of gold.

I checked my watch and saw it was 10.40 p.m. 'It's already past my bedtime, so I guess we could go to my place?' I offered, but the instant the words left my mouth, I regretted them. I had no interest in being with anyone but Georgia, and the thought of intimacy with someone else felt hollow and wrong.

She grinned and nodded, taking my hand as a cue for me to lead her out. Thankfully, the exit was on the other side of the room to where Carys and her friends were, so we could sneak away.

I turned and spotted one of Georgia's football friends, Ffion. Just my luck, I thought; now Georgia was going to find out that I had ditched her and the girls to go to a club.

'Is Georgia not with you tonight?' Ffion asked suspiciously, glancing from me to the lion-haired girl and back.

'No, I'm with work friends tonight.'

'Yeah? Is this one of your work friends?' she asked me, raising her eyebrows at lion-haired girl.

'Uh, yeah,' I said, bordering on hostile, hoping the girl would play along. I wanted to tell Ffion that it was none of her business, but I knew I'd probably get a whack if I said that – she was known for starting scraps on the pitch.

Ffion frowned. 'I hope you're not fucking around with Georgia like Ruth did. If you're going to do that, you should just stay with men.' She laughed flatly. 'You bi girls are all the same – you all go back to men in the end; you're all greedy.' I was suddenly a kid again, back in school, realising there was something about me that girls inherently didn't like. 'Have a great night with your work friend, yeah?' she said, walking away and shaking her head.

I watched her disappear into the crowd, and for a second, it seemed like everyone in the room had turned around to stare at me, as if a miasma of rumour was swirling above my head.

Refusing to act shaken, I drove lion-haired girl to my place, taking a few wrong turns along the way as I'd never driven that specific route before. I swear I suffered from some kind of geographical dyslexia; direction sense was not something I possessed in any shape or form. I'd even get lost in restaurants when I tried to find the toilets. My anxiety about losing my way ran so deep it even filtered into my subconscious. Ever since that boy did what he did when I was eleven – when my attempt to escape ended with him catching me – I'd been haunted by recurring nightmares. In the dreams, I'd run desperately, for miles, only to find myself trapped in a relentless circle, always looping back into the arms of my attacker.

As we were driving to mine, I practised saying in my head, *Look, I've had a change of heart*, but I couldn't force the words out. We walked from the parking space to my flat. I dragged my thumb over the ridges of the keys in my hand anxiously, and I willed my mouth to speak. *Stop!* I wanted it to say. *I don't want to do this.* If I said nothing, I was probably going to have sex behind the love of my life's back any minute.

'Drink?' I asked awkwardly, while still fumbling to open the front door of the building. It was a clumsy, poorly timed question, especially as there were still two flights of stairs between there and the actual door of my flat.

'Yeah, sure, do you have any wine or anything?'

'I have sparkling,' I said, the bald bulbs in the foyer flickering on and humming overhead. 'I always prefer sparkling as the bubbles go to your head and you get more of a buzz,' I continued, rambling, filling the time as we climbed the stairs – the same ones Gwen had died on. I swallowed hard, picturing her falling, the recycling bag splitting open, milk bottles and tin cans tumbling down the steps, and her clutching her chest in pain, dying alone. If I hadn't been out with Daeva Valentine, I might have been there for her, might have even managed to resuscitate her.

'Make yourself comfortable,' I said when I let lion-haired girl into my flat. 'I'll get the bubbles.'

I poured the wine and sat next to her, swallowing past the dryness in my throat. *Ask her to leave! Ask her to leave!* my brain chanted at me.

'I think it's drinking game time,' she said, grinning, tucking her feet under her. 'You've played Never Have I Ever, right?'

'Yes. Drink if you've done something?'

'Yep, drink if you've done it,' she confirmed, her green eyes catching the light like tumbled sea glass. 'Right. I'll go first. Never have I ever been to a girl's flat after just meeting her.'

Neither of us drank. That made me feel better – she hadn't done this before either.

'Never have I ever been with more than one woman,' I said.

'At the same time?' she asked, laughing.

I smiled awkwardly. 'No, just ever.'

She drank alone. OK, so she had been with at least two women. What if she'd been with loads?

'Never have I ever slept with a girl who I met an hour ago,' she said, a smile forming at the corners of her eyes. Neither of us drank. We held eye contact for a moment, but I couldn't physically seem to keep my eyes on hers; after a second, they drifted about her face like just-released butterflies. I was intimidated, I was nervous; I didn't want things to go any further. She glanced at my lips and licked hers, pressing them onto her tongue.

In one slow and steady move, she brought her face to mine, her hair tickling my neck and chest, and she kissed my cheek softly, her glossy lips leaving a sticky mark there. This was happening. We placed our glasses down on the coffee table at the same time, clinking them accidentally, and she climbed on top of me. She slipped my hair over my shoulder and pecked my neck, holding the back of my head. I felt nothing. Then it hit me: this was the place, the very seat, where I had shared my first kiss with Georgia; it was the moment I knew for sure that I had to be with her. My heart sank, and I felt my mouth turning down. But I remembered Li's words: *You deserve to live your life*.

'Bedroom,' I ordered quietly, and she dismounted. I grabbed her hand and hurried her down the hallway – not with passion or excitement, but with a determination to see it through, like I owed it to myself to try, just once.

I didn't turn on the bedroom light but I left the hall light on.

'Get back on top of me,' I said. She did what I told her. I was lying down while she straddled me, her wild tumble of caramel hair backlit and gleaming. She pulled her top off and unhooked her bra, letting it fall off her. Her tight nipples pointed forward and ever so slightly upward, and her skin was like burnished brass.

I felt as if I were watching it all play out second hand – as if she were on top of my avatar, and the real me was behind a screen somewhere, emotionless, just observing, moving my character around using a finger-pad controller.

When she leant down towards me, her scent was unfamiliar to me. I thought I'd liked it at the club, but when we were about to get intimate, I realised how little I knew about her. I'd been fantasising about doing exactly this my whole life, but as soon as I had the chance to act on it, I felt all but asexual.

I kept imagining Georgia's face. And I couldn't even remember this girl's name. I wondered whether the girls were still at Li's house watching bad horror movies and making each other jump; I weighed up whether I could still make it over there before they called it a night. A memory of one of our movie marathons flashed into my head; it was at my place. Bex always chose the seat closest to the window because she liked to use the curtain to cover her face when a scary part came on. I went to the bathroom during one part of the film and they paused it for me. When I came back, Bex was missing. I knew they were having me on. 'Where is she?' I'd asked, on my guard, and she'd jumped out from behind the curtain, having been crouched on the windowsill, and her momentum made her topple over the back of the sofa. We were all in hysterics.

I laughed through my nose at the memory.

'What's so funny?' asked lion-haired girl, smiling.

'Nothing.' I gave her a perfunctory smile in return.

She slowly brought her lips to mine for the first time, but I turned my head. She backed up and scrutinised me. I guided her off me with my hand and rolled onto my side, telling her the drink had gone to my head. I closed my eyes.

I woke up next to her in the middle of the night to see that the hallway light was still on and the duvet was down around her hips. Her incredible breasts rose and fell as she took gentle breaths. I woke her and drove her home.

I felt uneasy. It wasn't a new feeling, per se; more like a new recipe of familiar ingredients: a dash of mortification, a teaspoon of internal disgust, a cup of worry and a pound of guilt, seasoned with regret and apprehension to taste. I sifted through them, trying to separate and assess them, but it was no use. They all folded together in my mind as if in a large mixing bowl, making me feel sick.

All I wanted to do was see Georgia and explain that I'd made a terrible mistake and that I wanted – *needed* – her back more than anything. I was done with searching for new experiences; I'd just had a beautiful woman in my bed and wanted nothing to do with her. If that was anything to go by, then I needed to stop immediately.

But were two stabs at a one-night stand enough to base this entire experience on? Vile Daeva Valentine, and one hot femme? Maybe it would be best to consider them both trial runs. I couldn't take a second break from Georgia, so I'd have to be sure before going back to her. Maybe just one more try, just to be certain, and then I'd go back to what I really wanted.

Chapter 33

The music crashed through the speakers, a storm of electrifying guitar riffs, powerful chords and thunderous drums that seemed to shake the entire space, vibrating against the soles of my shoes. Hundreds of bodies jumped and swayed and sang around us in shared euphoria as vibrant lights painted them in pulsating hues, their passion contagious, amplifying the band's energy to an even higher level. The crowd screamed wildly whenever Polka Dot Sneakers' vocalist, with her split-tone peach and magenta bob, appeared on the big screen above the stage, or when the glitter-moustached drummer launched into an epic solo.

In the centre of the whirlwind of energy, Georgia was sitting quietly in her allocated seat. I dropped down beside her and shouted over the music, 'Are you OK?'

'Fine,' she replied, her voice flat. 'Just not really in the mood for this.'

'Do you want to leave? We could catch a taxi back to the hotel.'

She shook her head. 'We bought expensive tickets. Let's just stay.'

I nodded, though her answer didn't sit right with me. There was clearly something really wrong. 'Just say the word if you change your mind,' I added, my voice tight with concern.

I stayed in my seat beside her, the music blaring around us, but I couldn't enjoy any of it. Not with Georgia like this – so distant, so sad. Especially knowing I was the reason she felt this way. The guilt twisted inside me. What made it worse was that I hadn't stopped what I was doing. I still thought I owed myself just one more attempt at a fling with a stranger before I committed to anything long-term. That stranger, I'd decided, would be Frankie, who I'd met at a media event earlier that week. Frankie was non-binary and used they/them pronouns, something which was new territory for me. They'd approached me at the end of the event, handed me their number, and we'd exchanged a few texts since. There was no real excitement, no spark – just a hollow, detached sense of obligation, as if I needed to go through with it to prove something to myself.

But when I looked at Georgia, sitting there with that empty, distant expression, I knew – down to my very marrow – all I truly wanted was her. What I was doing, what I was planning to do, was wrong. My heart knew it. I had just been ignoring it, locking it away, choosing to act on something far less meaningful.

Months earlier when we, the Fab Four, had bought the tickets for Polka Dot Sneakers' gig in London, everything between me and Georgia had been perfect. We'd even planned a whole night around it – drinks and a meal before, then a hotel afterwards, one room for Li and Bex, and another for me and Georgia.

I'd considered cancelling or just driving home after the concert, especially since I was still feeling the weight of attending Gwen's funeral a few days prior. But in the end, I chose to stay.

'Anyway,' Georgia said now, 'I'm surprised you're not ditching us tonight to go to a club on your own.' Her tone was matter-of-fact but laced with disappointment.

A jolt of shame twisted through me. 'What?'

'You know what I'm talking about. Scissor Club?'

Ffion must have mentioned she saw me. I knew she would. 'I'm so sorry,' I said, my shoulders slumping. 'I should never have gone; I feel terrible about it.'

Georgia shook her head and just stared ahead, her silence suddenly louder than the band.

I glanced over at Li and Bex, who were having the time of their lives, arms around each other, jumping up and down. Those two were so good together. I could have what they had, but I was choosing to ruin it.

In the hotel room, the awkward quiet thickened. We were sharing a bed, but the distance between us felt endless. I wanted to reach out and hold her, kiss her, but I couldn't. I was being selfish. I couldn't confuse things. One more shot at being single before I begged for her forgiveness. Not that I would ever deserve it.

With my back to her, I pretended to sleep. My phone lit up on the floor next to the bed, and I peered down at it without moving. It was a text from Georgia – she'd texted me while lying next to me:

'All I wanted to do tonight was kiss you.'

I felt my insides melt. She didn't hate me. She still loved me. But if I turned and kissed her, my freedom would be gone. I stayed still, feeling a fat, searing tear seep out and run over the bridge of my nose. I ground my teeth together to keep from saying something. I heard her trying to muffle the sounds of her cries into her pillow, but I kept my back to her, my own tears silently flooding out. Why was I being so selfish? I was letting the woman I loved cry next to me in bed. I was *making* her cry. We both wanted to kiss and hold each other, but I seemed to care more about meeting and fucking a stranger. I hated myself. I was a bad person.

In the morning, both puffy-eyed, neither of us mentioned the text. All I wanted was to rewind time; I had chosen to ignore such a perfect opportunity – my heart had been begging me to seize it, but I went with my head instead. I repeated lines over and over in my mind that I wanted to say to her: *I'm so sorry; I don't know why I've done this to you; please come back to me; I love you so much; I don't know what I was thinking; I'm a cunt.* I said none of them.

Georgia drove the four of us home. I was in the passenger seat, and Li was in the back, next to a sleeping Bex. Georgia was on edge because we were coming back from London later than planned, and she had student work to mark. Bex had a brutal hangover and, before we could check out of the hotel, she'd had to run to the lobby bathroom, leaving us waiting in the reception and listening to her retching for half an hour.

On the drive home, I received a message from Frankie:

'So, where do you fancy meeting?'

I replied:

'I've got a press ticket for the opening night of Lagoon Lounge in the city centre this Wednesday, and I can bring a plus one...'

'Count me in.'

Via text, there in Georgia's car, Frankie and I arranged to meet, and I was disgusted with myself. I angled my phone away so none of the girls would see. Georgia was too caught up with mumbling to herself about a slow driver in front of us – who was going fifty-five in the outside lane – to look over at my phone anyway. She was always so even-tempered and reasonable, even in her road rage moments. I loved that about her. She could keep her cool so well. I saw Georgia glance at the time on her watch. Her eyes widened, clearly appalled at how late Bex had made us, and then she beeped the horn at the slow driver in front, waking Bex with a start.

'The middle lane is fucking clear, you prick!' she shouted, as though the driver would hear. 'Get over and let me fucking pass!'

It wasn't like Georgia at all. I'd never heard her swear like that before.

Chapter 34

Already tipsy after two Sunset Breeze cocktails, I spotted Frankie weaving their way through the crowded, tropical-themed bar, craning their neck to find me. I was immediately struck by their confidence, their androgynous good looks and the general suaveness they exuded. There was something so attractive about the melting of genders. I waved them over from the booth.

'Hello, my plus one,' I teased as they reached the table. I was already surrounded by a mix of acquaintances from the media and networking world: a local radio DJ, a woman from the city's tourism board, a couple of social media influencers, and Julie, a larger-than-life, fifty-something marketing manager at the council. And all of their plus ones. 'No problems with the ticket I left at the door, then?'

Frankie settled on the wicker stool next to me and adjusted the flower garland they'd been handed at the entrance. 'No bother at all, hostess,' they said cheekily. 'Sorry I'm late.'

I introduced Frankie to the group, and within moments, they were chatting away like they'd known everyone for years. Frankie had the gift of the gab. I was impressed, and a little turned on. I snuck off to the bar.

A few minutes later, I returned with a tray of drinks. 'Come on, then,' I said with a grin. 'Tequila shots!'

Julie let out a wild cheer.

'Oh, here we go.' Frankie chuckled, bracing themselves.

Everyone grabbed a shot, clinking glasses and tossing them back in unison, each person pulling their own variation of the classic post-shot grimace.

'My round next,' Frankie said loudly over the calypso music thumping in the background.

'What, at the *free* bloody bar?' Julie said, cackling. 'Make mine a double in that case.'

'Right you are, Jules, my lovely,' said Frankie, rubbing their hands together.

Julie barked a laugh.

'Coming?' Frankie said, just to me, in a quieter register, and I followed.

Once we'd pushed our way through the crowd and reached the thatched-roof bar, surrounded by hanging plants and softly glowing lanterns, Frankie turned to me and said, 'Not to be rude, but your tits look amazing in that outfit.'

'What, these?' I teased, pulling the neckline of my dress open to expose my cleavage for just a moment, straightening it back out when Li's voice echoed in my mind – *morals, morals, morals.*

Frankie inhaled sharply, a playful grin spreading across their face. 'And you expect me to keep my hands off you when you're doing things like that?'

I smiled and glanced at their lips. I liked the feeling of them wanting me.

'What can I get you?' asked the bartender, who was wearing a short floral dress and a huge pink flower in her hair.

'Love the 'fit,' Frankie replied, standing up on their tiptoes to admire the bartender's entire look.

'Thanks,' she said flirtatiously, twirling her plait and flashing a bright smile.

'We'll go for two tequila shots, please,' Frankie said with a wink, while I silently handed over two of my drink vouchers, resting my forearms on the sticky wood of the bar. Why did I feel a little jealous?

Frankie held the two shots up, grinning at me. I took one and offered the salt-sprinkled back of my hand to Frankie. They lapped at it slowly, their tongue warm and gentle over my skin, their eyes glancing up at me while taking their time to remove every grain.

'Uh, excuse me, can I get through please?' said a woolly-haired spectacled teen – a newspaper intern probably; they all looked the same – fighting for a space at the bar.

We drained the shots and Frankie took my glass from me, dumping it down before clutching my hand and leading me through a sea of people to the dancefloor.

'Wait, Julie's waiting for her next round,' I yelled, laughing, trying to pull back.

They held me tight to their body on the dancefloor as others careened around us, occasionally bumping into us. The beat of a new song kicked in, and Frankie bent me backwards as if we were at a '50s dance. People started making space for us, watching us smoothly move together as if performing a well-rehearsed routine. I wasn't enjoying the attention; I didn't appreciate all those eyes on me. What were people thinking? What if someone videoed us? It was a room full of journalists and gossips, after all.

Frankie twirled me back to face them, our noses nearly touching. With their hands, they guided my hips to the rhythm, never breaking eye contact. I stepped back, distancing myself a few metres to dance solo – running my fingers through my hair, lifting my arms above my head, hitching my flowy dress to the top of my thigh, and flashing parts of my body as if unintentionally as I moved. The alcohol had kicked in just enough to dull my worries about being watched, but not enough to let Frankie touch me.

Frankie stood there, half dancing, half gawping, their eyes only unlocking from mine to travel down the length of my body. They grabbed my hand again and pulled me in by the waist.

'You're so fucking gorgeous,' they said. 'We should go.'

I backed away casually, continuing to dance, smiling.

'Come home with me,' Frankie said.

I didn't want to take things any further, but we headed for the exit nonetheless.

Frankie pulled me back by the hand. 'Hold up, let's have a picture in here.' They pointed to a bamboo cabana in a corner of the surfboard-strewn lobby. We pushed our way past the crowd, pulled back the curtain and stepped inside. I swiped the selfie mode onto my phone camera in readiness to take a picture. Frankie lowered my phone and went to press a kiss to my lips. I dodged it, acting as if I wasn't aware of what had been coming, pretending to admire the surroundings, unsure how to turn them down after I'd sent out all the signals for them to do just this.

With a gentle sweep, they tucked a strand of my red hair behind my ear and boldly opened the top button of my dress. I glanced towards the veil-like curtain, watching the silhouetted figures move past us; anyone could have walked in. Noisy, drunk bodies bumped and shuffled against the sides of the cabana, adding to the thrill. Only, it wasn't a thrill. I knew it should have been, but it wasn't. It would have been exciting if the person about to ravage me was Georgia. I loved having secret sex in public with Georgia.

One of the many great things about being with a woman is nobody looks twice if you go into a private space together. A clothing shop's changing room was my favourite; we only did it once, but it was so hot and spontaneous, especially as it only had a thin curtain to conceal us – anyone could have pulled that back, peered through its gaps, or even made out our shadows moving together behind it. Georgia had had me up against the wall of it; she'd tugged down the cup of my bra and circled her tongue over my exposed nipple before switching between light and firm sucks. She'd slipped her hand into my underwear and had used the heel of her palm to knead my clit while dipping a finger into me.

'You're so wet,' she'd whispered, pulling her glistening finger out of me and bringing it to her face to inspect it. 'We definitely need to do something about this.' She'd smirked sexily before dropping to her knees in front of me, as though worshipping at my feet. She'd reached up under my dress to pull down my underwear, which she left at my thighs, lifting the front of the skirt to kiss me there; at the perfect angle to slip her tongue right onto me. If someone had opened the curtain, they'd have had a full view of everything; there would have been no way to hide.

I wanted to want Frankie; they were desperately attractive, un-apologetically themselves. I wondered what they would want, sexually. As they identified with neither male nor female genders, or maybe with both (we hadn't had that conversation), would being penetrated emasculate them? Would a certain touch make them feel defeminised? Were emasculate and defeminise even words that made sense in enby terms? I didn't want to make them feel any sort of dysphoria. Would my sensitivity come across as offensive? Was I overthinking? So many questions ran through my head, but I worried they were ignorant questions, which would have been distasteful to ask. Or perhaps communication was key? Not that I was going to say a word about sex anyway, because I wanted out. I felt trapped all of a sudden, and the moisture hanging in the air of the cabin became instantly heavy.

Frankie had already unbuttoned their shirt. They opened it and skimmed it off their shoulders, keeping it hooked over the crooks of their forearms. I looked at their chest, at the pink scars which told of their journey to self-discovery.

'I only had the op six months ago,' they said, smiling.

'Wow. You look amazing. How do you feel?'

'Free.' Joy sparkled in their eyes as they said the word.

Someone outside fumbled with the curtains, trying to find the gap between them. I straightened my dress over my knees. The perfect saved-by-the-bell moment.

Frankie shrugged their shirt back on, leaving it open. 'Come on, let's get out of here.'

We slipped through the curtains and snaked our way through the crowd to the exit and into the cool gust of night air. As I stepped onto the pavement, leaving the commotion of the bar behind, I felt the effects of a night spent in a loud, airless, crowded building; the outside world felt muffled and dull by comparison. Frankie didn't stop leading me by the hand until we were at the side of the building. With a slow shake of their head, Frankie gazed at me with a mix of disbelief, passion and wide-eyed excitement.

'If we hadn't been interrupted, that would have been insane,' they said.

I forced a gentle laugh through beginning-to-tremble lips. Frankie cleared a few strands of wind-swept hair from my face. They were an inch or so taller than me even though I was in high heels, a similar height to Georgia. I liked the way Frankie looked at me. But the difference was, with Georgia, I knew I'd be the only person she looked at like that – if we were in a relationship, that is. She wouldn't even glance at another woman when she was with me; she was loyal, respectful and considerate, embodying all the traits of a devoted partner. Frankie probably looked at everyone like that, just as they did with the bartender; their confidence suggested they were skilled at drawing people in.

I needed my Georgia.

I'd tried three times to have a one-night stand, and I hadn't been able to go through with any of them. Not even so much as a single kiss. That said it all. It was over.

I'd been sabotaging my happiness with Georgia for experiences that I hadn't even wanted – forcing encounters into my life that didn't belong or fit, like missing puzzle pieces I'd found in lost property boxes. I knew what I wanted; I'd known it deep down, but at that moment, finally, I had concrete confirmation that Georgia was my one and only.

'Come home with me,' Frankie said, skating their fingers over my jaw and chin.

'I need to head off,' I said, trying to tone down my smile as the thought of Georgia danced through my mind. 'I'm so sorry, something's come up.'

I pictured how I would finally come out to my family – for Georgia, for myself. My heart felt as if it might burst. The fear and apprehension had melted away. I was ready.

I texted Georgia before I went to sleep that night:

'Thinking about you all the time. Looking forward to seeing you. Are you free soon? Xxxxxxxxxxx'

I woke in the small hours, my brain dehydrated to a raisin-like quality, and I spotted that a reply from Georgia had come through:

'I'm fine. Can you stop messing with my head please? See you at Bex's birthday party.'

No kisses – eleven cuts to my heart. But what could I expect? I'd been awful. I didn't want her to think I was messing with her head; I had been, but that was over now. I was all hers again. All I hoped, to the powers that be, was that she would take me back; the space between us was unbearable.

Chapter 35

I made a beeline for the seat next to Georgia at the strip club. She was clearly less than thrilled to be there; it definitely wasn't her scene. I'd wanted to meet her beforehand, pick her up from her house and drive to the club together. I'd had it all planned out, yet again, how I would arrive at hers and ask if she would accept my apology, and then we'd cry tears of joy, and the warmth would instantly return between us. And then we'd arrive at Bex's party hand in hand and everyone would cheer. But I wasn't about to broach the subject of getting back together while we were in a strip club.

I couldn't help but think Bex had been a bit insensitive to Li's feelings by choosing that venue for her birthday party. But judging by Li's excited grin, she seemed just as enthusiastic as Bex for whatever the night had in store.

We were a party of twelve, nestled in a curtained-off horse-shoe-shaped booth. I recognised most of their faces from the gay bars or from Georgia and Bex's football games, but I'd never really taken the time to get to know any of them beyond surface-level chatter. The other women, clearly straight, were from the insurance firm where Bex and Li worked.

Three strippers – Desiree, Cleo and Pippa – introduced themselves over the music. Desiree, who seemed to be the head stripper out of the three of them, explained that we'd be 'sharing the trio' for the next forty-five minutes.

'We'll be dancing for all of you as a group,' she said in a sultry voice as smooth as velvet stroked the right way. 'And, if you're lucky, you'll be getting one-on-one attention too. Are you all ready?'

We responded with varying degrees of enthusiasm – Bex being the most eager and vocal, while the straight women from the Cymru Protect office offered only awkward murmurs. And with that, the show began.

Desiree was at one end of the group, Cleo was in the middle – in front of me and Georgia – and Pippa was at the other end. I couldn't seem to look Cleo in the eye, her being so close to us and all, so I mainly watched the other two instead. Cleo had mid-length dark hair, a huge tattoo of a jaguar on her back and was dressed in a black leather-look bikini-style top and a matching miniskirt – short enough to show the underside of her bum cheeks. Lit up in pale purple, she gyrated her hips while turning in a slow circle, gazing over her shoulder at me and Georgia while pulling on the knot of her string top, undoing it from behind before lifting it over her head, turning to reveal her small, perky breasts and hard nipples.

I think she saw my lack of eye contact as a challenge. She crouched in front of me, her hands resting lightly on my bare knees as she gazed up with her dark-brown doe eyes. Then she stood and reached beneath her tiny skirt, hooking her thumbs into the sides of her thong. Slowly, she slid it down her smooth thighs and calves before lying back, lifting her heeled feet into the air and spreading her legs wide, shaking her thighs to the beat of the music. I finally couldn't look anywhere but at her; I stopped myself from squirming in my seat as I stared down between her legs. As she gracefully rose to her knees and crawled towards us, she blew a playful kiss at me before continuing her performance for the girls next to us.

All three of the dancers had seamlessly switched places, Desiree now dancing in front of me and Georgia in a blood-red bodysuit and lace suspenders, her platinum-blonde hair falling to the small of her back.

It was hard to miss that Pippa, the one dressed all in white, had been doling out the personal lap dances. She wore a white babydoll negligee and an innocent smile, and as she approached me, her pigtails bouncing, I couldn't shake the thought of how Georgia would feel watching another woman all over me. Politely, I stopped Pippa before she could reach me.

'Sorry, I've got to go to the bathroom,' I said, getting up.

Glancing back as I passed through the curtained exit, my heart sank. Pippa was now on Georgia's lap, and Georgia wasn't objecting. A cry of shock and anger escaped my lips before I could hold it back. 'Fuck you!' I screeched, my voice raw and desperate, feeling the whole group's eyes land on me.

Georgia peered around the stripper's tiny waist to meet my eyes for just a fleeting moment before redirecting her full attention back to Pippa, a flirtatious smile on her face. The sight hit me like a punch to the gut. She'd never belittled me like that before, never disregarded my feelings, never shown me such blatant disrespect. I pushed my way through the curtains and stormed off to the toilet.

'Jesus, how much?' a man with drunk eyes said in the corridor.

'I don't work here,' I said forcefully, before adding, 'Sorry,' in a sweeter tone.

'Well, you should. You'd make a fortune.' He staggered a little and then reached out with both hands as if to hug me. I backed away and put my hands out in front of me, but he tutted and slid a five-pound note under one of the straps of my bra.

I flashed a hesitant smile before speed-walking to the toilets and slamming a stall door behind me, taking deep, ragged breaths. I'd never seen Georgia look at me like that.

'Jess? Are you in here?' It was Li and Bex, their voices thick with concern. 'Are you OK?'

I emerged from the toilet stall, tears spilling uncontrollably. 'I walked away from my lap dance, and she just stayed there, even though I told her I was offended.'

'You told her that?' Li asked, gently rubbing my back.

'Well, I screamed "Fuck you" at her, so that was pretty much the same thing. And she still didn't stop the dance, knowing I was hurt.'

'Yeah, I think everyone in the club heard that,' Bex said with an endearing giggle, trying to lighten the mood.

I smiled at her, sighing. 'Was it really that loud?'

'It nearly cracked my cocktail glass.'

'I can't go back out there,' I said. 'Sorry, I know it's your birthday, but I can't just sit there with her for the rest of the night like nothing happened.'

'Georgia left,' Bex said, to my surprise. 'Come on, come back. Have a lap dance.'

'No, I can't. I've got to go.'

Chapter 36

I dragged myself out of bed the next morning, the hurt still lingering in my chest. I knew I had no real right to be mad at Georgia, but the thought of being around her after what I'd seen the night before felt almost unbearable. I had to, though; I'd promised to help her move into her new house that day.

By the time I arrived, the front lawn of Georgia's dad's house was already cluttered with cardboard boxes. I took a deep breath, steeling myself as I unfastened my seatbelt and stepped out of the car.

'And when I went to look in the fridge, the doorbell rang, and guess who it was?' Bex's voice carried over to me as I made my way towards them, her audience consisting of Georgia's dad and sister.

'Who?' Mike asked eagerly, waiting to hear the highlight of Bex's story – one I'd already heard.

'Li, holding a takeaway bag filled with curried goat, jerk chicken—'

'No way!' Mike interrupted, laughter bubbling up as Bex continued.

'—ackee and saltfish, rice and peas, and rum cake for dessert.'

Mike shook his head, grinning in disbelief. 'How did she know?'

'I'm telling you – she can read my mind,' Bex said, her gaze landing affectionately on Li.

Bex was recounting the time she'd been craving Jamaican food, like her mum used to make, and had spent an afternoon browsing restaurant websites before ultimately deciding against ordering to save money. Just as she was about to rummage through the kitchen for something to whip up, Li had shown up with a feast in tow.

'It's like we share the same brain or something,' Li said, hugging Bex tightly before spotting me and jogging over to greet me. 'Jess! You made it.' She lowered her voice, concern on her face. 'Are you feeling OK?'

I nodded, managing a small smile. I acknowledged everyone, except Georgia, who was still inside the house, and added that I was a bit worse for wear but would help as much as I could.

'I'll get you a cuppa,' Mike said, smiling as we gathered our energy for the task ahead.

There was no need for a moving van since Georgia was relocating only five houses away from her dad's, in the same street. So we all dutifully ferried her belongings across the short distance.

Georgia would barely look at me. I wanted to tell her I was sorry for the night before, sorry for everything I'd done recently, but I needed to wait for the girls to leave first so I could do it in private. As I trudged between the two houses carrying her clothes, furniture, pillows and Pickle's dog bed, I couldn't help but hope this was all for me – her getting her own place, I mean.

At the start of our relationship, she told me she hadn't moved out of the family home yet because she was saving to buy a place – she thought renting was a waste of money. What if she'd chosen to do it now to show me what life could be like, where we could live together and what she could offer me?

Carrying more than I could comfortably manage – belongings crammed under my arms, and heavy bag handles cutting into my fingers – I squeezed myself through the door of her new home and shuffled down the hallway, dumping everything in the nearest gap I could find.

I gazed around inside the house, picturing how amazing it would be to build a life there together. I imagined how we'd decorate it; how we'd dance in the kitchen while drinking wine, dinner simmering on the stove beside us; how we'd have sex on the countertop halfway through cooking, unable to resist each other's touch; how we'd take baths together after long work days, both insisting on taking the less comfortable end where the taps were; how we'd brush our teeth side by side; how we'd snuggle in bed and pillow-talk in the dark about the best bits of our days; how, in the mornings when she was still asleep, I'd sneak downstairs and make her breakfast in bed; how we'd have Fab Four dinner parties with Li and Bex; how we'd fall asleep with Pickle, *our* dog, at the foot of the bed; and how, although we'd never say it, we'd both know that the spare room would one day be our baby's nursery.

I saw the image of us there together so clearly that I felt like I was predicting the future.

I waited impatiently for the girls to leave, hoping to apologise to Georgia privately, but they seemed oblivious to the hint I was trying to give.

'Right,' I said, rubbing my hands together in frustration. 'I think it's time for us to head out. Shall we leave you to it, George?' I said, although I had no intention of actually leaving.

'Sure,' she replied, avoiding eye contact. 'Li, Bex, did you want to stay a bit longer?'

I hesitated, feeling the tension in my chest. I couldn't very well admit that I wanted to stay too, considering I was the one who'd suggested we all leave. So I had no choice but to go. I trudged to my car, mentally berating myself, while Li and Bex stayed behind.

I should have told her right then and there, on the pavement outside her new house, that I would do anything to have her back. I kept waiting for the perfect moment, but I should have just dashed back to her and confessed my feelings. Instead, I slumped into my car and drove away.

The days that followed were a blur of regret and frustration. Georgia had all but blocked me from her life, even as a friend, and it made me so miserable, even though I knew it was my own doing. She wouldn't answer my calls, barely replied to my messages, and never answered the door to her new house when I turned up unannounced – granted it was only one time, and she may well have been out, but still.

I would text her variations of:

'Please, Georgia, I need to talk to you so badly!'

And she'd reply:

'Then talk, Jess.'

'I would much prefer to tell you in person.'

'Sorry, busy tonight.'

And repeat.

My chances were slipping through my fingers like sand. I'd type out things like *I love you so much, please let me come back to you*, and then delete it, tears flickering in my line of sight as I read it over and over. I couldn't do it via text.

The moment I opened my eyes to the new day, a burning determination surged inside me: Georgia would be mine again, no matter what it took. I wouldn't waste time planning or waiting for the ideal moment; I was going to take action, finally. The thrill of my newfound clarity sent a bolt of excitement through my stomach.

Chapter 37

'Mum, Dad, I have to tell you something,' I said. I couldn't look at them; my eyes were fixed on the mat in their living room, tracing the abstract patterns and the tuft of white dog fur in the middle – which I knew Dad wanted to pick up but was stopping himself because he could tell this was serious.

'Oh, please don't be pregnant,' Mum said worriedly. 'You're not even in a relationship.'

'What is it, love?' Dad asked, and in my peripheral vision I saw him put a gentle hand of cessation on Mum's knee. 'You can tell us anything.'

'I... I...' I faltered, my voice trembling as I buried my face in my hands. I couldn't bear the thought of seeing their expressions twist into that same look of horror and distress. The one that had haunted me since I was eleven, since the day I'd told them what that boy did to me. The memory of their shock, their tears, the way they wouldn't stop hugging me – it all came rushing back.

Quick footsteps padded across the room and I felt the sofa depress on either side of me before two hands rubbed my back.

'What is it, my angel?' Mum asked tenderly, feeding me the question like a spoonful of warm soup.

'I think I'm – no, I know I'm – in love with someone.'

'Well, that's wonderful news,' Dad said gladly. 'Who is he?'

I didn't correct the pronoun in that moment of prime opportunity, I just continued. 'It's... complicated.'

The kettle whistled in the kitchen. 'Cup of tea, love?' Dad asked, ever the believer that a good cuppa could fix anything. I always said yes because I knew it comforted him to think it might comfort me. I nodded, and he bent to pick up the clump of dog fur before heading to the kitchen.

Mum's hand was still moving in circles over my back. 'No matter what you're going to say, we'll handle it together,' she whispered, pressing kisses to the side of my head.

Dad handed me a steaming mug. I took it, avoiding his gaze, feeling my heart race. 'So... I... well... it's a woman,' I said, feeling the blood drain away from my veins before rushing back in.

'What do you mean?' Mum asked, her voice soft but confused.

'The person I've fallen for,' I said quietly, still not looking at either of them, too scared to see their reactions. 'I don't think I'm straight.' I couldn't bear saying words like 'gay', 'queer', 'lesbian' or any of the other terms I thought I might have aligned with. 'Not straight' was the best I could do.

'Since when?' Mum asked, shattering the few milliseconds of excruciating silence.

'Since always, I think,' I mumbled, listening out for clues in their voices in hope I could guess their expressions.

'Why haven't you ever said anything?' Mum asked, turning a little more towards me and patting my knee. 'Did you not think you could come to us?'

'I was just scared that...' My voice cracked in half. '...that you'd see me differently,' I said, starting to cry.

Dad took my mug out of my hands, set it down on the floor and hugged me with both arms. Mum joined him, the two of them holding me close.

'You,' Dad said, pulling back just enough to look at me, 'you couldn't do anything to make us see you differently.' His hands were still gently gripping my arms as if grounding me. I finally looked at him, and his face was doing the opposite of what I feared; it was bright, full of pride. 'You are our daughter, and we will always support you.' He stopped for a moment, as he always did when his voice started to wobble with emotion, collected himself and continued. 'All we ever want is for you to be happy. It's our only job as parents. I would say "we love you no matter what", but that doesn't cut it; "no matter what" almost sounds like something's wrong, so, instead, I want you to know we love you just the way you are.'

'Jess,' Mum said, her voice as soothing as a balm, and I turned to her then. There was a gentle smile on her face that grew as our eyes met. 'Thank you for trusting us with this. It takes courage to be true to yourself, and I'm proud of you.'

Relief washed over me. 'I wasn't even being honest with myself,' I said finally, swallowing sobs, my voice thick. 'It's taken this long for me to accept it. But there's a girl out there that I'm in love with. She wanted me to come out, but I was pushing her away because I wasn't ready for the world to know. And now I think I've lost her.'

'Oh sweets,' said Mum, squeezing me as I sobbed. 'There's always another chance. Go get her. I know she loves you back – how couldn't she?'

Then the dog, who Dad had let in from the garden, pushed his wet nose into my hands and wagged profusely like he knew the moment called for it.

Chapter 38

Feeling Georgia's lips on mine again after such a stretch of heartache and distance was quite possibly the best moment of my life. I'd had the opportunity to try my backup life on for size and then I returned it for a full refund. She allowed me to do that. Well, she didn't allow me, not at all in fact, but I did it anyway, behind her back.

And the kiss didn't actually happen; it arose in a vacant daydream on my drive to meet her at our place, Lake Calon. It felt so real, as did all my fantasies. When I actually saw her, though, the reality was very different.

She was sitting next to me on the bench, with her elbows resting on her thighs and her eyes pointed to the gravel path.

'I can't,' she said.

Her words hit me like a bucket of ice water. The cold shock stabbed its way into me, crunching through my flesh. 'You... can't?'

She glanced at me and shook her head.

'Please,' I said through a throat squeezed so tightly I could barely force the word out. 'Please take me back. Please let me make this right. I made such a terrible mistake. I'm so sorry.'

'I've honestly longed to hear you say those words, Jess. But it's too late now.'

'But surely your feelings for me can't switch off, just like that?' My voice sounded peculiar and muted in my ears. 'Is there someone else?'

Her eyes slid away from mine sheepishly. 'Look,' she said calmly, my heart falling through a trapdoor with the syllable. 'Even though I still care about you, I'm crushed inside, and I feel anger towards you. I need to move away from that. I've always believed in the saying that "the moment you start to wonder if you deserve better, you do."'

My heart continued to plummet. She believed she deserved better than me – just like when she said I deserved better than Joe. She thought I was toxic. And I was.

'Who is she?' I asked pleadingly, the world going hazy behind a veil of tears.

'Stop, Jess.'

'Just tell me. Please just tell me.'

I could see the bench stretching longer and longer, and she was moving further and further away, drifting so far into the distance. I knew I wouldn't be able to catch up with her. I wouldn't be able to reach her anymore.

The grey water of the lake was swallowing the sound of her voice, as though I were underwater listening to it. But I caught a few words: 'Speaking to me', 'So horrible', 'How could I be with you?'

Wait, what? What was she saying? I strained to get my brain to string her words together and repeat them back to me. I managed to merge them: 'The way – you've been speaking to me lately – has just been – so horrible. How could I ever be – with you after that?'

I realised she must have still been mad at me from when I screamed at the strip club.

'Honestly, it's not like you,' she said, her voice suddenly as clear as a bell, everything shuddering back to shape. 'It's just been so awful. I've never been spoken to like that in my life.'

'I'm so sorry, I didn't mean to speak to you like that, it won't happen again, I swear. I didn't even mean to say it.'

'I don't care about that now; I don't care about any of it. I'm numb. I just didn't understand; it was so out of character for you, I couldn't believe it.'

She was ending everything between us because I'd said 'Fuck you', once?

'I was in a weird place that night,' I said. 'I couldn't stop myself from saying something; I was hurt.'

'Which night? There have been too many to count. You've been genuinely awful.'

'What? This must just be an excuse you're using to lie to yourself that you hate me, so it's easier for you to let me go.'

'It's not an excuse, Jess. It gave me the push I needed to find happiness outside of you. I would have kept holding on otherwise. So even though you've been speaking to me like I'm a piece of shit, I can't hold it against you, because it ultimately helped me. It helped me to move on.'

I was dumbfounded. What did she mean?

'If you can be civil towards me,' she said, her voice chiselled and sharp, 'we can still be friends.'

The words punished my ears and echoed around my mind. *We can still be friends. We can still be friends. We can still be friends.* Those five simple syllables, when brought together, created an unassuming bomb, a Molotov cocktail, that shattered on impact inside me.

Fire raged through me, spreading frenzied flames as the fuel burned. Friends? But she was the love of my life. And I was supposed to be the one in control, for once in my life. For once in my fucking life. Now our relationship was just over? Just like that? This wasn't supposed to be happening. I thought I was worth waiting for. I thought I was her everything.

I searched for my words; they usually presented themselves neatly for me to choose from, but at that moment, they were in a disorganised heap, all tangled and twisted together like necklace chains in my brain. I didn't know where one ended and another began. I rustled around in my mind and picked up a small loose fragment.

'No!' I yelled. 'No.' It was the best I could do; all other language was jumbled and matted and lost.

I could still fight this. Maybe that was what Georgia wanted. For me to fight.

Over the next week, I sent flowers – blue orchids, our favourites – left presents at her front door, sent a letter (which she posted back to me, with a stamp on it, so I knew she hadn't come to my flat in person), and performed many other quixotic, hopeless acts.

I felt so desperate and fraught, my panic and passion mingling to create a volatile monster. After draining all my last-ditch ideas, all I could do was tiger pace and stare sightlessly into the darkness I had created. I held on to the fact that at least she was open to us being friends; the door wasn't closed if I had her as a friend. I could build us up from there. I just needed a plan.

Chapter 39

M y phone buzzed on my bedside cabinet. It was a text from Georgia. My heart leapt, and I sat bolt upright. Maybe she'd changed her mind:

'Hi Jessica.'

She'd never called me that before.

'My girlfriend thinks it would be better if you and I called it a day. I'm afraid we're going to have to cut ties. I'm sorry.'

Everything stood still. Heat burgeoned from every pore on my skin. Vomit burned in my throat. My heart liquified in my chest, dripping down until it pooled like lava deep down in the pit of my stomach.

I didn't know what part of the text to focus on first. *Girlfriend*? It hadn't even been a week since she'd told me she didn't want to get back with me, and she now had a *girlfriend*? I was going to throw up. Who was she?

It would be better if we called it a day? This was it? She'd cut me out forever? We couldn't even be friends now? Did Georgia ever even love me if she was willing to remove me from her life like a mistake she could just erase?

My mind shot back to the time she offered not to speak to her ex, Ruth, ever again after I had my moment of jealousy at their football game. I wondered whether Georgia had readily offered to cut me out for her new girlfriend, and the girlfriend had said yes. *Girlfriend.* The word hurt to even form in my mind. It didn't bear thinking about. How could she just throw me away like that? How could she prioritise someone she barely knew over me? Enraged, desperate thoughts fizzed in my stomach. Although, who I was angrier at, I'm not sure. Probably myself.

I texted her back:

'Please Georgia, don't do this! Please can we be friends? I can't bear not having you in my life. I won't try to get you back, I'll let you be happy, but please can we still talk – as friends?'

The message read as undeliverable. I tried again. Undeliverable. I tried our messaging app instead – it read as *message sent*, not *message delivered* as it usually would. I dialled her number, but it didn't ring; it went straight to a robotic automated voice that said, 'The mailbox you're trying to reach is full.' I tried again – no rings. She'd blocked my number. Already? She didn't even have the decency to wait for my reply?

I replayed what she'd said that day she'd offered to cut Ruth out of her life for me. *I will just tell Ruth straight; it doesn't bother me. I don't owe her anything. You matter more.* I pictured her saying the equivalent to her new girlfriend. *I will just tell Jess straight. You matter more.*

I searched my social media accounts; Georgia's name didn't come up on any of them. She had blocked me from them all. Why was she doing this? Why was she moving so fast, as if I were some ferocious predator coming to kill her? What was going on? I wasn't ready for the love of my life to become a life lesson.

Chapter 40

I didn't want to see anyone. I didn't want to listen to music. Food made me feel nauseous. Every ounce of joy had been sucked out of my life. I took sick days from work whenever I could get away with them, and when I had to go in, I faked smiles and cried in the toilets.

Despite me telling them not to visit me, Li and Bex turned up at my flat most days. They were my rocks throughout the breakup; I thought Bex would disappear when Georgia did, but we became closer than ever. Georgia had all but cut them both out of her life; she hadn't blocked their numbers, but she blanked their invitations to see them in person. Whenever I heard the buzzer ring in my flat, I knew it was them. Every time I opened the door, I hoped with every fibre of my being that it would be Georgia standing there, full of regret, wanting me back, but it was always Li and Bex. As much as it disappointed me not to see her, I couldn't deny how grateful I was for them. They showed up with meals, stocked my freezer, brought chocolate and magazines, and most importantly, they let me spill my heart out, over and over again.

It couldn't have been easy for them to be in my company; all I did was cry and beg them to pass on messages from me to Georgia – which they dutifully did. They'd been texting her on my behalf for weeks; she wouldn't respond to their messages from me, but it helped to know that she had read them. If I kept sending them on, she couldn't forget about me.

But one day, Li and Bex told me it had become too much; after passing along so many of my messages, Georgia finally snapped – she said she didn't want to hear from me anymore. 'You have to leave it alone,' Li had said gently. 'Enough is enough.' But how could I just stand back and watch all the potential doors back to Georgia close in my face?

Maybe I could have stomached it better if Georgia had just told me who the girlfriend was. She could have just had the decency to tell me that at least, to allow me a chance of closure (not that I wanted it); she wouldn't even tell Li and Bex.

The three of us had no idea who it could have been, even though we'd spent hours trying to work it out, using social media to help us track down whoever it was. We viewed the profiles of pretty much every lesbian we knew, and everyone on Georgia's friend lists, and we were still none the wiser. Whoever it was, I hated the thought of the four of them together, hanging out – this new girl taking my place in the Fab Four. It hadn't happened yet, but I could feel it coming.

I didn't know whether Li and Bex hadn't visited Georgia because the two of them were showing me solidarity or because Georgia was holed up having too much sex with her new girlfriend to even think about having friends over. I dreaded the day it would happen. Li and Bex had promised me they wouldn't entertain the idea of double dates with them, but how could I know for sure?

That day at the spa, Li had urged me to make a concrete decision when it came to Georgia. 'Indecision is still a decision,' she'd said, pressing me to be honest with her. What if Li had told Bex about my uncertainty, and then Bex encouraged Georgia to break away from me? The worst bit is, Bex would have been in the right to do that; if I saw my best friend being kept hanging by a string, I'd probably have taken scissors to it too.

I couldn't trust anyone. I needed to know who the girl was. I wasn't able to sit and suffer.

Chapter 41

I climbed into my car and drove to Georgia's house under the cover of darkness. I just wanted to sit outside and look through her windows, that was all. Or maybe I'd be lucky enough to see the girl arriving or leaving. And when I had a glimpse of who it was, I could leave, and go on living my life.

As I was turning the corner to pull into her street, I turned off my headlights. I knew I couldn't park right outside because she'd recognise my car, so I parked three doors down from hers, on the opposite side of the street. But then I had to back up even further because I was under a bright street lamp. It wasn't a good angle – the neighbour's hedge was in my way and I could barely see a thing – but if I'd crept any closer, or even passed her house to find a better spot, she might have noticed me, so I stayed put.

I slumped down in the seat and craned my neck to see. Her car was in her driveway, and the living room light was on, but the curtains were drawn. There was no second car on the driveway. Or maybe the girl didn't drive? Maybe Georgia had picked her up and brought her over?

I strained to see shadows behind the curtains. I saw none. But if I kept watching, I was sure I'd see something.

Minutes after I parked, the porch light of the house I was in front of came on. And their door was opening. Realisation clicked into my mind. How could I be so stupid? I was so focused on Georgia's house that I'd parked directly outside her dad's house.

I unbuckled my seatbelt and flung myself down so my head was on the passenger seat. 'Please don't come over, please don't come over,' I muttered under my breath in prayer. I reached through the gap between the seats, groping around for the picnic blanket I usually kept in the well behind the passenger seat. Where was it? *Shit*, it must have been behind the driver's side. I felt the edge of it, but I couldn't quite grip it from the angle I was lying at. I twisted and stretched painfully, my fingers fumbling. In a final burst of effort, I managed to grab the blanket. I kept my head down and unrolled it.

Then, from outside came an almighty crash. I couldn't risk looking to find out what it was.

'What the fuck?' It was Gemma's voice. She must have clocked me. Shaking, I frantically unfolded the blanket over my body and head, curling my feet up onto the driver's seat so that I could cover them too.

I heard her footsteps approaching my car. 'You absolute bastard.'

Then, *thud*. I heard the outside bin lid bang against the garage wall – I knew that sound from staying with Georgia at her dad's house on bin night; her room was at the front of the house, so I once asked her what the thudding noise was and she said it was her sister's job to put the bins out, and she hated doing it.

'These bastard bin bags are shit,' she yelled. OK, breathe; my best guess was that a bin bag must have broken while she was putting the rubbish outside, hence the crashing noise, and she'd called *it* a bastard, not me. I heard her mumbling under her breath while she picked up what sounded like tin cans and glass bottles. 'A little help, please,' she called into the house.

No, don't bring anyone else out here.

'Gem. How have you done that?' Her dad's voice.

'It wasn't me,' Gemma said. 'It's these piece-of-shit own-brand bin bags you keep insisting on buying to save a few pennies.'

'It's not a *few* pennies,' Mike said. 'They're half the price of the other ones. I'm not made of money, Gem. I brought you girls up by scrimping and saving. You should be thanking me.'

After what seemed like an eternity, I heard them dump the last of the spilled rubbish into the bin and they closed it again with a bang. Their voices trailed off, and the door shut. I waited a few minutes under the blanket just to make sure they were gone. I thanked my lucky stars that they didn't realise it was my car, but in that moment I missed them almost as much as I missed Georgia.

I needed to leave. That was too close.

***

I pep-talked myself into trying again the next night. I dressed in all black – in a hoodie, leggings and a cap. I fleetingly thought about putting something over my number plates, but it wasn't worth being stopped by police over, and Georgia would recognise my car regardless – blanked-out number plates would have just made me look like even more of a weirdo.

Before I opened my front door, I took three deep breaths and said in my head, *You can do this. You're not doing anything wrong; you're doing this for peace of mind.*

The door buzzer sounded, right next to my ear, and frightened me out of my skin. I yanked down my hood and threw off my cap. I would have asked who it was, but I knew; and besides, the intercom was broken, so I buzzed Bex and Li through the building's main entrance and waited for their knock. I opened my door. It was them; of course it was them.

Why wouldn't they ever text or ring before they came over? I hated it. I liked a chance to tidy up and make sure I looked semi-presentable before someone came over.

'We just wanted to come and check on you,' Li said caringly.

'Thanks so much, girls,' I said, blocking my doorway, knowing they'd just walk in otherwise. 'But I'm fine, you don't have to keep doing this. Just text me if you want to talk, you don't have to keep coming over.'

'You barely reply to texts, and you don't pick up your calls, so that's why we come over. I always know by looking at your face how you really feel, and I can't tell that through a text.'

That was actually quite sweet.

'Were you going somewhere?' Bex asked, glancing down at the trainers on my feet.

'No, I've just come back from the shop, that's all,' I lied. 'I was out of milk.'

'Come on, let's go sit down,' said Li, holding on to my arm and guiding me to the living room, as if I were a nursing-home resident wandering the halls after lights out.

I valued their support, but they were getting in my way. It didn't even cross my mind to tell them where I was really going because they would have just tried to talk me out of it; they'd repeat their new 'enough is enough' or 'leave it alone' catchphrases, and I didn't want to hear that.

'Honestly, I'm fine,' I said, a bitter twist to my words. 'I just want to get into bed early tonight and read a book.' I looked at my watch and stretched open a yawn, hoping they'd pick up on my cue for them to leave.

'That's a nice idea,' Li said. 'Are you going to make it into work tomorrow?'

'Yeah, I'm going to try.'

'That's good, nice to get back to some sort of normality when you're going through a tough time.'

'You're out of milk,' Bex called from the kitchen, peering into my fridge. 'I was going to make you a cup of tea. I thought you said you just went to the shop for milk?'

'Uh, yeah, the shop didn't have any,' I said as convincingly as I could.

'Well, is there anything you want us to do for you while we're here?'

'No, I just want to turn in for the night.'

'We'll leave you to it, then.'

'Actually,' Li said, 'before we go, I saw something earlier I thought you might like. It was an article online.' She unlocked her phone and scrolled. 'Here, I'll send it to you. It's about how deleting photos and videos of your ex could help you let go and start focusing on yourself again.'

I frowned at her, whatever patience I had left disappearing. 'I'm not ready to let go, you know that,' I said, trying hard not to push the words through gritted teeth. 'I want her back. I'd do anything to have her back. Why would I start deleting—'

'Alright,' she interrupted calmly, putting her hands on me gently. 'I just thought maybe it would give you some peace.'

She rubbed the back of my shoulder. 'We're going to keep trying to find ways to help; we've got you, OK?'

I pursed my lips and nodded, not looking directly at her.

'Come here.' Li squeezed me in a hug so tight it hurt. Bex waited for it to finish and then put her arms around me – she was more of a back-thumper than a squeezer. I'm not sure which hug I disliked most out of the two.

Something about their faces seemed off – like they wanted to tell me something. What if they had found out who the girl was? What if they had come over to tell me, but I was rushing them out? What if Georgia had seen me in her street the night before and had told them, and they'd come to check I wasn't about to do it again? Maybe that was why Bex questioned me about why I was wearing shoes.

'Is everything alright with you two?' I asked.

'Uh, yeah,' Bex said, smiling. She didn't sound confident.

'What's up, girls?'

'Nothing, we just wanted to see if you were OK and if you had anything to tell us,' Li said before quickly lightening her tone and rephrasing. 'I mean, if you *wanted* to tell us anything...'

I stared at her blankly.

'Honestly, it's nothing,' she said, her voice too bright, too cheery. 'Tuck yourself up and get some rest tonight.'

I waited ten minutes before I even thought about heading down to my car. I put my cap back on and made my way downstairs. As I came to the top of the second flight, I saw the front door of the building opening. It was Bex. Someone from another flat must have buzzed her in when I hadn't. She was carrying a bottle of milk. I didn't think she'd noticed me, so I ran back up the stairs, taking care to land my feet as softly as I could.

I fumbled to unlock my door and then I softly closed it behind me, flinging off my hat and kicking off my shoes. I wrenched my hoodie aggressively over my head, ripping out a chunk of hair as I did so, and threw my dressing gown on quickly over the rest of my clothes.

She knocked. I answered, faking a yawn as I did so.

Bex looked at me. I searched her eyes, trying to detect if she'd seen me running from her. I couldn't work out her expression.

She handed me the milk. 'Just wanted to make sure you had some for the morning.'

'Thank you so much, that's so kind,' I said, feigning surprise, as if I'd only just noticed what she was handing me.

'Night, then.'

'Night. Thanks, Bex.'

I shut the door and pressed my back against it, breathing out forcefully. I decided to go to bed.

***

The next night, I drove to Georgia's street once more, opting for an unfamiliar route that circled around to approach from the opposite direction. That way, I could avoid passing by her dad's house or hers. Inevitably, I ended up getting lost on the way, arriving in her street close to midnight – likely too late to see anything significant.

I chose a parking spot six houses away from hers. It was a satisfactory view, but I was sure I could crawl the car closer for a better look. One or two houses closer. Better. I could see that her living room light was still on, thankfully.

I gasped as a shadow moved past the window, my eyes stretching out on stalks for a better look. Then a second shadow appeared – I knew that meant *she* was inside too. The curtains shifted, and I slumped down, realising someone was peeking through. It was Georgia. She pulled the curtains wider, revealing her face fully as I peered over the steering wheel, tugging the brim of my cap down.

She was peering up and down the street through the window. Then she was coming out of the front door.

I started my engine and began a three-point turn. I glanced towards her house; she was on the pavement staring straight at me. I stalled the car while it was horizontal in the street. I looked towards a flash, startled; she had taken a picture of me.

Chapter 42

Thoughts raced through my head about what Georgia was going to do with that picture, why she had taken it in the first place, or why she had even looked through her curtains. What had alerted her to me? There were so many unanswered questions.

I buttoned up my work trousers; they were much looser than the last time I'd worn them – there's something to be said for heartbreak diets. I took a sip of milky tea, holding the mug between my hands, hoping it would be a cuppa that made everything better, like Dad always said. But I wasn't counting on it. I had a horrendous workday on the cards, in court covering an assault trial where the victim would have to relive every awful detail in the witness box, her abuser sitting just yards away. Cases like that always twisted my stomach, made me question my career. But I couldn't call in sick again. I had to push through, wear the mask of composure, and act like I was holding it all together.

The buzzer to the door went. It wasn't even 8.30 a.m. Why had Li and Bex come over so damn early? I buzzed them through the main entrance, ready to give them a piece of my mind.

I pulled a top over my head, shoved my phone in my pocket and waited with my fist wrapped around the door handle, yanking the door open on the first knock.

'Girls. You can't just—' I stared in shock.

'Jessica Davies?'

I nodded, wide-eyed, gawping at the police officer.

'Jessica Davies, I'm arresting you on suspicion of stalking and harassment. You do not have to say anything, but it may harm your defence if you do not mention when questioned something which you later rely on in court. Anything you do say may be given in evidence.'

I turned sick with fear and confusion as he cuffed me. How could parking on public property near someone's house be an arrestable offence? Oh god, what was going to happen to me? Was this going to be on my permanent record? What if they notified my boss? Would I lose my job?

'Miss Davies,' said PC Bevan, who had introduced himself once we were in the stark, sterile interview room. 'We've received multiple complaints about you from an individual.'

Multiple complaints?

'These pertain to stalking and harassment, in the forms of surveillance, intimidation and cyber abuse.'

WHAT? A chaos of panic whirred through me. Surveillance, OK, fine, I watched Georgia's house from my car once (twice). But intimidation? Cyber abuse? They had the wrong person.

'The individual who has made these claims has submitted evidence to us.'

My heart was beating out of my chest as he laid out an array of papers in front of me. On one of them was the picture Georgia took of me from the night before, resembling a deer in headlights. One sheet had on it what looked like a call log, and the rest of the papers showed screenshots of texts between me and Georgia.

'As you can see, the individual has submitted the texts you've been sending, in which you threaten both violence and the distribution of sexually explicit material of the individual.'

'I threatened what?' My words caught in my throat. 'I don't know what you're talking about. I honestly don't.'

My eyes grew wider still, and I grasped at the printed text conversations, holding them closer to my face. One, from my number, read:

'I have that video of me and you. You know, the one where you're the police officer and I'm the prisoner? What would your boss – the headteacher of a school – think of that? Maybe I should send it to her to find out? Or maybe I should just post it on the student forum? Or on a porn site for everyone to enjoy?'

What. The. Fuck?

Underneath the text was a still of the video Georgia and I had recorded, of her handcuffing me. What on earth was going on?

Another text from my number read:

'You better fucking watch out; I could be anywhere. Every time you come out of your house, I'll be waiting. I'm going to fuck up your life!'

I pushed the papers away, horrified. 'I've never seen these texts before in my life!'

'And there's this,' he said, passing me the call log.

'What *is* this exactly?'

'That's your phone number, isn't it?' He pointed with a pen.

'Yes, but—' I paused to study the pages, noticing that every call was from my number. There were hundreds of them, all with recent dates.

'I swear, I haven't done this.'

I hadn't called her since the day she broke up with me, the day she said we had to cut ties; I didn't call after that. And besides, her phone didn't even ring on that day. And come to think of it, my messages didn't go through that day either – they were undelivered – so how had she had all these texts from *my* number? She'd blocked me.

'The logs tell us times and dates for everything.'

'No. It's not possible, I—'

And then I saw it. The text that clicked the realisation switch in my brain:

'You're the reason Joe and I broke up, and you're going to fucking pay, bitch! We would have been happy if it weren't for you!'

'It's my ex,' I said loudly. 'He must have done this somehow. He's a technology expert – he started his own tech company – he must have found a way to copy my number and frame me.'

'Right, right,' said the officer, unconvinced. 'How do you explain this, then?'

He held up the photo of me, the one mid three-point turn, looking straight at Georgia's camera, horrified that she'd caught me red-handed.

I tried to keep calm. 'I'll admit I was outside her house last night, and that looks dodgy, I know, but it was only one time. Two times. But I promise you that's it. I haven't sent any of these texts or made any of these calls. It's all a big coincidence.'

He picked up one of the text sheets again and tapped his finger on a particular one. 'This one was sent to the individual at—' He double-checked the paper. 'At eleven fifty-six p.m. yesterday. The text reads: "I'm going to get you. Look outside your window right now – I'm waiting for you. I know you're both in there."'

He picked up the photo of me again, tapping the timestamp on it. 'And this was taken at eleven fifty-eight p.m. yesterday. So, this photograph was taken two minutes after the threatening text was sent to the individual. And you're saying you didn't send a text while you were outside her house? A text *telling* her you were, in fact, outside her house. Just a coincidence, eh?'

'I didn't send it. How is this possible? I don't understand.' Beads of sweat trickled down my lower back. 'I've been set up. Please. It's my ex-fiancé, I just know it. His name is Joe Griffiths. I need your help in finding out how he's using my number and how he's doing this because I swear that's the explanation for everything. Please believe me. I'm a victim of identity theft and phone hacking.'

He shuffled the papers together without looking at me.

'Please. I made a complaint about him a while ago; I called the police and told them he'd broken into my flat and urinated on my clothes. He's an evil guy. He's done this, I swear.'

The tangle of dread in my chest tightened, only allowing me to take shallow breaths, and the drumroll of impending doom raced.

'We're going to release you under investigation for now, Miss Davies. We'll have to hold on to your mobile phone; I'll let you know when it can be returned. Do you have someone you could call to collect you?'

I thought about calling my mum and dad, but I didn't want them worrying. I called Li instead.

Chapter 43

I stared out of the car window, turning myself as far away from Li as I could. I was horrified by what had just happened, and even though I had done nothing wrong – apart from sitting outside Georgia's house, which at worst was inappropriate – I was mortified and didn't want to talk.

'Jess,' Li said sympathetically, laying a hand on my knee while she drove. 'How are you feeling? Talk to me. What's going on? What happened in there?'

I wiped away tears and rubbed my wet hands on my trousers. 'Joe hacked my phone and has somehow been sending Georgia abusive texts, pretending to be me.'

'Oh god!' she said with surprise. '*That's* what's been happening? That makes much more sense.'

'What?' I turned to face her sharply. 'More sense than what? Wait. You knew something had been going on?'

'No, no, I just meant, because you were at the police station—'

'No. You knew something.'

She took a deep breath. 'Look, when we came to visit you, it *was* for a reason, but we didn't know how to broach it.'

I knew Li's and Bex's expressions had looked strange that night. 'What was it?' I asked, equal parts demanding and confused.

'Georgia had texted us earlier that night saying you'd been threatening her; she asked if you'd said anything to us about it. That's why we came over to check how you were, but it didn't feel like the right time to ask questions.'

I felt queasy. 'So you believed I'd been threatening her?' My voice was strained and high as I tried to hold back tears. 'Why would I do that when all I ever talk about is how much I love and miss her? You two have been my rocks during this breakup. I would never have thought you'd believe something like that – I've been open about everything.'

'We didn't believe it. But then—' She hesitated.

'Then what?' I demanded, fed up with how slow and indirect she was being.

'Then Georgia sent us screenshots of the texts. So obviously that was harder to get our heads around because the texts were coming from your number. Love does funny things to us all, so we didn't think badly of you, we just wanted to see if we could help at all, or if you wanted to chat.'

Was that why Li had encouraged me to delete pictures and videos of Georgia, because she thought I'd been using them to threaten Georgia?

'Why couldn't you have said something to me, Li? That would have been far better than getting a surprise knock on the door from a goddamn police officer this morning.'

'We had no idea she was going to get the police involved – I promise you.'

'Honestly, I don't know what to believe at the moment. Just take me home please.'

She pulled into a parking space near my flat. I unbuckled and got out of the car quickly, giving Li a curt goodbye before slamming the door. I was so mad at Li and Bex, but really, I knew I was just directing the anger I felt for Joe at them, and they didn't deserve that.

When I closed myself inside my flat, a realisation hit me: if there was ever a chance of getting Georgia back, it was finally over – she'd caught me outside her house and she'd thought I'd threatened to ruin her life.

After splashing cold water on my cheeks and quickly touching up my makeup, I grabbed my bag, ran down the stairs and stepped out into the cool air, forcing myself to breathe deeply. I knew I couldn't miss any more work. I slid into my car and drove to the office, my thoughts still racing. The morning's events felt surreal – a nightmare I couldn't shake off.

When I arrived at the office, I braced myself for Glyn's reaction. As I walked in, he looked up from his desk, his expression more annoyed than concerned.

'Look who finally decided to grace us with her presence!' he called out, making the whole room look at me. 'I was beginning to think you'd run off to join the circus.'

'I'm sorry, Glyn. I had a... situation this morning,' I said, trying to keep my voice steady.

'Meeting room,' he said, standing. I followed him. Once the door was closed behind us, he sat at the desk, his eyes glinting with curiosity. 'So, a situation?'

I hated how he seemed to relish it.

'You know, I'm always here if you need to talk about your "situations". Maybe over drinks after work sometime?' He smiled, tapping his pen on the desk while staring at me.

I couldn't even force a smile. 'I'll manage, thanks.'

He frowned, leaning forward so the edge of the desk pressed into his dough belly, his tone shifting into something much more serious. 'Just don't let it affect your work, Jess. You've got a Crown Court trial to cover this afternoon, and I need you focused.'

'Understood.'

I reminded myself of my purpose. I was going to court to report on a high-profile case that would hopefully put a woman-beater behind bars. I couldn't let Joe's twisted behaviour derail me. I had a job to do.

***

Ever since I'd turned down Glyn's date offer – which was essentially what it was – he'd been assigning me the worst tasks. Or maybe it was just that I didn't smile and *politely* decline his advances; I wasn't sure. Either way, it felt like he was punishing me with the most dreaded duty any reporter had to face: the death knock.

I was sent to knock on the door of a couple whose little boy had accidentally hung himself on the living room blinds. I was expected to show up and ask for a comment from parents grieving the unimaginable. It was a violation of their privacy, an intrusion into their raw pain. It's a horrific, ridiculous thing for a reporter to have to do, yet newsrooms expect it, thinking that just because it used to happen, it's somehow still acceptable.

I never wanted to upset people or make things worse. There's a world of difference between knocking on the door of a widow whose elderly husband passed away peacefully to offer a tribute piece and knocking on the door of parents who've just lost their child in such horrendous circumstances.

Death knocks are often pointless anyway. You drive thirty minutes each way only to be met with slammed doors. But that time was different. I didn't get the door shut in my face. I was run out of town.

I pulled up to the house in a sketchy cul-de-sac and, as always, parked facing the way out so I wouldn't have to drive past the house again afterwards.

I knocked, and a man in his twenties answered – the father of the boy.

'I'm really sorry to bother you,' I said, my voice barely above a whisper. 'I'm Jess Davies from *The City Post*. I know this is an incredibly difficult time, but if you wanted to say something, we're here to listen.'

'Fuck off!' he shouted, spitting at my feet.

I raised my hands in a placating gesture, my heart starting to gallop. 'Of course, no problem.'

'I saw you coming a mile off, knocking on the neighbours' doors looking for the right house,' he continued, his eyes blazing with anger and pain.

'I'm so sorry,' I said, feeling smaller by the second. 'Sorry to bother you, and so sorry for your loss.'

As I walked quickly back to my car, a Ford Fiesta came barrelling down the street, filled with men. I glanced back at the father, who was pointing me out to them. My stomach dropped as I saw the car screeching around the cul-de-sac, coming to follow me.

I put my foot down and got the fuck out of there.

Chapter 44

An unknown number was calling. I stared at it. Georgia? Joe? The girlfriend?

'Hello?' I said calmly.

'Miss Davies, it's PC Bevan. Are you free to come down to the station, please?'

'Yes. Now? Have you found anything?'

'Now would work; best if we talk in person.'

I arrived at the station and the uniformed woman at the front counter walked me to a room where PC Bevan was waiting.

'Miss Davies,' he said. 'Thanks for coming in. Please take a seat.'

He had kind eyes, far too gentle-looking to be a big, intimidating police officer. He had a bristle of short salt-and-pepper hair, a strong nose and a dimple on his shaved chin – details I hadn't noticed when we'd first met.

'We gave our cyber specialists your phone and they've been looking into your claim that your former fiancé hacked it. They didn't find any evidence of threatening messages in your device's sent items; even if you had deleted them, our analysts would have been able to recover them, so we now know for a fact there was nothing sent from your phone. Same with the calls – no evidence of those being made from your device either. We believe your phone number was cloned, allowing the perpetrator to impersonate you from a separate device, which explains the texts and calls that came from your number.'

'How did he even do that?' I asked, mortified.

'Our specialists discovered that sophisticated spyware was downloaded onto your device, allowing the perpetrator access to your phone and its number.'

I sat there listening, gobsmacked. The invasion of privacy was astounding.

'There's more, unfortunately,' he continued. 'Via the spyware, your phone's location was consistently tracked. We have confirmed that your location was traced the night you were outside Georgia Morgan's house – the night that she took a picture of you. If you recall, Miss Morgan received a text from someone claiming to be you, which said—' He moved his fingertip across the paper in front of him, stopped at a particular spot and read out mechanically, '"Look outside your window right now – I'm waiting for you."'

He cleared his throat. 'So, our belief is the perpetrator tapped into your location that night, saw that you were near Miss Morgan's house, and then sent Miss Morgan a threatening message – which looked to be from you – so that she would see you outside her window.'

Joe had probably been rubbing his hands together and evil-laughing that night; what a master manipulator he was – pinning me at the scene of the crime.

'The perpetrator would have needed uninterrupted access to your phone for hours to have had time to download something as advanced as this,' he continued. 'Do you have any idea if your former partner,

Mr Griffiths, would have had the chance to access your phone for that amount of time?'

'He could have done it while he was still living in my flat, while I was sleeping maybe?' I doubted it, though – I slept with my phone under my pillow because I distrusted him so much.

'Oh my g—' Realisation smacked me in the face. 'I left my phone at home on the day Joe broke into my flat and pissed – sorry, urinated – on my clothes. So he could have hacked it then.'

'What date would that have been?'

I gave him a rough estimate.

'Great, that will be a big help; I'll pass that information on to our tech team who can aim to confirm a correlation.'

My first thought was *Thank god* – proof for Georgia that I wasn't a malicious stalker. My next thought was how much I despised Joe for this. What an evil bastard. I wanted him dead for what he'd done; I was ready to rip his face off.

'The moment I saw the texts you showed me, I knew it was Joe, but I didn't know he would go this low,' I said. 'Can we prove it's him? Is there a way to trace it back to him?'

'Unfortunately, not at the moment,' he said. 'It's incredibly so-phisticated tech that has been installed on your phone; it's proving watertight so far, but we're working on it.'

'Could you take him in for questioning? I can give you his address. I'm pretty sure he lives with his mum.'

'There's no hard evidence pointing to him yet, so we need to find some proof first.'

I started pleading that they did something. I wanted Joe caught and punished.

'Look.' His voice softened. 'If we alert him too soon, he'll have time to delete evidence, won't he? And we wouldn't want that. This way will give us our best chance at proving it's him.'

'He used to abuse me, you know! Mentally abuse me. He's a manipulative, malicious person.'

It occurred to me that when Joe looked through my phone the day he broke into my flat, that must have been the moment he confirmed that there was someone else in my life. He must have seen all the text conversations between Georgia and me and realised I had feelings for her – although I never technically cheated on him, apart from kissing her, once, before ending things with him. He must have been livid, humiliated and demeaned – especially as it was a woman I had feelings for – and I knew that was why he'd decided to download the malware and why he'd pissed over my belongings. It made sense then – he went from love notes one day to piss the next. Of course he'd seen my messages to her. Of course he wanted to ruin us.

I knew he wouldn't leave my life as easily as he'd made it seem; I knew it was too good to be true. And I should have known he wouldn't let it lie after I called the police on him. I should have just let him have that disgusting act in the bathroom as the last word. It was always safer to let him have the last word. And deep down, I knew he'd keep trying until he had it.

I bet he'd downloaded the spyware just to have it in his back pocket, in case he needed to take things further. I didn't put it past him that he would have used it for his own perverse pleasure – to feel as if he had control over me until he got bored – but if I hadn't phoned the police on him, I bet this whole impersonation development wouldn't have happened.

And then his voice rang in my head: *If you're dumping me because you've met another man, I'll kill him. I'll fucking kill him.*

'I think Georgia's in danger,' I told PC Bevan. 'Joe threatened to kill the person I was ending our relationship for. And that person was Georgia.'

'Right.' He wrote something on his notepad. 'Thank you, Miss Davies. Call us if there's anything you wish to talk about in the meantime, and we'll keep you in the loop about any updates. Please keep all of this to yourself for now as it's an ongoing investigation. We'll get in touch with Miss Morgan directly.

'And Miss Davies,' he added, mollifying his voice again, 'easier said than done, but don't worry, OK?'

I nodded, rearranging my expression as best I could into one of gratitude, and turned to walk out. Glancing back at him for a second, I added, 'Oh, do you think I'd be able to have my phone back yet?'

'Best we hang onto it for now.'

'But what if Joe tracks the phone's location and sees that it's at the police station? He may start deleting evidence – like you said – if he thinks he's been found out.'

'I wouldn't worry about that,' he said. 'The perpetrator will have expected you to have been brought in by police after the impersonated text placed you at the scene, outside Miss Morgan's house.'

'I just, I just can't work out how he knew I was *outside* Georgia's house, rather than *in* her house?'

'It was probably a well-informed guess considering he could see your texts and call list.'

'What do you mean, sorry?'

'Well, the perpetrator would have known if you'd contacted Miss Morgan, or been invited over to the house – because of the spyware. The absence of interaction between you and Miss Morgan would have led him to guess you were just outside. You said you'd parked outside Miss Morgan's house twice recently, yes?'

I nodded, feeling a wave of shame wash over me as the indignity of having hidden under a blanket from Georgia's sister and dad flashed vividly in my mind, causing my cheeks to burn with embarrassment. 'I wonder why Joe didn't "out" me the first time I went to her street,' I said, trying to make sense of it.

'There's no rhyme or reason to that, not as far as we can see anyway.'

'What scares me is how he knows where she lives. He traced *my* location, but how did he know that the location was her address?'

'Hate to say it, but you may well have been followed by him – numerous times even. In our experience, cyber abuse isn't an isolated incident; it's normally paired with some other sort of in-person harassment or stalking. What car does he have?'

'A black pickup truck,' I said.

'Hold on,' said PC Bevan, as if a memory had popped into his mind. He opened the folder of papers again. 'I thought I saw... Yes, there.' He pointed at the photo Georgia had taken of me doing a three-point turn in her road; he held it out to me and drummed on it with a fingertip. 'A black pickup truck, in the background.'

My skin flared into goosebumps, and my stomach twisted into a tight knot. Joe was there? He had been watching me while I was watching Georgia? How had I not noticed him? How had I been so blind? The room began to rotate, the edges blurring. How many other times had he followed me to her house? How many times had he followed me full stop?

Chapter 45

'Wait,' I said, looking more closely at the photo of the truck. 'It's not his number plate.'

I couldn't see the number plate of the car in the picture – the letters and numbers were just fuzzy markings – but I knew it wasn't Joe's. His was much shorter than the normal number plate format. His was 800 BS – he'd spent a small fortune on that, or his mum had – just for the laughs from the boys, a plate that said *BOOBS*, how mature – but the plate in the picture was a standard length.

It was bittersweet. If it had been Joe's car, it would have been undeniable evidence that he was the ringmaster of it all. But it was a relief to know that he hadn't been there, because if he had, who knows how many more times he'd been just behind me, watching and waiting.

***

I fixed an empty daze onto my steering wheel. Even though it wasn't Joe's truck, he'd still impersonated me and intimidated the love of my life, turning her against me. How could someone be so callous and calculated?

There was no time to dwell on it all; I had to warn Georgia that she might be in physical danger. Joe had said he would kill the person I was leaving him for, and that may well have been the next step in his playbook as far as I knew. He'd already threatened violence in the texts he'd sent her, so what if he was now planning to hurt her for real?

To hell with what PC Bevan said about keeping this to myself and waiting for the police to update her themselves. Georgia had to know as soon as possible. I needed her to be on her guard and to know who to look out for, because at that moment, she still thought I was the culprit.

I didn't have any way of contacting her; I was blocked from all angles. And I couldn't show up to her house, not while she thought I was some raging stalker. I'd have to ask Li and Bex to pass her the message. Li knew what was going on anyway; I'd told her about Joe on the day she'd picked me up from the police station.

I dialled her number.

'Hey, Jess,' she answered quickly. 'I'm at work. I can't really talk right now.'

'Li, it's urgent. Please, give me two minutes and I'll let you go.'

'Oh! Are you OK?'

'I need you to do me a favour as soon as you can. I think Georgia's in danger. She needs to know that these abusive texts weren't from me, they were from Joe. She needs to know to look out for him. I have no idea what he has planned. I need to warn her.'

'Shit. Of course, I'll tell her. I'll ring her right now, and if she doesn't answer, I'll go over to her house.'

'Will you do it as soon as possible, please?'

'I promise. Of course, of course.'

'But you have to be discreet about it, Li. And tell Georgia she needs to keep it to herself too. If this gets out, it may ruin our chances of nailing Joe to the wall.'

I turned the key in the ignition and drove, thinking over all the new information that my brain had to process, wanting to organise it neatly, compartmentalise it, attach colour-coded sticky notes to it and give it structure and a timeline before it overwhelmed me. What was the furthest back I could go in all of this? What had happened first? Joe had downloaded the spyware onto my phone the day I left it in my flat. OK, that was first. Then, through the spyware, he'd monitored me via location tracking. And then he began impersonating me. I wondered when he sent the first impersonation text; how far back would that have started?

Wait.

I thought back to what Georgia had said when she broke things off with me. I groped about in my memory for her wording. *The way you've been speaking to me lately has been horrible. How could I ever be with you after that?*

I had thought she was referring to the one time I'd screamed at her in the strip club, but I distinctly remember that when I apologised for 'that night', she'd replied, 'Which night? There have been too many to count.'

I turned around and headed back towards the police station. I parked up and ran in, asking to speak to PC Bevan.

'Sorry, his shift has finished,' said the woman at the front desk.

I was about to leave when I spotted him walking down the corridor, his back to me.

'PC Bevan!' I shouted.

'Miss, you can't just—'

'Sorry,' I said to the woman, tilting my head and holding my hands in the air apologetically.

He thudded back down the hallway, searching the room sternly for the person who'd yelled his name.

I waved impatiently to him and he approached.

'Miss Davies?'

'I'm so sorry, something's just occurred to me and I wondered if you still have those text screenshots please?'

He glanced at his watch. 'Come through.'

I followed him to the interview room, and he passed me the text printouts from the file. I flipped through them, trying to find ones that pre-dated Georgia breaking up with me. There was nothing from that far back.

'Do you have any earlier ones than this?'

'No, that's all we have,' he said. 'What's this concerning?'

'Is there any chance you could ask Georgia for screenshots of any abusive texts she received from my number before the fourteenth of last month?' I asked with pleading eyes.

The fourteenth; I knew the date she broke up with me by heart. She'd said on that date that I'd been rude to her 'countless times' – and I just knew that must have been Joe texting her. I needed to see those texts. She said the way I was speaking to her was what drove her to break up with me; she'd said, 'It gave me the push I needed to find happiness outside of you. It helped me to move on.' I needed to know what he'd said to lead her to that point.

His texts were the reason she'd ended things. And yes, I was the one who went behind her back to try to hook up with other people, but she didn't even mention that as the reason she was breaking up with me. For all I knew, she was still none the wiser that I'd tried to do that.

She said the reason she was ending things was because of the way I'd been speaking to her. Only, that wasn't me. That was Joe. So maybe I still had a chance with her.

PC Bevan sighed. 'I'm not sure asking her for those texts is going to help us with our investigation,' he said. 'And I'm not an errand boy.'

'I'm so sorry, I didn't mean it like that,' I said, trying to ingratiate myself to him again, hoping he would return the softness to his voice – I thought he was beginning to like me, and I didn't want to lose that.

'Look, I'll do what I can.'

***

I drove home, chewing at my fingers and glancing at my work phone, mentally willing Li to call me back. I pulled into my parking space outside my flat, took my keys out of the ignition and texted her:

'Have you told Georgia yet?'

She replied instantly:

'She hasn't picked up. I tried her like ten times. Heading to hers soon.'

There was no time to waste; this was an emergency. I needed to just go to Georgia's myself. If she wouldn't answer the door to me, I'd just shout through her letterbox and hope she was home to hear. I didn't feel right posting a note through her door in case it was used as further evidence of harassment.

I messaged Li:

'I'm driving to hers now.'

I dug my key back into the ignition, the scrape of metal on metal setting my teeth on edge. My phone vibrated on my lap; it was Li calling.

'On my way to Georgia's now. I'll ring you after I speak to her,' she said.

'Thank you. Please hurry. Ring me when you're done.'

When she finally called me back, she said, 'I told her everything. I told her about Joe and to be on her guard and to lock the doors, and not to tell anyone about what's going on.'

'Thank you so much,' I said, sighing in relief. 'How did she take it? You told her I had nothing to do with any of it, right?'

'Yes, I told her. She said that made much more sense because it wasn't like you. She was obviously spooked by the fact Joe might get physical, but the police will take that seriously now that you've told them – you did the right thing by doing that.'

'Did she seem like she wanted to talk to me about it?'

'She didn't say – but I'd leave things for now, Jess. Everything's so complicated as it is. Just let the dust settle first. This is nearly over now, surely. The police will get him, don't worry.'

Over the next few days, I found myself checking my work phone every couple of minutes to see if there was an update from PC Bevan. Finally, my phone lit up.

'Hello? PC Bevan?' I said, a millisecond after the first ring.

He was talking to people in the office, clearly not realising I'd picked up. 'Oh, hello? Miss Davies, there's been a development we thought you should know about. Can you come down to the station today?'

I told Glyn I had to go for personal reasons, and then I ran out of the office before he could say a thing. I couldn't face another lecture.

***

'Would you mind if Cara, our wellbeing officer, sat in on this chat because of the sensitive nature of the information I'm about to share with you?' PC Bevan asked, gesturing to a woman with a benevolent face.

While my nails sank into my palms in apprehension, I told them I didn't mind.

He sat down and waited for me to do so too. 'This won't be easy to hear, I'm afraid.' He swallowed, and then, as if reading from a memorised script, he continued robotically. 'We already know that advances in technology mean that perpetrators have access to a broader and more complex range of tools to harm victims, and instances of tech-related harassment have been increasing. The number of individuals – mainly women – who have discovered spyware, or stalkerware as it's also known, installation attempts on their devices has increased by forty per cent in the last six months alone, compared with—'

Cara cleared her throat and gave PC Bevan an encouraging look as if to urge him to get to the point.

'The thing is, unfortunately, the spyware that was downloaded to your device is so advanced that not only has it allowed the perpetrator to impersonate you from their own device and track your location – as you already know – but it has also allowed for covert monitoring of your messages and screening of your calls.'

He gave a compassionate pause before continuing. 'The perpetrator has also had access to all of your password-protected accounts and your photo and video albums. And – Miss Davies, this will likely be the toughest piece of information to hear – they've had access to your phone's microphone and cameras.'

I sat there trying to listen to him, but his words felt like bullets – as if I were standing against a firing-range wall while he unloaded ammunition rounds into me.

'So, you mean, he's been taking photos with my camera?' I asked, stunned.

'More like, your front and back cameras have been utilised like webcams.'

'So – so he's been watching me?' I asked, shock jolting through me like lightning.

PC Bevan contorted his face into a sympathetic expression. 'With access to your device's cameras and microphones, he would have had the ability to watch and listen to you, yes.'

He waited while the worst of my sobs tore their way out. Cara pulled her chair nearer mine, handing me tissues. This meant that Joe would have witnessed my most intimate moments, and he would have seen me – or at the very least heard me – with all of my would-be one-night stands. My blood curdled.

'I'm so sorry this has happened to you, Jess,' said Cara.

'Can I leave now, please?' I asked, staring at the floor.

'Of course,' said Cara. 'We can resume the conversation at a time that feels right for you.'

'Hold on, would you be happy to stay for me to tell you one last thing, Miss Davies?' asked PC Bevan cautiously, leaning forward in his seat. 'It's the most important piece of information we've received so far.'

Cara shot him a look. 'If Jess is not up to continuing this conversation right now, then we should recommence at a more convenient time, PC Bevan, when Jess has had time to absorb the overwhelming information she's already received today.'

'No, it's fine,' I interjected. 'I want to know. I need to know now.'

Cara pursed her lips and gave PC Bevan a brisk nod.

'Right,' he said, glancing uneasily at Cara before giving me back his full attention, 'as you know, we've been working closely with our specialists from a cyber security company who have been looking into the spyware on your phone. Unfortunately, we have now learnt that there is a major conflict of interest that we had previously overlooked.' Apprehension carved itself deeper into his face. 'The company we've been working with is called—' He cleared his throat. 'JoMatTech.'

Shock raked its nails across my ribs.

'And the co-owner of the company is—'

Don't say it, don't say it! You'll make it real if you say it!

'A Mr Joe Griffiths.'

Chapter 46

This absolutely couldn't be happening. My head was spinning out of control. The next thing I knew, I was waking up on the hard floor, the side of my skull throbbing from where it had met the unyielding vinyl surface.

The interview room blurred back into focus and Cara's concerned face came into view. I felt her patting my arm in an attempt to comfort me as I struggled to make sense of the situation. Cara helped me ease into an upright position, the world still swirling around me. Struggling to blink away the haze, I accepted the plastic cup of water she offered, sipping shakily. Gradually, the spinning started to subside.

'Let me get this straight,' I finally managed when I was back in my seat. 'Joe hacked my phone, and then *his* cyber company was tasked, by the police, with tracing the culprit?' The words emerged tentatively, a deliberate effort to compose myself before fully delving into this surreal revelation. 'No wonder they were having trouble finding the source – it was a cover-up!' My breath buckled again.

'In through your nose and out through your mouth,' said Cara tenderly.

Why hadn't PC Bevan connected the dots before now? He knew Joe's name, so why hadn't alarm bells rung when he was liaising with Joe's fucking company? It was my fault; I'd never mentioned the name of Joe's company; how could he have known? I bet he didn't even communicate with Joe directly; it would have probably been the co-founder, Matty, he spoke with, or one of the female staff members. Or maybe he'd had no contact with them at all – maybe that was the job of one of his colleagues.

'We hadn't made the connection until now,' he said, looking more than a little embarrassed. 'We're so sorry this has happened. A wider investigation into this is underway as we speak. And it goes without saying that JoMatTech has been removed from your case, and suspended from all cases.'

I wanted to tear all my clothes off; everything felt too tight against my skin. 'How did this even happen?' I asked, spluttering. 'How – what? I don't understand.'

'We started working with JoMatTech quite recently,' he explained. 'We'd put the cyber security contract out to tender, and JoMatTech secured it.'

I held my head in my hands and squeezed at the roots of my hair.

'There is a bit of good news among all of this though,' he said, as soft as a kitten. 'Miss Morgan sent over those extra text screenshots you wanted to see.'

I looked up and he was already holding the pages out to me, like some sort of apology gift.

As I'd expected, they were dreadful. No wonder Georgia had accused me of talking to her as if she were a 'piece of shit' – the texts were plain evil. I read through them; they were mingled with texts that I'd sent from my own phone, too.

The first one on the list was:

'Would you be up for hangover out tomorrow?'

I remembered sending that one; predictive text had changed the word 'hanging' to 'hangover'. The next text was from me again, correcting myself:

'Hanging out*'

After that came pure vitriol, from my number again, from Joe impersonating me:

'About tomorrow, not so sure we should be alone. I don't want you trying to kiss me. Will your sister be there? I also can't be bothered to see you if you're going to be moping.'

He was so fucking awful! I noticed his text had come through to her phone in green, but my texts had come through in blue.

Georgia replied with:

'Don't worry, I know we're not together, you've made that perfectly clear. Gemma's going to be here, yes, so you won't have to be alone with me.'

It was baffling that she'd even entertained the idea of having me over to her house after thinking I'd spoken to her like that. She must have felt broken by that message. I remember that day clearly; I went over to see her – the day after meeting Daeva Valentine – and sat through a rom-com with her and Gemma. Despite my best effort to get her alone that day, to ask her if she'd be my girlfriend, I couldn't persuade her. Joe's text explained why she had been so cold with me.

I remember she even said to me, 'You've changed your tune after last night,' when I arrived at the house, and I didn't have a clue what she'd meant. When I questioned her on it, she'd said, 'The text you sent me.' This was the text she'd been referring to all along.

'I'm trying to wrap my head around this,' I said to PC Bevan. 'Was she replying to the two phone numbers separately without knowing it? And if so, how's that even possible when the two phone numbers are the same?'

'From my limited understanding of it, the green texts were from the perpetrator, and they were green because they were sent via SMS, from an Android phone. And the blue ones, sent by your device, were sent using iMessage. When Miss Morgan replied to the green messages, her texts would come through to the perpetrator, and when she replied to the blue messages, her texts would come through to you.'

His explanation went over my head. I couldn't grasp it at that moment; my brain was too saturated. I just wanted to keep looking through the list.

Another one, from Joe posing as me, said:

'Don't tell the girls, but I've ditched takeaway-and-movie night tonight to go to that new gay bar in the city centre – Scissor. Single life is so much fucking fun. I've finally got some excitement in my life! I'm dancing with a smoking-hot girl right now.'

After that text, there was a picture message Joe had sent Georgia – a photo of me and lion-haired girl. I could have cried endless tears over what my poor Georgia had been subjected to. I could barely stomach looking at many more of the texts; they were getting worse as I read on. Further down the list, there was a text from Georgia to my number:

'All I wanted to do tonight was kiss you.'

That was from when she was lying next to me in the hotel bed after the Polka Dot Sneakers' gig in London. I'd pretended I hadn't seen the text that night, and neither of us had mentioned it to each other the following day either. The text after that, from Joe posing as me, read:

'I can't believe you texted me saying you wanted to kiss me. You don't know how to respect boundaries, do you? Guess what I'm doing right at this very second (while I'm sitting next to you in the car and you're chauffeuring me back to my house LOL)? I'm texting someone called Frankie and arranging a date. *That's* how much I want to kiss you.'

I clenched my jaw, screwed up the paper in front of me and let out a shriek in front of PC Bevan, who was politely looking off to the side, feigning deafness. My poor Georgia. I thought back to that car ride home from the gig. She had been murmuring to herself about the slow car in front of her, and then, all of a sudden, after checking the time on her watch, she'd flipped and started beeping at him and shouting. Could that have been the moment she'd received Joe's text from my number? Oh my god, of course. She hadn't been looking at the time on her watch at all. All of her texts came through on her smartwatch. She must have seen the text message flash up on her wrist.

It made me wonder why on earth Georgia had been agreeing to see me after all those horrible texts she'd thought I'd sent her. She *must* have loved me to have endured all of that.

I couldn't stop myself from reading on – even though it was agonising to do so – as before my eyes was my own breakup story. I knew I was the one who'd started our downfall, but maybe I could have pulled it back if Joe hadn't ruined everything.

I continued to read them:

'Frankie, who I'm on a date with right now, just said I have amazing tits. Ha! Single life, baby! So much better than being tied down to you!'

I wanted to murder Joe. I thought about how, if I saw him, I would lunge at him and dig my thumbs into his eye sockets until I felt his eyeballs pop. How I would stab him through the neck and rip out his windpipe.

I read on. A blue text came next, from my actual phone, that said:

'Thinking about you all the time. Looking forward to seeing you. Are you free soon? Xxxxxxxxxxx'

And Georgia's reply:

'I'm fine. Can you stop messing with my head, please? See you at Bex's birthday party.'

The next one, a green one, from Joe, read:

'Glad you left the strip club so I could properly enjoy my lap dance tonight. PS, I really don't think we should hang out together anymore, we're just not compatible – not as partners or as mates. I meant what I shouted in the club – FUCK. YOU!'

I threw my head back and stared at the ceiling, taking deep, growling breaths, trying to calm myself. There were no words to describe his vileness.

***

On the drive home, still reeling from what I'd just learned, I stopped at a red light and saw a group of builders catcalling a girl in a school uniform. They were still doing this? Had men made no progress since the time I was a kid?

I got out of the car. It was the bravest thing I'd ever done.

'Hey!' I shouted. 'HEY!'

They looked at me, confused.

'She's in a school uniform, you fucking paedophiles!' My voice shook as I yelled across the road at them. 'You think it's OK to shout at little girls? She could be your daughter, you sickos!'

One of them laughed, a cocky grin spreading across his face. 'What's your problem, love? We're just having a bit of fun.'

'Fun?' I shot back, fists clenched at my sides. 'You call it fun to objectify a child? You should be ashamed of yourselves!'

Another one spoke up. 'Relax, will you? We're not hurting anyone. She should learn to take a compliment.'

'It's harassment! You're all fucking disgusting!'

The girl turned and gave me a small, grateful smile as she hurried off. The lights turned green, but no one behind me beeped. It felt like they were all on my side. I got back in the car and thrust my middle finger up at the builders as I drove away.

Ever since I could walk and talk, people had been telling me how beautiful I was. The way they said it always felt like a warning. Memories came to me in flashes then: the ice cream man asking me if I wanted to come inside his truck, and my mum running out of the house when she saw that I'd said yes; the old man in the long coat at the park who flashed his penis at me and Li; my reception school teacher, Mr James, sitting me on his lap and asking for a kiss on the lips by pursing them and tapping them with his finger; and the workmen and blokes in white vans wolf-whistling at me in my uniform. I remember thinking I'd wanted those compliments, like I'd earnt those wolf-whistles. I'd been conditioned to think it was a good thing, a positive thing. But I was always afraid. I'd both wanted them to look and I didn't.

Sexual attention in childhood became so regular that I came to expect it. I believed that the way fully grown men acted was not only normal, but that it was also some sort of validation for myself. I grew to crave their attention.

At a certain point, all that mattered was how good I looked for boys. I was wrapped up in the superficiality of it all, especially when I'd first realised the boys in school were ranking the girls' looks against each other. It became a competition, and I knew I didn't want the prize – boys – but the desire to fit in, to be liked, overrode that minor detail. I was compelled to take part, in the same way that a self-harmer is compelled to run something sharp over their skin, and I was always navigating the delicate balance of fending off boys (or men) and attracting them. All the girls in the race would swap diet, exercise and beauty tips in the school bathroom, all contributing what little factoids they could find, and the teenage magazines – which we were far too young to be reading – were more than helpful too. I learnt the perfect way to stuff my bra, how to hairspray my face so that my makeup wouldn't come off, how to pluck my eyebrows bare, how to straighten my hair with an actual iron, how to use pro-Ana websites to motivate me to starve myself for the perfect clavicle display, and, best of all, there was this revelation passed around that you could eat whatever you wanted and then just throw it up. Bulimic by my twelfth birthday, but at least I had a boyfriend.

Chapter 47

My work mobile buzzed with a text. I didn't recognise the number; it wasn't in my contact list:

'Meet for lunch tomorrow?'

'Who's this?'

'It's Bex. I'm on my work phone, I didn't even realise. Anyway, want to meet us tomorrow? We haven't had a weekday lunch in a while.'

'Hey Bex. Yeah, sure. Where?'

'Meet outside my work office at 12? I'll drive us somewhere nice.'

'Yep. Cool.'

'Great. Don't tell Li. I want it to be a surprise.'

I swallowed hard. I knew what was going on. Bex was going to propose to Li – it was so obvious. Li had always said her favourite type of proposal would be one where her friends hid in the bushes and then jumped out in celebration after the ring was on her finger. If Bex was going to propose, wouldn't that mean she was going to invite Georgia too? We were the Fab Four; until the breakup, we were each other's closest friends. Georgia was going to be there; I just knew it.

***

When I pulled up outside the Cymru Protect office, I saw Bex standing on the steps outside the front door. She looked anxious – of course she did, she was about to propose. I yanked up my handbrake and got out of the car, watching Bex dart down the steps and across the street to where she was parked. She beckoned me over hurriedly.

'You're late. Get in, quick.' Her tone was raw and urgent, opposite to her usual happy-go-lucky one. I waited for a van to go past before I opened the passenger door. 'Get in!' she shouted from inside, her voice muffled in the car.

I opened the door and ducked my head inside. 'Bex, what's going on, why are you rushing? And where's Li?'

'I'll tell you when you get the fuck in.'

'Bloody hell, OK.' I thudded myself down into the seat and slammed the door, inhaling Bex's airborne anxiety.

Her seatbelt, gripped in her fist, locked with her every frantic tug.

'What's going on, Bex? What's wrong?'

'Put your belt on, we have to be quick.'

I did as she said and she drove us off in a screech of tyres.

'Bex! Tell me what's happening; you're scaring me.'

'Right. Fuck. Right.' She took a deep inhale. 'You're not going to like this, Jess. You are not going to like this one bit. I followed Li yesterday.'

'OK...'

'I was suspicious because she took her car to work, but normally I drive us both, seeing as she's pretty much always at my house – and even when she's not, her place is on the way to our office, so I pick her up from there. We've done the commute in my car every day for months. But all of a sudden she wants to take two cars.' She was talking double-time as she squealed the car around a corner. 'Li said it was because she had a work meeting, but she kept on getting the details muddled when I asked her about who it was with. First, she said "he", then she said "she", and she couldn't remember the name of the place they were meeting. Anyway, I followed her to her so-called work meeting and saw her walking into the botanical gardens, of all places. I knew I was right to be suspicious – who has a meeting in a botanical garden?'

I waited for her to continue.

'And who did I see her secretly meeting at this park?'

'Who?'

She shot a look at me, and my heart dropped. No. It couldn't be.

'Georgia,' she said. The name breathed itself across the back of my neck, snaking up like a noxious vapour into my ear.

'Georgia?'

'I watched them together,' she said, ducking her head to peer up at the red traffic light that she'd stopped a bit too close to, impatiently waiting for it to change, tapping her fingers on the steering wheel. 'They didn't kiss or anything, but I just knew, you know?'

I glared at her, not wanting to believe what she was saying.

'When she came back to the office, she was in such a good mood. I wanted to march up to her and scream at her, but I kept it together and just asked her how her meeting went. She told me she went to a coffee shop to meet a guy she'd gone to school with, who'd been looking to get into insurance and wanted some advice from her. I don't know how I managed to keep my cool,' she continued, barely stopping for breath. 'Last night, she stayed at mine, and I was casually asking questions about Georgia, like, "I wonder who Georgia's in a relationship with" and "I wonder when she's going to invite us over to meet her," and so on, and Li acted dumb.'

Hot tears tussled for space as a storm of hurt and confusion whirled inside me.

'Then,' she said, her voice barely audible over the screech of tyres as she whipped around a corner, narrowly missing an old woman at a zebra crossing. 'For fuck's sake!' Bex yelled, slamming on the brakes. 'Stupid bitch!' She glared at the lady before flooring the accelerator again. 'Then, last night, Li said she was going to take her car in again today, for another meeting. So I texted you quickly last night and asked you to meet me so we could confront them together.'

'But there's a chance nothing's going on between them,' I said shakily. 'You said yourself you didn't see them kiss or anything.'

'I could see it in their eyes, Jess – their smiles, their closeness. And why would she lie to me if she were meeting Georgia? Georgia is our friend, I introduced them; there would be no need to lie.'

I swallowed against the rising of vomit. I couldn't lose my girlfriend *and* my best friend. To each other. This would be the biggest betrayal of my life. It would mean that Li had been play-acting as my rock throughout this breakup, when all the while she was sleeping with the very person my heart was breaking for. It couldn't be true. It simply couldn't.

My head replayed all the questions Li had been asking me. I thought she was asking them because she cared, but if this was true, she was asking for insight – to see how much I knew, or if I had any clues as to who this new girlfriend was.

'If they're there together again today,' Bex continued, parking up and wrenching the handbrake up, 'then there's no fucking doubt they're having an affair, and they've gone behind both our backs to make it happen. Our fucking girlfriends and our fucking best friends. Fucking.'

'I – I don't know if I can see this,' I said, shaking my head, my voice a little strangled. 'I can't see them. Together. No. Not after everything that's happened. I couldn't bear it. I can't – please drive me back to my car.' I heard how disjointed my sentences sounded, falling out of my mouth like pieces from an upended jigsaw box.

'No. We have to, Jess. They can't get away with this. At least Georgia had the decency to tell you she wanted to call it quits; Li hasn't said a word to me, or to you. Quick, we have to go now, before they leave.'

I followed Bex, who was jogging along the pavement to the garden's entrance, beckoning agitatedly for me to keep up. We trailed a winding path lined with towering, oppressive trees. 'Through here,' Bex said quietly, veering off the path into a mulchy wooded area, damp from recent rain. 'This is how I followed them yesterday without them seeing me.'

I stumbled after her, the thick haze of ripe petrichor filling my nostrils, my high heels sinking into the soggy leaf litter, and twigs cracking like wet, fragile bones beneath my feet. My dress caught on a branch of a fallen tree and dragged me backwards, snagging a hole in the material. Bex didn't stop, she just beckoned me faster, mouthing, 'Come on!' frantically.

And then, through the trees, we saw them. We were behind them. They were sitting on a bench in a rose garden on the other side of the wooded area we were in. Their faces were turned towards each other.

'Look,' whispered Bex.

I glanced down to where Bex's finger was pointing. Through the slats in the bench, I saw Li stroking Georgia's hand. I stared, feeling a burning hotness behind my eyes. This was really happening. I screwed my fists into my eyes, wanting to bruise and distort the image that had just seared into them.

Chapter 48

'Having a good work meeting, Li?' Bex shouted sarcastically, her voice poised to shatter like thin glass in a gale. She must have found her way through a clearing in the trees when I wasn't looking. She was on the other side of the woods, in the rose garden, standing next to them.

Li tore her hand from Georgia's and sat bolt upright. 'Bex. Hi!' I couldn't see Li's face but it sounded as if she was smiling.

'Tell me exactly what's going on,' Bex said calmly.

'What? Nothing,' Li said innocently, brightly, moving her body in a way that shielded Georgia from Bex. 'Georgia just wanted to talk, after all the stuff that's been going on with the police and what Jess has been doing.'

What Jess has been doing? What? *I* hadn't been doing anything. Li knew full well it had been Joe all along. Had she not told Georgia about this? She couldn't have told Georgia. She'd promised me she did. She'd said she'd told her everything.

'And Georgia wanted to talk to me because I know Jess so well, that's all,' Li said, cheerfully.

'Hang on,' Georgia started, staring at Li.

'That doesn't explain why you were holding hands, or why you lied about meeting a guy from your old school,' said Bex, ignoring Georgia's comment. 'Still waiting for those two crucial explanations from you, Li.'

'We weren't holding hands,' she said, chuckling a little. 'And I told you it was a school friend because I didn't want you to worry. And it was only this one time.'

'Hang on,' Georgia said again, louder than before, standing up.

'Lie after lie after lie,' Bex shouted over Georgia. 'One time? I saw you both here yesterday. I gave you a chance to come clean, multiple chances, but you didn't. And another lie that you weren't holding hands; I *saw* you.'

'You must have just thought you saw that,' Li said, waving a hand to shoo away the accusation.

'I was looking directly at your hands as you were holding them, you liar!' Bex shouted the last two words. 'I saw your hands through the back of the bench. I was behind you, watching. We both were.'

Li and Georgia turned to look behind them. I was standing there, silently.

Georgia gasped. 'Jess. What the hell?'

I was frozen in place, aware that I must have looked like the disturbed stalker Georgia had thought me to be, hiding in the dank, shadowy woods, peering through dead leaves at them. I thought I'd be hiding in bushes for a very different reason that day, ready to jump out and shout 'Congratulations' after Bex's proposal.

'What's going on?' Georgia asked uneasily. 'Someone needs to explain.'

'Jess and I don't need to do any explaining, Georgia,' Bex said with a disgusted look on her face. 'It's you two that have been caught red-handed – don't try to turn this around on us! You were both going behind our backs. *You* explain!'

Georgia's face was painted with a genuine look of confusion. 'Li?' she said, locking eyes with her. 'You told me you'd broken up with Bex. You said it was mutual.'

'I know,' Li said. 'I just couldn't do it.'

Bex let out a noise of exasperation over the private conversation they were having right in front of her. 'Are you two enjoying your heart-to-heart? This is unbelievable. You should be giving *me* an explanation, Li, not *her*.'

'I'm sorry, Bex,' Li said, hanging her head.

Bex laughed through her tears.

'I rang you that night, Bex,' Georgia said, 'the night that Li said she'd ended things with you; I rang you three or four times, but you didn't answer. I told Li that I'd tried to contact you and that I would try again the next day, but she told me that you didn't want to talk to me, so I didn't call again. I was giving you space.'

Bex stayed silent as Georgia continued. 'And you haven't been coming to football practice, Bex, so I thought you were avoiding me, like Li said you were.'

'Li!' Bex said loudly, her voice cracking in distress. 'You were telling me not to pick up Georgia's phone calls that night. I remember it. There were three calls, one after the other, and you stopped me from answering any of them. Then you rang her from your phone. You told me she was just upset about something Jess had done, and you wanted to be the one to talk to her about it because you knew Jess's side of the story better than I did.'

Bex turned her eyes to Georgia. 'And I haven't been to football because Li has been sick on practice days for the past few weeks.' Realisation dawned on Bex's face like a clouded sunrise. 'Oh dear god, Li, were you faking being unwell? No, you couldn't have been faking it, I saw the sick in the toilet. Unless – did you… did you *make* yourself sick so I wouldn't go to practice and see Georgia?'

Li's face said it all.

Bex shook her head. 'Did you honestly go that low just to stop me talking to her?'

'I'm sorry,' Li said, sighing. 'I just needed to hold you two off from seeing each other for a little longer while I thought of what to do.'

Bex crouched to the floor, as if her legs gave way.

A teen tossing a rugby ball in the air walked past, silently observing.

'I don't understand, Li,' Bex said, her voice twisting through tears. 'We practically live together. When have you two had the chance to be alone together?'

I stayed out of sight, just listening and watching from afar, my heart in my mouth. The idea that this was my reality was weighing down on me with such enormous pressure I thought it might push me right through the ground.

Li sat with her face in her hands and stayed silent.

'It's not—' Georgia began.

'No,' shouted Bex, dropping the weighted word from her mouth like a guillotine blade. 'I don't want to hear it from you; I want to hear it from her.'

Li lifted her head and took a breath. 'You know how I've been going to the gym more regularly in the evenings? Well, I haven't been going to the gym…'

Bex grimaced in pain.

'And I've been going out while you were asleep,' Li added unnecessarily.

Bex discharged a growl. 'It's all adding up!' she shouted, exasperated. 'All the little things – like when you told me to stop texting Georgia after she'd ended things with Jess; you told me you were taking charge of the texts on our behalf, as a couple, because we'd been sending Georgia duplicate replies and it was getting confusing trying to keep up with who was replying to who. "More streamlined", that's what you called it – you said you were going to "streamline" our texts. But you just wanted me to stop texting Georgia, didn't you?

'And you said you'd take charge of forwarding Jess's messages on to Georgia too. You said you'd send all those on, to help Jess fight for Georgia. Did you even do that? Or were you trying to keep Georgia away from Jess so you could have her for yourself?'

'What messages from Jess?' Georgia asked Li gravely.

My heart dropped. Georgia hadn't received any of my messages – none of my pleas to get her back. Li hadn't passed on a single one. She had promised she'd given them all to Georgia; she said she'd given her so many that Georgia had reached snapping point and didn't want to receive them anymore. But Georgia obviously hadn't said anything of the sort. 'Leave it alone, enough is enough,' Li had said to me so many times. She had just wanted me out of the picture so she could be with Georgia herself.

I lowered my chin, set my jaw and glowered at Li, how the tiger at the zoo had once stared at me, readying itself for the kill. My nails dug into the dough of my palm. I couldn't hold back my anger, an anger so complete that it burned white hot. I stood rigid, feeling my searing fury emulsify with the cold urgency ripping through my veins. The power of a thunderstorm churning beneath my skin. I couldn't take my eyes off her, seeing only her, my peripheral vision distorted in a rage so all-encompassing that it consumed every other feeling in my body. I felt it opening swiftly within me, like a monstrous flower unfurling into its full atrocious beauty. Then it used my legs to walk itself forward. I felt so sure of myself, so fixated on this one thing that I felt I had to do. I saw it playing out so clearly in front of me. So clearly that it felt like a premonition – my knees on her chest, my hands around her neck, crushing the breath out of her, watching her turn blue, her life fading away beneath my unrelenting grasp. How right that would feel.

And then, like a lit fuse, I propelled myself towards her, charging over the decaying carpet of sludge beneath my feet and through the twisted trees.

Bex grabbed my arm as I lurched towards Li, and then she hugged my body to hers from behind, stopping me dead in my tracks.

Screaming, I thrashed my arms and kicked my legs to free myself, but Bex held me with all her might.

'You didn't give her any of my messages!' I screeched at Li, spitting the words like acid, all the veins in my face feeling ready to burst. 'And I bet you didn't fucking tell her what the police said either!'

'I'm sorry,' Li said, hiding behind Georgia pathetically. 'I didn't know what to do; I was stuck. I knew she still loved you, and if she saw your messages, she might have come back to you. And you didn't deserve her, Jess. Not after you "paused" your relationship to go sleep with other girls. It was wrong. Dishonest. Immoral. Why would I have helped you to get her back when you'd treated her so badly? You can't do that to people.'

All I could do was stare at her, dragging in breaths through my teeth.

Li continued. 'All of your attempts to get her back – leaving presents and flowers on her doorstep – I knew she'd be better off not seeing them because she'd have been sucked back in. I had to get rid of them.'

She turned to Georgia, who looked horrified. 'It was for your own good, Georgia. I hope you understand why I had to do that.'

'What about the letter I wrote?' I cried out, unblinking. 'Don't you dare say you're the one who posted that back to me...'

As Li looked at the ground, I felt my body disintegrate from the inside out. That letter was my final attempt at saving the relationship.

'It wouldn't have been good for her to read it,' Li said. 'It was all about how "you belong together", and that simply wasn't true.'

'You read it?' I said, seething, trying to free myself from Bex's grip so I could fucking throttle Li.

Georgia stepped away from Li, exposing her.

'At least you didn't turn up in a black-and-white outfit pretending you were a prisoner,' Li added, almost chuckling under her breath, 'or have Georgia handcuff and strip search you.'

What the fuck? I'd never told Li that Georgia and I did that together. And I knew for a fact Georgia wouldn't have told her – she was too private a person; she never talked about sex outside of a relationship. And I could tell by Georgia's expression that she was just as shocked at Li's comment as I was. How would Li have known about that?

I tried to control my voice as much as possible. 'I'm just going to ask you one question, Li. Did you tell Georgia about Joe?'

She rolled her eyes as if it was a meaningless question. 'There was no need for me to tell her that. The police would have told her anyway, Jess.'

'Told me what about Joe?' asked Georgia.

Li made an exasperated sound and looked at her. 'The police got in touch with you to say that it wasn't Jess sending those threatening texts or making those calls, right? That they had proof it had been Joe all along? That he somehow "hijacked" her phone? They must have told you. They would have had to tell you; you were the victim.'

'No,' Georgia said, equal parts aghast and severe. 'I wasn't told that.'

Until that very minute, Georgia had thought it had all been me. I wanted to tear my heart out; it ached too much to stay in my body.

'The police would have told you eventually,' said Li. 'They must have just been too busy with other – far more pressing – issues; they'll contact you soon to go through everything, I'm sure. It's no big deal.'

'No big deal?' said Georgia, her chest heaving. 'You think that's no big deal? You knew that huge piece of information and you didn't think to tell me, knowing how anxious I've been about this? I've been constantly looking through my windows worried that Jess was going to act on all those threats I thought she'd sent.'

'Can you all just stop ganging up on me please.' Li put her hands over her ears like a child. 'I made a mistake – several mistakes – and I'm sorry. I'm sorry to you all, OK?'

'No, not fucking OK,' yelled Bex, letting me go, distracted by her own indignation. 'You've cheated on me, you've betrayed your best friend and you've lied to Georgia. Why on earth would any of us just let that go?'

'Because I'm not well,' Li said, squeezing her face into a tearful expression while her eyes remained dry. 'I'm damaged. This has all spiralled out of control and I never meant for it to happen.'

'What do you mean you're "not well"?' asked Bex scathingly.

Li exhaled, waiting to speak because a woman with a puddle-jumping toddler was walking by. 'Fine. I'll tell you. A few weeks before I started dating Bex, I found out... I found out that Nathan – the fucking love of my life who I'd dedicated nearly a decade of my life to – had been cheating on me. I was going to marry him, have babies with him, and he was fucking cheating on me, and guess what, he got that girl pregnant and left me. It broke me. It made me mentally unwell.'

She started crying – her first tear since we'd confronted her. 'I loved him. He threw away everything we'd ever had. He left me for that bitch.'

'But you said you'd left *him* for me,' said Bex. 'You didn't tell me he had cheated.'

'Well, I couldn't face the truth at the time. Anyway, that's my sob story that you all wanted so much; happy now?'

'What?' Bex said incredulously. 'Far from it. You think that because you were hurt it means you get to hurt all of us? Have you lost your mind?'

'I don't want to keep talking about it. I'm sorry to you all and there's nothing more I can say.' Li tried to leave, but Bex blocked her path. Li tried again, running this time, but Bex grabbed at the back of her jacket.

'No. You don't get to just leave like that,' Bex said, yanking her back, the force of it causing Li's bag to slip off her shoulder onto the ground, the contents of it spilling out – an umbrella, a lip balm, tissues, tampons. And three phones.

Chapter 49

Li lunged to the floor but Bex managed to swipe the phones up in an instant.

'Give them to me!' Li screeched, panicked.

Bex held them high, out of Li's reach. 'So, I know this is your phone,' Bex said, moving one phone into view.' Li pulled at Bex's arms, trying to bring the phones down to her level, but Bex's strong arms barely moved. 'And I know this is your work phone.' Bex looked at the second. 'But this one? My best guess is that *this* is the secret phone you've been using to have an affair behind my back. Tell me I'm wrong.'

Li scratched and smacked at Bex's arms. Bex quickly held the third phone – an Android model – to Li's face, and the phone opened via face recognition.

'Give it back. That's private!' She tried to smack it out of Bex's hand, but Bex held it high again.

'Just as I thought. Hundreds of secret messages to Georgia,' Bex said, scrolling. 'Wait.' A look of horror climbed over her face. 'What the fuck are these?' She scrolled a little more, looking up in the air at the phone held high. 'Oh my god.'

Bex read a text out as Li continued hitting and pulling Bex's arms. '"You're the reason Joe and I broke up, and you're going to fucking pay, bitch!" What is this?'

Coldness crept through my blood.

She read out another, her eyes wide. '"You better fucking watch out; I could be anywhere. Every time you come out of your house, I'll be waiting. I'm going to fuck up your life."'

I felt helpless, staggered at what I was hearing. My life was sagging and crumbling and collapsing before me.

'What are all these, Li?' Bex asked, stunned. 'Why did you send these?' She stared at Li, who was avoiding her gaze. 'Answer me! What is this shit?'

'I'll tell you what it is,' I shouted, finding my voice finally, jabbing my finger towards Li. 'It wasn't Joe that hacked my phone. It was her! It was her all along!' I lowered my finger and snarled at her as if I were a wild animal. 'It was you!' I screamed. I leapt at her, my hands a blur of motion, clawing at her hair and face with savage desperation. She stumbled backward, letting out a startled cry. I heard Bex and Georgia rushing for me, their voices urgent, but I hurled Li to the ground, raised my fist, and slammed it into her eye socket.

Bex and Georgia pried me away from her before I could lash out again. Their hands were firm on my arms as I struggled against their hold, my breath coming in erratic bursts. I wanted to badly hurt Li, to make her feel a fraction of the pain she had inflicted on me.

'It was you!' My screech turned into a cry as they held me back from her while she writhed on the ground. 'How could you do this to me?'

Li fought to sit up, covering her face on one side. She didn't make a sound.

'Is it true?' Bex asked as if willing it not to be real.

Li stayed quiet, looking at the ground with her good eye, swaying a little.

'Is it?'

Li still didn't say a word.

The fight suddenly drained out of me and my knees buckled. The weight of my body sagged between Bex and Georgia, forcing them to lower me to the ground. My anger turned to terror – I was terrified of Li. Even though she was sitting there like an injured baby bird that had fallen from its nest, she frightened me.

Georgia sat beside me, her hand resting on my shoulder, whether out of compassion or to make sure I wouldn't make a run for Li again, I couldn't tell. I could only sit there, the adrenaline fading, leaving me hollow and trembling.

For several minutes, nobody said a word. The only sound was Bex's gasps of shock as she continued scrolling through Li's phone. I didn't have the energy to ask what else she had found.

'What... what are all of *my* personal messages doing on here too, Li?' asked Bex. 'Why am I looking at a replica of the contents of my own phone? I don't understand.'

Li stayed quiet.

'Answer me.' Bex took a deep inhale. 'Answer me!' she screamed.

'I had to!' Li said raspingly, still cradling her face.

'Had to what?' Bex looked at her as though she were a ghost.

'Bex, I couldn't take my chances after what happened with Nathan. I had to know you weren't cheating on me.'

'So you *bugged* my phone?'

'Please understand. It was just for my peace of mind. I couldn't go through a repeat of what had happened with him. I just needed to know that I could trust you, and I've realised I can – I have proof,

proof that you're amazing, Bex. Please don't be mad. You can't blame me; you know you're a flirt when we go to bars. I just needed to know that nothing ever went further than flirtation. That's all. And you passed the test.' Li smiled meekly, one hand still blocking her eye.

'You fucking hypocrite,' said Bex, almost growling. 'You were so concerned about checking up on me, but you're the cheat.' She started pacing. 'Oh god. Is this the reason you didn't know I'd be gatecrashing your little meeting today – because I'd used my work phone to text Jess about the plan? If I'd have used *my* phone, you'd have weaselled your way out of being caught, wouldn't you?'

Li shook her head and sighed.

'Did you impersonate me, like you did Jess? Send messages in my name?'

'No. Never. I just used it for light observation when it came to you, nothing more.' She smiled sycophantically.

'Observation? Could you see me through the phone?'

'No! I... I had *access* to your camera, but I didn't use it. Well, barely. I listened in a couple of times to what you said to other girls when I wasn't around, and you never did anything more than harmlessly flirt – not in person, not on your messages – so I was happy with that. And now I know that, I'll never have to do it again. Trust me. I'm done with all that. You can just throw my phone in the bin now.'

Bex glared at her.

'Go on.' Li pointed to a bin a few feet away. 'Just smash it and throw it in there.'

'We're taking it to the police. We're not fucking idiots.'

'Just because I tapped your phones?' Li retorted, lightening her voice as she continued. 'There's no need for that. It's all over now anyway. I've said sorry.'

The three of us looked at her disbelievingly, sickened by her.

'Look, I only bugged Bex's phone to check if I was being cheated on. And I bugged Jess's phone to see if she was cheating on Georgia, which she was – Jess was having sex with other people. I did this for good reasons, moral reasons.'

'I didn't sleep with anyone, Li!' I said loudly, realising that she must have assumed I'd followed up on whatever flirtations she'd heard or seen via my phone. 'And our relationship was none of your business!'

She staggered to her feet, took her hand away from her face and stared at me. The skin around her left eye was already darkening to a deep purple, her eyelid partially closed from the swelling, and a split in her skin dripped a tear of blood. 'Because Georgia doesn't deserve to be treated badly,' she said in a low voice, unsteady on her feet. 'Just like I didn't deserve to be treated badly by Nathan.'

Her face flared with hate as she continued. 'You and Nathan are the same – out for yourselves; you don't care who you hurt. You didn't deserve Georgia. It's not my fault you didn't see how good you had it.'

She looked at Georgia. 'Georgia, you're such an amazing person; you've got to realise I was doing this to save you from getting hurt. I'm sorry I had to send you those texts, but you would have never walked away from Jess otherwise. I was just trying to help you. Please say you can see that?'

Georgia shook her head, tears in her eyes.

'I know it might look like I've done some awful things,' Li said with her arms spread, almost like she was a performer on stage, 'but I was just standing up for what was right, even if it meant going about it in a way that seemed wicked to others.'

'You're a disgrace, Li,' Georgia said. 'You need help.' She began to walk away but stopped, turning back with a fierce look. 'I can't believe you called the police and said Jess was behind all this.' *Li was the one who'd reported me.* 'And you practically pushed me out of my own front door, forcing me to take that picture of Jess. Did you send that picture to the police too?'

Pain whirled in my chest as I realised Li was the second shadow I'd seen behind Georgia's curtains that night.

Then Georgia walked away.

Li waited until Georgia was out of earshot. 'I made a mistake,' she said, making a desperate plea directly to Bex, stepping towards her and stumbling. 'It's you I want, Bex. We can get through this together. It's not that big of a deal when you think about it; people sneak a look at their partners' phones all the time. It's not something to break up over.'

'Of course it is,' said Bex, letting out a delirious laugh. 'And even if I could get over the phone hacking, you still slept with my best friend, and you framed my other best friend.'

'It meant nothing, Bex. I was just so confused. I'm so damaged. I just need love to heal me. You can heal me.' She touched Bex's arm.

'Get away from me,' Bex said, snatching her arm away.

The two of us turned and walked away from Li, catching up with Georgia.

'Bex, please,' she called behind us. 'Please understand.'

Chapter 50

It had been a year since the day Georgia last spoke to me, and I was cutting to mark the occasion.

I let out small noises involuntarily as I repeatedly whipped the tip of a knife over the flesh of my inner thighs. For some reason, I'd chosen that as the place to relieve my pain, through more pain.

I worked with careful strokes, the way I might if I had a pencil in my hand. The blade moved over the flesh of my inner thighs, delicate but deliberate, as if I were tracing a line. Each stroke felt like a dark, twisted art form, the way the dark buds of blood rose up, blooming in little crimson dots, beading together before spilling down in thin streams. Some left parallel streaks of red, like perfectly placed brushstrokes, some met in confluence and joined to form a thicker rivulet, and the rest overlapped each other's paths and then drifted apart forever.

I had to be quiet when cutting; I was back living with my parents after everything that had happened, and I didn't want them hearing or worrying. I was only making superficial cuts; there was no reason for them to know about that.

After the day in the rose garden, I'd tried to stay in touch with Georgia, and I did for a little while, but she realised she couldn't do it. Her mind was lost after everything that had happened.

It was all too much. Her life had been turned upside down; she needed a fresh start, away from the three of us entirely. Our connection was an open wound, and we had to allow it to breathe and heal on its own. She was traumatised. We probably all were.

Even though all of it stemmed back to the terrible decision I'd made to leave Georgia and pursue other women, Georgia didn't blame me. She had tried to let go of the negative feelings she had towards me, which she'd built up during the period she thought I was her harasser, but she said it was hard to do with me still in her life. She wanted to go through the process alone, let go of everything that had happened. And she said, maybe after that, we could find friendship again.

'My brain needs to come to terms with everything, Jess,' she had said one day at Lake Calon. 'I need time to heal now. And you do too, I think. I hope you understand.'

Her words were warm and kind and gentle, like a hand on my face, and when she turned and walked away, it left the coldest of sensations in my body – sensations that were still in there, deep inside, ice-cold and haunting.

The day the three of us had left Li in the rose garden, we'd called in sick to each of our workplaces and then huddled in the corner of a coffee shop, poring over Li's phone inch by inch. Thankfully, Bex had the foresight to change the password so she could access it without needing face recognition. I couldn't believe what I was seeing. My Li. Why did she do this? And *how* did she do this? She had hacked my phone, impersonated me, sent vile texts to Georgia, and she had *watched* me through my phone, used it like a webcam. She invaded my privacy to the most extreme extent possible. She had lost me the love of my life.

When we discovered the nude pictures of me and Georgia on the phone – photos we'd sent to each other months before – I cried out so loudly that a waiter came over to check on us. The shock of it was like being slapped awake from a nightmare. To see those intimate moments – moments meant to be shared in the privacy of our relationship – sitting on Li's phone was a violation I couldn't fully process. My heart pounded violently as I saw them, the images searing into my mind with a painful clarity. It wasn't just the invasion of privacy, it was the brutal betrayal. Li, my closest and lifelong companion, had done this. Had she ever truly been my friend? If she could do this, had our entire friendship been a lie? I felt like I was being gutted on the spot.

And there was more. The police-and-prisoner role-play video Georgia and I had recorded was on Li's phone. That was how Li knew about it; not because Georgia had told her – I knew she hadn't – but because Li had accessed all my videos. Everything that had been on my phone was also on Li's. She had seen and listened to it all. Every private moment.

I picked through every text message from my cloned number to Georgia's phone, scrolling back to the very first one Li had sent:

'About tomorrow, not so sure we should be alone. I don't want you trying to kiss me. Will your sister be there? I also can't be bothered to see you if you're going to be moping.'

I looked at the date. It was sent on the night I'd met up with Daeva Valentine. Li had clearly wanted to punish me for not being truthful with Georgia, and that was why she'd sent the first text – because she knew I'd been on a date behind Georgia's back.

I angrily wiped away my tears, then scrolled down and read more:

'Don't tell the girls, but I've ditched takeaway-and-movie night tonight to go to that new gay bar in the city – Scissor. Single life is so much fucking fun. I've finally got some excitement in my life! I'm dancing with a smoking-hot girl right now.'

Ffion – Georgia's football friend – hadn't been the one to tell Georgia that I'd been at Scissor that night. It had been Li, posing as me.

I kept reading, sickened:

'I can't believe you texted me saying you wanted to kiss me. You don't know how to respect boundaries, do you? Guess what I'm doing right at this very second (while I'm sitting next to you in the car and you're chauffeuring me back to my house LOL)? I'm texting someone called Frankie and arranging a date. *That's* how much I want to kiss you.'

Li was in the car with us when she'd sent that text to Georgia. I imagined her in the back seat, typing out those cruel words while Georgia drove. As I pawed through the texts, I realised that messages had been sent out to Georgia every time I'd met up with someone new – the night with Daeva, the night with lion-haired girl, and the night with Frankie. This was some sort of vendetta against me for not being 'moral'. Li couldn't punish Nathan for cheating on her, so she was punishing me for attempting to cheat on Georgia.

I sipped my tea shakily.

Bex's thick fingers traced the rim of her cup as she finally broke the silence.

'So how did the affair start?' she asked Georgia.

'We weren't having an affair,' Georgia said, looking up at Bex. 'I tried to tell you earlier. I could tell you thought that's what was going on, but nothing like that has ever happened between us. Li and I have never even kissed.'

Bex blinked in confusion. 'What?'

Georgia sighed. 'She just started showing up at my place unannounced, often really late at night, crying. Told me you two had broken up. She said she needed a friend. I didn't feel as if I could turn her away. And she said you didn't want to talk about it, Bex; she said you didn't want to talk to anyone. I tried, but you didn't answer, and you weren't coming to football practice so I believed what she said was true.

'She said to give you space,' Georgia continued, 'so I did. I had no reason not to trust what she was saying. She even told me you'd gone to stay with your auntie up north. I never knew she was so manipulative. I don't know why I listened to her, but it all seemed to make sense at the time.'

Bex leaned back, arms crossed, the disbelief clear on her face.

I set my cup down, the *clink* of it hitting the saucer ringing louder than I'd intended. 'So if Li wasn't your girlfriend, who was?' I asked.

'What? No one. I didn't – I don't – have a girlfriend.'

'But your text.'

'What text?'

'The one you sent me saying your "girlfriend thought it would be best if you and I called it a day".' I watched Georgia's eyes widening. 'And then you blocked me after sending it.'

'I didn't text that,' she said, shaking her head. 'And I didn't block you.'

'You didn't?' I paused, momentarily confused, and then it dawned on me. 'Oh god. It was Li.'

We looked at the phone again, and sure enough, Georgia's phone had been bugged too. Li had done it to all three of us. I felt stripped bare that day, skinned alive, my nerves exposed to the air, disbelief raw and pounding, my brain mush.

We wouldn't be able to think rationally about the 'signs' until much later – like how Li seemed fine with Bex flirting at Freedom that first night we went, because she had been listening in on her phone. I even remember Li holding her phone to her ear that night in the club – apparently 'listening to a voicemail from her boss', but in reality, she'd been eavesdropping on what Bex was saying to a girl on the other side of the room. And how Li always appeared so carefree and relaxed in her relationship with Bex, even though she had been the jealous and worried type when she was with Nathan. And how Bex had affectionately thought Li was able to read her mind, like when Li brought her the exact Jamaican feast she had been craving – but really, Li had been able to see what websites Bex was browsing.

After hours of investigating the phone, we finally took it to the police station. PC Bevan brought Li in for questioning soon after, and she confessed to everything. She admitted she'd taken my phone the day we went to the spa together; she had made me think she was putting it on top of my kitchen cabinets – out of sight, out of mind – but actually, she had slipped it in her pocket and had taken it to the spa with her. She'd skipped her massage and had locked herself in a changing room to download the spyware onto my phone. She'd had the software at her fingertips because she had already downloaded it onto Bex's phone, so she was well-practiced in it by that point.

I was wholly expecting to discover that Joe had at least played a part in the hacking, but it turned out that he'd had no involvement at all – at least, not in the way I thought. I wanted to feel relief, but instead it left me hollow, knowing how deeply I had feared him for so long, always terrified of what he might do if I ever left him. But nothing ever came of it.

When the police began investigating him as the lead suspect in my hacking case – something they likely wouldn't have taken seriously if it weren't for his ethical breach in collaborating with them – they confiscated his laptop and phone. I didn't expect much to come of it; I'd always believed Joe was too careful to leave a trail. But the police discovered that while he hadn't hacked my phone, he'd illegally manipulated the investigation. JoMatTech was supposedly made up of experts, so there had to be a reason they didn't find out that Li was behind the hacking. That reason was, Joe had sabotaged the investigation. PC Bevan described Joe's tactics as 'small, subtle diversions' that steered JoMatTech away from key clues that might have implicated Li, creating just enough of a smokescreen to render the case unsolvable.

His deliberate oversight stemmed from a desire to avoid a conflict of interest that could jeopardise JoMatTech's police contract and their reputation in the tech world. So Joe kept quiet, hoping he could manage the situation without the truth emerging. It was classic Joe: control through deception, always two steps ahead.

But that wasn't even the worst of it. His ultimate downfall came when the police uncovered his far more extensive cybercrimes. For years, he had been living a double life, manipulating and controlling others just as he had with me. Every contract JoMatTech secured – whether with banks, high-end brands, entertainment companies, private hospitals, or even the police – was an opportunity for Joe to steal their top-secret data and sell it illegally, for hundreds of thousands, all while hiding behind his polished, professional image. The kind of thing only a tech genius with no conscience could pull off. JoMatTech traded in security loopholes and sensitive data like it was currency.

I felt a smug sense of satisfaction that his crimes came to light only because *my* case prompted the police to dig deeper into his digital footprint. Seeing his mugshot on the front page of *The City Post*, courtesy of my lovely colleague Aled, with the word 'Cybercriminal' slapped in bold letters beneath his guilty face felt like the poetic justice

I hadn't realised I needed. Now the whole world knew exactly what kind of person he was. I didn't have to fear him anymore. With a combination of serious offenses, he would be behind bars for a minimum of two years.

As for Li, she received a thirteen-week prison sentence, charged with tech abuse under the Stalking and Harassment law, along with a restraining order against me, Georgia, and Bex. It was gut-wrenching to learn how far Li had gone to orchestrate the hacking. She wasn't tech-savvy enough to pull it off alone; she had help. She'd roped in the IT specialist from Cymru Protect where she and Bex had worked. The guy, Richy, had been involved in some shady dealings of his own, siphoning off small amounts of money from the company for months, exploiting gaps in the system only someone with his access would know about. A few thousand here and there – nothing that would raise flags unless someone was looking too closely.

And someone had been looking. Li.

She'd backed him into a corner, threatened to blow his secret wide open unless he helped her. She promised she wouldn't say a word as long as he gave her the spyware to install on Bex's phone – and then on mine and Georgia's after that. If he didn't? Well, she had all the proof she needed to ruin him. So he caved. He'd helped her turn our lives upside down to save his own skin, and in the end, she dragged him down with her anyway.

I didn't miss her. What she'd done had killed me. It wiped away all of our good years. At least that was what I forced myself to believe. On the surface, it was easy to feel nothing – to tell myself that our friendship was over the moment she betrayed me. But deep down, beneath the anger and the shock, there was Li holding me through bad dreams at our childhood sleepovers, Li comforting me through breakups, Li always saving me a seat on the school bus, Li leading the happy birthday song with infectious joy, Li moving to the same city as me for work because she missed me so much after I left. Li. Li. Li. My best friend, my sister – part of me.

I hated her. How had everything we'd had crumbled so easily? She was the one who had been there since the beginning. We had built our history together, supported each other through thick and thin. She was my most trusted friend and, through many chapters of my life, my only friend. Back in school, she defended me from the relentless bullies who'd made those days a living nightmare, putting herself in harm's way to protect me. And after all those years, she became my worst bully of all.

After her release, I still saw her car around from time to time. The Besties for the Resties sticker was still in place on the front bumper; it always made me shudder. She was clearly holding on to hope that we could reconnect one day. I knew how that felt, though – the longing to rekindle a lost relationship, to imagine that somehow things could go back to the way they were, even when you knew they never would.

Chapter 51

M y therapist, Maureen, didn't have an outdated-looking room in an NHS hospital building like my childhood counsellor did. Instead, my appointments were held in her cosy conservatory at home. Whenever she answered the door to me, she was always so ebullient – all rosy cheeks and soft eyes which crinkled at the edges – ushering me through and shifting a pile of something out of my way, wafting about hints of her lavender perfume as she moved. As she nestled in her purple armchair, filling it out, she would smile broadly, clasp her hands together under her pillowy bosom and ask in the homeliest of timbres, 'So, how are things, Jessica?' as her opening line, adjusting her thick-rimmed glasses with a gentle push as she spoke.

That day, I was sitting across from Maureen, telling her about how, before I met Georgia, I could only remember being truly happy in childhood – young enough that self-awareness hadn't taken root yet; the age at which you run at full speed, making aeroplane noises as you go, or belt out your favourite songs, not caring about anyone watching you – and how that innocence had come to an abrupt end at age eleven.

'A group of teenagers, my babysitter and her friends, took me with them to a skate park,' I began, feeling the words press against my throat. It had been years since I'd spoken about this. 'They were playing a game called keg – like tag, I suppose, but when they caught someone, they pulled the person's trousers down.' I paused, biting the inside of my cheek, the humiliation creeping back in, as vivid as it had been that day.

Maureen nodded encouragingly; this was the breakthrough I think she'd been hoping for.

'I didn't want to play,' I continued, my hands fidgeting in my lap. 'And then my babysitter caught me.' As I spoke, I could almost feel the girl's hands gripping me under my armpits, lifting me off the ground like I was nothing. 'And another girl yanked at my jeans. I held on to my waistband, screaming, but the jeans came off, and my underwear came off with them.'

Maureen shook her head. I swallowed hard, trying to maintain composure while the flashes of that day – their laughter, my fear – grew louder in my mind. The shame, the panic, it all felt as raw as it had then. 'Everyone acted like it was the funniest thing they'd ever seen.' I slid my hand over my mouth to cover its downward turn.

'Take your time,' Maureen said gently, giving me space to move through the rush of emotions I hadn't allowed myself to face in so long. The room seemed still, like it was holding its breath, waiting for what I wasn't sure I could say next.

'One of her friends,' I continued, remembering his kind-face, his wispy sapling beard and how he was the only one not laughing, 'a seventeen-year-old boy, he helped me pull my clothes back on and shouted at them to leave me alone. They went on with the game while he wiped my eyes with his T-shirt and offered to take me to a shop to get a bottle of water and some sweets. I agreed, feeling grateful to him. I knew about stranger danger but it didn't occur to me in that moment.

'We walked together for a long time, so long that I saw the street lights come on. I told him I had to get home because the lights signalled that it was past my curfew. My parents would be worried, especially if they found out I wasn't with my babysitter.'

Maureen nodded reassuringly again, her eyebrows turning up sympathetically.

'He led me across a field, insisting it was a shortcut, and I had no reason to doubt him,' I said, but deep down, I knew – like all girls know – that danger was looming. 'Then he told me I was beautiful.' At least, that's what he'd said with his mouth, but his hand, gripped painfully tight around my arm, said something else. 'And then it happened.' A tear fell down my cheek, which I quickly swiped at.

'It's OK, you don't have to say any more if you're not ready,' Maureen said gently.

I cleared my throat, shaking my head to let her know I wanted to keep going. 'He leaned in to kiss me. I let it happen because I felt his grip on my arm loosening, and when he let go to take my face in both his hands, I ran.' My shoulders tensed, and my breath became shallow as I forced the next words out. 'But he caught me.

'The next thing I knew, I was behind the bushes, on the ground, and he was unbuttoning and yanking down my jeans that he had so carefully helped me put back on earlier.' I crossed my arms protectively over myself. 'And then I was under him, under his weight.'

I put my head in my hands, pressing my palms against my temples as if trying to block out the images that were swimming in my mind. I ground my teeth together to keep from breaking down as the memory of me screaming and fighting beneath him played on an endless loop.

'You're safe here, Jess,' Maureen said. 'And we can take this one step at a time, at your pace.'

I nodded and took a minute to breathe. 'When it was over, he left me lying in the dirt. I felt as if my body wasn't mine anymore. I couldn't stand up – the pain was too much. I had to crawl. By then, it was dark out, and I had to drag myself across the field, calling out for anyone who might hear me.'

'Oh, Jessica,' Maureen said, looking as if she was on the verge of tears herself. 'I am so sorry.'

'My babysitter was the one who found me. She never asked what had happened or spoke a word to me. She phoned my parents from a phone box and stayed with me on the roadside, and when she saw their car approaching, she ran.

'Even in the dark, I saw the colour drain from my parents' faces as they looked at me. Dad lifted me into the car and put me in the backseat.' As I talked, more vivid memories rushed in. I could picture myself leaning over to rest my head on Mum's lap and catching a glimpse of my reflection in the rearview – already a ghost of the little girl I used to be. There in Maureen's conservatory, I almost felt Mum's fingers stroking my hair, picking out small twigs and leaves, her warm tears falling on my face. I could hear Dad's voice shouting 'Hospital or police?' to Mum, could see his eyes wide with panic, could hear Mum repeatedly asking, 'What happened, baby?' through her sobs. Back then, I struggled to find the words to explain what happened, not really knowing how to describe it to them, not even fully understanding what 'sex' was, but I said enough that Dad turned the car around and headed straight for the police station.

'I remember feeling like I was floating outside of myself,' I said to Maureen, 'detached and numb; I wasn't able to hear the police officers' questions.' They referred us to a sexual assault centre then. I pictured the paediatric doctor, with a teddy bear broach pinned to her white coat, crouching down to my level and telling me I was brave, saying I reminded her of her own daughter. As she collected the boy's DNA from under my fingernails – which turned out to be crucial in securing his conviction – I felt a fragile comfort in her kindness, a reminder that not all strangers were bad.

'I had to hand over my clothes for testing,' I continued. 'I remember feeling repulsed when I was given spare clothing – donated clothing, second-hand underwear and all – to wear.' It's so sad, looking back, that they had child-size clothing readily available at a rape centre. 'I remember my dad wrapping his coat around me too, his big hands shaking as he tried to keep me safe in the only way he knew how.

'After two nights on the children's ward, I was home, and the police came to interview me. I was scared, but my parents encouraged me to tell the officers everything – every horrible detail. The tears never stopped for my mum and dad, but I was numb. My mind was stuck in that moment, the scene replaying in my head over and over, and I became terrified of being alone with men, of the dark, of my own shadow.

'The babysitter – a neighbour – never spoke to me or my family again. Whenever she saw us on the street, she'd run inside or pull the curtains closed. Her parents came around with a card and flowers, though.'

'What happened to your attacker?' Maureen asked.

'The police arrested the boy – the man,' I said, remembering how Dad had wanted to kill him; I'd overheard him saying so, his voice cracking under the weight of his rage and helplessness. 'But the legal process dragged on for months, and I missed a lot of school – my parents had to take turns staying off work.' Their faces flashed into my mind again, carved with worry, pain and exhaustion.

'When I did go back to school, everything felt different. The other kids were still carefree, still unafraid, and it baffled me. How could they not see the danger lurking around every corner? I couldn't relate to them anymore. I only stayed close to Li.'

'Were you having therapy by that point?' Maureen asked.

'Yes, every week; I felt like a freak because no other kids my age had a therapist. I remember her suggesting I start a feelings diary. On the first page, I wrote *I think the world is full of monsters.* And I still do.'

'Did the diary help?'

'A little. More so when I started drawing in it instead of writing. Drawing seemed to let out more frustration.'

She nodded. 'And when was the trial?'

'I don't know exactly, but by the time it came, the boy had turned eighteen, so his sentencing was harsher than it might have otherwise been.'

Maureen gave me a sympathetic look. 'It must have been overwhelming, having to wait for that long, not knowing how things would play out.'

I nodded.

'And how did the trial go, Jess?'

'I didn't have to be in the courtroom. I spoke via video link.' I thought back to how my voice trembled as I recounted the worst day of my life to strangers. 'I worried he would be let off because I "led him on" when I'd let him kiss me, but he got ten years.'

'Did he serve the whole ten?'

'Released after five.'

'Oh gosh.'

'My parents were furious that he was out, back in our city, and I was petrified that he might come looking for me. But it wasn't long before he was locked up again.'

'Do you know what for?'

'Killing a girl.'

Shock flickered in Maureen's eyes, but she kept her voice calm. 'That must have been terrifying to hear. How did it feel when you found out... that he'd taken a life?'

'A twisted sense of luck and relief that I was the one that got away.' He was sentenced to life for taking hers, but that didn't erase the guilt I felt for being glad it wasn't mine.

My fear of people, not only of men, grew as I got older. It reached a point where I thought my very existence was a problem. My presence would irritate girls, and my very same presence would attract attention from boys. It was like I was seen as either a threat or a commodity. It made me not want to exist at all.

Chapter 52

I lay in bed that night feeling a little better after sharing with Maureen what I could tell she'd been longing to hear. She had been waiting for the breakthrough. The last thing I saw before I turned out my bedside lamp, the same thing I saw every night, was the blue orchid Georgia had bought me all that time ago; it was still thriving. I wondered if she still had the one I had given her.

The pills I took allowed sleep to swallow me whole, and when I was lucky, I'd dream about her. And when I was really lucky, they would be lucid dreams, in which I'd be aware I was dreaming, and I could touch her skin, and I'd make it so that she asked me to come back to her. I always wondered if we both secretly dreamt of each other.

The days ached and terrified me like nothing I'd experienced. I yearned for a do-over, to find a way to rewind and have a second chance to meet her again for the first time. What if I loved her for a lifetime and we never found ourselves in the same room again? It frightened me. I thought I'd know her forever.

I'd almost become accustomed to the pain and wasn't sure what I'd do without it; it felt like my new persona – my crutch, my addiction. I would set aside many moments every day to think of her, spending longer in my fantasies than in reality. I never longed to be over her or to receive closure, because holding on meant she was still in my life in some way. In my daydreams, I got to keep the best parts of us – we were always smiling, nothing was ever hard, life was perfectly simple, and we wouldn't argue or feel jealousy. We'd sit across from each other at the kitchen table and eat the incredible meals she cooked for us, or go over the shopping list, or make the most mundane moments enjoyable without having to try. The thoughts were always bathed in sunset orange, like being inside a golden bubble of energy with her, safe and secure. And in that bubble, she loved me back; she hadn't forgotten about me. She prioritised me. And we could act like we'd never broken each other's hearts.

I allowed the thoughts to glide and swim about in my head, on play and rewind and play again, for hours. But whenever I was snapped out of my daydreams – be it by a car nearly running me over, or by Glyn raising his voice at me, repeating his question because I hadn't been listening – I came back to coldness and greyness.

My brain felt like it was short-circuiting when I was doing anything other than thinking about her. When it came to her, my mind was pin-sharp and could think up magical scenarios and beautiful story-lines, the all-consuming thoughts flowing so freely that I could have stayed awake for a hundred hours straight and written a book about them. But when it came to writing for *The City Post* – about plans to redevelop the city centre, or controversy over hospital waiting figures – I couldn't think of a single word. I felt dumb and unresponsive, coated in a veneer of professionalism.

I'd always been a daydreamer, but this had gone so far beyond the dictionary description of the term. I knew it, and yet I couldn't snap out of it – and if I didn't, I was certain I'd lose my job.

Maureen kept trying to tell me that the world was so much bigger than what went on in my brain, and to stop living inside my head, but she didn't understand that my daydreams were my only source of happiness. I lived for the visions, and I wouldn't allow any person, any circumstance or any thing to remove me from them. A day of daydreaming, as far as I saw it, was a day well lived.

I was usually so aware of myself as a person, so aware of my facial expressions, my posture, my choice of words – conforming to societal expectations of how all three should appear – but I could feel myself slipping, checking out while I thought about her. Despite knowing logically that I had to try to get back to reality, I felt myself sinking deeper into a warm bath of obsession, hoping that one day I'd slip under, fully immersed in what could have been. I would have happily chosen to live in that space, a space where only my thoughts, not my body, lived on. My physical form could stay in a vegetative state in some hospital somewhere, attached to wires and tubes, and my mind could swim away into magic and love, in a realm where Georgia and I could try again. Maybe death held that pleasure.

I could imagine how serene it would feel to submerge completely into the dream of us. It would be calm and placid in there; light would ripple and dance across the surface of it, my limbs would float weight-lessly, the sounds from outside would be muted, and the outlines of everything would bleed into one another. There would be no more pressure to climb out, dry off and return to a dull daily life and the aching reality of facing a future without the person I'd planned it with.

I would just happily plunge down and down into it, and it would become cooler and darker and tighter the deeper I went. I could drown under the waves of my secret thoughts, the ones about her, the ones no one really wanted to hear about anymore, not even Maureen or my parents.

I don't think they were *tired* of me talking about her, I think they were worried that they'd feed my 'fixation' – as Maureen had referred to it. There was apparently a socially acceptable timeline attached to loving someone you lost, and I was outside of it. So I kept her to myself instead. I yawned the feelings deep down into my body. It was for the best, I think, because my love for her couldn't be put into words anyway; it was ineffable, so much more profound than anything I could ever say – like trying to describe the unfathomable vastness of the universe, or trying to translate from English when you don't know a second language. I couldn't express the inexpressible, or explain the inexplicable. Even if I'd had the words, no one would have fully understood them. I kept her name safely in my mouth, like a boiled sweet, rolling it around on my tongue and savouring its sweetness, tucking it into my cheek when I had to talk to someone.

In one of our therapy sessions, Maureen told me that my fantasies about reuniting with Georgia made me feel alive; they erased other, less easy-to-process emotions, and that was why my brain latched onto them. She said that obsessing over someone for too long stopped looking like love at some point. Not true; I still loved Georgia to my core. I'd never be willing to let go, or be capable of it, for that matter. I didn't blame Maureen for not understanding; she probably hadn't been in love before – not really. The 'real thing' is probably something very few people get to experience.

Maureen also tried to reason that my 'addiction' filled an emptiness inside me, which wasn't a long-term solution to being happy. She was wrong again; I was, in fact, *only* happy when I was thinking about Georgia, and it would always be that way – until the day Georgia walked back into my life for real, or until the day I died, whichever came first.

I touched myself to thoughts of Georgia. I imagined the ways we might bump into each other and the reunion we would have, and the romance that would follow. Not that I even cared if we ever had sex again; I just wanted to hold her body, see her face and smell her skin. To think I ever used to have daydreams about other women when I had her. I hated myself for that. Before I'd met her, all I'd fantasised about was a future with women. After losing her, all I fantasised about was the past we shared.

I often saw her from afar. She was everywhere I went – which wasn't many places, granted – at the bank, at the doctor's office, at the supermarket, at work's car park. I even saw her when my parents forced me to go on holiday with them to the Bahamas. Georgia had her back to us at the pool bar; she was ordering a Diet Coke – she didn't like to day-drink all that much. Her innocent, delicate skull showed its pale seams through wet hair. She was wearing a bikini, but I didn't linger on her body – just her head. It wasn't her, of course. It never was. Not in the supermarket, not in the car park, not at the five-star luxury resort halfway across the world.

Chapter 53

I would clutch my arms around Lucy's neck when she was on top of me. Lucy must have thought it was because I was in a moment of deep passion, but it was just a good position for my nose to reach my wrists, to inhale my perfume – the same one Georgia used to wear – and harness the power of smell to transform Lucy into the person I actually wanted. That way, I could feel Georgia in my arms again, bite into her neck and nuzzle my face into her skin, her hair, her ears.

Lucy wasn't my girlfriend. I could, in different circumstances, have let myself fall in love with her, but I needed any ties to be loose in case Georgia was ready to come back into my life, even though two years had passed since I last saw or spoke to her. I needed either no one around or someone easily severable. Maybe I was just becoming so familiar with pain that I was blocking out anything good that tried to find me.

Lucy was poly anyway, in open relationships with multiple people, so it wasn't as if I could have settled down with her. I didn't care about that, and I got on well with her two girlfriends; sometimes we all even went on dates together. And sometimes we'd all get in the same bed at night. I was in an unintentional polycule.

I didn't want – or wasn't capable of, I'm not quite sure which – emotional sex. It would have felt as if I were cheating on Georgia. After her, I didn't want love. Just fucking. In the main, it was just me and Lucy alone. It was easier to pretend she was Georgia when we were alone.

It was ironic that I was living the sexually liberated life that I had craved when proposing a break from Georgia, but when I actually had it, I didn't want it. The allure of the forbidden had existed solely in my imagination. I would have traded all the women in the world for one more moment with her.

I sat on the edge of the bed, my legs spread, watching as Lucy pulled the harness on with the ease of stepping into underwear, her hands moving with quick, practiced confidence. She skilfully fastened it, adjusting it around her hips – a thick, sturdy leather that hugged her waist and thighs snugly, each buckle polished and glinting faintly under the low light. The glossy black dildo protruding from the harness was long, thick and slightly curved, with a pronounced head and prominent ridges like bulging veins along the shaft. As she took a step towards me, it bobbed subtly with her movement, somehow seeming even larger as she came closer, as if daring me to look away. It felt almost alive, a formidable presence between us. Lucy ran a hand along it as if to make sure I'd noticed, her fingers tracing the outline slowly, emphasising its size and shape. The head was rounded, tapering slightly before giving way to the full width of the shaft – a shape meant to push boundaries, to stretch and fill.

Lucy wrapped her fingers around it, testing its weight as if to make sure it was as solid and imposing as it looked. She gave a slight tug, adjusting it in her grip, and the entire length shifted slightly, a heavy, quiet sway that drew my gaze and made my pulse quicken.

'Happy birthday, Jessie,' she said, her voice low and teasing. 'It's bigger than you expected, isn't it?'

I nodded, offering a faint smile.

She traced her fingers over my breasts and nipples, then along my thighs, her touch slow and deliberate, but I barely registered the warmth. This was just a moment, a physical release – a way to occupy myself and silence the noise in my head, even if only for a little while.

When she knelt between my legs, her hands spreading me open even wider, I let my head fall back, closing my eyes. Her lips brushed against my skin, but it felt distant, as if the sensation couldn't quite reach me. I went through the motions, my body responding on instinct, leaning into the touch, but there was nothing deeper than that – no spark, no urge for anything more.

She used her thumbs to open my pussy before pressing her mouth against it, and I felt the first flick of her tongue, quick and precise, moving in rapid, pulsing strokes. She worked with such speed that it was almost a blur, each motion seamless, pressing and flicking with unrelenting rhythm.

She wrapped her lips around my clit, creating a tight, throbbing suction that sent a shiver through my entire body. Each time she pulled away just slightly, I could hear the soft, wet sounds of suction breaking, only to feel her lips seal back around me again. The sounds echoed through the quiet room, wet and insistent. When she came up for air, she spat on my pussy, then licked her own saliva off me and let it trail off her tongue again, back on to me.

She rose to her feet and looked down at me. I started to pull at her leather-strapped hips, encouraging her to start to fuck me.

'You have to earn it first,' she whispered before biting her bottom lip. 'Suck it.'

I slid myself off the end of the bed, getting to my knees on the floor before taking the dildo into my mouth.

'Look up at me. Show me how that tongue can play with it.'

I tapped the glossy cock on to my tongue, licking in circles around its head, not breaking eye contact with her, licking up the shaft from base to tip. Lucy smiled and closed her eyes as I slipped the hard, girthy appendage to the back of my throat; she seemed to be enjoying the sensation, as if it were an extension of her. I slid it in and out of my mouth while staring up at her, knowing it was soon going to be buried inside me.

'That's it,' she said breathily. 'Eyes on me.'

I held her gaze, my expression calm, impassive, offering nothing beyond what was expected.

'Take it as deep as you can,' she said. 'Choke on it for me.'

I pushed it to the back of my throat again and gagged on it. And again, and again, until my own drool was landing in wet puddles on my thighs and my eyes were watering.

'Keep going. I want to visualise myself shooting down your throat. That's it, Jessie. That's it.'

Then she made a noise that sounded like an orgasm, though it surely couldn't have been, before saying, 'Now take it out of your mouth and turn around, bend over.' She drew me up, her hands guiding me over the edge of the bed, my feet on the floor and my torso on the mattress.

She placed the tip of the dildo against my opening. 'Beg me for it, Jessie,' she whispered, her fingers pressing into my hips.

'Please,' I murmured automatically, my voice even, controlled.

'What do you want?'

'Please, Luce, please fuck me with your huge cock.'

She grabbed my hair, wrapping it around her fist and pulling as she eased the dildo into me in one long, delicious move, and then took it all the way out again. She repeated the movement again and again. Long, slow, deep thrusts. I heard it squelching into me each time. I clutched at the sheets, focusing on the physical sensation, letting it wash over me without meaning.

'I love watching my full length disappearing inside you,' she said in a husky tone.

I swallowed, anticipating another hard thrust to bounce me up the bed, but it didn't come. Instead, she inserted the tip into me and left it there, not going any further, just barely resting it inside me, holding it there with a maddening stillness, not even an inch deep. She didn't move or speak. She let go of my hair and held on to my hips, squeezing them. Every nerve in my body tensed, expecting her to move, to give me more. But she didn't. She simply held her place, her hands gripping me tightly, her breathing heavy but controlled.

Seconds stretched on, each one intensifying the ache, making me hyper-aware of every little sensation: the heat of her body close to mine, the way her fingers dug into my skin, the sound of her breathing. I tried to push myself back against her, to force her deeper, but she held me firmly, denying me even the slightest movement. I started writhing with how much I wanted her to continue, feeling a burning anticipation deep in my cunt.

'Please,' I whispered, voice breaking.

Nothing. She just stayed there, unmoving, torturing me with her silence, making me feel the emptiness inside as if it were a physical ache. My hips were moving instinctively, searching for any friction, any relief, but her hands kept me firmly in place.

'Louder,' she said, her voice barely above a whisper, but filled with command.

'Please!' I begged, my voice raw with desperation. 'Please, Luce. I need it.'

'Need what?'

'I need you to fuck me. Please fuck me. Please, Luce!'

She slammed the dildo into my pussy, her hips meeting my body. I screamed out. She manoeuvred her hands, gripping onto the fronts of my thighs, yanking me towards her with each thrust, fast and deep. So fast. So deep. Ploughing into me. I could feel it bruising my cervix.

'I know, baby, I know,' she said through quick thrusts when I screamed out. 'I know it's a lot, but you can take it. I know you can take it. I know you like it rough.'

'Yes!' I cried.

Then I felt the pad of her saliva-wetted thumb slipping over my asshole, circling and tickling.

'You want me in both holes, Jessie?' she asked, slipping her thumb into my ass before waiting for my response.

'Yes,' I growled, grinding my ass against her pelvis, feeling her thumb firmly pressed into me. I heard her spit on her free hand, and she reached it around to play with my clit. I moaned, tingling all over, gasping and swallowing as she thrust into me. From what I could tell, she was shaking her whole hand so that it felt as if her thumb was vibrating inside my ass, and she was doing the same with her other hand on my clit, while continuing to ram into me from behind.

When it was over, she held me close, her breathing softening, her fingers trailing down my arm. I lay still, unmoving, letting her draw whatever comfort she needed from the closeness, but I felt barely anything in return. That was enough. That was all I needed.

Each night, while Lucy lay sleeping, I'd squint my eyes, focus on her features and try to blur them just enough so that they morphed into Georgia's. I'd squeeze my eyes almost shut until my vision distorted, and Lucy's straight nose would develop an adorable bump on the bridge and adapt to a more aquiline structure, her cheekbones would rise, and her lips would become shapelier. The longer I stared, and the more my eyes attuned to the darkness of the bedroom, the more her features would dissolve into mist, and the sharper the new ones would become. It was like studying an autostereogram – those magic-eye optical illusions that require you to relax your vision so you can discover the hidden butterfly or whatever else is concealed inside its repeating pattern. It always seemed futile at first, but when I loosened my eyes enough, the secret attraction would reveal itself, only in flashes at first, and then all at once, in wondrous 3D and perfect detail, full of depth and dimension and bathed in gentle moon silver. My Georgia.

As I transformed Lucy into Georgia night after night, I began to realise that I was undergoing a transformation of my own. I was done pretending for people at that point – for my family, for partners, for colleagues, for strangers, and especially for men. If anything, I'd gone the other way with my people-pleasing attitude, and I cared so little about what men thought that I bordered on offensive, rude and confrontational most of the time. I knew it was dangerous, but I didn't care anymore. I was released from the chokehold of constantly trying to impress.

I refused to move to the other side of the pavement for men; I refused to speak when men would ask questions about my sex life; I refused to smile at them when their jokes were distasteful; and I refused to leave a public setting when men purposely tried to make me and Lucy feel uncomfortable – when they'd say things like 'I could turn you straight' or that we 'just hadn't met the right men yet' or 'can

I watch?' Thankfully, Lucy was happy to stand her ground around men as much as I was, and fortunately, no physical harm ever came to us. I used to think it was my duty to back down, bribe, befriend, or flirt to ensure my safety, but when I stopped all of that, I was OK too.

Chapter 54

M y phone vibrated, startling me awake. I brought it to my right eye, the other still squashed into my pillow. It was a text from Bex:

'I'm so sorry to tell you this, but I knew you'd want to know. Georgia's engaged – to one of the teachers at her school.'

Pain bouldered its way into my throat, dragging its solid weight upwards, looking for an escape. I was already in fragments without Georgia, but in that instant, I burst into dust. I closed my eyes and hung in the stillness of the moment, my particles static and motionless in the air, my life on pause.

I stopped myself from thinking or moving or breathing because I knew as soon as I did, the reality would hit. And I couldn't bear that. I wanted to stay right there, floating under a spell of numb nothingness for as long as I could.

I felt my first thought start to squirm its way in, like an insect slipping beneath a door seal meant to keep it out. Once it had entered, it freely crawled about, unhindered. It was a thought about Bex, how even though I'd all but shut her out of my life, she hadn't allowed herself to be fully pushed away, always checking in on me via text. I felt grateful for her in that moment and allowed the legs of the feeling to scamper over my senses even though it disturbed the void that I wanted to exist in. I permitted it to distract me from absorbing the message I'd just read, news so colossal it couldn't be perceived as real.

Chapter 55

A faint, buttery light bathed my bare thighs and breasts as I knelt, sitting on my heels on a cream faux fur rug, my head bowed, awaiting Danni.

I was in her dungeon again, and I wanted pain and punishment in the form of being tied up and rhythmically beaten by her. Physical pain helped me process my emotional pain. It helped me process the dreadfulness of the choices I'd made behind Georgia's back, choices that had ultimately led to her finding love outside of me. Georgia was engaged, and I had been sentenced to a life without her.

You threw away a dream life, hissed the voice in my head. *You, and you alone! Georgia wanted you more than anything. She would have given you the world. You need to be punished for your mistakes. I hope you will forever grieve the life you threw away.*

How many times could the same thought break my heart?

Somehow, all that time ago, I'd thought I was being brave by taking the risk of attempting to cheat on Georgia during our break; I'd thought I was doing myself a favour – 'courageously' freeing myself from confinement for once in my life. Not only was Georgia the first girl I'd dated, and the first girl I'd slept with, but she was also the first person I'd fallen in love with. Back then, I told myself that I deserved the chance to explore my sexuality, to experience being single without Georgia knowing, without losing her. I told myself that I'd be living in wonder and regret had I not orchestrated the situation exactly the way I did – a way in which I could secretly live a double life, keeping her on the sidelines, unaware of my true intentions or actions, until I was done with my exploits. There was no other way as far as I had seen it.

At one point, I even thought of my plan as a favour to her; I thought that once I'd acted on my fantasies, it would mean I could fully immerse myself into the life we both wanted. I had just been too scared to grow a spine and be honest with her. Maybe she could have even respected my decision to want to discover my sexuality if I'd had some fucking *morals*. Maybe saying how I actually felt wouldn't have ruined us. I hated to say it, but maybe Li had been right all along.

I had to answer for my actions. My choices had consequences – I didn't get to erase them just because I'd realised my choices were mistakes. I could scream and beg and plead, but I could never go back to that life, that perfect life I'd had with her. I'd thrown it all away. And I wanted pain.

I heard Danni's heels thudding across the floor with purpose. I glanced up at her latex mini dress that had a neckline so plunging I could almost see her belly button. She had worn a similarly deep neckline the night I'd met her, at a queer fetish night called Hanky Panky. Everyone there wore hankies, or pieces of material, hanging out of their pockets, as per the rules – right pocket for those interested in receiving a certain sexual act, and left for those interested in giving.

Everyone wore a certain colour hanky to represent what they were into; there were so many colours that I made a note of them all on my phone and had to keep glancing at it through the night. There was white to signify virgins, or people looking for virgins; yellow for golden showers; grey for bondage; and black for heavy SM. There were plenty of others, too – to represent the likes of rimming, foot stuff and breast play – but I forget the colours. It's safe to say there was no judgement in the room.

I was alone, leaning at the bar, sipping a too-sweet cocktail when she approached, enticed by my green flag – symbolising 'newbie'. Danni played circus clown and pulled a rope of different coloured hankies out of the sleeve of her black blazer – which she wore over a crisp white shirt, unbuttoned almost all the way, with no bra underneath. Her hanky gag indicated she was open to anything. I was out to sabotage myself that night, to fuck a stranger, to drink until I couldn't feel, to escape the real world.

Danni told me what she liked to do in the bedroom – or rather 'The Dungeon' as she jokingly called it – and I realised she could give me what I needed. I'd always felt tongue-tied and embarrassed talking about my fantasies; they'd always been a source of shame and enticement, and acting on one of them had lost me the love of my life. But Danni helped me forget for a moment and cracked open a door to voicing some of my desires again, in a safe, supported way.

'Fantasies and fetishes should never be seen as shameful,' she'd said that night, smiling, lifting my chin with her finger so that I looked her directly in the eyes – those dark, sparkling portals, framed perfectly by her angular obsidian bob. 'Our deepest thoughts and secret hopes draw us to people we're meant to meet.'

The Dungeon wasn't half as scary as I was expecting it to be; it was a gorgeous room – in the basement of her big, beautiful house –

featuring a bed with actual sheets and pillows, plus a bondage bench, and a reclining chair with stirrups. My favourite thing about the room was how wonderfully clean it was.

It wasn't how I'd pictured a BDSM room to look. I'd expected black and red décor, exposed brick, low-level lighting, heavy chains hanging from the ceiling, easy-clean plastic wrap over any furniture, and for some reason, I thought there'd be medieval-style wooden stocks, and metal cages around the place too. There was none of that at Danni's though, apart from the low lighting. It was pared-back, clutter-free and chic – Scandi, even – with a classy, muted colour scheme of mostly off-whites, smoke greys and woods.

The place was all clean lines and minimalism everywhere you looked; even the whips, crops and floggers were arranged by order of length on a wall-mounted rack, each with their own hook. And the toys were concealed neatly inside a solid wooden chest. She had plenty of toys that I had never consented to be used on me – from pussy pumps and Wartenberg pinwheels to ribbed urethral plugs and anal hooks; Danni had taught me all the lingo – I found it all pretty freaky.

We went on casual dates occasionally, but I only really wanted to be Danni's plaything, with no strings attached. I'm sure she invited a hell of a lot of girls down to The Dungeon, but I was emotionally numb to it. We weren't anything serious, and I had no jealousy about not being her only sub. She got a kick out of holding the power, and I wanted to relinquish control, so we both won.

She was a 'stone top', a 'dom', a 'touch-me-not' – terms I hadn't heard of before I met her – meaning she was exclusively a giver, and didn't consent to being touched during sex, under any circumstance. Underneath all the rigour and armour, she was a soft-centred sweetheart, a kind and decent human. She wasn't a professional dominatrix by any means; it wasn't her 'job' – she was a lawyer by day – and she never took payment from any of her subs. Danni and I just went with the flow, and I'm sure she gained as much experience as I did during certain play sessions – or 'scenes', as I realised they were called.

We always discussed and negotiated the particulars of our scenes beforehand – sometimes for hours. There's a whole lot of etiquette and structure in the BDSM world, with consent at its core. It's a kink that allows people to experience both safety and adventure at the same time. That's not exactly a combination you get the opportunity to experience in the daily grind that we call life. It's normally one or the other – safety *or* adventure – and often, as I did, you have to risk it all if you choose the latter in real life.

Before I'd tried out BDSM for myself, I'd wondered why the hell someone would enjoy pain – I'd thought it must be for people who were a little sick in the head, a little strange. But I came to realise that bodies have the ability to process such a stunning scope of sensations, and whether those sensations are perceived as pleasure or pain is utterly subjective. I liked to feel myself rush between the two, riding the fear-meets-thrill endorphin rollercoaster. There was something about the overwhelming intensity of the pleasure-pain duality that moved me to a stripped-back, pure, transcendent space where I could access my authentic self – not my mind, not my body, but my raw consciousness.

The first night that Danni took me home, after wooing me with her rainbow of hankies, we sat in her living room and talked through our intimate boundaries for hours before she so much as touched me. As our sessions went on, I became much better at describing what I wanted; I think it was because I started to let go of my shame. By session four, I happily told her how I wanted her to make me feel: like I belonged to her, like I was her property – but also, I needed her to balance that out with acting as if she loved and respected me, treating me as if I were the only woman in the world. We tried it once without affection and I fell apart; it made me feel like a worthless object. I'd said my safe word within minutes.

'Are you going to let me do everything I want to you this evening?' Danni asked now, crouching next to me while I was on my knees. She licked at my neck and gripped my jaw firmly, holding it upward.

'I am,' I said acceptingly, diverting my eyes, hoping what she had planned for me was going to do the utmost damage.

'That's my girl.' Her thigh-high boots creaked as she stood back up. 'Very good answer. But remember what you must call me.'

'Sorry, Miss.'

'Very good. I'd like you to be on your best behaviour this evening. I'm going to need you to do everything I ask, and do it exactly as directed, OK?'

'Yes, Miss.'

Danni knew my limits – both physical and psychological – but she also knew that I liked them pushed, and that I consented to them being pushed.

She eyed my naked body – which was shivering, not with cold but with adrenaline. 'Stand up now and walk up and down so I can see you.'

I felt the bounce of my full, firm breasts as I paced, the visceral nervous-eager concoction sparkling in my stomach.

She ordered me to the Inspection Slab, as she called it – a kind of padded table, with enough room to lie on as long as my knees were bent. I set myself down, the cold material under my back making my skin tighten.

I kept my knees together as she cuffed my wrists with cool-to-the-touch leather restraints, securing them to the corners of the structure behind my head.

She stood above me, to my side, and brushed her fingertips along my thigh. 'Settle in now, you beautiful thing.'

'Yes, Miss,' I said breathily, obsequiously, my heart thumping.

'Now open up for my inspection, please.'

I did as she said immediately, planting my feet wide apart.

'There she is,' she said, looking between my thighs and smiling. 'Look. At. You. That's my girl. You are eager for me tonight, aren't you?'

'Yes, Miss.'

'I'm going to get you even wetter down there now. I'm going to have my way with you and you're going to allow me to please you – isn't that right?'

I nodded, feeling the heat of her words infuse into my skin.

'I'm going to make that beautiful little pussy drool for me. Do you remember your safe word?'

I gave my answer without hesitation.

'Good.' She stroked my hair. 'I expect you to try your hardest not to use it. Understood?'

'Yes, Miss.'

The playlist began – dark, deep and throbbing – and she pulled on her black nitrile gloves, securing them over her wrists with a snap.

I watched her while I was so exposed, feeling the air of the room breathe and play against my openness, all my attention on that sensitive spot, feeling myself clench and spasm involuntarily in anticipation.

She poured something oily onto her hands and glossed them together, the squelch intoxicating. More of the substance was drizzled on my stomach, pooling in my belly button and dribbling over the sides of my waist, tickling me.

She began to massage me, swiping the oil up to my breasts – squeezing them, working the flesh like dough, letting them bounce and slide out of her hands repeatedly, pulling on my nipples. She glided her hands down my torso to the tops of my legs, her gloved fingers sweeping from my inner to outer thighs, and her thumbs slipping into the soft creases of my groin.

'Wider now,' she commanded, peering between my legs, using her palms to press gently on them, encouraging them further apart. My thighs were convulsing and my knees were shaking with expectancy.

'Thaaat's it.' She drew out the words in a low, slow voice, not taking her eyes from my centre. 'Well done. You look fucking sensational.'

She stood in front of me and slipped full, flat hands over my inner thighs, her thumbs on either side of my pussy, putting pressure on the borders of my outer lips, squeezing them together purposefully. Up and down, up and down. I felt myself relax internally. If my wrists hadn't been in restraints, I'd have had to fight the temptation to touch myself where Danni was so carefully avoiding, but I was helpless to do anything.

I couldn't work out whether it was the pulse of the rhythmic music or the sound of my heartbeat in my ears; either way, the commanding and enveloping reverberations deepened my other senses.

After making me wait, she ran her hands smoothly over my desperately wet, sensitive centre. I trembled at her touch – so gentle yet so powerful. She slowly pushed her slippery hands over me with her open palms, one after the other, stimulating me with upward strokes. She stopped, then ran a slow fingertip from my opening up to my clit, pressing onto it and then flicking her finger, making me jump. I was so very close.

She worked two fingers downward into me – the index fingers of both hands – massaging down and out to the sides, gently stretching me open in preparation.

She ordered me to put my feet in the air, legs together, and then rhythmically pinched my pussy lips closed with her slippery fingers, trapping my clit between them, waiting for it to retreat from her grip with a pop before she pinched at it again. I felt a reverb bouncing through my clit each time.

I obeyed her 'legs apart' command, keeping my toes pointed towards the ceiling as she stood back to admire me, tilting her head from side to side to see me from all angles.

'As wide as you can,' she instructed, looking down her nose at my open pussy and ass, which were fully served up to her. Then she placed my ankles into stirrup loops, tightening the straps onto my skin until I was securely fastened. I couldn't have been more exposed, more splayed; my yearning for the pending maltreatment deepened further.

There was such an eroticism to being tied up, at Danni's mercy, trusting completely and abandoning modesty at her command. She started patting my needful pussy with her whole hand, picking up force until they became stinging slaps, waking up every single nerve ending, causing my skin to shiver and my pelvis to rise to meet her controlled, spaced-out smacks.

'That's my girl,' she said. 'You take it so well.'

I subdued my cries and listened to the sharp sounds of palm on pussy, the erotic charge always in proportion to the degree of pain.

'Just beautiful.' She parted me with her fingers. Her leisurely, heated inspections combined with her praise drove me wild, the balance so perfect between feeling like her property, yet so cherished.

'You're nice and swollen now, and there's a lovely stiffness to your little clit.' She swiped her finger back and forth over it. 'You have such a perfect cunt.'

She reached for a light overhead – similar to that above a dentist's chair – one with a long flexible neck to pull down close to her sub. She brought it between my legs and turned it on. My pulse pounded in my throat and pussy simultaneously as I silently waited for her touch.

She sat on a creaky chair in front of me, angling the light just so, and wiped the excess lubricant from me before using her thumbs and fingers to pinch my lips and prise them apart gently, slowly, keeping them open and staring down at me, telling me how she'd never seen something so perfect before. She manoeuvred her fingers, finding different ways of opening me to my fullest, flirting them around the borders of my opening.

'I could look at you all day,' she said, 'and I'm going to inspect even more of you now.'

Then came the speculum. She eased it into me, the lubrication cold and plentiful, and gradually opened it inside me until I felt the solid pressure on my inner walls of flesh. She shone the light inside me.

'You're doing brilliantly,' she said after peering in for what must have been minutes, her eyes penetrating me, making me tingle all over. 'That's it; keep staying nice and still for me. Every inch of you is perfect. And it's all for me. Your cunt is primed and ready for me now; you're wide open for me.'

I throbbed in waves against the heat of her gaze – her powerfully sensual stare poised to burst the orgasm inside me. All the energy centres of my body were activated at once; I vibrated and purred with electricity and longed for relief so much that it ached. She slipped the medical device out carefully.

From the toy chest, she picked out a modestly sized smooth dildo. She poured the oil over it before slipping it into me, bringing her body over mine, and using her hand to fuck me with it slowly.

She gazed into my eyes, grazing her teeth over her bottom lip. 'That's my girl. Now, don't move a muscle.' She slowed her rhythm further while twisting the toy inside me gently. I groaned. 'Shhh, nice and quiet now. Do you know what's coming next? Do you want me to play with that lovely clit of yours? Stroke it while I slip this cock in and out of you?'

'Yes, Miss,' I said, begging.

'No answers yet. I'm going to give you all the options first. Perhaps you want me to kiss up your thighs and for my tongue to tease your clit with the little circles you like?'

I whimpered and stopped myself from nodding.

'Or maybe you want to be fucked with something a bit... bigger?

'Here's the thing,' she said, licking her lips, her body still between my legs and her hand still sliding the toy into me deeply, slowly, delectably. '*I'm* going to choose what happens next – because you're mine, and I decide everything. Nod if you understand.'

I bobbed my head quickly, closing my eyes in sweet anticipation.

'Well done.' I heard the smile in her voice. What was she going to do with me? I was clueless. No two times in The Dungeon were ever the same.

She gradually slid the dildo out of me and picked up a too-large vibrator. She eased the oil-slathered tip inside and worked the length into me, inch by rock-hard inch. I strained against its girth and the intensity that its tremors brought, writhing my hips madly. It was as if my body was pushing against the feelings while simultaneously opening up and engulfing my welcome intruder. I let out a moan so loud and long that she shushed me again.

I listened to her praise and guidance.

'You're taking it so well.'

'That's it, just like that.'

'Relax onto it for me.'

'Good girl.'

'In The Dungeon, you belong to me and only me,' she said as she pushed in and pulled out in a measured, painful, yet mouth-watering rhythm, stretching me wide as I rolled and rocked my hips. 'Whose are you?'

'Yours, Miss.' My mouth forced out the words through a closing throat.

She increased her pace until she was fucking me rough and hard, pounding into me and knocking the breath out of me. I wanted to scream my safe word; she smiled and stroked my face when she saw it in my eyes. The seconds seemed to be decelerated with that huge toy inside me; it felt like it was in my stomach – I was stuffed, surfeited. Then came the shock of another vibrator, on my clit.

'That's better, now, isn't it? I want to see you cum in this position before I torture you. You're on the brink; I'm going to let you release. You've been so patient, so well-behaved.'

I didn't think I could climax on cue, but my whole body tensed at the two overwhelming sensations, inside and out. The waves of pleasure-pain coursed through me; they flowed and surged and swelled until there was a violent crashing wave that made me scream out. My cry pierced the air, soaring and swooping like a bird set free from captivity. I couldn't stop the muscles in my face from contracting; my mouth seemed fused in a perfect O as if the muscles in my lips had locked into that position. Ecstasy rippled through my limbs, sparks shot through the ends of my fingers and toes and all my negative thoughts loosened.

'We're not finished yet; far from it,' she said as she added more lubricant to her gloved hands before circling my asshole with a slippery fingertip.

'Ah, look at that beautiful little hole; relax it for me.'

I did as she said, as best I could, the pathways of my brain disrupted. And then she pushed into me gently.

'I feel you pulsating all around the tip of my finger. Do you want more?' she asked, smiling, taking her time to insert one finger into my ass. Then came two. She left them in there, unmoving, as she dipped into my pussy with the fingers on her other hand. She began to thrust both sets, slowly; while one set plunged in, the other set eased out in a delicious pattern, back and forth, in and out, the fullness almost unendurable, the slip of the lube luscious.

My groans pressed and squeezed their way out; I wanted to gag from the pressure and pleasure. She entered so deeply and filled me with such width; it felt like her fists were inside me. Maybe they were. I couldn't decide whether it was too much to bear or if I wanted more, the two feelings so closely combined I had no idea where one started and the other stopped. It shook the very roots of me. I was about to climax again but she pulled out slowly, keeping me suspended at the brink of release.

'Uh-uh,' she said, shaking her head. 'I haven't permitted you to cum again. I want to make those beautiful ass cheeks red first.'

She released me and ordered me to my knees over the bondage bench. When I was in position, she blindfolded me and then cuffed my wrists and ankles, attaching the cuffs to the eye hooks on the bench until I was helpless again – defenceless yet protected, vulnerable yet secure.

Something leathery made sensual strokes up and down my back; I knew what it was: the riding crop. It caressed my ass cheeks, the backs of my thighs, the soles of my feet, my shoulders, and the sides of my breasts. Danni called that type of stroking 'pacing'; she always liked to let me recover in a new position before moving on to the next sensation.

I felt the tap of the long, slender crop on my back. 'Arch it, and stick that magnificent ass out for me,' she said, and I acquiesced, the expectancy heaving inside me. Whenever the crop came out, the fear of knowing that no one outside of the room would be able to hear or help me would intensify the experience and make my heart hurtle in my chest, especially as I knew it would only get more painful from there on. My fight-or-flight response was on red alert, which only underscored the fact that I couldn't resist or run. I was fixed to the spot, powerless.

She began to slap my ass cheeks with her palm – quick, broad strokes that thumped more than stung. There was something about her hitting me with her open hand that amplified the power dynamic between us even further. She picked up the intensity, the sharp, repetitive spanks directly translating into clitoral surges. She stroked her palm in soothing circles over my skin before pelting it again, the caresses making me feel loved and cared for, adored and used at the same time.

I sensed her behind me. She opened my ass cheeks with two hands. 'Look at that ass. This is such a good view of your pussy too; I think I'll keep you like this for a little while and just look at you, watch how that cunt pulses and drools for me.'

I wanted to beg her to touch me.

'I think it's time for a taste. After all, you're mine to do with what I want, and if I want to taste you, I will – isn't that right?'

I moaned confirmation as best I could, though it was likely incoherent.

'Stay still and keep being good for me.'

Then, answering the demands of my imagination, I felt her tongue plunge into my pussy from behind, luxuriously soft, hot and wet. I *heard* her tongue-fucking me, the wetness of her mouth and my pussy combining.

'You taste as delicious as you look, as always,' she said between wet slurps and 'mmm' noises as if she were enjoying a meal. She pushed her tongue onto the whole of me, flattened out; I felt its tip touch at my clit. She ate me eagerly, combining leisurely licks with internal, rotating tongue dips, and then she slid her tongue up to my ass and started to circle it around my asshole, tickling and licking the delicate skin. I revelled in the silky wetness and heat her mouth generated.

She left for a moment and I heard her dig into the toy chest again. I knew that sound well. At her command, I relaxed my asshole, and she pushed something smooth against it – a butt plug. She pressed the bulbous tip of it delicately inside, bobbing and twirling it before slowly easing it forward until I was filled and my muscles settled around it. I whined against the pleasure of the burn and stretch. Her fingertips or knuckles – I couldn't tell – tapped on the toy's base, sending internal drumbeats through my bones, making me feel both hollow and crammed, reminding me I was just flesh, just a shell.

'That'll open you up nicely, ready for me to fuck you in there soon.'

She left the plug in place and picked up the crop again, stroking the leather tip along my neck and down to my lower back. 'I'm going to punish you now, my gorgeous one.' On the last word, she thwacked it across my ass, shocking my cheeks with its sharp bite. I got off on the whoosh-and-snap noises it made as it cut through the air before making violent contact, its stiff, wide leather tip aiding the precise, targeted hits.

She alternated steady, rapid tapping with hard strikes in no particular rhythm so that I wouldn't be able to guess when the next blow was coming – *tap tap WHACK, tap WHACK, tap tap tap tap tap tap WHACK* – leaving me flinching and craving. She focused it all on one point on just my left ass cheek, before moving on to the right. I could feel two perfect bruises colouring. Then it made its way between my legs, and she cropped my inner thighs from behind, springing the long, flexible implement from side to side rapidly.

Next came the flogger, the super-soft leather fronds fast-tracking from delicate, tickling strokes to sharp strikes and confident blows, leaving flashes of adrenaline sparking over my quivering cheeks. Tears glossed my eyes beneath the blindfold. I must have been making too much noise, as she strapped a gag into my mouth. I didn't complain or try to say my safe word, but she knew she was pressing on a serious boundary.

She stroked my hair. 'You're pleasing me tonight. Keep being good for me.'

She lanced across my raw cheeks again, the fronds finding their way to flick against my tender open pussy every few strikes, jolting me with gratifying stings, the fast shock of it against my clit, the intensity spectacular.

Next was the rattan cane, which left lightning-quick hot slashes of pain exuding over my cheeks, snapping down again and again as I twisted and screamed against it. It burned against the backs of my legs and over the tender surface of my ass, which juddered under the assault.

Danni continued to arrange the searing lines of agony across me while telling me how well I was taking it and how much it pleased her. My tears surged as I actively inhaled into the sensations, riding with them, even though my instinct was to hold my breath and tense my body up tightly.

The worst – or best, depending on how I looked at it – implement came last, the plaited bullwhip, which cracked down and decorated me with burning welts until I was fully tenderised and trembling with hurt. I lost track of the whips she used to torment me, the last's rigid leather handle finding its way into my available opening while the butt plug remained in place.

She touched, teased and tortured parts of me I barely knew existed, both physically and mentally, altering my state at a neurochemical level.

Danni knew about Georgia; she knew Georgia was the reason I was the way I was – the reason for the misery I felt inside. And she knew I wanted, *needed*, to feel punished for what I did to her, what I did to myself, to our relationship. Danni was well aware of the army of guilt that still raged in my veins, and of the loss that still clawed at my heart, forcing me to endure reality over and over again in an excruciating loop. She understood my need for release – not just on the surface of my skin but all the way to my core – and she didn't judge me for it.

After each session with her, I would come closer and closer to empty. The bodily pain she inflicted on me helped to release my deep-set emotional pain. One would replace the other, purging me bit by bit. That's why I preferred her not to be gentle with me – 'The harder the better, as always,' I would tell her in our pre-scene negotiations, so I got more bang for my buck with each blow. Upon impact, hot shards of my embedded emotional hurt would loosen and liquefy and then seep out of me like lava, each burning rivulet's path interrupted somewhere along its way to freedom by a pudgy, freshly made whip welt or a self-inflicted scar. The inside tops of my thighs had the highest concentration of the latter – a hidden-away interlacing display of despair, carved on me like ancient pictographs on cave walls. Even though there were many, they paled in comparison to the deep slash across my heart – my deepest wound, forever to remain unhealed.

Every time I visited Danni's dungeon, I experienced a trace of healing in the stripping away of daily life's armour that I had to wear to get by, but in receiving it, I sank further into a pit of loneliness. And what's the point in healing if you're at the bottom of a pit, all alone, by the time you're whole again?

I didn't want to heal fully. I wanted the guilt and shame and sorrow to pump around my body, in my blood, and give me sustenance – the pain being the only surviving link to what I'd lost.

After gently removing the toys from both holes, I heard Danni opening the chest again, its hinges creaking as she did so. I closed my eyes tightly and squirmed in anticipation. I could hear the buckles of her strap-on harness clinking, and the sound of lubricant being squeezed out of its tube. After a moment, she took a position behind me and spread my ass cheeks firmly with her palms. Slowly, she traced the full length of a dildo along my pussy, slicking the shaft in my wetness before setting the tip against my asshole. With a gentle pressure, she slowly pushed in, deeper and deeper, building pace until she was fucking me hard – fucking me free of regret's insidious hold for a moment. Her fingers stroked at my slippery clit, marginally ameliorating the deep, pulverising ache that pounded into me from behind. I barely remembered a time before I was at her mercy.

'Cum for me now, gorgeous,' she said through thrusts as she sped up, fucking my ass into oblivion. My body obeyed and I was quickly consumed into a flickering space in my brain as if I were watching my blood cells burst into fireworks. Eruptions shattered through my body, experiencing the limits of sensation, every muscle turning rigid and to jelly at once, exploding and melting at the same time, dissolving the edges of my identity.

I tumbled down a dark, vertical portal, a rabbit hole, which stretched for miles, heading towards the centre of the earth. Down, down, down, like Alice. All I could hear was Danni's muffled voice repeating, 'Atta girl, just like that.'

Spasming, and drooling from either side of my gag, I opened my weighty eyelids to distortions and hazes, my sight rolling from side to side.

I felt Danni unlocking me, laying me down and tending carefully to my damage – 'aftercare', she called it.

With only a nebulous recollection of what had happened, it took a few moments to realise where I was – like when you've been driving on autopilot and you wonder how you've travelled so far without concentrating on the road.

My muscles were sapped and my body was a heap. The lasting sensations of the whips were singed into my skin, and my orifices thudded and radiated. The afterglow of the pain, combined with the feeling of being cared for and cuddled, and the lethargy drifting through me, sent me into a trance-like euphoria, a subspace, where only Danni and I existed.

There was such catharsis in it – a pureness. Letting go was the ultimate act of self-cleansing, allowing me to relinquish control, submit to my fears, be pushed to – and beyond – my limits, attune to my dark parts, and embrace the shadowed side of myself. I never had to hide when I was with Danni. I was safe. I was free.

But no matter how safe I was in The Dungeon, there always loomed the anxiety that I'd have to face the real world again soon. It was always a ticking time bomb. I'd feel the despair kick in when ascending The Dungeon's stairs. When I reached the top, the gloom would hit me in the face like that hot, humid rush of air that enfolds you when you step off a plane in some faraway country, and you know a transition has begun.

Chapter 56

'A re you waiting for a taxi, too?' a girl asked me and Danni.

'Yes, but we're not ready to leave yet,' I said, slurring, squeezing one eye shut to ease the spinning sensation. 'We want to stay out and party.'

'Come back to my house,' she squealed, jumping on the spot. 'Loads of people are back there – it's a student house, so it's always party central. We've got so much booze already, so you don't need to bring anything.'

Danni and I looked at each other. We'd only met this girl five minutes ago, after leaving our bar date.

My newfound impulsiveness spoke on our behalf. 'Fuck it, yeah.' What harm could it do?

We pulled up outside the girl's place. The house's thinly curtained windows glowed red then green then blue, light spilling from them into pavement puddles. The music thumped through the walls and I could already hear how many people were in there from the roar of voices. Suddenly, I didn't want to go in, but I followed the girl through the front door anyway.

A buzz of wild, chaotic energy hit us square in the face and the voices and music grew louder as we opened the porch door. The girl kicked glass bottles out of our way in the hall; there was a smell of stale sweat and spilled beer.

We walked past rooms thick with bodies chatting, laughing and dancing to tempo-pushing music built of synthesiser riffs, deep basslines and no lyrics. All the house lights were off, replaced by spinning disco-ball lamps on the floor of each room, illuminating colours and patterns over the walls and ceilings.

Danni and I pushed our way to the kitchen at the back of the house. The windows in there were steamy with condensation from all the people, people I didn't know, packed into one space. I made straight for the back door and stepped out into the cold shot of air. There was no garden, it was just a poky, paved area which led to a back gate, and it stank of marijuana.

'Yo,' said the one guy out there.

'Um, yo.' I offered a faint smile.

He held out his spliff between his thumb and forefinger. 'Drag?' he asked tightly, trying to keep the smoke in his lungs.

I glanced down at the soggy end that had been in his mouth. 'Sure.'

I sucked on it and handed back the joint with a friendly nod, heading inside before he came any closer.

I spotted Danni talking to a little group of people in the far corner. I made my way to join them but bumped straight into someone as solid as a brick wall. Blood crept into my face and a shiver ran down my spine as I saw who it was. Daeva Valentine.

'Oi oi!' she bellowed, all venomous smiles and arctic eyes. 'What are you doing here? Jess, right?' She hugged me with her tattooed arms while I turned as stiff as a board. 'You never kept in touch.'

I gathered myself and painted on my most convincing unruffled mask. 'Oh, hi Daeva! Yes, life's been so crazy,' I said with a wave of my hand. 'Anyway, really sorry but we were about to head off,' I lied, eager to make my immediate escape from her.

I went to move towards Danni, but Daeva grabbed my wrist and pulled me back to her, just as she'd done the night when I'd tried to leave her house. Overt hostility poured from her but it was trapped, bulging and sloshing inside the watertight layer of sociability she wore cloaked around her.

'What are you doing here?' she asked, lighting a cigarette before locking in on me with her predacious gaze, wisps of her black wolf-cut grazing her sooty eyelashes as she blinked.

'I was just randomly invited back here after a night out.'

'Got to love a house party, eh?' she said, smiling. 'I just came in here uninvited and no one said a thing. Who are you here with?'

I pointed to Danni. 'The one in the white shirt.'

She rubbed one papery lip against the other. 'So you have time to go on dates and to house parties but no time to message me back, no?' She smiled sardonically, taking a drag of her cigarette.

'She's just a friend. Anyway, I—'

'You know, you could have just told me if you didn't want to see me again,' she said, cutting me off. 'It's not nice to ghost people.'

'Sorry. Life just sort of got away from me. I didn't mean to.'

'So you *do* want to meet up again?'

'It's still complicated right now,' I said, trying not to show any fear.

'Fucking hell.' She rolled her eyes and drew on the fag, letting the smoke flare from her nostrils. 'Go with the flow a little, for fuck's sake. You're so uptight, mate.'

I was spontaneously at a stranger's house party; if that wasn't me going with the flow, I'm not sure what was. I concealed my annoyance with a tight smile.

'So have you fucked anyone lately?' She blew smoke upward and diagonally, in the general direction of the open kitchen window. I was unfazed by her vulgar directness; I was expecting it.

'No, actually, I haven't,' I said calmly, hoping that I wouldn't trigger the bubbling rage that always seemed to simmer just beneath her surface. I had a feeling that if I'd said yes, she'd have been angry that it hadn't been her.

She peered at me silently through the smoke, as though marshalling her thoughts. 'I can tell you like to do unhinged shit in bed, just by looking at you. You're into weird stuff, aren't you?'

'Uh,' I said, caught off-guard that time. 'No, not really.' My mind flitted to my last session in Danni's dungeon – where she had me spread-eagled on the bed, arms and legs bound to all four corners of the bedframe, unable to move, hers to do with whatever she wanted. 'Anyway, my friend's waiting for me, so I better dash.'

She must have noticed my mask of composure slipping, and it emboldened her. She grabbed my wrist. 'Do you want to know what I like? People say it's strange but then they try it and I convert them for life.'

'You don't have to tell me your personal stuff, that's OK.' I glanced over at Danni, hoping she would notice my subtle 'help-me' eyes, but she just smiled and waved. For a split second, it made me miss Li, who understood my needs with a single look.

I shifted from foot to foot awkwardly, trying not to show my unease.

'Knife play,' she said, those piercing pinprick pupils of hers dilating for a second. 'It sounds mental, but it's so hot.' She chuckled and shrugged.

I smiled agreeably, wriggling my wrist a little, hoping it would serve as a cue for her to let go without me asking her to.

She came a little closer and semi-whispered, 'Lightly running the tip of a knife across a woman's skin is like an aphrodisiac. Not always drawing blood, but just leaving little white scratches and seeing her squirm because she realises she likes it too.'

'I have a weak stomach when it comes to stuff like that,' I said, stepping back and trying to appear casual, even though I knew I had more welts and scars on my skin than anyone in that room.

'One drink before you go,' Daeva said, releasing her grip by half. 'Then I'll forgive you for ghosting me.'

'I really can't, I just need to—'

'It wasn't cool to ignore me. You owe me one drink.'

'OK.'

She let go of my wrist but clasped my hand in hers instead, entwining her fingers with mine. 'I knew I'd get a second date with you. I always get what I want.' She swung my hand back and forth in hers.

'I guess I'll just get us some drinks then, shall I?'

'Hang on,' she said, another smile stretching across her face. 'I haven't finished telling you about knives in the bedroom yet.' Her voice had claws all of a sudden. 'Honestly, it's nothing gruesome. It makes you feel alive, you've just got to be open to it. It's more visual than anything and involves a lot of trust. Do you trust me?'

'I don't really know you, but you seem trustworthy,' I said cooperatively. 'My tastes are a lot milder than that. Anyway, that drink won't pour itself.' I went to pull my hand away, but she gripped it tighter.

'I once "turned" a girl, y'know,' she said. 'She was against knife play at first, but after she tried it, she was more into it than me. She wanted it every time we went to the bedroom. I reckon she developed a proper fetish.' She laughed, pausing as if to reminisce, her eyes lighting with lust. 'She grew to love blood so much that she always wanted to go down on me when I was on my period. And she wanted to try play piercing, but that was past my limits.'

'God, that's crazy,' I said robotically, beginning to turn away. 'I'm just going to grab those drinks.'

I felt her gaze stalk me as I walked across the room. While I was helping myself to the booze in the fridge, the music suddenly shut off and a well-built guy – who looked as if he had been abusing steroids – shouted, 'Right, who wants to come in on buying some blow?'

Half of the room, including Daeva, began to lay down banknotes on the table, and others announced that they'd just wired certain amounts over. Within minutes, they'd racked up hundreds of pounds between them like it was no big deal.

'Yeah, so, anyway, would you be up for having your mind changed about knife play?' Daeva asked as I placed our gin and tonics on the table. I couldn't find any glasses, so I'd poured the drinks into mugs – hers yellow with a daisy painted on it, and mine with a picture of an avocado and the words *Avo nice day* printed across it.

'Right, done, going to meet the dealer,' shouted the muscular guy, switching the hardcore playlist back on.

'I'll come with you,' I yelled at him without conscious volition; anything to get out of the next phase of the bloody – literally – conversation with Daeva.

'Come on then, Jessica Rabbit,' he said, flashing me a grin. There was that nickname again.

Without giving Daeva a chance to interject or grab me again, I seized the opportunity and walked out with him, the music drowning out any protests she had.

As we left the house, I checked over my shoulder to make sure Daeva wasn't following us, and I had to break into a light run to keep up as we zig-zagged through the backstreets of the neighbourhood. A few minutes later, in the picking rain, he said, 'Stay here,' and he jogged across the road over to a parked car. He got in. I realised I hadn't been paying attention to the direction we'd walked, so I didn't have the first clue how to get back to the house.

My whole life, all I'd done was try to keep myself safe, but now I was constantly, deliberately, compulsively putting myself in these dangerous situations. I was out on the street in the dead of night with a meat-head man-mountain, waiting, alone, for him to finish up his drug deal. I thought about what might happen. What if the muscly guy and the dealer were, at that moment, thinking up a plan to bundle me into the car and rape me? They wouldn't even need a plan, the muscly guy could just literally pick me up and pop me into the vehicle and there would be nothing I could do about it.

I hastily looked around for the best direction to run in. I coughed a few times, clearing my throat to give my screams a clear exit if needed, and I circled and loosened the bones of each ankle to prepare myself for a sprint.

'Let's go,' the guy said, jogging back to me. Thank god for that.

Back at the house, I did a bump of coke, my first ever. It shot through my bloodstream and exploded in my brain. The next thing I knew, I was standing on the dining table watching everyone clap at me as I danced. I had so much energy – wide awake and wired, as if

I could take on the world. My nostril was numb and glowing warm from the drugs; the feeling spread to the roof of my mouth and my gums, and my teeth on one side of my mouth didn't feel like mine – as if I'd chewed on anaesthetic.

The exciting feeling wore off pretty quickly; there were no lasting effects apart from itchy teeth and feeling incredibly thirsty. I crouched down, still on the table, and picked up my avocado mug, necking the whole thing in one before attempting to climb off the table, but as I did, it was like the whole room sloped, and then the end of the slope melted away and disappeared as if over the edge of a waterfall. I tried to blink away the vertigo, staggering up to the top of the slope for safety. And then Daeva appeared in my eyeline, smiling her horrible smile. 'You good, girl?'

Even with my brain in the state it was in, I knew what this was. How could I have been so stupid? I'd left my mug unattended next to Daeva. I couldn't stop my eyes from closing. Then everything went dark.

Chapter 57

I was upright and moving, but I couldn't open my eyes to look. I was leaning on someone – my arm around their shoulder – and they were propping me up, taking my weight, hauling me somewhere. Wherever we were, there was an oven-heat in the air. Managing to peer through the slit of one eye, my head hanging down, I saw my feet; they were dragging behind me, the toes of my shoes bouncing along a mosaic of brown, orange and blue Victorian tiles – the type my late grandma had had in her hallway. I recognised that floor. Every inch of me tightened in dread. I was at Daeva Valentine's house again.

'No,' I said with what little energy I could muster, my heart racing in my chest. 'No.' I didn't even know if I was making a sound or just thinking I was.

'It's cool,' Daeva said, her arm snaked around my waist as she pulled my limp body along her swelteringly hot hallway. 'You asked if you could sleep here tonight, that's all. I'm taking care of you. You trust me, right?'

I tried to take my arm from around her neck, but it was no use; I could barely move a muscle. What the fuck did she put in my drink?

'Up,' she said enthusiastically and repeatedly, hoisting me up each step of her staircase, her voice straining, but only ever so slightly. She was so strong.

I felt my rag-doll body flop down onto a bed as my panic centres continued their relentless, silent plight. My eyes wouldn't open more than a fraction; I tried to lift my eyebrows, hoping that would help open my lids, but nothing.

'I'm just getting you ready for bed,' she said softly. 'I know you'd do it for me.'

I felt her slipping off my shoes before unbuttoning my jeans and wiggling them down my legs.

'No,' I attempted to scream, but nothing emerged from my mouth. I was trapped in my body, trying to claw my way out of my skin.

'Arms up,' she said cheerily, picking my deadweight limbs up and flopping them onto the bed. She used my torso to balance her weight for a moment; I could feel my ribs bending beneath her hands and was frightened by how fragile I was compared to her.

She peeled off my sweat-soaked top. 'I don't know about you, but I like to sleep naked. I'm guessing you're a naked sleeper too, so I'll get you nice and comfy – out of that tight bra and kickers; I find underwear such a pain to sleep in, don't you?'

She hooked her fingers into the waistband of my thong, as if to pull it down, but stopped herself, clasping her hands together.

'But first,' she said, with a brightness in her voice, like she was about to find a fun way to explain the times tables to a class of kids. 'I know you said you didn't think you'd be into knife play, but...' She giggled through her nose. 'I bet I could change your mi-ind.' She warbled the last word in a sing-song tone, which shot even more fear through me. She was a human version of a lullaby in a horror movie.

'I'll be super gentle with you, this being your first time and all – I won't even draw blood. It's going to make you feel alive. I promise.'

I wanted to kick and fight against her, but my limbs were disconnected from my brain, and my mouth felt stitched shut. My heart was beating out of my chest and the coldness of fear crept over my skin like spiders as I felt her icy gaze upon me, operating on me. It was like one of those nightmares where you can't shout out when the murderer is approaching.

I could barely make her out; my eyes wouldn't adjust. She was just a cold, dark outline shadowing the burn of the lights behind her. But I could see the knife in her hand. My screams were trapped inside. I willed my body – any part of it – to move, but the whole of me felt stapled to the bed. My tongue was so heavy in my mouth that it started slipping down the back of my throat. I began silently choking on it; I couldn't breathe.

The cat-claw-like drag of the knife stung my belly. I tried to gasp for breath but my tongue blocked my airway. I felt myself passing out. *No. Please, stay awake. Turn your head to the side. Come on, Jess.*

I couldn't do it.

***

I awoke to light, quick slaps across my cheek, dislodging my tongue from my throat – Daeva must have finally noticed that I wasn't able to breathe. I gulped for air as my head lolled to the side.

'Fucking hell, your lips practically went blue then, Jess. What are you playing at?' she said through a laugh. 'Tell me if you need to move next time, you silly sausage. You scared me.

'So what do you think about knife play so far? You're into it, aren't you?' She nodded and smiled, observing me from the corner of her eye spiritedly. 'I knew you'd like it. What do you think, shall we move to level-two intensity? It won't hurt. Ready? I love that you're trusting me; that's such a compliment. You're going to be ringing me tomorrow and asking for more, that's how much you're going to enjoy it.'

I felt tingling in my legs, as if they were coming back to life.

'Here we go, then...' she said.

Someone banged on the front door.

'Open up!' It was Danni's voice.

'Why do people have to ruin everything, eh?' Daeva said with an exaggerated shrug, each word inflated, as if she were a children's TV presenter.

The banging and shouting went on, and my legs continued to wake up.

'Yeah, yeah, yeah, I'm coming,' she said, huffing.

The next thing I knew, Danni was helping me downstairs, my legs like jelly, before plunking me into the backseat of the waiting taxi. The fact that only a bra and thong were covering my modesty was the least of my worries.

Chapter 58

I slowly blinked my eyes open, the brightness assaulting my senses, and peeled my tongue from the roof of my mouth. The sterile whiteness of the room greeted me, its cleanliness almost blinding against my groggy vision. Confusion flickered in the recesses of my mind as I struggled to piece together where I was. The clinical smell of disinfectant hung heavy in the air, mingling with faint wafts of food, sick and death. Machines beeped rhythmically, their persistent tones punctuating the steady hum of murmurs, groans and shuffling feet coming from beyond my curtained-off space.

I shifted in the bed, the rustle of stiff sheets and the squeak of the plastic mattress startling me.

'You're awake.' It was Danni's voice. She was sitting to the left side of me, just out of my line of sight.

And someone else was there too, on my other side. I felt the familiar warmth of Lucy's hand resting lightly on mine. I blinked again, my gaze landing on her. Her face was a mixture of relief and something deeper that I couldn't quite name.

Danni explained how she'd seen Daeva dragging me through the back gate of the student house and into a cab. She said she couldn't get to us in time, so she'd called the taxi company and asked them to trace the car that had been called to that address.

I didn't end up pressing charges against Daeva; I didn't even notify the police about what happened. I couldn't have coped with any more drama in my life at that point. Besides, the authorities might have blamed me – maybe I led her on, laughed too hard at her jokes, stayed talking with her too long, or wasn't firm enough. Plus, since I had done coke, they might have even had reason to arrest me.

From then on, I tried my best to signal to the world that I wasn't interested in anyone else coming into my life. I didn't want anyone else to want me, to desire me, to assault me. Unapproachability was my aim, setting my face in a frown and pressing my lips together. I wore sunglasses everywhere, scraped my hair back, and wore baggy clothes. I wished I could have been invisible.

Why couldn't I have just had Georgia back in my life, even just as an acquaintance? Life would have been so much better if Georgia had been around. I missed her. I missed her so much it was agonising. I also missed the parts of me that only showed up when I was around her. They were the best parts of me.

I wanted the hurt to kill me.

Now and then, I'd unfold the letter that I'd written to her in my last-ditch attempt to apologise and get her back – the letter that Li had intercepted and mailed back to me without letting Georgia read it. I don't think Georgia ever knew what she really meant to me. I wished I could have sent her another letter, and I wished for her to send me one back. Maybe she never knew that she was the love that burst in on me without warning before I'd even had the chance to process it or realise what it was. She'd had my heart before I truly knew it. One morning,

I woke up and she was all I could think about, and that never went away. I wanted so badly to recreate everything that could have been, and make it work the second time around.

Chapter 59

Since Daeva Valentine's violation, I'd been chaste and all but terrified of sex. It occurred to me that my connection with Danni wasn't real. Neither was my relationship with Lucy. Not one romantic bond existed in my life. It was all a pointless lie; it was all make-believe. And I could either pretend to hold on to my nothingness, or I could let go entirely. I chose the latter, and the fact that neither of the girls even tried to put up a fight hurt me even more.

In self-protection, my mind detached itself from real life for a while; I couldn't bear living, and so some other force besides me took over. I thought I was experiencing psychosis when it first started – when I would hallucinate – but the doctor assured me I wasn't.

'You're normal,' she explained. 'You're having a normal human experience; this is just anxiety, which will pass.'

But I wanted there to be something really wrong with me, something diagnosable so that I could be cured.

***

It wasn't that I'd sit and ponder how to kill myself, but in the haze of a triggering moment, I would impulsively and without thought search for the easiest way to escape life. Like when I ran out of shampoo in the shower one day; I threw the bottle down in a fit of rage, grabbed the door of the shower and ran my wrist down its glass edge, fast and hard, longing for it to be sharp enough to slice through my skin and artery in one stroke, but when I checked, there wasn't even a cut, just a pathetic pink dent against the thin blue streaks. I stood there sobbing under the water until my ribs ached, watching the blood-that-could-have-been pour onto the shower floor, diluting and swirling with the water, lamenting the missed opportunity for a way out that would have been so damn easy. In just a few minutes, I'd have slipped away, as effortlessly as the blood down the drain.

I never tried to end things twice in one sitting; it would always be a single act of crazed immediateness, and then I'd wallow in the outburst's failure, and then be glad it didn't work, and then take it as a sign that I was supposed to live.

But then it would happen again, maybe the next day, maybe the next hour.

I saw all the ingredients to wellness on imaginary shelves in front of me: a box of sunlight; a pack of good nights' sleep; a jar of friends; a jug of hobbies; a container of positive thoughts; a tin of coping skills; and a carton of daily exercise. They were all within reach; all I had to do was pick them up. But I didn't want them. I didn't want to allow myself to get better. I wanted to wallow and deteriorate and hibernate.

The doctors and the people on the other end of the free suicide hotlines weren't really there to help me, they didn't care about me; in fact, they all hated me because if I hadn't kept calling in, their jobs would be easier. I was just making it harder for them. I was just another case that was adding to their workloads and interrupting their water-cooler chats. They all judged me and recorded their captious criticisms on my permanent record for me to be forever ashamed about – for potential new bosses to read and use to refuse to hire me; for the insane asylum I was destined to be locked away in to deduce just how crazy I was; for the social services workers to baulk at if I ever had a baby in years to come, and then to arrange for the child to be taken from me by court order.

Why would I tell anyone what was going on in my head? They'd all use it against me. They'd all profess they were on my side; they'd use soft voices and make gentle movements before pouncing on me and locking me away. It was safer not to let the world know what was wrong. I'd even stopped going to see Maureen, who was likely in on it too.

One day, a well appeared. A well so dark I couldn't tell where the bottom might have been – deep enough that no one would ever find me again if I fell in. The Well would switch locations depending on which room of my parents' house I was in. I didn't leave the house, so I'm not sure whether The Well would have appeared in the outside world, but I'm betting it would have. I tiptoed and balanced on the edge of it – its grey, cragged stones rocking under my weight as I tried to make my way around its circumference without falling in. Sometimes the stones slipped and plummeted into the hole, and I'd never hear them land as it was so far down.

It wasn't death that awaited me down there; it was madness. If I fell in, it would mean I'd enter a realm of complete and utter insanity, where my soul would be trapped for eternity.

The mouth of The Well was always growing larger, and there was more chance of being pulled in by its petrifying gravity. Maybe it would even happen while I was sleeping; it would just open up under my bed and I'd drop right in. Or maybe it would start sucking me in one day, fed up with my stubborn resistance.

I was always on the cusp of madness, and I knew if I slipped in, I'd never be able to get back to myself. That would be it. Forever. It would seal up and shut me in, and no one would be able to find me, or the mouth of The Well, ever again. It would simply disappear and be walked over. Feet would traipse aimlessly back and forth over where it had once been. Mum and Dad would call my name in desperation while standing right on top of where I'd fallen in.

The longer I managed to survive, the angrier The Well seemed to become, and the fate that lay within the abyss worsened. If I succumbed, at least it would be a gentler descent – like an innocent person who pleads guilty in the hope of a lesser sentence – but if I waited until the very last second, it would no doubt pull me in, swallow me and digest me in stages in its acid, and I would burn from the outside in, in eternal pain.

***

There wasn't a moment or revelation that pulled me out of that dark place – it wasn't as simple as waking up one day and realising I was cured. The process was more like learning to navigate a maze in slow motion, where every turn revealed both light and shadow, but the path was always there if I looked for it.

It started small, almost imperceptibly. I started doing little things that I had forgotten brought me comfort – sitting with a book, taking myself into sunlight, and most of all, drawing – letting the quiet act of creating something on paper soothe the chaos inside me.

I thought I had to wait for a major breakthrough, but the healing was in the simple, slow, digestible process of rooting for myself over and over again. I started to look for the glimmers in life, the little moments of awe, the pleasure in the ordinary, the magic in the mundane, the micro-moments that breathed bliss into me and offered dashes of hope. I collected and treasured them, allowing them to elevate me. It was the feeling of the freezing sea against my skin, it was listening to the rain patter onto the window when I was warm in bed, it was a hug from my parents, it was beautiful song lyrics, it was a dog lolloping towards me, it was a baby waving at me, it was the realisation that bad times don't last forever. I'd forgotten it was so simple; I'd forgotten there was so much to see, so much good in the world.

When I focused on The Well, the more power I seemed to give it, like I was feeding the very thing that was trying to consume me. So instead, I began to nurture other things. I opened up to my parents, who had always been there, waiting for me to emerge from my isolation. They had been standing on the sidelines, never pushing, but always ready with open arms when I was ready to take that first step back. Then I phoned Bex, and I reached out to Lucy and Danni. Three wonderful people that had never deserved to be thrown away by me.

And then, there was acceptance. Not of The Well, not of the darkness, but of myself. I stopped waiting for some version of myself that felt 'better' or 'whole' or 'fixed'. I learned to be OK with where I was in the moment, to honour it for what it was, instead of wishing it away. Slowly, I realised that my sense of worth didn't have to come from defeating the darkness – it came from living despite it. That shift changed everything.

The Well still existed as part of the landscape of my life, but its mouth wasn't always gaping open. And it was shallower. I began to believe that if I ever stumbled again, I could find my way out. That was the greatest gift I could give myself: not the certainty that I'd never fall, but the belief that I'd always find my way back up.

All I would say to that well now is, 'Thank you. Thank you for breaking me to the point where I finally learnt to value myself. Thank you for helping me realise I needed to feel at peace more than I needed to feel in control. Thank you for trying to make me disappear because it made me appreciate that all I really wanted was to be found.'

Chapter 60

I wipe my hands on the front of my paint-splattered pinafore, a happy sigh escaping my lips as I survey the room and the people in it. Easels are spread out in a semi-circle, each holding a canvas, some blooming with bold strokes of colour, others marked with more hesitant beginnings or charcoal scribbles. There are eight of us today, a small group – intimate enough for everyone to feel safe, even when the act of creating stirs up deep emotions. The gentle hum of concentration fills the space, brushes meeting paint, paint meeting canvas. It's quiet here, but a good kind of quiet, the kind that feels full.

This is my space. I built it from the ground up, from the empty, echoing walls of this old studio to the thriving community it's become. After getting my certification as an art therapist, I knew I wanted more than just a traditional clinic. I wanted a place where people could heal through expression, where the act of creation could be a form of therapy – both for them and for me.

There was a time when I'd thought being promoted to news editor of *The City Post* was everything I'd ever wanted. I was so ambitious, always pushing myself, aiming high, and berating myself for every missed opportunity. But deep down, I knew it wasn't right for me. It was too hectic, too full of negativity. There were moments that made me feel awful, like the unwritten rule of calling the newspaper before calling 999, or the death knocks, or the court cases. It wasn't in my blood. The more I tried to force myself into that world, the more it felt like I was betraying something inside me.

But art, that had always been my outlet, my sanctuary.

I walk over to Ellie, a regular in the class. She's young, in her twenties, but she carries a heaviness of someone much older. She's staring at her half-finished painting with furrowed brows. She's one of the most talented here, but she rarely shares the meaning behind her work.

'How's it going, El?' I ask softly, standing just to her side.

She glances up at me and offers her usual shy smile, but it's tinged with something else I can't put my finger on. 'I don't know,' she says. 'It feels different today.'

'Different can be good,' I say, leaning in to study her painting. Swirls of deep blues and greens blend together, with bright streaks of gold cutting through the dark. 'It's beautiful. Lots of movement in this one.'

'Thank you. I think I'm understanding what the piece means to me now.'

I nod, understanding the feeling. One of the key principles at Healing Arts is that people can talk if they want to, but they don't have to. I never push. Instead, I offer the option at the end of each class – just like today.

I step into the centre of the room. 'Alright, everyone,' I say calmly, smiling. 'We're going to be wrapping up shortly. As always, if anyone wants to share what they've created or what it represents to them, you're welcome to.'

I pause, scanning the room, ready to accept the usual silence. Most people here use this space to process without words, and I respect that. But then, Ellie clears her throat.

'I think... I want to share,' she says, her voice small but steady.

I nod, offering her a reassuring smile. 'Of course. Whenever you're ready.'

The room goes still. Everyone turns towards her, but in this space, it's never with judgement. Ellie glances at her painting, her fingers nervously playing with the edge of her apron, and then she starts.

'I've been coming here for a while now, but I've never really talked about what I paint.' She takes a breath, steadying herself. 'I think I was afraid to. But today feels different. I've been thinking a lot about my sister. She passed away when she was fifteen.' Her voice falters for a moment, but she pushes on. 'She was an amazing person – bright, always laughing, and then one day, she was gone.' She points to the streaks of gold in her painting. 'This... this is her light. Even when everything else feels dark, memories of her joy cut through it.'

I glance at the other members of the group, and I can see the empathy in their eyes. I step forward.

'Thank you for sharing that, Ellie,' I say, my voice soft. 'That's incredibly powerful.'

Ellie nods, her face a little flushed from the effort of being so vulnerable, but there's a small smile on her lips.

I give the rest of the class a chance to speak, but no one else feels the need to today, and that's fine. Everyone's healing process looks different.

As the class filters out, Ellie lingers for a moment, and before leaving, she says,

'Thank you, Jess, really. I feel... lighter.'

I rest my hand on her shoulder. 'You should be thanking yourself. You're doing the work.' I smile warmly. 'I'm so sorry to hear about your sister, Ellie. What was her name?'

'Angharad. Angharad Thomas.'

The name ripples through me and my breath catches in my throat. Angharad Thomas. The child whose name had been in the headlines. The child *he* killed. The child whose life was taken by the same man who once shattered mine.

I keep my expression steady.

'She was... murdered. They said the man should have never been out of prison. He was supposed to be locked up for ten years, but they let him out after five... after he attacked some poor girl when she was eleven. My sister would still be alive if they'd kept him in.'

I hold the weight of the shock carefully, keeping it close. It doesn't shake me like it once might have. Instead, it feels like a full circle, like the final piece of something I've already healed from. This is Ellie's moment, not mine.

'I'm so sorry, Ellie. I can't imagine how hard that must be.'

She nods, her lips pressed together, but there's a hint of relief in her eyes – relief from sharing the burden, even if she doesn't know how much of it I already understand. After a beat, she gives me a small smile. 'See you next week.'

Chapter 61

As I leave the studio, the weight of Ellie's revelation lingers, but not in a way that overwhelms me. *Angharad.* The name echoes softly, and for a moment, I pause, allowing myself to acknowledge the past. The past is a part of me, yes, but it no longer defines me. And as much as the memories stir something deep inside, I feel... strong. I've faced so many of these painful pieces already – like finally reporting Daeva's assault, a reminder that justice, though delayed, can still be served. I've returned to old wounds, not to reopen them, but to feel them heal.

And now, there's one more piece to face.

Lake Calon.

The lake that was once 'our place'. Georgia's and mine.

I've been putting off visiting; it felt too painful, too poignant. But a huge step in my healing process has been to push myself to smile in the places I had once cried. I started with my old bedroom at Mum and Dad's house, a place where I had sunk into and lived through my illness. I went back, climbed into the bed, and just allowed myself to feel grateful for that turbulent time I had faced, because without it, I wouldn't have been able to rebuild.

Another big one was revisiting the rose garden, where I'd found out Li had been the one secretly ruining my life.

I even parked outside the police station where I'd been bombarded with awful news after awful news.

There has been true romance in the journey back to myself, and I now understand that past me did her best with what she knew at the time. I'd lived in regret for so long, but I had to move past it and free myself from the shackles that I'd locked myself in, giving myself permission to unlearn who I'd been. And most importantly, I forgave myself. I hadn't deserved all the horrible things I said to myself.

And now, the final thing on my list, the one I've been delaying, trying to find the courage to face, is the lake. The last time I came here was five years ago – the day Georgia told me she couldn't cope with seeing me anymore.

I take a deep breath, step out of my car and feel the last rays of the afternoon's sun on my skin as I walk towards the place that holds some of my most precious – and painful – memories. Time to face it. Time to finally let it all go.

I begin to walk the border of the lake. Tufts of dandelion fluff float like ethereal ballerinas in the breeze as I gaze out at the golden, sun-sparkled quilt of water, the molten orb of amber in the sky casting its final glow of the day.

I can sense the magic that lingers here – the magic that has always seemed to exist at Lake Calon. I sit on a grassy verge in a shaft of saffron sunshine, out of view of passers-by, and I simply take it all in – the birdsong; the musical vibration of youthful laughter; the bobbing ducks painting delicate ripples across the water; and the breeze weaving gently through the trees, casting dancing shadows on my face.

I breathe in the peace and the memories, and I simply smile. I smile through the ache that bubbles up in my heart, and I smile at the tremendous loveliness of the place.

It was here Georgia and I had laughed, played, picnicked, loved, cried, and broken each other's hearts. And now that I'm finally revisiting it, I feel my heart fill with tender memories. There was no other place that had been more significant in our relationship – other than maybe her dad's house and my old flat, neither of which were accessible anymore. The lake had truly meant something.

I still hold Georgia in my scarred heart, but the desperation and pain that used to bind her to it have been released. She made this world feel like home to me, and I've had to purge myself of homesickness for a place that doesn't exist anymore. Amid planets, stars and universes, I feel fortunate to walk the same earth as her, grateful to have been born in the same lifetime, and blessed to be under the same sky and breathe the same air. Knowing she is out there is enough.

Whenever I miss her, I remind myself that it's not a sign to seek her out; it's just a memento proving that we had been a great thing once upon a time. I know it's OK to cry over her; crying doesn't mean I'm still stuck, it just means I am human.

We had imagined that Lake Calon would be where we'd say our vows. The lake, as far as I see it, is a place I *had* to revisit – as if I were following my own twelve-step programme, and this was the final step on the list.

Above me, the sunset sky is an ever-changing canvas, and below, the water seems supercharged with energy, as if it were located on ley lines. It feels enchanted, somehow more so than ever. I stare out for what seems like hours, and at the same moment that my eyes intuitively glance over my shoulder towards the path, I see her.

Chapter 62

She walks towards me, like something from a dream.

My heart starts to pound and time seems slowed. I rise as she nears, and we lock eyes. I'm not even sure she'd seen me until that moment. She stops in her tracks and her hand covers her mouth in gentle shock.

'Jess,' she says tenderly, a smile gradually engulfing her face. 'Oh wow. It's... it's so amazing to see you. It's really you.'

I brush grass blades off the back of my trembling legs. 'Georgia.' I beam, shaking my head slowly in disbelief. 'This doesn't feel real at all.'

She steps into me and hugs me. I feel her hands clutch at my back and I melt into her, with tears in my eyes. I've waited a lifetime for this moment. My heart feels like warm butter. I'm half expecting Pickle to bark at us, as he always did when Georgia and I hugged, but it occurs to me that Pickle is probably long gone.

Being in her arms feels like make-believe – like watching it on a film or having an out-of-body experience. Her perfume sweetens the air;

it's different to the one she used to wear, but it still somehow smells like her.

We both speak at the same time.

'I come here—'

'What are you—'

We laugh in sync over each other's shoulders while still holding on to the hug. 'You go first,' I say.

'I come here almost every day,' she says, releasing me but keeping hold of my arms, her eyes soft and gazing. 'I've never seen you here.'

'This is the first time I've visited for five whole years if you can believe that.'

Her eyes gloss as she smiles.

'How are you?' I ask, stunned but trying not to stall. 'How have things been for the last half-decade? Any news?' I ask, laughing at the absurdity of my question.

'Has it really been five years?' she asks, her eyes carrying a mixture of shock and despondency. 'Gosh.' She pauses, shaking her head, and then, as if stepping out from a deep memory, continues. 'All's good with me. I'm lecturing at Cardiff University now. And I teach a night course at the college a few days a week.'

I recognise her hand gestures as she speaks, and the way only one of her dimples indents itself when she smiles a certain way. I'm completely absorbed in her eyes, her smell, the music of her voice, her mannerisms, the way she swallows between sentences, the shape of her words, the faint pink veins on her eyelids, and the few stray brow hairs just above those veins. She's so lifelike. She's really real.

'That's amazing.' I touch her arm. 'You've always been so great at teaching. Your students are so lucky to have you.'

She stares at my face as if admiring a painting at a gallery. 'You look so different, Jess. Good different,' she adds reassuringly.

'Thanks,' I say, smiling, picturing what she's seeing at that moment: my once-long crimson hair, now cut into a tousled bob that barely brushes the tops of my shoulders, no makeup, a long-sleeved T-shirt with jeans and high-top trainers – a low-maintenance aesthetic that I've been fully embracing. I feel more 'me' than ever, celebrating the parts of myself that I used to deem as imperfections. I look the way I want to look, rather than the way I know impresses others – what a burden that used to be.

'What are you doing these days, Jess?'

'Well, the news editor position at *The City Post* came up for grabs,' I say, my thoughts drifting back for a second to the day Glyn was escorted out of the office by security after being fired for misconduct. My complaint against him had sparked a wave of similar reports from other women in the office, ultimately leading to his dismissal. 'But I didn't apply for it. I handed in my notice, moved out of the city, and retrained as an art therapist, and I have my own studio now.'

'That is bloody incredible, Jess. You always loved art.'

'It's so rewarding; I don't even feel as if I'm working. I feel like I'm doing a bit of good in the world.'

'I'm so proud of you.'

I let her words wash over me. It really is the little things.

'So where are you living now?' she asks.

'Swansea, in the Marina. I just needed a change – a new start, you know?'

'Sounds like it was a great choice.'

I offer a gentle smile and a nod.

'And who's this?' she asks in a baby voice, crouching down.

'This is Elmo, the most gorgeous boy in the entire world.' I stroke his soft, beige head as he snorts in greeting.

'Oh Elmo, aren't you a distinguished gentleman?' She scratches his little ears and he dissolves into a delighted mess at her feet. She continues to talk to him as he shakes his curly tail, his entire body wiggling. 'Your mum has wanted you forever. You're a very lucky pug with a lovely mum like that, aren't you?'

She stands, smiling. 'Shall we sit?' she asks, pointing to the patch of tucked-away grass where I'd been perched.

Chatting with her feels as if no time has passed between us at all, as if the last five years had never happened. I still feel our connection; it's as if we're being drawn together by an invisible force – as if the very threads of my DNA are reaching out to her, tenderly, like iron shavings drawn to a magnet.

'How's married life?' I ask.

She holds her left hand out, palm facing down. It's bare save for an indent where a ring used to be. 'Florence and I were never married. We were just engaged. And we officially separated a little while back.'

I feel my heart leap in my chest but I try not to show my surprise. 'I'm so sorry to hear that.'

'Thank you. My dad and Stace got hitched though.'

'Really? That's fantastic! I'm so happy for them.'

'What about you, Jess? Are you…'

'No. God no. Single,' I say, my mind flashing back to how I once believed I should be married with a baby by twenty-five – an expectation I felt I had to follow to fit in, convinced that a woman's purpose was to be a wife and mother. Now in my thirties, I see how far I've come from that narrow idea of how life should look.

We smile clumsily, both barely making eye contact.

I feel the remnants of the past sparkle in my heart, and I think I sense them glow in hers too; there's just something in the way she's looking at me.

'Do you want to know a secret?' she asks, gently stroking Elmo's back as he stretches out next to her sleepily.

'Of course...'

'Every time I come here, I look for you.' She bites into her lip as if to stop it from quivering. 'I always hope to see you.' She laughs through her nose without smiling and stares straight ahead, her eyes varnishing with tears. 'I actually used to think I was seeing you everywhere, but it would always turn out to be someone else.'

My stomach flips as I think about all the times I'd done the same – believing I'd seen her in the supermarket aisles, or halfway across the world.

'I really am so sorry that everything happened the way it did,' I say, the corners of my mouth vulnerable. 'You meant so much to me, and I'm just so sorry I ruined it.'

She's just staring at me, breathing shallow and quick, and I worry for a moment that I've gone too far and that she might make her excuses and leave.

Instead, she pushes up the left sleeve of her jumper and presents her inner forearm, on which there's a tattoo of a blue orchid. 'Just like the ones we bought each other all those years ago,' she says, with droplets brimming in her eyes.

I can't speak. She had a symbol of our love permanently drawn on her.

'I regret so many of the choices I made all those years ago,' she says, turning to face me but looking at the ground. 'I should have given you the chance to explain everything; I should never have believed those texts were from you. And I shouldn't have pushed you away after everything that happened with the police and with Li. I'm just so, so sorry.'

Tears roll down my cheeks as she speaks; I wipe them away before responding. 'No, *I'm* so sorry,' I say, sniffing, trying to compose my voice so it doesn't shake too much. 'If I hadn't hurt you in the first place, none of it would have happened. We may have even still been together in some parallel life.'

My heart blooms when she raises her head to peer up at me. I can see the universe in her eyes; I'd forgotten just how blue they are.

'If only,' she says, which makes my blood stop pumping for a moment before my heart starts to pound with a mixture of caution and hope.

We exchange a look, the affection and nervousness contained within it letting me know the love is still there, for both of us.

'I'd always wanted to reach out,' she says, 'but I thought I'd missed my window with you, and I didn't want to disrupt your life, so that's why I started coming here, to our favourite place, hoping I could just bump into you. I'd even dream about it sometimes.'

She had dreamt of me just as I had dreamt of her. I wanted to cry out, overwhelmed with relief and joy.

'Well, it finally worked,' I say, laughing louder than I mean to, wiping my eyes.

She laughs along, tears dripping down her ruddy cheeks. 'I never stopped thinking about you.' She shakes her head and meets my gaze. 'You were such a huge part of my life.'

'I've never...' My tongue locks in my mouth for a moment, unable to form the words. 'I've never stopped thinking about you either.'

She reaches out and places her hand on mine, further stirring the electricity that had always existed between us. I squeeze her hand and search her teary eyes. A thousand unspoken words hang in the air between us, and the weight of half a decade's worth of longing seems to press down on us.

'Do you think—' She looks at the ground again, wiping the wetness off her cheeks and chin with the back of her free hand. 'Do you think we could ever try again?'

Shock seeps through me. I dart my gaze over her face and nod quickly, smiling, feeling another long tear fall. I try to restrict the sensitive noises that prowl in my throat, trying to claw their way out, but I fail; they burst from me in colossal relief, and I collapse into her as she holds her arms out to me.

She clings to me, her whole body shaking as I flatten my cheek onto her chest, feeling my teardrops soak into the material of her top. Sniffing back her tears, attempting to swallow down her convulsive gasps and hiccups, she rocks me, rubbing my back as I squeeze her so tight I think I might crush her. I savour the way she feels in my arms.

In the pile of ashes inside my heart, an ember had always remained aglow for her, and while we sob into each other, I can feel that small, brightly smouldering spark being stirred up in the wind of emotions. It's light enough to be blown through the air, and it lands before being blown again, and blown again, igniting new little wildfires everywhere it touches until my body is blazing.

We clutch onto each other until we're both calm and breathing normally. I lift my head from her and realise our surroundings have dimmed as the sun dips below the horizon, painting the sky and water with dreamy hues of candyfloss-pink and lavender. She wipes away my tears using both hands and then cradles my face in them. My lips part at her touch. I lean my head into one of her palms and close my swollen lids, feeling the warmth of her skin against mine. The years melt away, and I'm transported back to a time when our love was everything. I cup her hand with my own.

And then I feel them. Softly, ever so softly, her lips touch mine.

She pulls away. 'I'm so sorry, I shouldn't—'

Before she can finish her sentence, I reach out, draw her mouth back to mine and kiss her deeply as hot tears stream down my face.

Our first kiss flashes into my mind – how the entire world stopped and how I knew she was the person I wanted to spend the rest of my life with. Nothing had ever felt so right. I'd felt the value of that moment in every cell of my body that night, and my cells had held on to it when it became a memory – as if it had been written into my genetic code. And this kiss is the same, if not more intense.

It's tender at first, the joining of lips, but as we lean into it, it engulfs us. Her body feels irresistible – just as good as it used to. I want this kiss more than I want air. In this moment, it's as though time is undoing itself, obliterating the entire empty chapter that exists between us. It feels as if we'd never left each other, never broke up, as if Li had never interfered, I never started dating Lucy, I never began visiting Danni, and never encountered Daeva Valentine.

Murmurs of emotion escape as our mouths meet tenderly and fervently, both our faces slippery with salty tears. It's an instant filled with the promise of second chances, forgiveness and the rekindling of a love that had always been there, waiting for the right moment to reignite.

I'm home.

She sweeps my hair back and gently kisses the curve of my neck as I dizzy underneath her. Her lips trace a path of adulation down to my chest, and before I know it, the full weight of Georgia's ardent body is pressing me down onto the grass. Elmo lifts his head for a moment, sighs dramatically, and flops back down as if to say, 'Get on with it.' I can't help but smile as I plant kisses up Georgia's neckline and hug her into me, aching to feel as much of her against me as possible.

When she glides her hand under the waistband of my trousers, every nerve in my body tingles. She stops kissing me for half a second, waiting for me to nod my consent.

'Please,' I whisper heavily, a raw desperation in my voice.

Then she's pushing her hand down, finding her way as I shake with need under her touch. I'm caught between breathless gasps and the urge to cry as I reach down her body and let my hands unbutton her trousers and explore her with equal intensity.

Her warmth presses against me, our forms aligning as she guides our rhythm, and we dissolve into each other's touches as the last rays of light cast long shadows across the landscape and the lake shimmers with the remnants of the day. She holds me close and envelops my body as we drift into the deep end, drowning in each other, oblivious to potential eyewitnesses or to the chill settling into our bones from the now crisp night air. Time slips by unnoticed as we remain nestled together in the promise of what could be, Lake Calon a silent witness to our love story.

I feel the weightlessness of freedom – the vastness of my own existence. For the first time, a relationship doesn't appear to me as a binding container, but rather an infinite sky where I can soar freely with her – intertwined, yet each in our own beautifully distinct skins.